ECHOES OF WAR

A STATE OF THE UNION NOVEL

BOOK TWO

ECHOES OF WAR

A STATE OF THE UNION NOVEL

BOOK TWO

NELLE NIKOLE

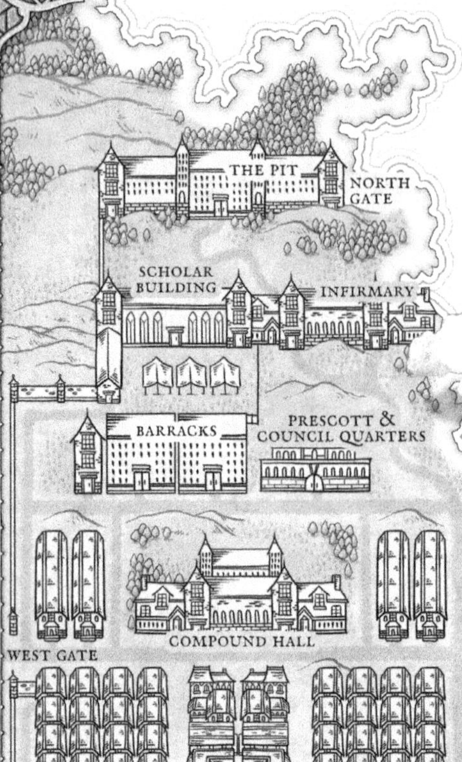

MONTEREY BAY
THE PIT
NORTH GATE
SCHOLAR BUILDING
INFIRMARY
BARRACKS
PRESCOTT & COUNCIL QUARTERS
THE KITCHENS
THE GARDENS
WEST GATE
COMPOUND HALL
THE ARENA
ENTERTAINMENT SQUARE
SOUTH GATE
THE MONTEREY COMPOUND

N
W
THE
DOCKS
FISHING &
AL QUARTERS
EAST
GATE
GARDENS
THE
STABLES
LIVESTOCK

CANADA
THE PACIFIC OCEAN
SALEM
TERRITORY
MEXICO

STATE OF THE UNION
THE EXPANSE
THE COVERT PROVINCE
TRANSIENT NATION
THE ATLANTIC OCEAN

CONTENT WARNING

PRONUNCIATION GUIDE

- **Amaia** — ah-MY-ah
- **Alexiares** — ah-LEK-see-ah-rees
- **Abel** — AY-bel
- **Elie** — EL-lee
- **Finley** — FIN-lee
- **Jax** — JAKS
- **Lola** — LOH-lah
- **Luna** — LOO-nah
- **Malachai** — ma-LA-kai
- **Prescott** — PRES-kut
- **Reina** — RAY-nah
- **Riley** — RY-lee
- **Ronan** — ROH-nan
- **Seth** — SETH
- **Sloan** — slown
- **Tomoe** — toh-MOH-eh
- **Yasmin** — YAHZ-meen

MAGIC INDEX

ELEMENTALS

- **Fire** (*Ignis*) masters of flames, wield the power of fire
- **Water** (*Aqua*) manipulators of water in all forms
- **Earth** (*Terra*) controllers of the earth
- **Air** (*Aer*) commanders of the air

SKILLS

- ***Umbra Mortis*** ability to make anything and everything a weapon with unparalleled precision
- ***Scholar*** knowledge is power
- ***Tinkerer*** (*Physiscus*) possess a knack for all things science and technology

THE OTHERS

- ***Supra*** heightened physical abilities–faster, stronger, taller
- ***Pansie*** zombie mutation
- ***Brujas*** wielders of the dark arts

WORLD OF RISING

You've come to the right place if you're a reader who craves vivid imagery and immersive worlds. Scan the QR codes below to discover the World of Rising and its characters.

Pinterest Board

Echoes of War Playlist

Origin Stories (Recommended but not required)

To the little girls who never took any shit.
Especially from a man.

Magic can only fight half your
battles, the rest is up to you.

CHAPTER

ONE

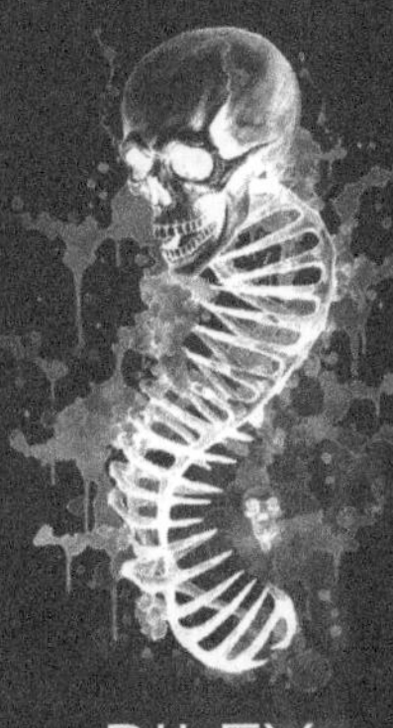

RILEY

Everything was lost. Our safe place, our haven, our place of peace, was no more.

I had yet to receive word from Amaia. The reality of our situation was my sister would not be returning for some time. My family that I had grown to love were gone, and the fate of our home was up to me. Amaia, Reina, Tomoe, and Alexiares would do what they could from Duluth, and Prescott and I would do our best to hold down the fort.

Seth would meet his own fate, soon enough. The universe did not reward evil. I had to believe that. Had to have faith in something larger, or what else was any of this for?

If we played our cards right, and the stars aligned in our favor, then we'd have a fighting chance of coming out of this with at least half of our people alive. This family of mine was full of sacrificial lambs. The life we had created was worth the risk. Amaia would always be my priority, but I could not protect her from here.

So I would focus on protecting the place and people she loved the most—The Compound.

"Your stance needs to remain adaptive, Eleanor. Leave your neck exposed, and you die."

We were in The Pit practicing among others. It'd been that way a lot lately, everyone using most of their spare time to brush up on their skills. Civilians and soldiers alike, doing their best to stay ready. Our people didn't have the luxury of getting ready anymore. It was stay ready or be caught off guard when they try to take down our walls, *again*. Wrong place at the wrong time and being surprised could mean your death.

Elie's golden curls bounced as she weaved out of my reach. "It's Elie, and you know that," she said, her endurance waning.

I'd come to find I had another sister to look out for, to take under my protection. After Amaia left, Elie had appeared lost, on edge. Nervous. And nervous energy was never good.

Amaia had spent a lot of time wrestling with the idea of Elie receiving substantial training. She'd been dead set on keeping her from being involved with her troops, discouraging her aspirations of being a soldier. Doing her best to keep Elie from becoming *her*. The way Amaia saw things, sixteen was far too young to understand what being a soldier meant, what doing the job consisted of. In Elie's best interest, Amaia had kept her away from everything except the basics.

I'd understood, but this wasn't The Before. The time for hand-holding was over. Not that I'd ever believed in that anyway. It was a point of contention for us in the past, but I figured Amaia would forgive me for training her if it meant Elie stayed alive.

Sure, I'd been training her physically, mentally. But I'd also respected Amaia's decisions. Decided to delegate her specialty in a way that gave the perception that she was involved, but kept her away from danger. I'd chosen to challenge her Tinkerer gene, using her to help build weapons that could be beneficial. And damn, did she have a knack for explosives.

Elie glanced down at her feet, checking her stance. I grabbed her fist before she had the chance to throw a successful jab, taking advantage of the hesitation. The weakness.

"In here"—I swung my right arm, the movement purposely slow enough for her to predict—"it's Eleanor. I am your teacher, not your friend. You know what Amaia once told me? That invisible feeling? In your gut? That's your primal instinct keeping you alive. That is the most innate survival tool us humans have. Follow that feeling. Fear is a gift. Always trust your gut."

I flipped her on her back, careful to avoid her head slamming into the ground but rough enough to prove my point. "Because had you listened to yours, you wouldn't be in this position right now."

Brown eyes stared up at me, tears welling up at the mention of Amaia. I'd told her the truth of the betrayal. The rest of The Compound had yet to be made aware. Prescott, The Council, and I had discussed it for hours. Ultimately, determining that without the general here, the revelation of Seth's act of terrorism would be the stick that broke the dam.

Elie had been furious. In her time around Jax and Amaia, she'd grown familiar with Seth too. Had at least trusted him, and he'd betrayed her by failing her favorite person.

She smacked my hand away. "Don't baby me, I can stand on my own. Again."

Her eyes were hard, focused, though the slack in her posture gave her away. She needed rest, yet here she was, ready to go. Relentless when it came to a fight. A soldier first, a person second. Except she wasn't a soldier, she was a kid, I reminded myself, promising not to cross that barrier again.

"You two are so alike, it's terrifying." I chuckled, grabbing her by the shoulder and guiding her toward a bench on the outer part of The Pit. "Take a breath. Get some water."

"Is there time to take a breath and get water in the middle of a battlefield, Riley?"

My eyes narrowed, glaring in her direction. She ducked her head, turning to follow directions. Elie plopped down onto the bench with a huff, rolling her eyes.

Over the course of the last few weeks, there'd been an attack at our gate twice. Our borders had known no peace, but we'd held steady. For now. I wasn't sure how much longer our soldiers could hold on. Every morning, our gates were greeted with flocks of people from beyond the walls across Monterey territory. The reason they arrived varied. Some came in search of sanctuary and safety, others were determined to have a base location to put up a fight. Thankfully, with Seth's departing words, I'd known to debrief Prescott without having to wait on hearing back from Amaia. Her instructions for the worst-case scenario had been vague, but enough to work with in getting things ramped up back home.

It was no longer a secret that war was headed our way. On our doorstep, one knock away. Under normal circumstances, I'd welcome any newcomers with open arms. The more bodies, the more work that would be done, the more solid of a settlement we'd become. Now though, they were just extra untrained bodies that would be in the way. More bodies that needed protection.

Elie gulped down her last sip of water, wiping her mouth and kicking her feet, watching the others sparring around us. The smell of sweat and tangy scent of blood filled the air as she sprang to her feet. I laughed at her attempt to catch me off guard. She lowered into position, a smirk passed over her lips, her throwing knife now in hand. Elie tilted her head, challenging me to take it from her.

Amaia had gifted it to her, leaving it at her doorstep the morning she'd left for Duluth. She'd sought me out right after, demanding I teach her how to use it, stating that if I didn't help her, she'd simply have to learn herself. The knife never left her side, her most prized possession.

"Let's do knives next," she teased.

I scoffed. This kid was a piece of work, truly. Saying nothing, I turned on my heels, leading the way toward one of the target rooms in the underground portion of The Pit.

Shrill screams rang out in the direction of the North Gate. *Not again.* Elie glanced toward me, eyes glimmering with mischief.

"If you try to stop me," she said, "you'll be wasting precious seconds those people don't have."

A groan escaped my throat, my locs dancing as I shook my head, "Keep up."

Elie ran at my side, ready to defend what was ours.

CHAPTER

TWO

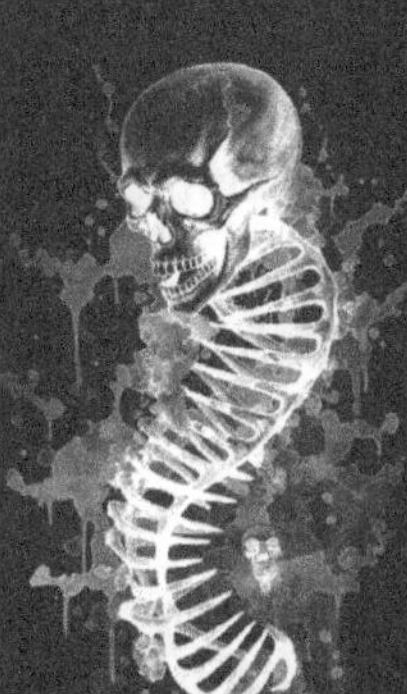

AMAIA

Three weeks had passed since Seth left us, abandoning the family we thought he'd grown to love. To be betrayed and then abandoned … there was no instruction manual on how to grieve a loss of that magnitude.

It was different from death. He had chosen this path. Deliberately set out to hurt us and left our hearts in tiny pieces. Left us to grieve the loss of a person who was very much still alive. At first, it was a shock. Reina refused to accept it, her denial unyielding.

She was convinced he would come back, that he wasn't truly on their father's side and instead would return having talked him down. *Seth will save us all. Just you watch*, she had said. The pain in Tomoe's eyes had let me know that wasn't even a remote possibility in our future. At least not at the moment.

That was a visage Tomoe displayed most days. Each word she uttered was laced with venom. Like it was painful for even her to say. Not because she cared if it hurt me, but because it hurt her to look at me. To talk to me. We interacted with each other when we had to, spoke when it was required to get the job done. Besides that, I was dead to my sisters.

Our days were busy. The first morning after Seth's departure we'd set straight to work. The message of the impending war had spread throughout the major networks in Salem Territory and The Expanse. Things had been kept quiet, for now there was no news of the fate bestowed upon my family and I.

The silence of the grapevine meant nothing to me. I knew Seth had already made it to their father, felt it in my gut. Ronan Moore knew damn well we were still alive. And now he would plot his next move while we remained here like sitting ducks, something I'd worked hard to keep us from being. I'd be damned to sit here twiddling our thumbs, waiting to see how Covert Province would retaliate. Now was the time to research, to gather evidence, to build up our own forces. Most importantly, figure out how I could put an end to that man and anyone who followed him.

Sloan had put together a small team to accompany us outside the walls to conduct field research and gather what we could from attacks nearby and passing herds. Things had changed quickly. At the forefront of this mess, it had been either the OG Pansies or the upgraded versions, not a mix of the two. Maybe a few would stumble into another herd here and there, but now, they moved as one.

It had become a common occurrence to see an even mix. The made Pansies guided the originals.

"Riddle me, how herd mentality makes any sense? It's a piss poor theory at best," Reina said, glaring at the three Duluth Tinkerers Sloan had assigned to our mission. "These are the best *scientists* you have?" Her voice was cold, detached.

"Reina ..." I warned, begging her to stop before things escalated again. Berating them wouldn't make them any smarter.

Her icy eyes glared back at me. "What, Amaia?"

"She's right," Sloan said, staring down her nose distastefully
at her cousin. "Herd mentality is psychological. It relies solely on
influence and behavior, not communication."

She had majored in psychology in college, and though those
years were far behind us, I trusted her judgment.

"Then we're back to nothing?" I asked.

A chair scraped across the floor, falling forward at my feet.
"Yes, Amaia, I'd imagine being back to nothing is precisely what
another disproved hypothesis indicates." Tomoe's thin lips pulled
into a snarl.

They were still furious with me over Seth. Not that it wasn't
justified, but I found that his betrayal heightened the severity of
their emotions. I'd grown used to it from her and Reina both. My
sisters hated me for my betrayal. So I turned the other cheek. If
their survival in this war rallied around resenting me, then sucking
it the fuck up would become my full-time job.

The two of them spent what little free time we did have these
days away from me and with each other. Oddly enough, Alexiares
had become my only companion in the wake of Seth's departure.
Reina and Tomoe only interacted with me when our jobs required
us to. Where everyone else looked at me with distaste or hatred, his
eyes had been kind. Soft. Proud. If the damn, warm, fuzzy feeling
I got when his eyes landed on mine was a sin, then call me a sinner.

Most days we just talked, often late into the night, finding
ourselves accustomed to falling asleep in my room. Nothing had
happened between us. The idea of sleeping at each other's side
had become comfortable. Routine. Yet, I couldn't help but get the
sense that we were treading dangerous territory.

Waking up nestled into him every morning had quickly become the highlight of my day. There was something so serene

about those moments, the gentleness to which he stroked the curls of my hair as he slowly came to. But with Seth lighting our entire lives on fire, now hardly seemed the time to explore *what ifs*.

I watched him, tracing the outlines of the ink that curved around the nape of his neck, reaching toward his ears. The way his hazelnut eyes shifted, processing the information we'd spent weeks digesting. He sat staring at some generic-ass dolphin painting that belonged inside a dentist's office. The room we'd grown accustomed to meeting in was full of odd paintings that didn't appear to belong. It was unnerving.

My brows scrunched. The thought of the clicking noises the Pansies made triggered something in me. Sounds that only nightmares could construct. They all made them, but the cadence of clicks and grunts from the created ones differed from those we'd spent the last five years fighting.

"I don't suppose echolocation is a plausible theory," I said, half-joking.

The room went quiet; I glanced up at Reina, eyes questioning. She said nothing as I took in the other Tinkerers. Their chatting stopped, now staring at each other, mouths agape.

"No … no, it's not. But you may be on to something else." Reina took a seat, her grief flowing throughout the room.

I bit down on a yelp of pain. Everyone around the room grasped tightly onto whatever their hands could find. Not a single soul spoke, growing accustomed to her newfound lack of control over her gifts under pressure.

Sloan's fierce blue eyes found mine, the tension from our previous conversations on how to handle Reina filling the space between us. To Sloan, grief was weakness. A pointless emotion that got in the way of getting the job done.

Gone were the two best friends, the roomies that shared laughs and inside jokes. There were so many memories. Now we were simply two strangers, with mutual interests who happened to trust each other. Allies.

Allies in war with history.

"Reina, talk to us. Where's your mind going?" I moved to her side, cutting off Sloan's view of her cousin.

Her head snapped toward me. "Give me a second, would you?"

Tomoe's inky eyes found mine over Reina's shoulder. On this, we had found common ground. She placed her hand on the upper portion of Reina's back in comfort.

"Reina, the more brain power, the better. What is it?" Her raven-colored hair spilled in front of her face as she peered down, trying to meet Reina's stare.

"My mom," she mumbled in response. "When I was a kid, she gushed about some study. Dolphins, they were her favorite animal. They figured out dolphins could replicate advanced spoken language. Conversations. Similar to what we could do. It was groundbreaking, though I don't remember hearing much of anything about it after … acoustic signals. They help with group coordination, ya know, hunting and traveling. The pitch and frequency vocalizations help them stay together or convey information about their intentions and movements to other pod members. Holy moly … the Pansies are communicating with each other through acoustic signals."

Her eyes danced at the thought. The other Tinkerers murmured, pulling books down from the surrounding shelves and flipping pages. We all remained quiet, waiting to see if she had more to add. Reina shot across the room, grabbing a chalk board and jotting notes down.

Tomoe's eyes went wide with annoyance, the red rims around them a clear indication that she wasn't as okay as she pretended to be. "Okay, I'll be the first to ask. What the hell does that mean?" She deadpanned.

"It means we're screwed." Reina said, emotion vapid in her voice.

There was no hesitation about what was discussed in front of Duluth. Information had flowed freely between our sides once we'd established the terms of us working together. Everything we'd known, they now knew, within reason.

The last few weeks had been spent trying to understand exactly how the Pansies were being made, how they differed from the ones this world had grown accustomed to. More importantly, how the hell Moe had power shared with Seth.

"They never lost the ability to form complex thoughts," I added, "only needed the chance to evolve a new way of communicating."

Just because their thoughts had turned primal, about survival, didn't mean the ability to think and comprehend no longer existed. I explained to Sloan and her team the story my family had already heard.

My first fiancé, Xavier, had turned practically upon nuclear touchdown. The radiation only gave us mere moments together before changing my life forever. He'd gone Pansie, and I ran, only to have to kill him later to survive. It was during that fateful fight that I discovered my magic.

Flames had ignited in my palms in the flurry of panic, and I'd brought my hand down, intending to grab his shoulder and push him away. When Xavier glanced down at where my hands had touched him, then back at me, an expression of astonishment crossed over his face at his safety. My flames hadn't burned him, because my magic only answered my desires. They would not burn those I did not intend to harm. But I did harm him that day. I drove a knife through his skull and started a new life. This life. And now I knew the truth.

That he'd still been in there.

Fucking hell.

This entire time, I'd been right. Years of people telling me I was crazy, trying to talk me down, and I had been right all along. The confirmation gave me no relief. I dusted my fingers over the tattoo that lay hidden beneath my wool sweater.

"Amaia …" Reina said, the distaste for my theory coming forward, ready to shut me down.

"Reina," I hissed, "out there, when we're off in the privacy of our own space, you can cut me off, you can ignore me. Hell, you can even cuss me out. But here, outside the four walls of your apartment, I am your general, and you will hear what I have to say before dismissing me."

Reina's eyes went hard, narrowing at Sloan, who smirked at the sternness of the command. A chill trickled down my spine. The resemblance between her and Seth at the moment was haunting. Alexiares cleared his throat, slicing through the tension in the room. He caught Sloan's attention, now glaring in his direction, with a scoff.

"Problem, Sloan?" Alexiares bit out.

"We're sharing the same oxygen," she said with a taunting smile. "I think I'll always have a problem with that, *Bloodhound*."

Friendly fire had a better chance of taking one of the two out than our shared enemy. He was known throughout The Expanse as a bloodhound. The Bloodhound. Part of the reason The Expanse was never able to get a real footing or an ounce of stabilization was because every time someone competent was put in place, they mysteriously came up dead. Brutally mutilated type of dead.

Alexiares sniffed, a fake smile pulling across his angled face as he observed me, reading the words in my eyes. *Not here, not now.*

"Go on," he suggested, proud of his efforts to give me the floor.

"What if all your father did was speed up evolution?" I asked Reina pointedly. "What if he merely enhanced what was already possible? Gave them the ability to vocalize what was already going on behind those soulless eyes."

For once, I hoped I was mistaken. The evidence suggested otherwise.

What a bitter pill to swallow.

"An upgraded version," Tomoe muttered.

I inhaled sharply, "Yep."

Reina chewed her bottom lip, considering.

"It *is* technically possible, given the world we live in," one of the Tinkerers said in between ruffling pages of the book their head was buried in.

Reina nodded slowly, coming to a decision.

"No, you're right, Amaia. As usual, you are right." The disdain in her voice was a punch to the gut. "He started turnin' people by injecting them with whatever Moe saw in the little vials in her vision. That much we're gonna have to piece together with the information we have. There's not a way to prove that on our own. Ethically. We also know he's using them to change the population, make it *stronger*."

Shuffling and a few dry coughs circled the room, the accusation in their eyes at who her father was. Who she had the potential to be, who they thought lurked just beneath 'good' facade.

She cleared her throat. "To *him*, in *his* opinion. The question remains, how many of your people, likely soon our people, will he change to accomplish his goal? Because the answer to that determines how much shit we're in if Amaia is right. Let me tell ya, we should all be hoping she's not."

"What happens if she is right?" Alexiares asked, sitting up straight.

It was a fair question. Reina's eyes brimmed with fear, though her magic calmed everyone. It wasn't a good ending. I could tell. If I was right, we were in for some shit. A disastrous ending. That was where we were headed. For we would not only have to fight other humans who had both modern weapons and magic, we would have to fight evolved Pansies too. Pansies who now had the ability to communicate. To strategize.

"Then this war will take a miracle to win."

CHAPTER
THREE

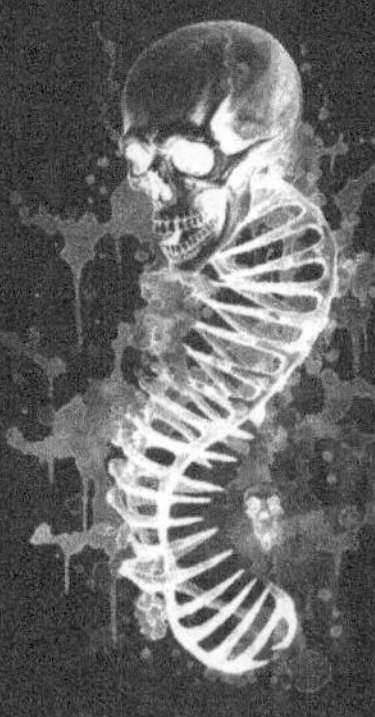

TOMOE

"We aren't entirely fucked. We still have power sharing." I said, chewing the side of my cheeks.

It was the last thing I had up my sleeve. I'd been avoiding it, hoping that we'd be able to run off the idea of a simple protection spell. Trying to powershare among the individuals in this room.

"Yeah, that you have no idea how to replicate. We've been running through your baseless theories for weeks, and what do we have? Nothing. Nada." Sloan growled, shrugging her shoulders in indifference.

Suddenly, I sympathized with her uncle. If you couldn't breed impatience out of their bloodline, maybe a punch to her fucking mouth would help. Her temper reminded me so damn much of her cousin.

Reina was quick to have my back. "Watch it, cousin," she snarled.

"Or what, you'll cry? Throw a grief fit? Bring everyone to their knees with your tears? Grow up. Your weakness won't get us far," Sloan said.

My sister strode over, chest pressed against her cousin. Their eyes were level, the icy blue in them spinning the same sea storm. Whoever this version of Sloan was painted a starkly different picture from the happy, carefree girl Amaia had talked about when telling stories of her life in The Before. True enough, this version of Reina was different from the one that had existed only a few weeks ago.

Suffering a great loss could do that to a person. To them both.

"Just because I cry doesn't mean I'm not strong," Reina declared decisively, unwavering.

I cleared my throat, a weak attempt to break the tension between them. Something I'd become accustomed to doing no matter the Moore member that stood on either side of me. Reina had already lost her brother, *again*, to Seth's persistence. She didn't need her heartless cousin furthering the damage.

"We've been operating under the assumption that power sharing was about vulnerability. Possible only because of the initial protection spell I put in place."

I paused. Given the current state of our family and the shattered state of Duluth, I'd been putting all my faith in the universe for the problem to be one of face value. We didn't trust each other. And to be vulnerable, one must trust. But that was only part of the problem.

It'd been an uneventful night. Nothing out of the norm, our typical Friday at the tavern. A stupid smile plastered across my heated, drunk cheeks as I peered around the table. Consider me shitfounded when I realized it was the first time that I'd been happy in years. *Truly* happy. That was an emotion I hadn't experienced since The Before. That night I'd rushed home and protected my family the only way I knew how.

I no longer practiced paganism. I hadn't in years, had given it up after I'd played with darkness for a touch too long. Part of me still believed I cursed myself with these stupid visions, my consequence being watching my family die. After all, it was my visions that trapped me inside my head, leaving me unable to help them in real time.

I wouldn't lose another family. That night I'd told myself no cost would be too high if it meant protecting them. Keeping them safe. So I bound them to my magic, my power, to help keep them alive. A lifeline. I'd been careful not to tie it to my actual lifeline. I'd simply provided them with extra strength, extra power.

Their magic fed off mine, a succulent to an eternal flame. It wasn't much. In fact, if my magic stopped running through my veins, it'd be of no help at all. Still, it'd be *enough* to keep them safe if they needed an extra spark to defend themselves.

Then again, how much could it have helped if Jax had still died? Whatever I'd done, it hadn't been enough to stop that. I'd felt him go, but his magic had remained. A small kernel that refused to fade.

"There's something I left out," I admitted.

Everyone turned to face me, and the size of the room tightened under their scrutiny. Sloan closed in on me, moving around Reina only to be stopped in her tracks by Alexiares. Something I'd seen him do a lot since we'd arrived. Another oddity we all pretended not to notice, but everyone did. Alexiares was the one person in this damned place that silenced Sloan. One would almost say, scared her.

I didn't know much about his past, hadn't given a shit enough to ask, let alone pry too deep with my magic. All that mattered to me was that he was now on our side, and all I could do was hope it stayed that way. Riley hadn't come along with us on this adventure, but he'd be in for some competition for Amaia's shadow when we got back. There was one place you could count on Alexiares being these last few weeks, and that was at Amaia's side.

Perhaps that was where the root of my anger stemmed from, why I let it linger for nearly a month. Only one of us would die happy, knowing an intense love. The understanding of completion, of having a home no matter where you went, as long as you went together. At least that's all I could see right now.

I braced myself, ready for the recoil. "About my practice, about paganism."

A few people winced, the thought of it still making them uncomfortable. Not the religious aspect, or the practice of it, but rather at the fact of more sci-fi shit being possible. Being true.

"The spell I used had an … extra component to it."

"Meaning?" Reina leaned forward in her seat, the scientist in her intrigued.

"It wasn't just a protection spell. I used blood as the binder. It strengthened the effectiveness of the spell. I think," I muttered.

Seconds passed before anyone spoke again. I knew Reina and Amaia were mulling things over, but the rest of them … yeah, they were probably thinking of the closest cross to burn me on.

"Why do you sound hesitant about that?" Sloan asked, her hands toying with the matchbook in her hand.

"Because I didn't write the spell down." I said, "It was my own creation, a mix of different practices found in my research. I called on different cultures throughout time—Aztec, Mayan, Roman, Egyptian, Greek. Even modern practices."

Recognition passed over Amaia's eyes. Somewhere inside her know-it-all mind, she was running through whatever historical facts she had from each culture. "The books that were scattered across your room before we left, when you were trying to channel more of the lab vision. You were studying something. What was it?"

I nodded, tugging on the sleeves of my black hoodie. "Yeah. I was trying to figure out which part of the spell allowed *this* to happen. Then how to strengthen it."

"I'm still not seeing the problem here. You can't channel a vision and watch a replay?" Sloan's voice erupted, the impatience creeping back into her monotone voice.

"Magic has its limitations. The magic that runs through our veins, it's natural. Well, natural in the sense that it only amplifies the elements of the universe. Relies on them. The same magic that practitioners over time molded and used at a much smaller scale throughout time." They all stared at me like I had four heads. I rolled my eyes, dumbing it down to what they could understand, "Witchcraft. But dark magic, bloodletting, that's not natural. It's forbidden, and thus the universe has consequences for its use. My current limitation being one of them."

"The larger problem is she can't remember which practice got us here. Since she didn't write it down, she'll have to test them out to see which one sticks." Amaia added.

Reina's knotted brown hair fell in front of her face. "I don't get it; you got it right the first try the last time you did it."

"I didn't know if it *worked* the last time I did it. It was something I did in a manic-drunken rush. I can barely recall the night itself. I was so spooked after I did it, scared I'd cursed my family once again … I trashed it all. Haven't practiced since."

"You're about to," Sloan commanded. "What research and resources do you need?"

Always to the point. Relentless. Whatever got the job done. Every interaction we'd had with her since we'd been freed from our little cell and placed into our individual ones had been transactional. Which was fine by me considering the stench of tobacco off her was unbearable in close quarters. Eating meals around her when our days were long was up there on the list of worst experiences I'd been through. Ever. And I've been through a lot of shit.

Not only was the stench, and sight, of her nauseating, but she insisted on having a pre- and post-meal smoke. If this war didn't kill her, her lungs would. I wouldn't tell her that though, not when she treated my sister the way that she did.

"If this is true, Tomoe, if you can figure this out, our armies will be unstoppable," Amaia said, a sly grin teasing the side of her lips.

She was already doing the math. The face of a general stood before me. She'd made it clear that she was capable of doing anything to win this war. Seth's departure had been nothing but a casualty of war to her. Instead of receding into a depressive, drunken state we'd feared her slipping into, she'd emerged the next morning unfazed. Determined to end anyone within Covert Province that supported Moore and his war. *And Seth*, she'd said. For with this betrayal and the certainty of his role in Jax's death, Seth was dead to her. Had only signed his death certificate the moment he'd walked away.

I sighed, shaking my head. "Even if I figure out the spell, I can only perform a few of the rituals myself. We'll need more power than what I have. A fuck ton more."

We'd never be able to connect an entire army. That was something even at my novice level I didn't think conceivable. What was possible, however, was connecting soldiers within units. Now *that* would be game-changing. Maybe even enough to win the war before it truly begun, before we lost too much.

"Okay, so how do we do that? Can't be too hard." Reina said, that hint of optimism still alive somewhere deep inside her.

"We'll need more practitioners," I mumbled, doing the mental math, "people comfortable with bloodletting."

They all stared at me with stupid, empty eyes. I huffed, their faces asking me, *what's the issue?*

"It's frowned upon," I said, making 'woo woo' hands at them. "Dark magic."

Reina took a step toward me, hope in her eyes. "There has to be someone willing, and I'm sure that someone will know someone."

"That's helpful." Sloan mocked, "We can't exactly place an ad in the local newspaper."

"I may know someone."

Every head in the room swiveled in Alexiares' direction. *Of course he does.*

"There's an underground network," he said, unfazed. "Something comparable to what the black market might offer."

"What? So we place an order? We're not searching for objects, we're looking for *people*. People we aren't even entirely sure still exist or will come out of hiding like this one," Sloan's words were acidic.

Amaia flashed a glare in warning, daring her to continue. Credit given when credit is due. She'd taken up for Reina and I, despite our differences as of late. It was noted and somewhat appreciated.

I could see how she and Sloan had been best friends. They fed off each other's energy. Their equal levels of intensity induced a never-ending spiral of chaos. Pushing each other to work harder, to make better decisions. Sloan was cutthroat, but the sad thing was, she was often right. As was Amaia, to my displeasure.

Realization set in. "More than objects are sold in the black market. They're selling us?" I mumbled.

"Not selling." Alexiares shook his head, his bright brown eyes glowing in the dim light. "They're running the damn thing. *Brujas.*"

CHAPTER
FOUR

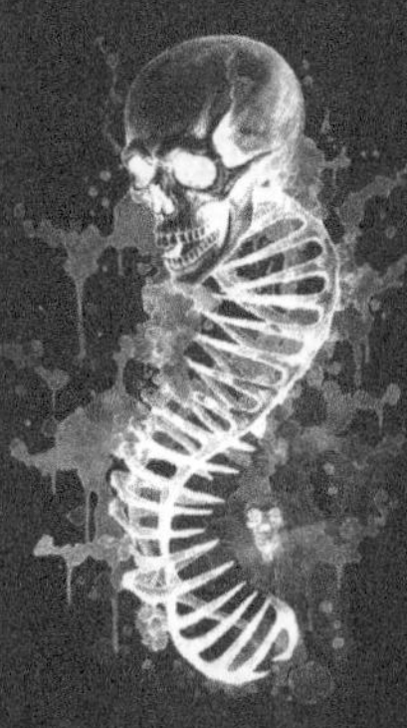

AMAIA

There wasn't much to say after Alexiares' little revelation. The only way for us to move forward was to wait until a connection was established and he got an idea on how many practitioners he could gather. *If* he could, otherwise the plan would fail. Grossly enough, I had faith in him.

A person as notorious as him didn't get by far without the resources to help them. There was also the fact that he would do whatever it took to keep the only friend he'd ever had, Tiago's brother safe. To him, there was no option but to succeed.

"Tomoe, keep working on the fine details. I expect to have something tangible soon. Amaia, figure out the rest." Sloan commanded, her voice dead as she turned to walk out the room. She waved her arm at me on her way out, brushing me off nonchalantly.

Her Tinkerers took one glance around at who they'd remain alone with if they stayed. Their gazes hovered between Alexiares and I, before scrambling after her. Not that they'd be much safer with her. I hated to admit it, but I wasn't sure who my friend had become.

I clenched my fists. Somehow, I'd become someone who answered to her, yet her troops now answered to me. *We* were the reason her people had stopped dying by the masses. *We* were the ones strengthening their forces and their defenses, sharing what knowledge we had to make their people safer. None of that changed how she looked down on us. Made sure we knew she thought us responsible for bringing this to her side of the world, for her people falling. Fair enough, we kinda were.

Alexiares briefly closed his hand over mine in support. A weird sense of calm washed over me in response. I was here to do a job, not to make friends. Few things mattered aside from keeping people safe, preventing the devil incarnate from taking over this land. Failing meant I would be single-handedly responsible for letting what remained left of society fall to the hands of evil. There was no freedom, no peace, in a government that operated off the absence of choice.

The rest was bullshit. I didn't need respect, people to like me, or hell, even acknowledge the help I'd been providing, to get the job done. Reina and Tomoe stared at me stone-faced, their shoulders slouched in defeat as they awaited their orders.

"If you need anyone to bounce ideas from, come find me," I said; Tomoe continued staring at me blankly. "Reina, focus on gathering materials she needs to perform the spell."

"Ritual," Tomoe ground out.

"*Ritual*," I corrected, "Alexiares, I'm assuming there's someone in the area you've established a connection with?"

He nodded at me, his brown eyes locking on mine then slid to my lips. The same level of amusement fixed on his face that had always laid there when I fell into general mode. Except, before it had been mocking. Tinged with disrespect. Now it made my damn heart flutter. I pushed the feeling away, this wasn't the time. Right now, I had to focus on the mission—keeping people safe. Free.

Against my own desires, the responsibility I had over thirty-thousand men, women, and children of Monterey Compound had shot up to include the entirety of Duluth overnight. Sloan had executed the former general when he'd declined to follow several of my recommendations. His refusal to work with me led to fifty of their men falling to a massive herd of upgraded Pansies. *He's outlived his usefulness*, my friend had said, emotion absent in her almond-shaped eyes.

Her heart had turned cold throughout the years, though I suspected most of it had come from the last few months. Deciding who lived and who died could fuck a person up, I got it too well. We were all susceptible to doing terrible things for the people we love.

In all fairness, his inability to accept a woman as a military advisor had been only a small blip on his long list of fuckups as a general.

"I need to send out some logistics with the next wave of emissaries to depart. The rest of my day will be spent trying to fix what I can of their mess of a military. You know where to find me," I said, waiting for them to object, a tendency they developed toward nearly everything I said these days.

The only response I received was uncomfortable silence.

"Anything else?" Reina asked, refusing to meet my eye.

"Yeah, one more thing," I paused, hesitant to pose the question at the tip of my tongue. "Has anyone sensed Seth try to connect?"

A collective chorus of, "No," went around the room. Alexiares' response wasn't necessary as Seth had never entered his mind before, but with us, it was so natural; it was possible he could be there without us knowing.

Reina and Tomoe were learning what had sucked the desire to live out of me in the months that followed in Jax's passing. The day that you lose someone, the day that person is no longer capable of holding space in your life, that's not the worst day. No, the worst is when you're left with nothing but time to think, to let your mind wander and convolute a series of *what ifs*. The worst are all the days they stay gone. Where the possibility of forming new memories somehow becomes impossible.

"Good, keep your guard up."

Keeping a mental shield up around our minds was the only way we could be certain that Seth wouldn't intrude. Much of our bare minimum, half-assed plan relied on making sure he didn't get a glimpse of anything important that may be discussed in his mental presence. He couldn't mind-read, but if he was already connected to you, had talked to you mind-to-mind in the past, his rare Scholar ability granted him access to whatever was going on in your current conversation. Like placing a phone down against your chest to have a private discussion without pressing mute. It was muffled, but if he focused, put some real energy behind the effort, he could put the pieces together.

I doubted he'd attempt it; though, under the influence of his father, who knew. He understood my thought process, the checklist I would go through once he left. Our defenses would be up. After all, he'd been the one to train us to be resistant against his gift all those years ago.

"Aye, aye, General." Tomoe snarled before turning on her heels, Reina's mousy brown hair flowing as she followed close behind.

Alexiares crept up behind me, his hand falling to the small of my back, the sensation sending a shock through my spine. So many secrets, so many lies. So much betrayal, from all sides. Tomoe had betrayed our trust too, but somehow, that had been an easier pill to swallow for Reina.

I guess I could understand that. Tomoe's betrayal had formed with both fear and love in mind. Love had blinded her. For me, it wasn't as simple. My friends didn't want to be protected. They'd never asked that of me.

I'd stolen their ability to make a choice for months, let them form new memories that they may not have wanted to form had they been the wiser to my suspicions. Possibly changed the course of their entire lives.

My choice had changed the course of at least one aspect of Tomoe's. Seth's too. Maybe he'd still be here had I confronted him in a more controlled environment, given him the opportunity to redeem himself.

But that wasn't what was best for the people of The Compound, and that was something I reminded myself to ease the pain every day. My decision may not have been the best for my family, but it had been the best for my people. Without the choices I'd made, Seth may have been able to rally soldiers from his cavalry and others around The Compound to support his cause. And *that* was something I could not have.

My family was safe and alive. That was the important thing. We were a broken family, but the damage was not irredeemable. *I don't think.* No, the love within my family was unconditional, we were stronger as a unit. Still, weeks had gone by and yet Tomoe and Reina remained at a distance.

"I'm fine," I said, not bothering to shake off his touch.

He moved to lean on the table in the center of the room, arms crossed across the wool lined coat I'd become accustomed to him wearing. He'd grown his dark brown hair out. The waves of it now tucked behind the tips of his ear, covering the part of the tattoos that traced up the nape of his neck. He'd cited the crisp December air as the reasoning behind needing the extra warmth. Despite how many times we'd practiced, keeping himself warm with his fire magic was a skill he had yet to master.

His chin tilted, brows furrowed as he searched my face. "Talk. You're worried about something. You're making the face."

"What face?"

"That one. Your lower lip pouts out and your brows scrunch together. Then you glance to the side, all perplexed." His pink lips pulled into a proud smirk.

I sighed, the son of a bitch had grown to know me better than I'd initially intended. "Riley should receive the letter any day now."

"Okay, that's a good thing, ain't it?"

"Duh, obviously." I pushed his shoulder playfully. "I just, I don't know. We've never been away from each other this long. He's my shadow, and it's odd to have to keep faith that everything with him is okay. Not only him, Prescott too. What if I never see them again?"

"You have to keep the faith that they're okay, because that's what's getting them through right now. Riley would rather die than let you down."

"That's exactly my fear," I said, suddenly ready for this conversation to end. "I have to go."

There wasn't much time I had to waste. Most of my time here had been spent convincing Sloan's worthless General that I was worth a damn. That had only made the battle of preparing their underwhelming soldiers to have some semblance of defensive value rather difficult.

They were sloppy, uncoordinated, and scared. Unfortunately for me, fear makes the wolf bigger.

Not only did I have to struggle against an incompetent, now-expired General and his troops, I had to add in the fact that I couldn't let it show that we were actively preparing for war. If word was to spread, Covert Province might have the urge to speed up whatever surely disgustingly intolerant bullshit they had planned. Our actions would aggravate them and I wasn't quite ready for that yet. It certainly wasn't anything Duluth could handle with their already diminishing population.

The half-truths and convoluted lies I'd spewed had helped hold off more of their people being killed for the sake of the Salem network. That wouldn't keep Covert Province at bay for long. Seth, slimy little asshole that he was, would one hundred percent run every course of action he'd known me to take in the past by his father. Without a doubt, he'd help him plan an attack against the place he used to call home.

"Hey," he said, his calloused hand gripped on my wrist keeping me from leaving, "I'll help you when I'm done. This isn't all on you."

I chuckled, my flames teasing his fingers, not burning them but causing them to release. "My idea of *help* Alexiares is having my Compound snipers take high ground on every path into this place to keep these idiots alive."

CHAPTER

FIVE

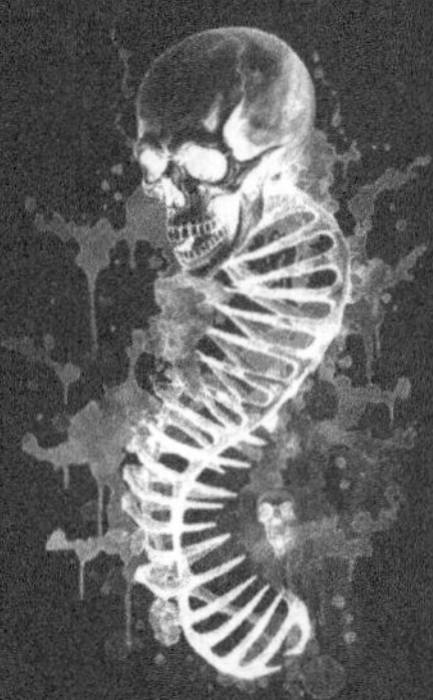

ALEXIARES

My favorite part about pissing Amaia off was watching her perfect ass walk away. Weeks of several meals a day, and the alcohol she pretended none of us knew about, had served my eyes well. Her cargo pants hugged the slender curves of her waist and cupped beneath her ass. It was hard not to admire the beauty of it. Maybe it was all the free time we'd gotten since we stopped running for our lives, but I found her to be a welcome distraction during all of Sloan's 'necessary' meetings.

Amaia knew it too and hated it. She flipped me off as she walked away, upset over my desire to head out beyond the walls alone today. The little princess would have to get over it; we couldn't afford to wait for her to get a free moment during daylight to accompany me.

Not only had December robbed any ounce of warmth from the cold-ass air, it'd managed to steal valuable working daylight hours from us. We'd already thrown away two days due to her helping Sloan's incoherent population get a fighting chance of survival on their own. For the life of me I didn't understand why she'd been so reluctant to allow the arming of her citizens, or at least basic combat.

Sloan had been vindictive in every interaction we'd had since we had all arrived weeks ago, yet when it came to the average citizen, she had been soft. Her and Amaia were the same in that aspect. Strong leaders who would do anything to protect those they deemed deserving of preserving their innocence and happiness. They couldn't care less if it came at the cost of their own peace. The difference between them however came down to something that could not be taught; knowing when you have to cross a line, blur a line, or pretend that you can't see a damn line at all.

This life and the life I'd led Before had taught me a lot, but the most important lesson had been simple. If you had never walked the path of a monster, never been hellbent, then you would never truly understand the courage it takes to hold immense power, yet still embrace tenderness.

That was one of the less infuriating traits of Amaia. She handled the suck, no matter the means. Hell, she made better decisions than I would if I were in her shoes, better than most people I knew would too. *Not like that was saying anything.* We all saw how St. Cloud had turned out.

Didn't matter much anyway, Sloan's people were thoroughly fucked. Double fucked if I couldn't make this connection with the *brujas.* I made my way through the city center, the pack on my back filled with essentials to last me a week-long trip.

Sloan had grudgingly cleared me to take one of their solar powered trucks, the roads were clear until around the halfway point. I'd have to walk the rest of the way, which would take a few extra days. There would be no complaints from me on that detail. St. Cloud territory was uncomfortably close to St. Paul. The less attention I could draw, the better.

Cold, bony fingers grabbed the back of my neck. I whipped around, latching on to a long leather coat, shoving my attacker into the wall of the closest building. Arrows clattered against the red brick and I met crazed electric blue eyes.

"Where are you going?" I asked, noting the small bag attached to the pouch for her arrows.

Reina's tongue graced over her teeth, "Where are *you* going, Alexi?"

I let her go with an exasperated sigh. The last thing I needed to do was place Reina on a psych hold when Amaia was on the fucking verge of losing her shit.

"To get you some witches. Now, where are *you* going?"

"Mind your business," she hissed. Her eyes darted toward the ground, she was up to something.

"Oh, you're up to no good," I said, a smirk pulling at the corner of my mouth. "I want in on it."

Despite the constant state of busyness that existed to keep this place from falling, I was bored as hell. For as long as I could remember, I wanted to be better, or at the very least be a better person than the one who had raised me. What a rude awakening it was to discover being good was boring. There had to be a middle ground. A slightly darker option.

The bad that fought for the good.

"I doubt what I'm up to will win you any favor with Amaia." Her words were sharp, maybe Amaia was right, maybe forgiveness *was* off the table for some. That would ruin her, and I refused to stand by and watch it happen.

"Who cares what she thinks? Trouble, as your father likes to say, was bred into me. If you're up to no good, chances are you'll need my help."

Though my offer was sincere, I couldn't help but hope I may find a way to get through to Reina in the process of helping her. She'd found out that the people she loved were no good. Now, she had to decide whether that meant she should love them anyway or hate them the way the world does. No matter the softer sides she'd seen to both her father and brother, the world would only see one version of them. Monster.

I knew what that was like. Hating your provider of life was a complicated thing. She would need family to help her through. To keep her from slipping from the light.

She snorted, "I don't need help from Amaia's little lap dog. I've gotten away with hiding my shenanigans my whole life, don't need your help now."

I eyed her curiously. Yeah, I guess she *did* have a knack for hiding things. Still, one thing bothered me.

"I'm not her lap dog," I ground out.

"Doesn't matter where I'm going. Now I'm coming with you," she drawled, brushing past me back toward the busy street.

"No. Do you know what she'll—"

Reina whirled around, the thick sweater and scarf peeking from beneath her coat. "Thought you weren't her lap dog?"

Rage danced in her stormy eyes, her long brown hair whipped in front of her face, stark against her pale flushed cheeks. I saw every drop of that Moore blood in her. There was no stopping her, she was coming whether I'd wanted it or not. It was easy to see how she'd talked Amaia into coming along the journey here, why Amaia hadn't pushed back more.

"Okay," I relented.

"See." She strode up to me, patting me on the head. "This is why I like you. Good doggy."

A glimmer of the old Reina shone through as I grumbled, shaking her off.

"This way." I gestured. "It's a week-long trip and there's not enough daylight left for you to go back and pack. Hope what you have is enough. If you can't keep up, I'm leaving you behind to pick up on the way back."

She scoffed. "Pshh, did you miss that entire journey? I kicked ass. *You* keep up with *me*, lap dog. If I'm feeling generous, I'll even share some of my hunt."

I was left standing in her wake, wondering how I ended up surrounded by so many unstable people. Nodding in disbelief, I followed the skipping brunette, taking off in the distance.

THE UNKEMPT BRIDGE OVER ST. LOUIS RIVER TOSSED THE WEIGHT OF the cargo in the bed of the truck. Problem was, we *had* no cargo in the bed of this truck. At least not when we'd gotten in and left the garage of Duluth's trade and military vehicles.

Reina could be born mute and she would still talk your damn ear off. Today's topic was everything but the only question I'd asked her once we'd gotten outside the walls; *Where were you going?*

I slammed on the brakes.

"Ow, what the heck?" Reina said, rubbing the back of her neck.

My hand flew over her mouth, her lips pursed beneath my palms to push it away. I shushed her, praying she'd for once since I'd known her to listen when someone's trying to keep her ass safe.

I'd always had shitty luck.

"Ew, your hands are dirty, get off—"

"Shh, damn it. Shut the fuck up." I mouthed, her head now backed against the window in horror, suppressing a gag.

She crossed her arms, ready to say more, but took one glance at my face and thought better of it. Her body tensed, leaning forward to grab the knife strapped on her ankle. My eyes met hers, *stay alert.* Reina nodded.

"Stay here," I silently whispered, pulling my knife out in return.

Best to keep whatever this was quiet. I didn't need the extra attention in our direction slowing us down further; this was time sensitive. The longer we waited, the longer Duluth would remain vulnerable to attacks. We all would.

Monterey Compound would be no more. And then what would have been the point of this all? Of Tiago leading me to his brother Tomás? My failure would ruin what was left of Amaia's heart. It would ruin her.

I didn't plan on failing any of them.

Reina rolled her eyes, shrugging in response. *Where am I going to go?*

Keeping my movements slow, I opened the car door, crouching low toward the back of the truck bed. Silent on my toes, I crept forward, listening for any indication on what awaited me inside. A rattled, hushed exhale sounded. *There it is.*

Springing in a swift motion, my knife found the collar of a black coat. I was ready to graze it across, not wanting to give whoever the fuck this was a chance to act first. They wouldn't be hiding if they just wanted to talk.

Kill or be killed appeared to remain the way of life out in The Expanse. I'd be lying if I said I didn't blissfully embrace that small rush that came from ending a life. If Seth and Reina's father had a chance to study my brain, my genetics, I bet he'd say murderous was hereditary.

"Woah, hey!" A strained voice said, arms up, surrendering, "I'm Riley's guy, I come in peace."

My eyes scanned him over. His coiled hair was cut low, military style. The black cargos he wore were tucked into tan hiking boots, the thick material of his coat hid his lean body. Staring down my nose, I took in his face. Not a single worry line on his brown skin.

Age meant shit these days when it came to power, but he was little more than a kid. Couldn't have been more than twenty, and that was being generous. He held up a crumpled piece of paper in his hand.

The kid was built for information, spying maybe, but not killing. Then again, Reina had an innocent way about her that went out the window when it was time to do what needed to be done. I smirked, deciding to take my chances. Amaia had been concerned about Riley's wellbeing the other day. While Riley would be getting our letter any day now, the letter he'd sent after our departure to announce our fake arrival should have arrived weeks ago.

We'd been awaiting a messenger, unable to seek them out ourselves without Seth here to communicate with Riley on who he was. Shit, a base-level description of him would've given us *something* to go on.

I sure as hell wouldn't be leaving shit up to a mind-leech ever again. Amaia couldn't glare her way into silencing me. Smirking, I snatched the letter from him, dragging him out the bed of the truck and dropping him onto the asphalt.

He pushed himself off the ground, dusting himself off. "Fuck, you're just as unhinged as they say."

"And you're either stupid or extremely confident in your abilities to be lurking after *the bloodhound*," I said, sarcasm lacing the words. "The only reason you're still alive is because I can't fuck *that* one up in the head anymore or I'll have to open up my own asylum."

He glanced behind my head toward the passenger side of the truck. "I had to wait to seek you all out, make sure it was safe. Sloan's watching like a hawk; now's not the time to let her know they have a spy among them."

"He's right." Reina's boots crunched under shattered glass as she approached my rear. "Don't want another Moore to be the reason someone else at Duluth loses their head."

The messenger studied her, sympathy crossing over his dark eyes. "I don't think you're one of the bad Moore's if that makes you feel any better."

"I thought I told you to stay put," I muttered through clenched teeth,

"What? Is your name Amaia or somethin'. Last I checked I don't take orders from the lapdog." She released a mocking bark, grinning as she swiped the letter from my hands.

"It's nothing we don't already know," I said, watching her thick brows scrunch as she scoured the letter again, "If you're here to help, why are you hiding?"

"I was going to speak up, but … you scare me. I was hyping myself up for it," he stammered, shadow-boxing the air on bouncing toes. "And there's nothing new on the letter because the knowledge I hold is up here. I just brought it as proof because, well, like I said, you scare me. I figured I'd need some tangible evidence." He thudded a finger against the temple of his head. *Scholar*, of the Seer sort, like Moe.

"Go on." My voice was rough, impatient.

Amaia wouldn't like this one bit. Riley having made use of a literal child as a spy. The way Riley had spoken of him, he'd been here since the end of the war. He would have been solidly under the age Amaia had allowed to staff her troops. Perhaps that's why she wasn't as hesitant as Sloan to arm them. Everyone in a position of power would have to bend over and let their morals fuck them at some point. Figure out which line is worth crossing and which one isn't. It was possible that, at one point, he was needed. Shit maybe it was his choice.

His stammering was probably endearing to some. I could see how he could be a good choice to welcome people to the area, but you don't leave someone at the gates who can't hold their own in some capacity.

I'd keep an eye on him.

"I'm Abel. Riley said you'd be expecting me. I'm his inside guy, I work Duluth's front gate. Mostly responsible for greeting new arrivals. More specifically tasked to escort each emissary that arrives. I know who can help us, and who we'll need to focus on using more … convincing tactics." He gazed at Reina knowingly.

"Why would Riley tell you that?" I asked, suspicion creeping in. They were a tight group, they didn't expose each other's gifts unless absolutely necessary.

"He didn't, he saw it." Reina grinned and looped arms with him. "Now tell me, Abel, who may I have the pleasure of seducing?" She tossed her head back, brown hair blowing in the wind as she let out a brisk cackle.

CHAPTER

SIX

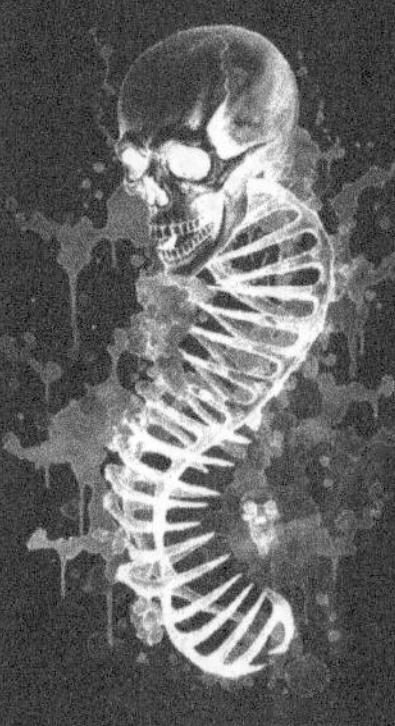

AMAIA

I glanced out the large arched window that took up a wall of Sloan's study. The city of Duluth was dimly lit by the night sky beyond it. People hunched around bonfires in the distance. I appreciated that about Duluth. During the day, they were serious. Despair filled their eyes as they moved through the settlement, the question of who was next at the forefront of their minds. But at night, shit, they partied like it was their last night. And maybe it was.

Smoke dissipated in the air as Sloan's whiskey burned down my throat, warming the depths of my chest. She ashed her cigarette, fingers tapping to the classic rock she played on the CD player when I'd arrived. I hadn't even realized how much I missed basic electricity. Building a dam should have been the least of their priorities, but I couldn't say I blamed them for wanting it.

This was becoming our thing. She'd call me to her office to debrief her, and I'd have to answer her summons. It was hard, pretending the space I'd previously dedicated in my evenings to Jax and Prescott was now dedicated to this … bullshit. I missed how things used to be.

There was a time where I wished that I could turn back the clock, go back to The Before, but now, I just wanted my life in the immediate After. When things had been good, when I'd had my family. *Shit*, at least in her office there was judgment-free liquor. It wasn't good booze, but anything was better than nothing.

"I need more people, Sloan," I said, leaving her little room for resistance.

This constant, never-ending conversation was growing tiresome. It was no longer a request. She needed to heed my warning, or her people would die.

"That can't happen and you know that." Her fire red hair grazed the ground as she leaned her head back in her chair, trying to tune me out.

"Sloan …"

"No, Maia." Sloan's voice cracked, her sad blue eyes met mine. For the first time in weeks, I saw the emotions that tormented her, the thoughts she tried to keep everyone from seeing. "I can't. You know that."

Violet, her daughter, giggled from the balcony, her dolls slamming into each other with force. Sloan watched her with caring, watchful eyes, a small smile forming as she lost herself to daydreams.

"There are over fifty-thousand people here, Sloan, and only eight-hundred soldiers. It's not sustainable. Hell, it's not even operational if you want me to be honest."

"I promised Morgan I would keep these people safe. Give Violet a shot of normalcy, a good place to grow up. Similar to what you have out in Monterey, in Salem. They deserve that, and we can't give them that if we arm the innocent. Arm *children*," she said in a hushed tone through clenched teeth.

Morgan was Duluth's fallen leader. I'd worked closely with him during the war between territories. He'd been a sensible man, still had his morals intact. Learning of their romantic relationship had taken me by surprise simply because I hadn't seen any remnants of romance in their interactions during the time I'd spent here. But things change quickly when life goes to shit, and I could see how she'd be drawn to the kindness I'd seen in him.

It was a good balance; where he was kind, she was hopeful. In their leadership, that hadn't been a good mix. In his death, she had realized that, making her wary of learning another lesson.

The lesson of balance. A lesson she was on the cusp of learning, whether she realized it or not. A lesson she needed to master. Ruthlessness must be checked by kindness. Hopefulness must be checked by reality. One without the other was a recipe for disaster in this world.

A good leader can be both ruthless and kind. Hopeful but realistic. Unfortunately for my friend, she only presented each flaw one at a time.

"Then keep them safe. Train them, help them be prepared. Eventually I have to leave, Sloan, go back to prepare my own people. Your citizens deserve a fighting chance, and you need to give them that. Because if you don't, when war comes to your walls, this place will fall."

Her round lips closed over the butt of her cigarette before she put it out. My old friend stared back at me, pleading to help make the decision easier. I would offer no help here. This was a decision she needed to make on her own. There was no one who could press the red button but her.

"We don't get to preserve innocence anymore, Sloan. I hate it too, but now is for fighting, for doing what we can to make sure at least some sliver of it will remain. Meaning, we have to nip this shit in the bud. Fast. And to do that, we need numbers. *People.* I agree, we shouldn't be arming children, but they still need to know how to fight should shit go bad. Everyone under sixteen can shelter, *Violet* can shelter," I said, reaching across the desk to grab her hand. "Besides that, get them ready to fight."

My chair dragged against the red and blue patterned carpet as I scooted away from the desk. Chugging the last of the liquor, I sighed, wiping my mouth before placing the glass down with a clank.

The brass knob of the door rested against my palm. Sloan's voice, cold and gravely, stopped me in place, "You'll get your soldiers. Give me a few days."

CHAPTER
SEVEN

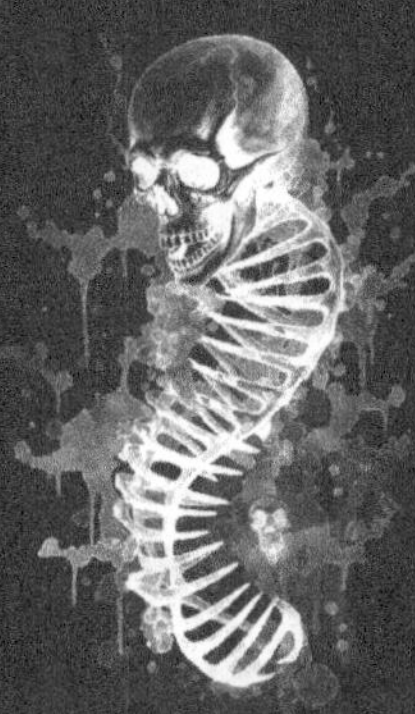

ALEXIARES

My fist tapped lightly against the dirty-ass door of one of the rundown apartments Sloan had stuffed us in. I'd never get tired of those toned brown legs. Biting my lip until it fucking hurt, I willed some self-control into my mind as I traced up toward the oversized sweater hanging down to her thighs. She rolled her eyes, curls bobbing in her bun as she scoffed, walking away toward her room.

Closing the door behind me, I locked it, letting out a small chuckle as I followed her inside. A fire sparked in the makeshift pit she'd put together to warm the room, the smoke trickling out the cracked window. She'd somehow found a way to make the place inviting, cozy even.

Amaia stumbled over her feet, an empty clear bottle kicked under the bed. I cleared my throat, forcing her to meet my glare. She wasn't fooling anyone, let alone me.

"Back already? Must have gone great." She humored as she slid onto the right side of the bed.

I kicked my shoes off, scooting in on the other side. "Reina didn't tell you?"

How we had gotten to this point fucking beat me. After our time on the road, it was all too easy to fall into the routine. The first few nights had been two tired people debriefing on the day. Even if Moe and Reina were talking to her, they didn't have the military or combat expertise she needed to lean on. Wasn't long before I realized she'd been drinking again, and I didn't want her to plunge into her misery alone. If she fell apart now, then we were all fucked.

But then, the conversations about preparing for war and the stunning idiocracy of the people here had turned deeper. *Good* conversations. She was fucking brilliant; I felt like the dumbest person alive conversing with her. And I was no dummy. There wasn't a single topic I could bring up that Amaia wouldn't have some knowledge of. Not to mention an opinion.

The sky would grow lighter until our eyelids gave up, falling asleep curled into the couch. Then one night, she'd led me into the room instead of toward the tattered sofa. *Fuck if I would ask questions about the invitation.*

"She told me to go ask the dog, and since Harley isn't here," she said, her brown eyes dancing as she teased. "I'm assuming she means you."

"Ouch, I thought she was joking." I would be lying if I said it didn't bother me at least a bit. I'd come to care about Reina. She was a good person and I didn't know many of those.

"Oh, she is, don't take it personal. It's more so because you're here … with me. I don't think she believes I deserve any comfort right now, not after what I did."

"Hey," I reached over, cupping her chin, forcing her to face me, "you did what you thought you had to. What you thought was right; they'll understand soon enough."

Her eyes were so damn sad. I saw every emotion yet nothing behind them at the same time. "It's more than that. I think now … I think they fear me a bit. Not what I'm capable of physically but—"

"Fear they may never know who you actually are."

The same argument could be made toward Reina and Tomoe. It was unfair what they held against her. They all had kept vital secrets that could have resulted in a different outcome. Personally, I believed Tomoe should be able to get that. There was no use bringing it up regardless. Dwelling on the past would get them nowhere.

"Fear lasts much longer than love, Alexiares," she whispered.

"Fear keeps people alive, Amaia, you of all people understand that. Sometimes it's better if love and fear go hand in hand. You can't have fear without knowing love. To have fear, you must have something you love. Something that can be taken."

She shifted in the bed, eyes darting down. "What happened out there?"

I explained how we'd found Abel and the information he'd been able to offer. Amaia winced when I brought up the fact that he was barely past the age of puberty. Around the age my brother Evander would have been, had he survived.

It appeared that our mission had become even more complicated. We had our work cut out for us, and now we were going to be stretched thin. The *brujas* still needed to be collected, Tomoe hadn't yet finished her research for the right spell. Everything Sloan had her hands on was a mess.

Now, not only would we have to make the journey back to Monterey, we'd also need to convince settlements to join a war they ignorantly believed wasn't at their doorstep. We'd been operating under the impression that our way back home would be faster, easier now that we'd be able to take direct routes. If each of the settlements were on our side, the treaty wouldn't be at risk as we passed through. Evidently, that was not the case.

As long as there were *some* settlements that would let us pass through without protest, then it would take us less than the three months it took to get here. In the meantime, heeding Abel's advice may be the best course of action. His vision had shown Reina and Tomoe acting as emissaries, trying to gain allies. If they didn't join our side, they would fall. Abel had seen it. If they fell, we were fucked. Covert Province would force them to fight on their side. Another variable that could go wrong in an already fragile plan.

"Makes sense," she said, oddly calm. "Reina used to do some of our emissary visits at the baby stages of The Compound. You've seen her—powers or not, she's a schmoozer."

"Schmoozer," I snorted, "you and your words."

"Jealous of my extensive vocabulary now, are you?"

I tossed my head up, releasing a sarcastic laugh with a mocking gesture. "If that's what helps you sleep at night."

"Seems to me like *I* help you sleep at night."

"Your bed just happens to be more comfortable than mine." It was a lie. They were both shitty mattresses. "And you talk a lot. Your voice reminds me of one of those audiobooks. Puts me right to sleep."

Amaia blinked dramatically, jaw slack. "Sorry, every time you bring up reading, it catches me off guard."

I smiled at the insult, closing my eyes as she talked about the moments I'd missed in her day.

THERE WAS NO SUCH THING AS PEACE IN THIS HELLHOLE. I THOUGHT The Compound was a magnet for attacks, but this place might as well have a blimp floating over it with a giant arrow saying *Attack Here.*

Rapid banging against Amaia's door startled me out of my sleep. Amaia sprung from the tuck of my body that she somehow always ended up huddled into. Her head smacked into my jaw in the process.

"Ouch, damn it."

She glanced up, tugging some cargos out of the dresser in front of the bed with a smirk.

"You've taken worse hits, you'll be alright," she said, before striding to the door.

I followed her, standing at her six as she cracked open the door. Sloan pushed her way in, Elliot paused in the door frame, an awkward smile on his face in apology to Amaia.

He was a real weirdo if you asked me. Elliot never said anything unless it agreed with Sloan. Professional backup.

"Good morning to you too," Amaia muttered.

Sloan glared at me, whipping around to face Amaia. "No, not a good morning, Amaia. We've got a problem."

"We always have a problem, Sloan. How are the shields coming?" Amaia yawned, brushing off Sloan's urgency.

Everything was an issue to her. If Sloan said jump, the only thing she expected in response was *how high?* It was exhausting. I would respect it if Sloan's demands ever came with working solutions. Instead, she made demands and expected others to solve her problems.

"There *are* no shields." Sloan shook her head in annoyance. "We pulled the scientists from working on them to train."

We'd been trying to replicate Finley's shield, to no avail. I hadn't been in the business of caring about what went on in Finley's lab. She'd never discussed the specifics with me. I wouldn't understand and she didn't exactly have the patience Reina had with breaking things down.

Amaia groaned, brushing past her to shove her pants and shoes on. "Move, Sloan. Must I do it all my damn self? Learn how to delegate properly. Why would you have your scientists training for physical combat?"

Amaia had long forgotten the hope that she may get her long-lost friend back, desperate to have someone here besides me to lean on, confide in, feel welcomed by. Instead, I'd seen two women who had once trusted each other and now chose to do so again for the sake of their people. Their past friendship had saved our lives, allowed us to have a chance in this war. Nothing more.

There was a chance it could have been redeemed, had Amaia chosen to push for it. But she didn't. She had lost respect for her friend. They both had been placed in a position of power without the desire to have it, but only one had stepped into their role with a mind of a leader. Amaia's trust in me hadn't exactly helped Sloan have confidence in her judgment. The tension between them only increased in my presence.

"Sure. If you want to go out there and die, be my guest. Your scientist is here, clearly had some training. Why should mine be any different?" Sloan said dismissively.

Something about the defiance in her eyes made me decide this was a cat fight that I didn't wish to be present for this damn early in the morning. I let out a sigh, moving across the room to put my shoes on for whatever order of the day Sloan insisted we tended to.

"What are you talking about?" Amaia asked, arms crossing over her chest.

"We're about to be surrounded by a hundred soldiers. Jig is up. They know you're here, alive. I'll take a guess and say my cousin is fine and made it to his father."

I stopped in my tracks. "Fuck."

"You're cursing doesn't help, *Bloodhound*," Sloan bit out. "Unless you have a solution, stay over there. Hasn't anyone ever enlightened you on the principles of being seen and not heard?"

I smiled at her. "If only Finley had handed me your name on a folded piece of paper. This is my—"

"Alexiares, hush." Amaia said, her hand going up as her brows pushed. She was thinking, doing some calculations.

Elliot pushed from the corner of the room, strolling over to Sloan's side with a "no bullshit" glare on his face.

My face flushed, heating with anger at her silencing me. Whatever was happening between us, whatever the fuck this was, didn't stop her award-winning attitude from shining through. This little act in front of others only fueled the canine nicknames people annoyingly attributed to my name.

"I was *going* to say that this *is* my territory." My voice was colder than I expected, but it was too early in the morning for their verbal assaults. "Before her shields, Finley was working on using the resources we had at hand. Can I continue or are you two going to keep telling me to shut my mouth?"

They both turned to scowl at me but said nothing.

"Pleasure, ladies. Now, there's enough snow on the ground that we may be able to form a natural barrier. That way, we can put snipers around to funnel them into a more manageable formation. They won't be able to surround the wall. Make an alleyway and they're target practice. How much longer do we have before they get here?"

Sloan scoffed, "This is ridiculous. I'm not risking the safety of my people by putting them out there to be protected by frozen fucking water."

"You lose a few or you lose a hundred. Those are your options today, Sloan, grow up and make a choice. Stop teetering back and forth over having a conscience or being a good leader. You don't see Amaia stuttering over her choices."

Hurt crossed Amaia's eyes as she gazed past my head, face hardened. I tilted my head, wondering what I said wrong.

"How you went from Xavier to *this*, I will never understand." Sloan burst into a choked laugh.

I glanced between both of them. Sloan's pale, freckled face set in a sneer. Amaia refused to meet my eye directly. She turned to Sloan, nodding her head absent-mindedly.

"Whatever, Sloan. He's right, it may work. I may not have a conscience," she said, looking at me pointedly. "But I wouldn't risk the lives of the majority if there was a way to prevent that from happening. The lives of a few are a calculated risk; these are soldiers. *This* is their job, *this* is what they signed up for. For the freedom of those they love. They don't take that lightly and neither should you. You need to let them do what they're meant to do. Protect."

CHAPTER
EIGHT

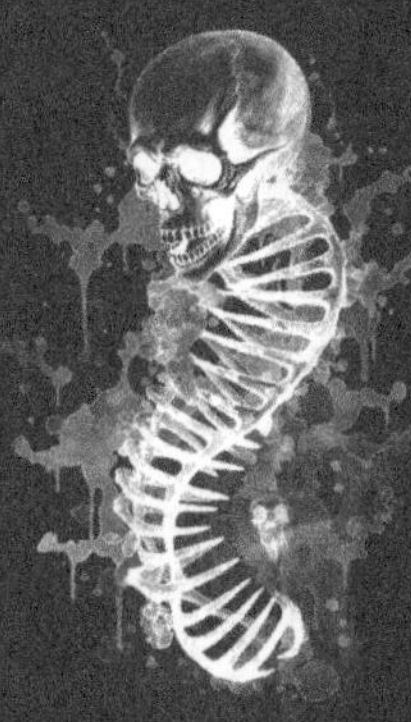

AMAIA

"Only high-power bullets can get through more than three feet of solid ice," Alexiares explained to Sloan. "As long as the temperature stays below freezing, then what we have here will be much stronger than that."

Sloan stared past his head dismissively, meeting my gaze as though I'd have anything to add. This wasn't my kind of thing. We didn't have snow, ice, or even freezing temperatures to work with out in Monterey Compound. Understanding the basic science behind this was fine and dandy, but that wasn't why I believed it would work. I didn't need to understand the intricacies of science to have faith in our plan. All I had to do was understand weapons and their functionality in relation to our environment.

"Given the little information we have on them, I think it's safe to say that they do, in fact, have high power bullets among other fancy shit." Sloan grumbled, doubt showcasing on her face.

I nodded my head in understanding. "The cold will slow their bullets down. Factor in the increase in wind deflection and bullet drop … we're set. You're fine. It'll give us the advantage of reduced energy on impact. Their accuracy would have to be impeccable. *Umbra Mortis* will probably stack their front lines, but that won't be an issue for long." Not with our own snipers in place, snipers local to the area. They were used to the weather. This may be the one advantage they'd be able to keep.

Being *Umbra Mortis* had its perks—we were walking weapons. But a weapon cannot fight against what it cannot see.

She met my stare blankly, still not comprehending how it would work. Alexiares moved off to the side, helping a soldier finish constructing the last of our improvised shields.

"High power bullets can get through three feet of snow, right?" I attempted to try another way of getting her to follow where our minds were at, "We have six feet. Adding in the calculations of the temperature, wind, and the bullet's response to gravity, ain't shit getting through here. Not unless they use their magic, a lot of it. Which makes them weak, vulnerable, easy to pick off. They don't want that, not if there's only a hundred of them as you say. Strength is needed for the journey back, and if they can't subdue us here, then we'll be able to fight back. Chase them, meaning they can't stop for rest. We lower their morale by picking them off. Once they see their bullets don't mean shit here, they'll retreat."

The purpose of our plan was to simply slow their approach to Duluth's walls and pick them off. If they had any sense of self-preservation, after the first few down, they would turn back to regroup, giving us more time to get things under control. I wouldn't hold my breath on that one. It may buy us a day or two, but not anything longer. If Dictator Moore was anything like Seth, brute force would be their first objective in pacifying us.

Alexiares returned to my side, his body too close for comfort. I rubbed my temples with irritation. There wasn't time for me to lose focus, lives depended on it. I circled around, moving next to Sloan. His honey brown eyes caught mine, narrowing in question.

Having a conscience or being a good leader. The words echoed in my mind, tormenting me. Had I been wrong about him? Jax had seen me as being good, and though I knew I wasn't quite that, it had still been nice having someone see me that way. Now I was the villain in everyone's eyes, including a villain himself.

So much for seeing the darkness with me, for embracing the beast. *You'll have to have to feed this beast alone.* Sighing, I decided to turn my attention back to the soldiers setting up our little death valley.

Elliot hovered behind Sloan. "We going to test this out or what?" he asked.

Alexiares' heavy stare weighed on me. "I'm not the one running this show," I retorted, refusing to meet Alexiares' eye. He was bundled in layers to fend off the freezing temperatures, his eyes and the bridge of his nose were about all that was visible.

Alexiares squared his shoulders, his head the last to turn away from me. "You're always the one running the show."

"Clear the area," I commanded the soldiers in the immediate blast zone scattered toward what we had determined to be the edges of this battlefield. Alexiares waited, eyes eager for my instruction. "Fire."

A small, but mighty ember of flame encased Alexiares' palm. I'd been working with him on mastering control over his magic. He was right, a weapon of mass destruction without structure is dangerous. And not dangerous in the way I needed him to be. We'd only been able to step away a few times, but each time he made progress, what little progress may it be. I would take what I could get at this point, though admittedly I'd grown slightly frustrated.

It was like he got it, was on the verge of mastering it, and then he would lose focus. As luck would have it, no one had been harmed. Yet. I was determined to not let it get that far ever again, not unless he wanted it to.

He released his power; the blast let out a sizzle in the seconds after it met the packed snow. Some of it had melted, but not more than a few inches. Alexiares followed up with a spray of bullets, tossing the AK-47 back over his shoulder when he was finished. It would take several clips and some magic to get through, and by that time, they'd already be down a quarter of their soldiers.

"Awesome, it works." I growled, bowing before Sloan. "Can we go now? I'm cold and I haven't had the pleasure of my morning coffee."

"What? We just leave them out here?" Sloan asked, jogging to catch up with me and Alexiares, who now walked at my side. I picked up the pace, wanting to be clear of both their presence if only by a few steps.

"Yes, Sloan, that's what soldiers do. They stay and fight." I halted in my steps, Alexiares ramming into my back at my abrupt stop. Fire simmered at my fingertips. My eyes squinted as I watched a figure in all black running straight for us. "Who's that?"

Alexiares grabbed my shoulder, trying to catch my attention. "That's Abel."

My flames went out. The last time I'd seen Abel, he'd been a boy. I took in his features as he got closer. Damn, even with the years of distance he was just like Riley. He was tall, not quite as tall as Riley, but he still had years to grow. It was hard to tell how healthy he was as the large black coat and thick sweater underneath swallowed him. There was a lot of bounce in his step. Every bit of his demeanor happy, excited to be here.

"You know Abel," Sloan said, accusation in her tone. Her blue eyes pierced mine, a chill going down my spine. I would have to answer for this later.

Fuck. Please be cool, please be cool.

Abel nodded in my direction as he approached. His brown eyes lit up with joy, followed by a wary glance at Alexiares, grazed over Elliot, then Sloan last. I honestly don't know how he made it this far undetected. The recognition in his eyes when he took us in was undeniable.

I hadn't known Abel would be sent here. It was protocol for Riley to only tell me *where* we had spies lingering, not *who* was there. All I knew was that he had begged Riley for a chance to prove himself on his own and help The Compound. He wasn't like Riley. Abel grew up with his parents, came from a good home until both his parents turned.

When Riley found him sneaking around and stealing food, he moved Abel in with him. The fuss he went through to make sure one of his men kept an eye on him at all times had been one of his more dramatic moments since I'd known him. Soon after that, Abel had made it clear he no longer found satisfaction within the bounds of safety. Of having a home. He'd had that before. The memory of it was good enough. Why would he want to be bored behind the walls of The Compound now?

While some people longed for a safe environment, a place that's theirs to call home, others had no desire to have that. They needed that adrenaline rush, that constant *what if*. Tomoe had told me of her time in Transient Nation. It was full of people who found pleasure in uncertainty. We couldn't stop Abel from leaving. He would do it if he wanted. Had always been a determined kid. But if we gave him a mission in a place with relative safety, we had a chance of preventing his premature death.

I didn't agree with Riley's decision, but at the time, I was new to my role. There were certain things I was willing to push back on, and shamefully during times of war, a sixteen-year-old enlisting wasn't one of them. I'd had my regrets. My rules on who was eligible to fight in my troops came shortly after.

"Tomoe has news," Abel said, out of breath from the quick pace he'd kept trekking in the snow.

Sloan looked bored, her fiery hair blowing under the fur hat. Alexiares side-eyed me, waiting to see if I was going to encourage him to continue. I shrugged. I hadn't known Tomoe was close to figuring anything out. She hadn't consulted me once.

"Okay? What is it?" Alexiares asked impatiently.

He'd been less than thrilled when he'd told me about the car ride back with Abel in tow. I found it amusing that someone was able to match Reina's energy. It was comforting that someone had been able to bring the Reina I'd grown to love back to the surface, as fleeting as it was.

"She thinks she knows the spell," he said, peering up at Alexiares like he would pin him down for talking too slow. *Nope, knowing him, he probably did do that the first time.*

Sloan's suspicion was still evident, her stare watchful, darting between the three of us. "Thinks or knows?" she asked, her voice raspy from the cold and constant smoke.

"Well … *think* I suppose," Abel said, not quite sure how to answer her. "We won't know until she tries … right?"

Sloan grumbled to herself, stomping off in frustration without us. Abel huffed, not having a moment to rest before returning to the miles long snowy trek back inside the walls of Duluth city-proper. He did his best to keep up, sensing the trouble he'd placed himself in. Alexiares studied me, searching my face for a hint of emotion. I rolled my eyes. We had work to do, and standing here staring at each other wasn't going to bring us closer to our goal.

"Ready to be test bait?" I teased, forcing him to follow.

CHAPTER
NINE

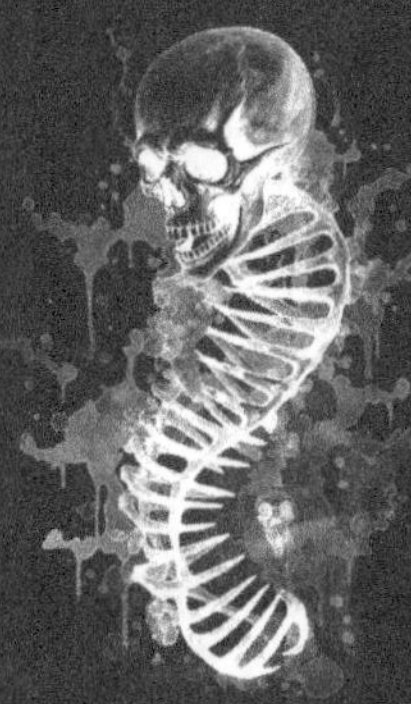

TOMOE

The heavy door slammed into the wall. Sloan tossed her thick wool coat on the nearest chair, a long blade tucked in a wide leather holster against her hip. Several of her lackeys filled the space in the room behind her, Abel and Elliot on either side.

At least in Monterey, I'd been granted a sense of privacy. Knocking wouldn't kill her, and if it did, shit, maybe she should knock twice.

A curly bun bobbed into the room. The tip of Amaia's ears were pink, sticking out from beneath the soft scarf wrapped around her neck. Her dark eyes scanned the room, marking each corner and point of entry. They softened as they found me and I forced myself to peer past her shoulder. Alexiares followed close behind.

"I see Abel found you," I said curtly.

Sloan's eyes rolled to the back of her big ass head, her raspy voice cut through the air. "Clearly. You have something to share?" she questioned, a smug expression crossing over her freckled face.

I sighed, already tired of being in her presence. "Possibly, yes."

"I didn't haul ass five miles in two feet of snow to be informed over *possibilities*," she said, her fingers making air quotes around the last word.

"Possibilities, Sloan, are the best I can fucking do until I see it in practice. As I said several times, I wasn't even sure my original spell worked until shit fell apart." I stopped, realizing we were missing someone. "Where's Reina?"

"Do you take me for my cousin's babysitter?" Sloan tossed her wavy, red hair over her shoulders, arms crossed as she leaned against the large high-top table in the center of the room. I couldn't help but imagine yanking her hair right out her head. Maybe if she was nice, Reina would offer her people a tip or two about homemade conditioner.

"Do you want me to answer that?" I mumbled, her sharp gaze meeting mine.

"You haven't seen her yet?" Amaia asked. "Sloan woke us up. We went straight to the field." She paused, realizing I had no clue what was happening. "There's about a hundred Covert soldiers headed our way. We'll be able to slow them, for now. Your update couldn't have come at a better time. It won't take them long to regroup."

"I'll go get her," Alexiares said, his thick brows gathered in concern.

Amaia nodded in acknowledgment. "Should we wait or …"

Her pupils dilated, eyes following Alexiares, trailing him as he crossed through the room and back out the door. Sloan nodded, sending some of her people out to guard the door. It was my turn to roll my eyes at her continued waste of resources. What did she think was going to happen,— Alexiares would bite off an ear? Her people would revolt?

Abel stood tucked into the corner, eyes down. *Ah, so that's what this was about.* She had ordered guards to keep any other undiscovered spies away from the door. I smirked, letting her know I was onto her fear and planned to fuck with her over it.

We had no other spies here, but what was the harm in her thinking that we did? And if other territories did, then I guess her paranoia was a good thing.

"I've got better things to do besides wait around for my cousin," Sloan snapped. "Let's hear it."

"Better things as in … Tell people what they need to do and how fast to do it? Delegate all your responsibilities?" I bit out, unable to catch myself this time around.

"We can fill her in when she gets here, Tomoe." Amaia tried to reassure me, her tone even. "She's right. We don't have time for this. If you have a new development, please share. We need some good news right now."

I folded my arms over my chest, bunching up the stiff, itchy sweater Sloan had provided. I'm pretty sure she'd given me the shitty batch of clothes on purpose. Maybe it was my bubbly personality that had inspired her distaste.

Of course Amaia thinks Sloan's right.

I walked toward the bookcase, my fingers traced the leather spines of a few books before landing on the ones I needed for reference. Lining them next to my notebook, I surveyed the room, ready to offer what I know.

"We have a few options," I said.

To be expected, Sloan cut me off before I could finish my train of thought. "Options as in?"

Impatience, in this case, did appear to be genetic. It was endearing on Seth—on Sloan, not so much. "I'm getting there if you would let me speak."

"Sloan," Amaia said in warning.

Sloan rolled her neck like she was fighting mental fucking demons. Her hair cascaded down her back against her white shirt as she motioned me to continue. A couple of the Tinkerers skimmed the pages of my shit. I smacked the closest one's fingers away, my other hand instinctively diverted toward Wrath. Sloan had begrudgingly re-armed us. After all, we were pulling more than our weight here.

I eyed Sloan with a pinch of repulsion. It was hard looking at her. Seth and Sloan's features were so similar. Reina had always said her and Hunter stuck out from their family like a sore thumb. After staring at her and Seth's faces for so long, I'd grown to see their similarities more than their differences. So seeing Sloan share Seth's fiery hair and fierce eyes, the same small but full lips, was unsettling. It made me want to vomit.

"Starting with weather," I continued, showing my notes in the beautiful vintage journal I'd found in Duluth's Public Library and claimed. It wasn't the most breathtaking library I'd ventured into, but it was *something*. "The snow, it helps with balance. We'll need that to keep people from burning out when they powershare. We won't have time to train them for mastery and without balance this could be … catastrophic." I bit my lip, peering up at their faces.

When no one pestered me with questions, I continued, "They're about to develop magic that's familiar yet unrecognizable to their mind. They won't know how to control it. Think of it like a string," I said, mimicking a thin strand in the air. "When we activate our magic, we tug at what feels like a string that starts in our mind and connects with the heart. That's the string we constantly stroke gently to keep ourselves under control. When we do this, that string will still exist, but now a new one will too. And that thread will be stronger, thicker. That string will become a rope. Without channeling the snow, without providing that assistance of balance, we'll have weapons that we cannot control, because *they* cannot control. Everyone will burn out their magic before realizing they're about to sever the string."

"Makes sense," Sloan said, nodding. "Okay, what next?"

The hazy glow of the sun tucked behind the heavy gray clouds in the sky illuminated the room through the tattered wooden window. If any of the gods out there were even halfway on our side, the snow would hold up through the weekend.

"The day of the week also matters; ideally, we'll want to wait until Saturday."

"Moe, it's Thursday, we need to test this out *now*." Amaia said impatiently, shifting side to side.

"Spell timing is important," I pushed. "Saturday gets us self-discipline. *Saturday* gets us protection. Not to mention the aspect of transformation. All three of which we'll need; we wait until Saturday."

"Fine," Sloan ground out. "And the rest? What's the actual spell?"

All the oxygen sucked out of the room as everyone focused on me. I hoped I was right on this. "I'd like to start by saying none of you will exactly love this. A protection spell in ancient times was typically complemented with food or a beverage, followed by a cleanse."

"Tomoe, I'm getting tired of having to bait this out of you." Sloan took a step closer to me; if it was a fight she wanted, I would happily oblige. I pushed away the desire to close my eyes, not wanting her to assume my inability to face her for long was a result of intimidation.

"The blood," Amaia said, her eyes trailed over my body. "You said the spell you performed had blood."

I nodded, realization crossed Sloan's face. Her lips stretched to a tight line. "Really? Blood? In the middle of an apocalypse caused by biological warfare? Fantastic."

"I said you wouldn't like it, but it's necessary. I'm sure Amaia would love that."

Hurt crossed over her face, but instead of flinging her pain back at me, she offered me some humor, the way she had consistently done over the last few weeks. "I'm sure someone else I know would love the blood aspect too," she teased.

"Hmm." I grumbled, ready to move on. "Anyway, I suppose all you care about, Sloan, is what we need to accomplish for a test. Send your lackeys to get the ingredients since your dear cousin isn't here to take my requests." I tilted my head, a sliver of joy going through me at the knowledge that she had no choice but to follow my command.

Elliot motioned for one of the Tinkerers who'd moseyed through my notebook. The woman flipped to an empty page in her notepad. Her green eyes met mine, genuine curiosity staring back at me as she awaited my list.

"I'll need a vial of blood for each person partaking in the spell. A white candle, rosemary, sea salt, black tourmaline or a small piece of hematite, whichever you can find. Doesn't matter which one. And a pen and piece of parchment paper. Specifically parchment, nothing else."

Her head moved absentmindedly as she mouthed over the list, she glanced at me for confirmation, then at Sloan who said nothing before dismissing her.

"What's the prep?" Amaia asked.

"Just need a quiet place to focus, no interruptions." I said, eyes trailing pointedly at Sloan, "and to center myself. Other than that, it's about testing it out to see if it works. I know the spell, if the ritual goes off without a hitch, we'll be fine. Dark magic or not, spell-casting is simple. The only requirements are intention, focus, and belief. Intuition is everything, but again, I have to warn, magic of this sort comes at a cost."

It was a damn good thing Reina wasn't here, or she'd see right through my bullshit confidence. Truly, I was terrified that I would fuck this up and hurt someone. Or worse, be wrong and end up being the reason our mission would fail. Why the alliance would fail.

The reason this war would be lost.

Unfortunately for me, my visions were of no use. The spell required dark magic, that meant we had to go at this blind. The universe would ensure there would always be balance.

"We know, we know," Sloan said, as if my warnings were minor inconveniences in the plan. "There's a chance they can't gain control, but I have full faith you and cousin dearest can use Alexiares' rings, maybe a quick peek into Finley's past to figure out the rest."

"Whatever."

Amaia moved near my side, her fingers grazing my notebook, trying to see what I saw. If anyone here would understand the complexities of this ritual, it was her. "Let's run through the spell and the ritual."

"I'll begin with casting a protective barrier for the duration of the spell, then we'll move forward with the blood binder. The blood needs to drop onto the parchment paper, then the rosemary, sea salt and black tourmaline or hematite go next. I'll touch each item, their energies becoming one in mind—it'll form a shield of defense around whoever I cast on. I'll then say the spell, seal it, then close the circle. Ritual complete."

"What could go wrong?" Sloan mumbled sarcastically.

Amaia's eyes light up with joy, "You brilliant-ass bitch, I knew you would do it."

Our eyes met briefly, Amaia's excitement over the realization of how I'd blended a mix of cultures for the ritual gave me a sense of pride. Full disclosure, also a sense of connection. These were the kind of discoveries and conversations that had formed our friendship. It was nice to have an intelligent conversation with someone who wasn't a prick. The other Scholars at The Compound could be so … ivy league.

I missed my sister damn more than I was willing to admit. Things weren't the same between Reina and I either, but it was weird. Reina's betrayal wasn't toward me, and it wasn't meant to hurt her brother, either. She handled the situation poorly, but it was as best as you could have expected for a twenty-one-year-old in the midst of chaos.

If you keep a lie for one year, it only makes sense to carry it to the grave. Reina had confided in me what had possessed her to keep her secret of what had truly happened the day her family fell apart. The same fateful day she'd lost her uncle, her mother, her brother, and as far as she knew, her father.

Seth would have left if he knew there was hope—he would never stop searching for both his father and their brother. That would become his life goal, to go after them because Reina would not be able to confirm definitively that they were dead. She had lied to keep Seth safe. I hadn't lied, I had omitted, and it was to keep Amaia and Reina focused. To keep *everyone* safe.

Amaia had lied and gotten countless people killed. Her lie had been selfish. It had stripped thousands of people from their choice. So, as much as I missed my sister, I could go another week or two without pleasantly co-existing in the same space.

"I'm not done … that's only the first part," I added. "The last part, um, the first go round, I sort of drank the blood after the spell was complete. Like I said, in ancient times, protection spells were sealed with food or drink. The only way to know if that small change in the ritual had aided in the spell or not is to do it again."

The room went silent, everyone looking around, knowing what would come next. Not ready to volunteer themselves as my sacrificial lamb.

"Lovely, I guess I have until Saturday to convince myself drinking blood doesn't gross me the fuck out," Amaia stated, her mind made up.

It was cute she thought she had a say in this, but two could play at her game. I didn't have a choice, and now, neither would she. "Hell no."

"Moe …" she tried to reason.

Sloan huffed in the background. *Yeah, yeah. She doesn't have time for this. Busiest woman of the year.*

"Amaia," I challenged, "doesn't matter, Reina would never let it happen and neither will Alexiares."

"I somehow doubt Reina gives a shit about what happens to me at this moment, and I'm not in the habit of caring about what Alexiares thinks. If you haven't noticed, his opinion weighs little."

The pain in her voice struck a nerve—she truly believed that. That Reina didn't care. It wasn't true, she still did. We both did; we were just hurt. Amaia had apologized, but only her actions could show us that she respected anything about our friendship, our family.

Sloan scoffed, the locks of her hair falling in contrast against her white shirt. She kept her head down and to the side, hiding the smug grin I wanted to smack off her Moore face.

Amaia's eyes darted to her, a blush reddening her thawing cheeks. "What's funny, Sloan?"

"The fact that you think we're all blind," she mumbled as she reached for one of her rolled cigarettes.

The side of my lip curled in disgust, "For once, I have to agree with the redhead."

"Why am I not surprised by that turn of events?" Amaia took a step closer to me, the pleading clear in her eyes.

She knew she couldn't do this without me, even if Alexiares managed to find a *bruja* closer to the city walls. Even if she merely showed them the spell. There were nuances that could only be repeated if taught, an intentional move on my behalf. If anything were to happen to my family, I needed that bargaining chip to bend the will of whoever stood in my way. What small moral code that remained left in our fallen world would not cease to exist because of my ex-boyfriend and his daddy issues.

"Sucks you can't do the spell without me. If I say no, it doesn't matter what you want to do." I challenged, closing the gap between us.

I'd seen what catastrophes lay ahead due to her decisions. So many fucking visions, so many options, it was hard to keep timelines straight.

"I thought we were all mad about people taking away choices, or is it just her actions we're picking over? Since you and Reina seem to be doing alright," Sloan taunted, an odd mix of defensiveness over Amaia, yet pure bitchiness too.

Looking over my shoulder, I mean-mugged the hell out of her. I wasn't fooled one bit; there was selfishness in her words too. If Amaia wasn't the test subject, then one of Sloan's people would be. Even if I had to drag them here myself.

"How many more people do you want us to lose, Amaia?" I asked, turning my back to Sloan.

"As many as it takes," Sloan said, lighting her cigarette, taking a deep inhale before blowing it into the back of my head.

My right eye twitched, leaning against the center table I took in Sloan's cruelty for what it was. Amaia had been Sloan's best friend for years, and now, they were … this. Whatever the hell this was. I couldn't tell, truly.

There were times I had walked past the large window to Sloan's study that overlooked the city center, her and Amaia tossing back drinks. Laughing, dancing to whatever Sloan had playing on her crappy CD player. A few times they'd sat unmoving, leaned up against the wall. What they were laughing at or what they had the energy to dance for, who knew. All I knew is I couldn't ever imagine having a friend as cold and uncaring at Sloan. Numb to all but a few things.

We'd all lost a lot. Her sorrow was no excuse for her heartlessness, only an explanation.

Amaia broke the tension, staring into the distance as she replied, "If it takes my death to keep everyone else safe, then I'd say that's a life worth losing."

"That's bullshit," I exclaimed.

"That's the truth, Tomoe, and eventually, you'll see that."

Amaia's words sent a chill through my body. My heart beat faster in horror at the situation unfolding before my eyes. I knew how this ended and I hated it. This would set the course for everything, and right now, the future was bleak as hell. The room fell quiet once more at the harsh possible reality. She turned toward Sloan, asking if there was anything else she needed. When she shook her head no, she announced her departure.

"Now, if you'll excuse me, I'd like to go enjoy a cup of crappy coffee. Send Alexiares my way when they get back. I trust you'll fill Reina in on the rest. See you Saturday," she gave me a mock salute.

Her words echoed in my head as I watched her leave, knowing they rang true. The thing was, Amaia's death would solve it all, but not before more lives were lost. Long ago she'd warned me against looking toward the death of the ones I loved, for it would only bring me pain. Cause me to spiral on figuring out how to stop it.

A thick ball of nothing caught in the center of my throat, making it harder to breathe as I fought off tears. These last few weeks, I had only seen my sister when our duties required me to do so. *I think … I think it's time for that to change.*

CHAPTER
TEN

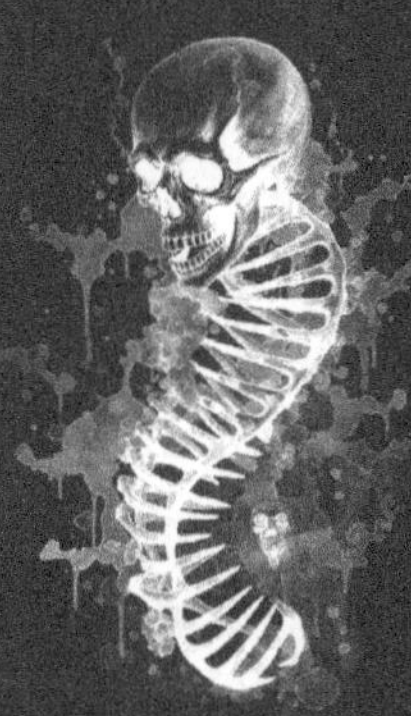

ALEXIARES

In my time heading toward the coast and my short stay at Monterey Compound, I had forgotten how much I fucking hated the cold. Yeah, I'd spent most of my life in Chicago and the weather had gotten ridiculously cold during some winters. But that was Before, now we were in The After and the cold was ten times what I had already considered ball freezing.

I wasn't sure where Reina had wandered off to. If the other day was any indication, I had an idea on where to kick off my search. Walking through the muted brown city, it wasn't hard to find the one person who managed to make a fashion show out of animal hides and thick fur coats. She claimed she wore them because if we had to kill an animal, it was good practice to use every part of it. I mean sure, but I was willing to wager that the appearance of the thick fur over the black wool leggings and bustier made her smile in the morning as she got herself dressed.

Keeping to the shadows of the brick and stone buildings, I stalked up behind her, snatching the bag off her shoulders, "I'll take that."

"Hey!" she exclaimed, spinning around trying to fight, but it was all too easy to hold her off.

One thing about Reina Moore is that she hated causing a scene.

She pulled at the beanie that had slipped off back over her mousy brown hair. "Pretty sure Amaia mentioned you thinking searching bags is a violation of privacy."

"No such thing as privacy when it comes to keeping people safe." I mocked Amaia, searching through her bag full of supplies.

Small rations of the food we'd been served were wrapped in plastic wrap at the top of her bag. A few canteens of water, an unreasonably large thermo sweater, some socks, an extra pair of men's shoes, some of her medical supplies and extra tips for her bow and arrow.

"You're trying to find him," I said, my head tilting to the side trying to figure out how to approach this gently on a loose cannon. "Reina, it's been weeks, he's back with your father."

Not going to lie, I was out of touch with the gentle side of supporting a friend. Not that I'd ever known that in my lifetime. My father had made sure of it. Each one of my mom's gentle touches toward Evander or me earned her a less than gentle lash of her own.

Alexander Drakos would not have weak, soft-hearted men for sons. Not even when they were children or sick or in need of their mom's comfort. So I'd kept my mom at a distance. Always there to protect her, keep her safe. But I would not let my mom dote on me, love on me. I knew she loved me. Loved us. That wasn't the problem. No, the problem was that I feared her love for my brother and me would get her killed.

Some people didn't get the privilege of knowing softness, kindness in this life. I'd learned early on that if I kept my knuckles bloody and my tongue sharp, then people would be afraid of hurting me. Of hurting the few people in this world I cared for. For the most part, that was true. Everyone feared me, and I couldn't say I didn't enjoy it. They say when everyone fears you, you have no one to fear except for the ones who don't.

My father had never been afraid of me. In fact, I was certain he viewed his beatings and my resistance as entertainment. Then came Finley. She hadn't feared me for one fucking second.

"You don't know that," she snapped, her icy blue eyes narrowing.

"It's what makes logical sense," I pressed. "Why would he hang around here? There's nothing left for him, just like he said."

Maybe my words were harsh, but I had the belief that sometimes people needed the tough truth to snap back into reality. Something she so clearly had slipped from.

"That's not true," she said, snatching the bag back from my grasp. "He has us. He just has to see it. If I can find him, I can convince him to—"

"I don't know your brother—or any of you—they way you do, Reina. What I'm saying is, objectively the one thing I noticed immediately about him is that he doesn't appear to be the type that you can convince of anything. Especially once his mind is made up."

"He's my brother, Alexi." Her voice was soft, muted. Nothing more than a whisper lost against the wind.

"Your brother was dead the second he left these walls. Whether it be the cold and snow, the Pansies, or Amaia—he is dead. You need to understand that." I stepped closer, trying to match her hushed tone.

It was imperative that I drove this point into her mind before some of the less sympathetic citizens caught wind of what she was attempting to do. They already thought she was a traitor by relation; this would only make matters worse. Selfishly enough, part of me needed her to pull herself together because, like each of us, if one part of our plan failed, it all failed. And she was an essential piece to the puzzle.

"And Amaia gets to what? Play God now?" Reina spat back. "Decide who lives and dies? Whose betrayal can be forgiven and whose is treasonous?"

"You don't mean that," I said, arguably somewhat defensive over the woman who'd become a pain in my ass.

She was a lot of things, and deserved a decent amount of pushback on the bullshit she did on the daily, but this wasn't one of those things. She only wanted to keep her people safe, this wasn't about her or being power hungry. Amaia couldn't give less than two fucks about that, that much I knew to be a fact. Everybody has a version of a story that is told, but only the objective observer would know the truth.

"Oh, but, Alexi dearest, I truly, truly do."

"Isn't that what you all made her be? Forced her to become?" I asked, challenging her to think outside of *her* side of the story. "Is that not the soldier you were begging for, trying to bring out of her when I arrived at The Compound?"

Reina for once in her damn life was quiet, her blue eyes lined with tears as they widened in contemplation.

"Every one of us has done some nasty things, kept some terrible secrets that all led us here. To this exact place in time. Each one of our actions made *this* version of reality possible. You, Tomoe, Amaia, all kept secrets from each other. Harbored information that could have stopped this all."

She took a step back, not a fan of the collective blame. "I'm well aware of that, thanks."

"If you're aware, then cut the shit. Your brother is the reason someone close to you is dead, the reason people at The Compound won't ever see their loved ones again. Your brother did that. Your father appears to be responsible for it all. I know you see how they all watch you." Reina glanced up, pulling at her hair. "I know how it feels, because they look at me like that too. The difference is, you have a chance to make it stop."

"How?" she asked, her sorrowful, tear-filled eyes meeting mine.

I sucked in a whisk of air, trying to fight off the sadness flowing from her body as I gently placed a hand on her shoulder. Wiping the tear slowly creeping down her face in a familiar way, I thought about my next words carefully. Truth was, I didn't have an answer for that. Hadn't quite figured it out myself, but fuck it, fake it till you make it.

"By being better than them," I said, forcing calmness into my tone. "Help us make this fragile-ass plan fall in place. We need you. You're the only one who's got a chance of making sure our alliances form and remain. Against Covert, we're only as strong as the weakest territory. If one falls, we all fall. It'll all trickle down."

Her reddened lips moved side to side. "You sound like her."

This time there was no malice in her tone, no bite. Only a lonely girl who now existed in a world without any ties to the family she adored and had been betrayed by the one she'd grown to love.

I let out a huff, half chuckle, half exhaustion. "The thing is, Reina, it's not possible for betrayal to come from your enemies. You expect to be blindsided by them and you plan for it accordingly. But when it's someone you care about, someone you think cares about you … that's what makes it a betrayal. You aren't helping anybody by sitting here, harboring hate for someone who loves you *very* much. She did what she had to do because she loves you. Isn't that what you did for your brother? Pick your fucking chin up, own all the bullshit, and let's go. Moe has news."

Damn, I'm good.

The snow crunched under my boots as I turned back the direction I'd come from. I made it to the corner of the street before she followed me. Reina stood taller now, her head high as she pretended not to see the glares and nasty words that came hurling her way.

CHAPTER

ELEVEN

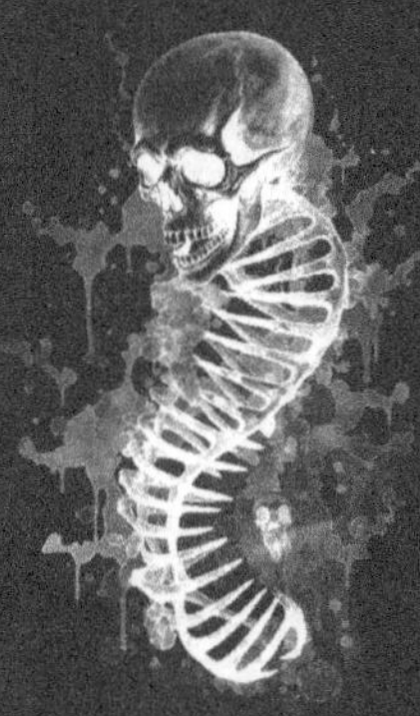

AMAIA

"You sure about this?" Alexiares asked, staring uncomfortably deep into my eyes.

I took a step back, turning away before he could read the hesitation in my eyes. Two days had passed since Tomoe had stumbled across a possible solution to making our plan work. We had everything we needed for the most part, the black tourmaline being last as that or hematite had been surprisingly hard to find.

Pretending to keep busy, I shuffled through Tomoe's notes. "Can one be sure about anything when they're about to be part of a blood sacrifice?"

She slammed the book closed on my fingers. I winced as Tomoe snarled. "A little respect might help the spell take easier, Maia."

Heat rushed to my cheeks. She'd called me Maia. A name that hadn't rolled off her tongue in three long weeks. A name I hadn't realized I'd become desperate to hear. Tomoe didn't linger. She moved across the room busy with preparations. I wasn't even sure she had realized she'd let it slip.

"Fine. Yes, I'm sure," I said, trying to reassure all the Nervous Nancy's in the room. "If there's anyone who needs checking in with, it's *you*, asshole."

I felt terrible about it. His decision had not been his own. It was made in a panicked, rash way. Alexiares had heard my resistance to involve anyone else in our matters and volunteered. *When the hell had he become so intent on teamwork?*

This was new territory for us. The last leg of our trip had forced us to work as a team, but I was used to his resistance at least a tiny bit. Pushing back on what I wanted to do or testing my limits was his thing, *our* thing. What he was doing now, trying to be a partner instead of a teammate, I needed him to stop. Expeditiously.

"What? And let you have all the fun?" Alexiares teased, the corners of his soft pink lips pulled into a mischievous grin.

"Can you two please stop passive-aggressively flirting?" Reina whined from her corner of the room. "It's making everyone uncomfortable."

"Pretty sure that's just you, cousin. I reluctantly find it endearing. Almost makes me want to have a soul again," Sloan teased.

Her fiery hair pulled into a knot at the top of her head, her freckles danced across her pale face as she watched Reina carefully. Less menacing than she had in the weeks prior, lovingly almost.

I fought off a smile at the glimpse of the dark-humored, snarky friend I'd once loved. Still loved, I suppose, just in a different way. A less friendly way, distant cousin you remember their name but nothing else kind of way.

"No one's flirting, Reina," I said firmly. "This isn't something we should take lightly. I'm making sure he knows what he's getting himself into."

Deny. Deny. Deny. I didn't even know what flirting was anymore. That was the least of my fucking problems.

"Only person taking anything lightly is you." Reina pushed, "Literally every single person here, except Sloan to no one's surprise, objected to you doing this. He's doing it because *you're* doing it."

Her eyes, there was something about her eyes. *Maybe it's time to cut back on the drinking.* I was clearly fucking losing it. I'd only taken a few sips before leaving my shitty apartment. Liquid courage. Who could blame me? If I was going to die, damn it, fuck being sober. But now I had half a mind to think there'd been something extra in that bottle, I needed to focus, stop reading into things. Reina's expression was … slightly unhinged. Over the last two days, the vivid blue of her eyes was alert. Five cups of coffee alert, and shifty, but her posture remained confident.

"Reina, we've been over this a million times. I'm not bringing someone from outside this room into it, not before we know it'll work. Otherwise, what's the difference between us and Covert?" I was careful not to mention her father.

The way she flinched every time those words left someone's mouth made my heart hurt for her. She didn't deserve this. Reina was not her father. She was not Seth. The woman before me wouldn't hurt anyone who didn't try to hurt her first, which was why I didn't know where her recent change in opinion had come from.

Whatever Alexiares had said to her had clearly changed things. She wasn't sad anymore; now she was just angry. It scared me a bit. I'd stumbled across enough evil Marie Curies to last me a lifetime.

Reina released an exaggerated sigh, tossing her hands up toward the other side of the room Tomoe had prepared for the ritual. I glanced over, checking in on my other friend. Her silky black hair hung in a simple braid down her back. She'd shed her heavy coat and left a fitted black turtleneck in its place. She'd removed her boots too, getting comfortable for whatever was about to take place. Her toes scrunched nervously into the ground and her fingers curled in and out.

I wanted to reassure her, tell her everything would be alright, but I couldn't. I was in over my head. All I could do was fake the composure to get people through this, pretend like I knew what I was doing, that I was brave. I couldn't reassure her because I couldn't even calm myself.

Tomoe would blame herself if anything went wrong today and would never forgive herself if something happened to me. To Alexiares. Her remaining family. But I couldn't think about that now, nor could I think about her mental toughness. It was bigger than that now, bigger than any of us. There were more people to protect than the people in this room, and it was time for me to act like it. Self-preservation of my family had gotten me nowhere for six months and it wouldn't get me anywhere now. I was general of two armies and responsible for the safety of eighty-thousand people across two compounds. Selfishness was not an option any longer. That card had played the fuck out long ago.

"I think it's brave," Abel said, taking in the expression of helplessness on my face.

Sloan's head shot up, brows raised as she willed him into silence. "Of course you do."

The smile that had creeped forward wiped from my face. I hated that for him. He'd been caught with his pants down that day on the battlefield. The little boy that had hugged me before going off on his own had been thrilled to see someone he once admired, someone familiar. Poor Abel couldn't contain his excitement, and now his future here was in the air because of it.

"What?" Abel questioned defensively. "It is. I don't know too many people willing to subject themselves to this kinda thing. I certainly wouldn't."

"That's because you understand that bravery and stupidity are two sides of the same coin. The only difference is the outcome," Tomoe said morbidly before grinning, conviction seeping back into her body language. "Now, you two, get in the circle."

She pointed toward the center of the room, where she'd outlined a circle in chalk on the wooden floorboards. It was merely guidance for us, so we knew where the metaphorical circle she'd be envisioning with her magic would appear. Tomoe claimed it served to protect us. From what? Fuck if I knew, as long as it gave us a shot of coming out of this alive.

We shuffled into position, the size of the circle forcing us to stand shoulder to shoulder. Tomoe turned around, scanning the room and stopping at Sloan. *Here we go.* Sloan had bitten her tongue with Tomoe far more times than I would have had the patience for. A shocking turn of events considering these days she was fresh out of patience. Perhaps it had something to do with the perspective I'd offered. Sloan and Seth visibly appeared more like siblings than Reina and he did. It drove me crazy that I didn't notice it before, but faces become blurry when you have no pictures and you're separated by thousands of miles.

Tomoe inspected her spell book, then glanced over at her notes, then back at Sloan, making a show of the whole charade. "I miss something? Last I checked, you weren't needed for this to happen."

Sloan opened her mouth, shock crossing over her delicate features. "Listen here, *witch,* I don't know what your problem—"

"Right now, my only problem is that you're here breathing my sacred, ritual air. Now beat it."

I pleaded with Sloan silently. Her only response was the roll of her eyes. "Whatever," she said, arms crossing over her chest. "Find me when it's done."

"Wouldn't dream of doing something and not informing you, Sloan," Tomoe retorted, clearly amused by the turmoil she was causing, "including taking a shit. Now out. Now."

"Abel, Reina, let's go," Sloan said, taking the opportunity to clear the room. If she couldn't be here, then neither could they. As far as she was concerned, they weren't necessities either.

Tomoe's face crinkled mockingly, nose scrunched. "Mmm, they're fine to stay. Thanks though."

Icy eyes shot toward Abel, who then followed her out of the room without a word or glance back at the rest of us. He would do what he needed to, for now. Reina remained, her movements twitchy and brows scrunched. She was lost in thought. It wasn't evident that she'd even heard Sloan's request.

"Ya know," she said, making me jump. "I like him."

"We know," we all said collectively.

"Can we keep him? Please?"

With this, we were all on the same page. Abel would be coming back with us. Coming home. We would not leave him here, no man would be left behind. Not on any of our watches. As much as I wanted to say Sloan wouldn't kill him, she one hundred percent would. It wouldn't be out of cruelty or enjoyment, but because she could no longer trust him.

He knew too much about the ins and outs of Duluth. In his revelation, he'd become a liability. The only reason he was still alive was because Sloan knew I'd raise hell if she raised a finger toward him, let alone a weapon. But the second we left, I was certain she'd make him a casualty of war.

Besides his safety, one thing remained true about Abel's presence. He'd been the only one to pull so much of a crack of a smile out of my sister since we'd arrived. When she wasn't with Tomoe, she could now be found with him. And when she was with either, I hadn't a clue where she went, and Alexiares hadn't budged on revealing any of the details he had discovered.

How cute, I'd remarked when he'd noted that friends don't share friends' secrets. What did he know about friendship? Please.

It's in the past; it doesn't matter as long as she has a plan on moving forward, he'd replied. And I'd left it at that, because he was right. It didn't matter, as long as her head was in the game now. I didn't need any more secrets disrupting my life. What was done in the dark would clearly always be brought into the bright ass light. I didn't need to go seeking any new secrets out.

"Come on, let's get this over with." I said, grabbing Alexiares' arm and pulling his entire body into the circle.

The tension in his body softened under my touch and his hazelnut eyes met mine. For a fleeting moment, I forgot that I was terrified. I felt … peace. Calm. Safe.

I shook my head, breaking that train of thought. "We're going to have to work day and night getting your magic under control now if this works."

"It will work," he offered, voice steady. "And I know the risks. You can repeat them thirty fucking times if you want, doesn't change my decision."

"Enough small talk. Let's begin," Tomoe cut us off, walking over with a small knife in and a silver goblet in hand. "Alexiares, I'm almost positive you'd like to do the honors."

His eyes danced as he took the knife and sliced the palm of his hand. Alexiares cleared his throat, fighting off the smile plastered across his olive skin. Drunk off the pain, something I recognized all too well.

Blood seeped from his hand as he squeezed what he could into the cup, hesitating once he grabbed my hand to do the same. I stood tall, forcing my stare to lock into his. Gently, I placed my hand over his, forming a deep cut over the palm of my opposite hand.

When the last drop fell into the cup, Tomoe stepped back toward her table, ready to begin. Reina sat on a stool near the center high-top, leaning forward with interest. Tomoe held the cup in her hand, gently swishing the red contents inside, her eyes closed as she focused on her power.

Her movements were careful as she poured a few drops of our blood onto the parchment. She lifted a sprig of rosemary next, followed by a pinch of sea salt from the wooden bowl beside her. The black tourmaline was last, placed directly near the paper. Her eyes flickered, and the room fell colder than outside.

Alexiares wrapped me into an embrace as my teeth chattered from the freezing temperature. We didn't dare use our fire to warm us, not when it could fuck with the spell. Tomoe's fingers traced each item.

She'd walked us through the entire ritual several times; right now, she was taking a moment to imbue each item with her intention for our protection. With each touch, she would have to envision merging their energies, forming a shield of defense around us.

Her inky eyes shot open, staring absently ahead. She chanted in Latin. Each word left her plump lips with confidence and clarity.

"Sanguine nexu vetustaeque doctrinae,

Clypeum texo, semper validum.

Ex culturis priscis et vigore hodierno,

Eam evoco, nocte et die,

Per Aztecas, Mayas, Romanos et Graecos,

Ex eorum sapientia, meum incantamentum quaero.

Elementa coniungo, haustu validum,

Custodi et protege, vetus et novum.

Sic fiat, hoc incantamentum emittitur,

Protege firmiter, ut perseveret."

Reina met my gaze. A tinge of fear of the unknown lingered in her eyes. Tomoe's eyes were pure white, no recognition of the situation around her as she strolled over, offering us the cup. I took it hesitantly, peering back in Reina's direction, who nodded in reassurance. Taking a deep breath, I brought it to my lips, stopping once the warm fluid touched. I gagged, my fingers trembling as my confidence wavered.

"Want some wine to swish it down?" Reina asked, no malicious intent concealed in her tone.

Sighing, I shook my head. I could do this. Ironically, I'd forgotten about my little party favor in my anxiousness. There was no time to spare. Tomoe had made it clear the spell was time sensitive.

Alexiares took the cup from my hands. "Together," he said, eyes on mine as he tossed it back, handing it back to me half empty.

Together, I thought back, too disgusted with what I was about to do to respond. The taste was worse than I'd imagined. Metallic and sweet at the same time. The overwhelming smell of iron influenced the taste of the thick fluid coating my tongue. Reina strolled over, her coat now folded over the back of her chair. She removed the cup from my hand, the corner of her mouth pulling in pity. Her head tilted, arm extending toward my shoulder before remembering Tomoe had warned her not to enter the circle during the ritual.

Tomoe had gone silent. Now, she was doing the most important part, sealing the spell. It was essential that she saw the shield around us as being impenetrable, repelling all negative energies and keeping us safe. She snuffed the candle out, closing the imaginary circle.

After a brief pause, she murmured words of gratitude to whatever entities she had decided to call on. The last thing I remembered before I hit the floor was Alexiares saying he felt like shit.

I woke up on the ground, Alexiares lay next to me, head propped on a pillow. My mind groggy but otherwise okay. Reina and Tomoe sat against the wall near the door, watching us. The former wearing a mask of fascination, the Tinkerer in her taking over.

"Fascinating," she murmured, walking toward my side.

Her hand waved over the entirety of my body, her powers kissing over my skin as she checked for any signs of something gone awry. When she found none, she glanced back at Tomoe, who still sat timidly in the corner, afraid she had hurt me.

"I don't remember that happening the last time," I said tentatively, not wanting to alarm her.

She shook her head in response. "That's because I only had Seth's blood. Riley and him fought that night, remember?"

I chuckled at the memory. I did remember. It had started off as a joke, well, as much of a joke as Seth was capable of. What had begun as drunken horseplay, Seth had taken to the next level, per usual. Riley, who happened to be slightly less drunk than him, had gotten a clean hit, breaking his nose. Tomoe had been covered in Seth's blood as she removed her shirt to apply pressure.

That had been the first time I'd noticed that they'd taken an interest in each other, when I knew the inevitable would happen. One glance at Reina let me know she saw it too, a fat grin smeared across her face at her brother's potential happiness. Now we knew why. Tomoe had been an opportunity to keep him distracted. Force him to settle down. She hadn't used Tomoe for her benefit. No one thought that. But their relationship surely didn't hurt her cause.

"How long until we know it works?" Alexiares said, his voice startling me.

I hadn't realized he was awake. He shifted his weight, pushing himself up and surveyed the room, eyes landing on Tomoe.

She shrugged, not having a solid answer for that. "Immediately, I guess."

"Why are you staring at me like that?" I asked. There was an odd look in her eyes. Let me know that I wasn't going to be excited about what came next for the forty millionth time this week. "Give it to me straight, Tomoe, cut the shit. What's next?"

Her hand slid over her face, resting on her cheeks. "You have to get into a … uh, intimate position. Seth and I were touching when it first happened."

"You expect soldiers to fuck each other in order to power-share?" Alexiares snapped.

I scoffed in agreement, not appreciating the expression of horror lining his features. *Lovely.* Not only did he think I had no conscience, he also now found me physically repulsive. I hadn't let him into my room since he'd made that statement days ago. I'd pretend to be busy or asleep. He could get in if he wanted to; I knew that as did he. But he didn't. Hadn't even tried. To me, that said a lot about where we stood in this stupid friendship.

"First of all, we weren't fucking," Tomoe explained, waving her hand through the air dismissively. "I was sitting in his lap. It was a moment of vulnerability like I said. And second, no. But until we understand how this works, we need to work our way up from ground zero."

Reina cleared her throat, chiming in with scientific reasoning. "She's right, ya know, think of it as a laboratory experiment. You have to replicate the same thing over and over again, make sure it's concrete before drifting out and changing variables. Once we know this works, we can consider other options."

"Fine," I said begrudgingly.

"What's wrong, princess?" Alexiares teased, his accent tilting on the word *princess*. The rasp of his voice sent a shiver down my skin. "I don't bite, not unless you want me to."

"Shut up," I ordered. "Sit back."

I pushed his shoulders back, slamming him into the ground as I moved to straddle around his waist. He smirked, a certain part of his body greeting me in response and heat swarmed to my cheeks. *Just the natural reaction of his body, that's all. It's human nature,* I reminded myself.

"Rough now, are we?" Alexiares' eyes shone, taunting me with a wink, trying to pull a reaction I had no intention of satisfying him with.

Despite not entering my room, he'd still shown up both nights. Three knocks on my door, waiting for me to answer. I stood on the other side, debating on if I should answer or not, ultimately deciding against it. And he would stand there, giving me a few minutes to decide.

If I didn't know any better, I'd have assumed he possessed the *Supra* gene similar to Seth and could hear my short gasps for air. He probably could even without any extra gifts given the shitty apartment doors. The doors were crap. Cold air slid through at all hours and they retained little heat in the room. These walls were thin as paper. I could hear Reina blurting out random country songs as she rinsed herself off each morning and night. He could probably hear me blink. He wouldn't need *Supra* enhanced senses to hear shit.

"Alexiares, focus." Tomoe warned, what little patience remained slipping from her tone. "We don't have time for this."

"Yeah, yeah. Amaia reminds me of that every day."

I pulled my hair into a messy bun, wanting my curls to be out of the way of whatever the hell it was we were supposed to be doing. Hollow eyes stared at me, no emotion behind them, and I replicated the deadness in mine. Minutes passed by, but nothing signaled to me that I was different from the moments before the ritual had begun.

"Nothing's happening," I said, shrugging. "I don't feel anything different."

"Me either," he replied, though it was pointless. If there was no change within me, then there wouldn't be with him either.

Leave it to Reina to point out the elephant in the room. "Maybe it's cause y'all won't even look each other in the eye for more than a few seconds," her voice boomed through the air.

"Try again," Tomoe commanded.

Her countenance was tired. Not in the sense of needing a nap or being overworked. But physically drained, her already pale skin was dull and clammy. The light that typically lingered in her hazy, inky eyes was gone. Even the color from her night hair was muted.

My sister needed to rest, and our inability to complete our portion of this task was holding her up. I grew frustrated with myself and with him, though it didn't leave my lips that way.

"We haven't really stopped now, have we?" I bit my tongue, not wanting to say anymore. I hadn't meant to direct my frustration toward her, but I was annoyed. Had we done all of this for nothing?

I turned back toward Alexiares, who was staring up at me from the ground, unmoving. That stupid smirk appeared again, and I wanted to smack it off his face. Rolling my eyes, I tried to focus again. As I peered into his eyes, I forced myself to think back on the fonder memories of him. Of us. They were few and far in between, and certainly not sweet. But they were there. Alexiares had shown me he'd cared in small ways. He'd saved my life on more than one occasion.

Another memory tugged at my mind, the first time he'd opened up to me down at the rocks. It had been a moment of vulnerability for the both of us, though it had ended on a sour note. Then there was the time he'd awaited at my bedside, making sure

I was on my way back to full health, our moment on the porch in Foley. The late nights he'd spent in my room since we arrived, listening to any and every thought that entered my mind, unable to be stopped by the voice in my mind that told me to keep them to myself.

A small tug awakened something in the center of my chest. Before I could explore what it was or confirm if it was in fact what Tomoe had said we would experience, a loud rumble rang through the air. The room shook, breaking my concentration, and the small tether I had receded.

"Damn it," I cursed, suddenly realizing Alexiares and I were now face to face, only a whisper of space left between us.

"You felt that too?" he asked, searching my eyes.

"I felt something. Don't know what though," I replied, turning back toward Tomoe and Reina, who still sat on the other side of the room, mouths agape. "The hell was that?"

Reina pushed off the ground, springing to investigate the cause. "I'll go check."

She let out a small yelp, taken by surprise by Abel, who lingered outside the door. His brown skin flushed as he took in the woman who opened the door. Abel's dark brown eyes scanned Reina's tight outfit, lingering over curves of her wide hips.

"Hey," he said sheepishly, obviously forgetting why he was here.

"You know she's on a peen free diet, right?" Tomoe called over her shoulder, her focus now back on me and Alexiares. "Like permanently."

Abel glanced down at the floor, watching his feet stroll into the room. "Oh. Well, still, hey."

"Hey yourself, handsome. Talk to me nice, and maybe I'll make an exception," Reina teased, never one to turn away an opportunity to snare someone in her lustful ways.

For most of us in this room, flattery would gain no one any favors. But with Reina, flattery could buy someone all the favors and then some.

Abel's voice had been a surprise the first time I'd heard him speak now that he was an adult. I'd missed those pubescent years, and thus the drop of bass in his tone.

Which is why it took me a moment to process that it was him who asked, "Has it worked?"

"Don't know yet," I replied, ready to toss a question back at him. "What was that?"

"Nothing." His words were clipped, eyes shifty, and the tip of his nose twitched.

I call bullshit. Some things *hadn't* changed from when he was a child.

"I can't believe Riley stationed you here. You're a terrible liar." Alexiares said, twisting beneath me, trying to pry himself free nonchalantly, but I refused to let up. We weren't done here. I smacked the side of his head, making him pause.

"Sloan ordered me not to worry you, well, not yet. But she did in the future. I mean, it just happened. I haven't seen her yet, maybe I should—" Abel took in the scowl on my face and decided who posed the greatest threat to him at the moment, "... don't freak out. A few labs exploded."

"Which ones?" I didn't move from my position, though I was pissed. Didn't matter which lab exploded, whether it was for the shields or magic disablers, either one would inevitably fuck up or delay our plans.

Abel glanced at Alexiares warily, then back at me. "Um, all of them?"

They were right next to each other in some old warehouses nearby.

"Amazing," Alexiares growled out, attempting to sit up and take care of it. He'd been essential in their development since he'd been present when Finley had begun working on them. She'd kicked him out of the lab when she'd gotten to the good part. Wisely so, I would do the same, but it still pissed me off.

I shoved him back down. He wasn't going anywhere. We needed to do this now more than ever. "Stay down. We aren't done. Anyone hurt?"

"We'll see once the fire is out," Abel said, taking the seat Tomoe had previously occupied.

"Even more of a reason to continue," I stated matter-of-factly. "Now, quiet so we can focus."

CHAPTER

TWELVE

AMAIA

We tried for hours to no avail until suddenly, we found victory. Three hours of awkwardly staring into the depths of those soft brown eyes and snarky remarks, and it turned out Tomoe had been right all along. Vulnerability was key, but that was only a piece of the puzzle. We'd had to let our walls down completely, let each other in without hesitation. Low and behold, the resistance had been on my end, not his. I may have trusted him with my life. The innate sense of trust required for this, however, did not come easy.

Alexiares had dropped his guard an hour into our efforts. He'd been halted because of my blockade once my power seeped into his veins. It hadn't been my intention, but subconsciously, my magic had fought back, refusing to submit and accept his presence that was now rooted within me. The push and pull of our magic, trying to find a way to merge peacefully was taxing. My magic drained at a concerning, unsustainable pace. Still, I couldn't bring myself to stop fighting.

Every time I let my guard down this way, trusted with completion, the poor soul on the other end died. Loving me was a death sentence. Riley was the only exception to that. He acted as my shadow for so long that, at some point, my subconscious no longer recognized him as a different entity. He simply became an extension of me.

There had been a flash of pain as I met Alexiares' eyes. For someone who had no control over his natural power, he sure knew how to agitate mine. Begging me to let him in and angry at my refusal.

Tomoe had fallen victim to exhaustion when I'd finally succumbed to his wishes. Reina's dismay was evident in her heavy sighs pointed in my direction. She did her best to simmer his frustration while trying to rein in her own.

I couldn't blame them. We'd been here half the day and now deep into the night. We were hungry and tired, but nothing we hadn't survived before. The only difference now was that morale was nonexistent, and they didn't want to be stuck in a room with me any longer than they had to. Abel had gone to update Sloan and come back with news from the explosion; no deaths but the labs were fucked, thus so were our chances of having shields anytime soon. *Perfect.*

We hadn't had the chance to explore the full extent of what power sharing had meant for us. Alexiares had noticed a deeper well of fire, but that could be explained away by his lack of understanding of how far his gifts even went in the first place. Our fire wasn't a real measure of how Tomoe's spell had worked anyway. The maximum potential we had was obtaining a score of one hundred if we were to test things out in the Element Room. There was a steady flow of water underneath my veins, but I'd had not a drop of energy to test it out. Although time was of the essence, the rest could wait for tomorrow.

The following day had been equally as exhausting. Sloan's soldiers finally returned. Holding off Covert had taken more effort than we'd expected. They were a determined bunch on both sides, I'd give them that. The men and women of Duluth had held their own. Both sides had suffered casualties. It was war after all. What mattered, though, was who lost the most, and this time we were lucky; we'd lost a few while Covert Province had lost almost every single soul.

I'd expected them to retreat. Smart soldiers would want to gather themselves a few miles back and wait for further orders, but no further orders had been needed. Covert's soldiers had one mission, a suicidal one; no surrender. For five days, they'd shown no mercy for themselves or for Duluth. In the end, the last man standing had shot himself in the head rather than answer any questions Sloan's soldiers had. Few had fled into the woods, but that had likely been intentional. Their role had been defined for them to do so as messengers.

That order had come from Seth. I could feel it in my bones. His cavalry had been instructed to operate under the same circumstances during times of war. I'd objected, but at the end of the day, his cavalry was loyal to him, not me. I wondered how that would change when we got back. *If* we made it back.

With losses on her side and the labs completely fucked, Sloan had nothing better to do than hover down our necks on Sunday. Now that we knew the ritual worked, Tomoe and Reina had undergone the same process. There was no snow falling from the dense gray sky and it was no longer Saturday, but Tomoe and Reina had come to an agreement. The same 'rules' would not apply. The protections that were placed on Alexiares and I would be different.

Scientifically speaking, we needed to see what changes in a variable setting, different weather, different day, would bring. See how much any of that stuff mattered. We needed something to compare ourselves to, a control group.

The only difference we noticed this far had been how much the ritual had taken out of Tomoe. To be fair, we weren't entirely sure if it were from the rituals taking place back-to-back or if it was her magic draining from constant use over the past few days. She'd been monitoring pieces of the future, making sure our efforts wouldn't be in vain.

Our chances of coming out victorious weren't great at the moment. As far as I was concerned, if we still had a chance, even just one, the cost would always be worth the price. I couldn't protect my family from any of this anymore. We were all in. All or nothing to protect Salem, to protect The Compound.

The Compound must survive at all costs. Compound first, always. What was left of humanity, the small smidgen of The Before that remained, relied on that.

Our idea of having a control group and creating a comparison group had turned up fruitless. There was no definitive way to see if the connection was technically weaker because Alexiares and I were not bonded to my sisters, therefore, we could not compare. Not accurately at least. Despite the risk of draining our power-mate of their magic, we were safe. The ritual had not exceptionally weakened us to the point of being on the brink of death. For now, I would take that win.

On the next snow-filled Saturday, we would perform the ritual as many times as we could for the benefit of the troops, just in case. Still, it was nice to know that we had another working option.

As with everything in this shitty life, there was good to balance the bad. While there was still a lot unknown about power sharing, we'd received more concrete evidence on what power sharing meant once bonded. There appeared to be an indisputable rule; power sharing was dependent upon the powers that were mixing. Which meant they could display differently on everyone, even between similar elementals. For Alexiares and me, that meant Steamfire.

I'd seen the evil glint in Sloan's eye at the realization. If done right, and everything aligned the way we hoped, this had the potential to make our forces unstoppable.

Our fire and his water merged in a delicate dance of destruction. Flames had burned an ethereal, sapphire blue, the water shimmering with a golden glow, suddenly a radiant mist emerged. The temperature of the brisk room rose rapidly creating an oppressive, oxygen-sucking heatwave, our flames intertwining with mist, licking objects in its path and leaving nothing in its wake. I fought hard to simmer them, but Alexiares was too strong. His power felt … endless. There was no bottom to his well.

"What the fuck, turn it off!" Sloan had shouted, angry at the piles of ash we'd created in the once eccentrically-decorated study.

This would be a problem. Alexiares had no choice but to get his powers in check or power sharing would backfire. It was pertinent that the mage flames and water harmonized or they would cancel each other out and spiral into chaos. We'd barely touched the surface but we could already see the possibilities that now lay at our feet with this gift. Mastering our Steamfire would take precision, skill, and an immense amount of control.

Reina and Tomoe had developed their own force to be reckoned with, though theirs would help with a mental battle instead of a physical one. If I was honest, their gift terrified me more than Steamfire ever could. Together, they had the ability of intense visions that heightened emotions. It wasn't channeling and seeing for themselves the way Tomoe's visions initially worked; no, these were visions they were able to push onto others.

The caveat was that these visions could only play to the emotions Reina was able to control. Primal ones. Fear, anger, pain, sadness, surprise, disgust, anticipation, pride, hope, curiosity, trust. Love. Instinctual emotions, things that were considered universal across cultures and time. Things that could destroy one's mental state, shatter you into nothing.

As Tomoe had predicted, with every leg up we gained with magic, there would be consequences. The more we practiced, the weaker we became. Nearly drained if used for more than a few minutes at a time, even when we remained in control. If we were to use these gifts, even with mastery, they would have to be used strategically, when the time was right.

His room smelled like him. I mean, obviously I'd expected it to have his essence, but with the little time he'd spent in here between our daily responsibilities and sleeping in my bed, I didn't expect this. It was a strong scent, though pleasurable. Rain and fire, an odd mix, but calming. Made my soul warm as much as I hated to admit it.

Alexiares was neat, nothing was out of place. He had hardly touched anything in the four weeks we'd been settled into Duluth. *Settled* wasn't quite the right word to use. I wasn't sure what it was actually. We kind of just … existed. A constant state of angst and not knowing when we'd have to pick up and leave. Not even Tomoe had those answers; *the future is different every day, several times a day,* she'd emphasized when I'd inquired on what the overall outcome of this would be. It was safer that she didn't tell me anyway; we weren't yet desperate enough to use her gifts to bend the war to our will.

I had no doubt that Covert Province was, however. And I planned to use that to our advantage—they *thought* they knew our next moves, had that advantage over us. But they didn't. Not when our use of dark magic would cancel any of their 'truths' of the future out.

Sloan had given us enough clothes to wear that we never had to wear anything too dirty. Everything needed to be layered up anyway. If one item got some wear and tear from all our training and experimenting, we'd tuck it underneath something else to hide it. I pulled the long, thermo leg sleeves she'd provided him out of the armoire in the corner of the room. Turning my head, I checked on the sleeping beast snoring in the center of the mattress, no movement. He slept like the dead instead of a bloodhound—I couldn't believe *this* was the man they all feared.

Smirking, I pulled out his cargo pants next, then a long-sleeved shirt, a hoodie, and his coat. He shifted in his sleep, wiping the drool from the corner of his mouth, and I tossed a beanie to cover his ears onto the bed.

"Wake up," I said, voice gentle as I hopped on the corner of the mattress making the bed sag.

His eyes sprung open, the usual hazelnut color in his eyes nearly green in the surprise. "Huh … what?"

"Huh, what?" I mocked teasingly, "I *said*, wake up. We gotta go."

I motioned to the clothes I'd laid out for him on the other side of the bed, he scanned the room, searching for signs of danger. When he found none, his gaze settled harshly back on me. Part of me wanted to retreat into myself. Okay, yeah, I could understand where some of their fear came from. I would not be waking the beast again; I was lucky looks didn't have the capacity to kill in this ever-changing, magic world we now lived in.

"What are you talking about?" He questioned, sitting up. A yawn formed and creased the lines on his forehead. "Go where?"

I pointed to the other side of the bed, but his eyes were barely open. I'd learned over the last few weeks that, yes, he could go days without sleep. When he did however, his REM cycle ran deep enough that made me question if he was still alive. Alexiares was far from being a morning person. "To train, come on. Your clothes are over there."

He rubbed the sleep from his eyes, finally adjusting to the light filtering into the room, "You went through my stuff?" he asked, a hint of uncertainty in his raspy, morning voice.

"If I didn't, it would be taking you even longer than it already is to get dressed."

"How'd you even get in here? I thought you weren't talking to me outside of when you had to." He rolled to the other side of the bed, grabbing the clothes and pulled them on.

Before his pants were fully on, he moved into the bathroom to relieve himself. Duluth still had electricity thanks to the dam not too far away, though not running water. We made it work, but cleaning our spaces was the least pleasant part of my week, and that was saying something considering the gore that often accompanied my duties.

"What?" I said, turning away as he zipped his pants up. He smirked at me, catching my stare at the v-lines down his abdomen that promised me a good time. "You think you're the only one that can pick a shitty lock? Please."

"You never answered my question."

"I don't have to if I don't want to. Like you said, you don't bite." I closed the door in his face, knowing he'd be right behind me and I'd already pissed him off.

We moved through the city in silence, the cold air warmer now that the snowstorm had passed and the sun fought to make an appearance. It was still early, but soldiers were now headed to change shifts and some of the dam workers and kitchen staff made their way to their stations.

I hated being here, not only did the air lack warmth but so did the people. A smile was a rare sight in these parts, even the children walked around miserable. I guess with as much death as they faced, it was hard to blame them. Still, it made me miss Monterey Compound all the more.

Maybe, if we were lucky and things played out in our favor, Duluth could be made in the image of Monterey too, as with other parts of The Expanse. They didn't have to live this way forever, not if they didn't want to. And it was hard to imagine that anyone *wanted* to.

"Where are we going?" Alexiares' voice interrupted my thoughts, causing me to break my stride. He'd realized we were heading outside the gates, something that had recently become a big no-no.

"I already told you," I stated matter-of-factly, "to train."

"Yep, understand that. I also understand that going outside the gates right now is a death wish." And he was right, it sort of was. But that had never stopped me in the past, and I didn't plan on letting it stop me now.

Call me crazy, but a dance with danger made for a stronger soldier. It was why I had my own soldiers train outside the walls; you could not defend against a force you had no idea how to combat. Certain things could only be taught in real-life scenarios.

"Alexiares, we *are* the death wish now." An evil grin found its way across my face, one glance in his direction showed a returning smile of agreement.

The hardening snow on the ground slowed us down, though we were in no true rush. Even Sloan understood the importance of having a day off. There was nothing waiting for us back inside the settlement. Two miles and an hour later we made it to the other side of Lake Superior. Duluth's city walls sat off in the distance, the steam rising above in the gray sky. Peeks of blue shone through the clouds. To my displeasure they added no additional warmth. I willed my flames to bring some heat back into my body but was careful not to expel too much. *I'm getting sick of this cold shit.*

This was the perfect place to train—the lake on one side, earthy terrain on the other and not a soul in sight. He glanced around, scoping out the scene before turning to face me for further instruction. *Good little soldier.*

"I can't train my soldiers to master this if I can't train you," I explained my impromptu training session.

He shrugged, not seeing the point in focusing on this at the moment. "You can't train anybody without knowing what the hell we're even capable of."

"Forget what we're capable of," I said, hoping he'd see where I was coming from. "We have to start with the basics. Once you can control your normal magic, then we can tackle the other stuff."

Other stuff, as if it were not the big advancement that it was. It was a game changer, yes, but as he'd told me during our journey here, power is nothing without structure. Without self-control. He nodded in agreement, handing me his rings to place inside my bag and moved a few feet away, ready to get to work.

Hours passed by and he was no closer to mastering his gifts. Sure he was a shit-ton better than the man I'd started training weeks ago, but he was still only scratching the surface of his control. Alexiares was capable, that much I knew, I'd seen it before. I only needed to figure out how to bring it out of him.

He slammed his hat onto the ground in frustration, his grown-out hair tousled. Beads of sweat flew from his dark brown strands as Alexiares shook his hair out, running his tattooed fingers through them to push it back. I sighed, taking a seat against one of the trees behind him.

"What are you doing?" he questioned, plopping down on the ground right next to me. A tad *too* close for me to focus.

"You are full of questions today, aren't you?"

"Sure," he retorted, always quick in this game of banter he so enjoyed. "And you're full of evasiveness, as usual."

"Pot, kettle. Sorry, I was just trying to avoid coming off as lacking a conscience. I figured the less I say to you, the better." I took a sip from my water, closing the canteen before tossing it into his lap.

He picked the bottle up, unscrewing the lid and glancing up to meet my harsh glare. "Amaia."

"Don't."

"Fine, I won't," he agreed reluctantly. "But you should know, that's not what I meant."

I shrugged, my hands waving him off dismissively. "That doesn't sound like an apology to me."

"Well, you told me not to." He studied my face, trying to judge where I was emotionally. "I am though. Sorry, that is. I didn't mean it that way."

We sat there for a moment, searching each other's eyes. There was kindness behind his gaze merged with regret. It took me a second to remember that the man who had meant to hurt me every time we talked had disappeared over a month ago. The Alexiares before me cared, was genuine and intentional with his words. Even when he wasn't able to get them quite right, he still tried. Was learning to be decent, to be good.

I shook the moment away, I wasn't quite sure why I still kept him at a distance. He had made it clear where he stood, and I had, in my own way, done the same. That didn't negate the fact that everyone I cared deeply about lived on borrowed time. I didn't want that fate for him.

Alexiares deserved to experience happiness in this life. He had never known it except for fleeting moments. I'd had my time, twenty-two years of love and joy in The Before. He had not. But he did deserve it in The After. So I would keep him at arm's length until his infatuation with me dissolved.

"Then humor me," I said, breaking the tension between us, "how could one mean those words to come across?"

"That you're stronger than Sloan. More capable. That she should turn to you as a mentor and not just lean on you the way she does one of her little cronies. There's a lot she has to learn, and she's under-utilizing your talents. You have what it takes, she doesn't. She'll get people killed—"

"So will I." I cut him off. I saw where he was coming from, but he was wrong. Sloan's treatment pissed me off as much as the next person; despite that, at the end of the day, she was still my friend. Not to mention, we weren't as different as everyone thought us to be.

"Yes, but not for lack of trying," Alexiares reasoned, his accent growing thicker in his intensity. "Not because you waver in your leadership. Yours will be casualties of war, hers will be casualties of her own indecisiveness."

"Watch it. That's my friend you're talking about," I snapped.

That was enough. I wasn't going to sit back and let her get slandered when she couldn't defend herself.

"Is it? Because the rest of us can't tell."

Silence. That was what filled the air. Silence and anger. Not directed at me, but coming from a place of confusion and defensiveness. Tomoe and Reina may have hated me at the moment, but they hated Sloan's treatment of me even more. Where my friends were concerned, I'd done nothing to deserve her impatience and indifference toward me. But I understood, my second had caused the deaths of hundreds of her people. Not only their deaths, but she'd never had the chance to grieve the loss of Morgan. A man she had apparently grown to love. If what Abel had told us was true, they were soulmates. That shit tugged at my heart, I could certainly understand the havoc losing one does to your life.

"Yes. She is. And I can relate to her loss. The difference between me and her isn't that she isn't capable, it's time." I said, my tone lethal. "Guidance. I had Prescott and Jax as a moral compass and years to grow into my position. Checks and balances and good people surrounding me when mistakes were made. Sloan has no one. She was thrust into this life and expected to make no mistakes. She has no one, except for me. That would be hard for anyone to adjust to, let alone someone who never expected to end up in this situation. For as long as I've known her, she's been a follower, not a leader. The fact that she stepped up to the plate makes me proud, so I'll take her harsh words and nasty glares if that's what it takes to keep her going. You of all people should know how much having a sense of hatred can propel someone into action. The force of fire under your ass can make a person unstoppable."

Alexiares said nothing, just nodded his head and stared off into the distance. He was learning when he should and should not push me, quickly understanding that this was a conversation he had no business continuing.

"I accept your apology."

My words brought a soft smile to his lips, lips that I desperately wanted to kiss but refrained from doing. Light filled his eyes, acknowledgment of the torture I was inflicting on myself by resisting.

He pushed himself off the ground, extending me a helping hand. "I'm ready to go again."

I watched Alexiares move into place, practicing drawing water from the lake in one hand, and lighting a silver and gold flame in the other. Carefully, he guided the flame along the dried branches I had strategically laid out a few feet away. He almost had it, his thick brows scrunched under the pressure and then he failed. Again.

Wait a fucking minute. I huffed a laugh, I knew exactly what to do.

"Alexiares," I whispered, coming up directly behind him. I couldn't get as close as I wanted, he towered over me even with the thick sole of my boots.

"Yes?" His body stiffened at my tone, head glancing over his shoulder, magic dousing, eyes trained on my mouth.

It appeared my words had the effect I'd been seeking after all so I pressed on, "I know what the issue is."

"Do tell." Alexiares' head tilted, curiosity lacing his words.

"Each time I've seen you in control, my life was in danger."

It was true. The night in the national park when we'd been chased through the forest by feral savages, when Finley's soldiers had come for us in the clearing near St. Cloud, then again down by the river. Each time, he'd remained in control. It had taken him no focus, no concentration, no thought. He had simply acted.

"Okay, and?" he questioned, shrugging it off, already having chalked it up to a coincidence.

"How were you feeling in those moments?"

The snow crunched under his boots as he shifted uncomfortably at the question. "What is this? A therapy session?"

"Again with the questions."

"Scared," his voice was soft, hushed. "I was scared that I wouldn't be able to save the last life I cared about."

"Well shit," I teased, "don't worry, I won't tell the others."

"You know what I mean."

"Do I?" I took another step closer to him, now chest to chest.

I turned my stare up, placing my hand over his heart. Even through the thickness of his layers, I could feel his heartbeat pick up. Alexiares' breaths grew short and shaky, his hand falling to the cusp of my lower back and he pulled me closer. Through my own layers, my skin grew hot and my face flushed despite the cool winter air. It was December, yet my skin burned as if I were back home in Monterey.

A snapping of branches caught my attention, I had picked up on low moans and groans earlier but it appeared Alexiares remained distracted. None the wiser. Taking a step back, I turned around, throwing knife in hand and tossed it directly in the center of a Pansies head. It had barely crossed the threshold of the tree line. In the next moment, I drew another knife from my side holster holding it over my wrist. I looked up, meeting confused honey brown eyes and slit my wrists.

It was time for the others lingering in the woods to know their next meal awaited.

He shouted at me, applying pressure to both my wrists. "What the fuck are you doing?" Something in the tone of his voice made me jump, and for the first time, I saw the *bloodhound* Sloan warned me about all over his face.

"Dinner time, boys." I grinned at him, shaking myself free and bringing singeing fire to the surface to keep him from attempting to grab me again.

One step, two steps back and I swiveled on my heels making a mad dash. I was unarmed, my guns back over near my bag at the tree we had rested under. I stopped in my tracks, ready to be surrounded by the five Pansies now headed in my direction. *He can do this, I know it.*

"Whatever you're surely going through right now," I taunted over my shoulder, this was fun. "Channel it. Let it guide you."

Closing my eyes, I smiled, and fell back into the snow.

I was at peace with whatever came next, but a voice in the back of my mind told me Alexiares would never let it get that far. If he couldn't handle the task, well shit, I guess I would become their next easy meal.

It was over in moments. I heard him yell, my eyes still closed and thuds sounded around me. One thud. Two. The sound of what was likely ice piercing the wet, soft skull of another. A burning, sickly sweet scent filled the air and my eyes flashed open. Alexiares stood over me, his face red with anger.

His hands shot out as he grabbed the necks of the remaining Pansies, and he turned them to ash.

Never had I seen him so flawless in his execution. He had total control. Alexiares' light brown eyes had turned dark, lethal. They were hard in a way I hadn't seen since before we'd left Monterey. He was furious.

My neck snapped back as he yanked me off the ground in one swift movement. "What the fuck is wrong with you? Are you insane?"

"Starting to think that's my new nickname," I mumbled, admittedly slightly frightened by him for the first time.

"You could have died."

I was left standing around the slaughtered Pansies, staring at his back as he stalked toward the tree to grab my bag. My words were lost to the wind, "I mean yeah, but I didn't."

He ignored me, turning back in my direction and grabbing my wrists to address my wounds. The herbs he placed under the wrappings burned against my open flesh. I examined the area around us, making sure no others lingered in the area after the commotion.

"Listen, we're out of time." I attempted to reason, somewhat apologetic. "I'm sorry but I had to force your hand. What happens if I'm not around, Alexiares? What happens if I'm dead? That's a real possibility you know? I could die before this is over."

"Stop it." He stopped wrapping my wrist, dropping it aggressively, but his face softened. Fear replacing anger.

"No. That's a reality in one of Moe's many, many possibilities. So what? If I die, are you going to give up? That's it? Fuck the world?" I needed to drive that point home.

It wasn't that I didn't think he understood the gravity of our situation, because he did. They all did. But what they all failed to accept was that my role in this had been made a turning point in this war the moment Seth had left. I now had a major target on my back, and the arrow was someone who knew every play in my playbook.

"Now who has all the questions," his voice was softer now, filled with understanding.

"My point is, Alexiares, yes, channeling that emotion is great. But it won't win us this war. I needed you to dig deep, know what control *actually* feels like. Manipulate whatever you're feeling in here," my finger rested against his heart. "And now that you know it, learn it. Then abandon it. Because banking your power off emotions *is* what gets people killed."

He glared at me, knowing I was right but not liking any second of it. Shaking his head, he brushed past me. Pulling the knife out of the first Pansie I had hit, Alexiares tossed my bag over his shoulder and took off.

"No."

"No?" He stopped, not bothering to face me. "No what." His words came out forcefully, it wasn't a question. It was a challenge.

"Again." I pushed, "We go again, and we keep going until you can't go anymore."

An unhinged expression crossed over his harsh features as his head whipped toward me. He smiled at me, eyes narrowing as he tossed my bag over to the side. Within moments Alexiares was in my face, only a whisper away.

"Soon enough, you'll learn I can go all night. I don't get tired, princess."

I threw a punch to his gut, and he dodged, arms lining with flame as water pulled from the lake soared over my head. A waterspout formed inches above me, my curls flying in the wind. I crouched low and lunged.

CHAPTER THIRTEEN

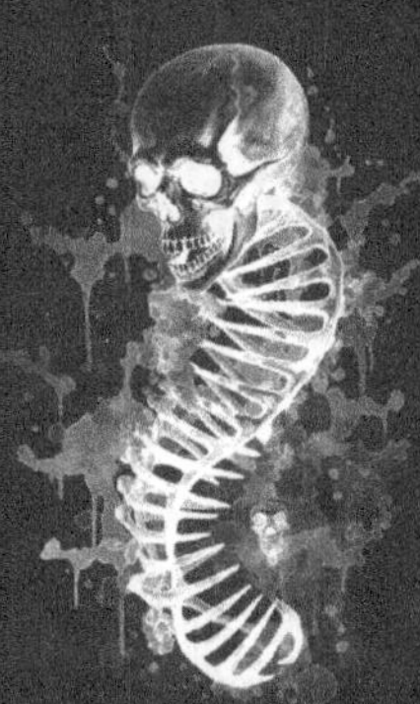

ALEXIARES

It was an odd feeling, being in control.

Since that day out by the lake, my magic had become mine again. I hadn't been in this much control since the immediate After, when my magic had first developed. Before I knew how deep my well really went.

Amaia was absolutely crazy. Fuck me, I loved every second of it. She was infuriating, and frankly, too self-sacrificial for my taste. Instead of running the other direction, against all logic, the woman drove me mad with desire. I needed that type of crazy in my life. Thrived in it. And she expected the best in me, required it. So I did everything in my power to make her proud.

I'd never had someone proud of me before. Not even my mother, I was a disappointment to everyone in my life in The Before. The outset of The After too. Tiago had never said the words, but I'd seen the disdain in his eyes the day I revealed I'd gotten hitched to Finley. *The she-devil.* That was the nickname he'd settled on for her.

But Amaia was different; when people made her proud, she was never shy on letting them know it. For her, I would be better. A shaky laugh escaped me; I saw where Riley was coming from now. Why he'd do everything to protect her, she brought the best out of people. Inspired you to get on her level, no matter how erratic her methods may be. That shit was getting old though, I'd make a point to nip it in the bud soon enough.

WE'D WORKED ON OUR STEAMFIRE EACH NIGHT, FINDING AN EMPTY part of the city where Sloan could give less than a rat's ass about what happened to it. I guess Covert Province had slaughtered them by section, not skill. There was no one left in that part of Duluth to be upset if our Steamfire melted their precious belongings or burned down their homes. Not that Amaia had let it get that far. She had an unprecedented amount of control.

She'd told me on the journey here that there was a time when she'd had no control. When Prescott had found her, he'd helped her. I found it hard to believe his training routine put his or her life at risk, but I digress.

The last few days were a blur. When we weren't working on our Steamfire, Amaia had me train with the rest of the soldiers on mastering their gifts. Tomoe had only started the process of linking people, helping them powershare. None of them had been soldiers; if we were going to do it, we needed to do it the right way. Tomoe was strong, powerful, but she was not enough to get the job done on her own.

Which was why as soon as Sloan stopped running her fucking mouth, Amaia and I could be on our way to get some help. I just hoped Lola wouldn't disintegrate us on the spot once we arrived.

I'd sworn to her long ago that I wouldn't bring anyone to her home who wasn't in need of safety. I mean, we technically were, but not in the way she defined safety. To her, it was possible this would be seen as bringing trouble to her doorstep.

Sloan had summoned us all to the lab Reina had been working out of. Turned out to be a good decision to put her right next to Moe's study, or all her work would have been lost in the explosion. She'd been tasked to work with a group of Tinkerers to figure out how to bridge the gap between Finley's gas and Duluth's magic-stripping powder.

Luck had not been on our side. Not that I believed in that shit. Whatever was meant to happen would happen, universe be damned. Tomoe's visions were only proof of that fact. The future was always changing, and there were too many variables at play to make trivial things such as luck or blessings be true.

"Right, and you expect me to believe you have not a clue how this all works?" Sloan tossed her hair over her shoulder, sneering at me in disbelief.

I shrugged, unsure why it was hard to ingrain the concept into her smooth brain. "Don't know how many times I have to repeat myself for you to understand Finley never let anyone into her lab to see the specifics of anything. She is the lone, as in singular, creator of it all. We were injected with vaccines that prevented the powder from working, and you have to be sure you only suppress the magic, not take it away. That's all I can tell you."

Abel released an audible gulp. "What happens if you accidentally take it away?"

Sometimes it was hard to remember he was a great deal younger than us, but I hated to say, the kid was growing on me. He reminded me of Reina, well, the old Reina. He brought a youthful vibe to the group. A reminder that there was positivity still vibrant in the bleak, gray world surrounding us.

The group. Damn that felt weird to say given I was a part of it.

"What happens when someone drains their magic without enough time to recharge?" Amaia's tone wasn't exactly harsh, but sure as hell not sugarcoating a thing, "They die."

Reina mumbled as she peered through her microscope; she was beyond her depths here. "It's a decent start, but I can't figure out how to get the full seventy-two hours she has. It's like whatever she's using attacks your cells, mutes them. In all my years, I've never seen anything like it."

"You're doing fine, Reina," Tomoe reassured her friend, placing a gentle hand on her shoulder and ignoring the flinch Reina returned in response. "Don't let *Sloan*, of all people, make you feel dumb for doing what she can't."

"I never feel dumb," Reina said in the least humble way possible.

A small grin tugged at Amaia's lips, a proud sister. "Good, you shouldn't. You've taken a powder that only lasts twenty-four hours to a solid fifty. We'll get there, you just need time."

"Time that we don't have, you said so yourself." It was a fair reminder, though it earned me a glare from all parties.

We were short on time, that was the understatement of the year. Our new team motto.

"Hate to say it," Sloan relented, her next words making my bones turn to ice. "It may be time to consider bringing Finley in for help. She's desperate for a trade, her people have no food."

"If you can't even work with me, I doubt you'll be able to stomach the woman who gave every order."

Amaia shrugged in agreement off to my side, Tomoe grumbled something about wanting to see that show. I could not imagine Finley and Sloan in the same room, let alone exchanging magic-sucking recipes. Finley would walk all over Sloan, especially if they were left alone in Duluth to their own devices. The only mitigator I could imagine containing the two is Amaia, and I never wanted to see the two of them in the same room again.

"Even the devil's words sing a captivating tune, *Bloodhound*," Sloan snarled, enough to shut me up for the moment.

I'd said my piece; if they wanted to destroy each other, it wasn't my fucking problem.

"We're not that desperate," Amaia added in support.

She looked tired, but still beautiful. Her jeans hugged her hips, the black sweater she wore accentuated the curves in her waistline outlining the lean muscle in her arms. Her curls had been revived now that we had a steady diet of nutrients. She was still annoyingly verbal about her ache for a different source of protein. I hadn't yet worked up the nerve to tell her the disaster Finley had caused that made fish a delicacy around here.

Duluth's farm saved them from starvation in the dead of winter along with the greenhouses. There was one farm not yet available to the public that would make her the happiest woman here. All I had to do was convince Sloan to give me access to it.

"Yet," Abel, added meekly; every soul in the room turned to stare at him instead. "I mean, just give Reina some time. I'm sure by the time the two of you get back, she'll have it figured out. I can help her."

Sloan tugged at her long wavy hair, shaking her head as she turned to face her cousin. "Fine. Get it done."

"I'll help too. If I focus enough, I can try to pull out the smaller details. She'll do what she has to; you worry about keeping another laboratory from blowing up," Tomoe offered up, wanting to help her sister where she could.

The two had been inseparable, yes, but Reina still kept her at an arm's length. She hadn't completely forgiven either of her sisters for their betrayals, though Tomoe got the better end of Reina's shit-on stick.

Sloan motioned in show of giving zero shits about what Moe spent her time on now that she had completed her portion of the mission and headed toward the door. She stopped before Amaia and glanced her over, then over Amaia's shoulder back at me. I tensed, waiting for whatever insult ensued.

To our surprise, she pulled Amaia into a hug then pulled her back to meet her eye. It was an uncomfortable display, like they both didn't know where it came from or how to receive it. Amaia would be coming with me to meet the *brujas*, with Sloan's permission of course. Not that we needed it, but she did have the authority to not let us back in the gates if we rubbed her the wrong way. Amaia's abandoning her promise to ready her troops would definitely count as doing so.

"I'll be fine, Sloan," Amaia said, rolling her eyes. "You don't have to worry about me."

Sloan sighed, frustrated that Amaia was clearly missing something. Her line of sight fell on me once more, and I moved away, pretending to be distracted by whatever Abel, Moe, and Reina were debating on the other side of the room.

I heard every word, everyone did.

"It's not you that I'm worried about. It's him. You don't understand what he put our people through."

"Then enlighten me," Amaia replied, iciness recapturing her tone.

I couldn't help but grin smugly at the back of Sloan's head. It was nice to be cared about, supported. Defended. Not that I deserved it though; Sloan was right. The things Finley had me do to these people still haunted me when my eyes closed at night. Hell, it had been my last mission here that had made me snap, fleeing home to Finley, and had kicked my desertion into a reality.

"He terrorized us," Sloan ground out, a thumb jutting out in my direction. "For months our strongest and brightest were slaughtered like animals. Limbs and fingers were found in loved ones' beds, the rest of their bodies never recovered."

My breath caught, waiting to hear Amaia's response. Reina glanced up at me, then shied away when I met her stare. Abel shifted nervously, eyeing me as though he remembered every detail. He probably did, probably knew some of them too. Some of them had been emissaries. There was a chance he blamed himself if he had been the one to let me in while I was under disguise. The only one to pretend none of it was happening was Moe. Hell, she'd probably seen worse in her own mind.

She understood me to an extent, wasn't bothered by gore. I mean how could she be? She chopped heads off like it was her day job, never hesitating as her blade swung down.

"As you said, Sloan, people change. He's not that person anymore." Amaia's voice was unwavering, she didn't care.

Everyone had a past, herself included though not as gruesome. It had been a job for me, a soldier completing their duties. I'd expressed as much when I'd woken her up with one of my many, many nightmares. Instead of kicking me out, she'd comforted me, saying nothing as I lay against her. Her sweet scent consumed my thoughts as I fell asleep in the comfort of her presence.

"People do change, Amaia," Sloan said warmly, "but not that much."

"I'm with him. For better or for worse, he's not leaving my side."

I fought to keep the widest grin off my stupid face.

"A starving dog is never loyal," Sloan slammed, lighting her cigarette as she leaned against the door. "If I had Tomoe's gifts, I'd likely be able to tell you concretely that it will, inevitably, be for the worse."

Amaia smirked at her, careful to avoid the butt of her cancer stick as she pulled her in for a final embrace. "I knew that the moment I laid eyes on him."

My stride was quick across the room, I huffed a laugh and pulled the door open moving Sloan aside in the process. Amaia understood my cue, walking beneath my arm and through the arch of the door. My heart damn near beat out my chest as I watched her lead the way. I was so fucked.

This girl will be the death of me.

FOR SOMEONE WHO HAD A STRONG CHANCE OF DISINTEGRATING FROM magic in a few days, I was riding an unsustainable, insatiable high. Amaia accepted me for everything I was and had told Sloan just that. Our family did too, even though it was fucked up at the moment.

I had a family. A real family. A dysfunctional family, but not anything similar to the one I'd been raised in. The thought was fucking crazy to me. I grabbed her hand, tugging her to the tunnel Abel had directed me to a few days ago.

"Oh shit, what's this?" she asked, her dark brown eyes filled with mischief as we reached the end of the tunnel that was our way out.

I grabbed her shoulders in excitement, shaking her gently. "What's it look like?"

"Ha ha, I meant, where did you get the gas for this?" She removed her gloves, fingers skimming along the length of the bike.

"I've been working on it with Abel." I offered some insight, "It's solar powered."

Amaia released a low laugh that let me know she'd forgotten that Abel was a Tinkerer. I had, too, honestly until our conversation had drifted to our lives in The After on the way to meet Amaia and the others earlier in the week. It wasn't his most powerful gift, in fact, he didn't appear to be powerful at all, *most* of the time. There were times he let it slip, showing there was more there than what he exhibited.

He'd bounced with excitement at the opportunity to help me restore what he'd referred to as a 'beauty' he'd stumbled across on one of his many unsanctioned adventures. After making me swear

I'd say nothing to his overlord, Abel had rerouted us to Indian Roadmaster. It wasn't my Kawasaki, but it would do. We need longevity anyway, not speed.

Wide, dark brown eyes stared at me with an expression that could bring me to my knees. No one, not even Finley, had ever looked at me with such warmth. With admiration. She didn't even realize how much she controlled me. I was merely a puppet in her show. Amaia was infuriating, and that was fucking perfect for me.

I didn't want a tender love or even a soft one. I wanted a love fueled by fire and intensity. Fire had always felt safe to me, kept the monster beneath my skin at bay and away.

"It'll only get us halfway there," I added, breaking the eye lock we'd fallen victim to. "The roads are blocked around Pine City, but it will cut our travel time down in half. I figured you wouldn't want to be away longer than we had to."

She smiled at me, "As much as I hate this place, they aren't quite ready to be left on their own. Not with Reina, Tomoe, and Abel behind these walls."

"Figured he wouldn't be left behind." I chuckled, glad that we were on the same page. "He's a good kid, Riley did well."

"Riley always does well."

"Tell me about it. You ready?" I asked, sliding onto the bike and tightening the straps of my pack to give her more room.

"Um, sure."

Amaia hesitated, taking a step closer and then recoiled.

"Don't tell me," I taunted, "miss fearless is actually scared of something."

"I'm not scared, I'm … nervous. I've never ridden a bike before, let alone a motorcycle."

I offered out a hand. "You trust me?"

Her lips twisted and her thinking face took over her expression. My heart sank to my ass. Of course she didn't, trust was asking for a lot after what Sloan had revealed. Just because she accepted me, cared for me, didn't mean she trusted me.

"You know I do," she said, breaking my doom-filled thoughts. Amaia bit her lip and I desperately wanted to bite it for her. She took my hand, sliding onto the back. Her fingernail pierced through layers of clothing as she held onto my waist for dear life. For someone who claimed we *were* death, it was comical how she was now hesitant to get on the back. We ran a slim-to-none chance of crashing without anyone else on the road.

I cranked the engine, ironically pleased by the silence it offered thanks to Abel's rain-man mind. "Then hold on tight."

TIME FLIES WHEN YOU'VE GOT THE WORLD'S TOUGHEST WOMAN clutching the air out of you in fear for her life. A little over an hour and we'd pulled the bike into a random garage in some neighborhood in Pine City. The roads had been clear for the most part until we'd reached the extent of Duluth's clearing efforts. Or maybe it was a strategic blockade, cutting off a major pathway to their shitty enclosure. Who knew? I doubted it, though; if they'd always leaned on Amaia's expertise, then there was a strong chance they hadn't thought to plan such an effort. Duluth had likely run out of resources and called it a day. As things stood, they were able to get far enough without resistance for trade.

We had to walk the rest of the day to our first stopping point in North Branch. It would take another two days to get to St. Paul from there. As luck would have it, those two days had flown by without a hitch. Amaia and I slept in shifts, four hours on, four hours off. With only the two of us, it left us vulnerable. Traveling in a small group gave you a fighting chance against humans and Pansies alike.

My journey to Monterey had been relatively sleepless. Over time, I became accustomed to running off the bare minimum.

Suckerpunch guarded as much as a guard dog was capable, but waking up to low growls was about the same as being caught with your pants down. You were fucked either way—one just came with a slight warning, while the other came with consequences.

I wanted to punch myself for letting myself get comfortable with decent sleep. It had made me weak, and now we would pay the price for it. She claimed she was okay, that insomnia had taken over her life in The Before, with not much having changed over the years. After our nights together, I knew the truth, Amaia loved her sleep. Now the dark circles under her eyes were proof that her body, in fact, did crave more than a few restless hours of shut eye.

St. Paul was an occupied city, but not walled in. There were different sectors that existed within the city. It wasn't total anarchy, but it was close. Some sectors got along with other divisions better than others. Then there were the occupants who had no friends in the city, only people who feared them. Occupants such as the *brujas*.

I get it, people feared what they didn't understand. As I said time and time again, fear is what keeps you alive. You just had to know when showing you were scared was okay and when it would damn you. In this case, fear got you far.

"This is …"

I interrupted, taking in the horror on her face as we strolled through the city. "Anticlimactic? Depressing? A piece of shit?"

"I was only going to say not like Monterey," she chuckled nervously, "but sure."

Her hair was free and bouncing against her shoulders. The last hair tie she'd had popped over a day ago. She'd yelled out as if it was her last piece of food. It felt silly to me because even though we both stunk and hadn't bathed in days, she looked divine. I knew it wasn't about aesthetics to her though, Amaia grew frustrated with every curl that betrayed her, popping into her face.

It's a hazard, she'd claimed, rolling her eyes at the confusion in my eyes and ignorance to the problem.

"Yeah, no place is *like* Monterey. I told you that."

She glanced up at me, questioning, not knowing where the bite in my reply had come from. I cursed myself, not wanting to fall back into this routine with her. She didn't deserve it. For once since I'd known her, she hadn't done anything reckless in at least a few days.

"You okay?" Amaia asked.

"I'm fine, just closer to St. Cloud than I'd prefer." It was a half-truth, but I didn't want to scare her. "Finley knows about this place, so we need to be in and out."

"St. Cloud is out the way; she has no reason to think we'd come here. We're fine."

I loved that for her, that she didn't know the real danger we were putting ourselves in by coming here. Finley was one concern, yes, but one of many.

"You don't have the slightest clue what she's capable of. Who she has around."

That caught her attention. She grabbed my arm, forcing me to halt. "Hey, what's going on?"

"Stay on high alert, I have friends in the area."

"*You* have friends?" she teased, trying to lighten my mood, though the question was genuine.

"Let's hope they still are, or she already knows we're here."

We approached the only fortified part of St. Paul, Como Park & Conservatory. Ironically, most of the *brujas* here had received earth magic, creating an elegant barrier. Intertwined branches, and thick brush lined the outer portions, creating what appeared to be a natural wall, but there were other protocols in place. Protocols you couldn't detect even when you'd become privy to their location. Probably another type of magic the rest of the world had yet to discover. Not dark magic, but what ran through someone's veins. A gift of nuclear warfare. Monterey weren't the only people to keep certain gifts under wrap.

"It's beautiful." Amaia said breathlessly. Her eyes widened, mesmerized as she reached to touch it before I could stop her.

I knew what was coming next. "Just you wait."

The crisp clicks of several gun chambers being locked filled the surrounding air, and we suddenly found ourselves surrounded. Several people emerged from the wall, a few from holes in the ground I'd been none the wiser to, others appeared from thin air. My hands flew out to push Amaia behind me, but our fingers clasped as she reached out to do the same. Magic flowed through our veins, ready to protect each other.

A middle-aged woman with deep, bronze colored skin and straight black hair emerged through the hidden door tucked in between the corner of the barrier. She approached, her stride confident, and I took in the lines of wisdom that populated along her eyes and forehead. She was beautiful, yet weathered in a way that only came from the stress this way of living offered.

Amaia whispered low enough that only I could hear, "She is exactly what I'd expect a witch to look like."

The woman was covered head to toe in thick, loose layers of black. Her camo poncho was thrown over her shoulder like she'd whipped it off the moment she saw me. "Sabueso?"

I really wish everyone would stop calling me that.

"Sí, Lola," I replied, unsure what mood I'd be faced with, especially with a guest in tow who was clearly not in distress. "Soy yo. Este es mi amigo, venimos en paz."

I saw Amaia side-eye me in my peripheral. I'd forgotten she was only aware of a couple of the four languages my father had forced down my throat at an early age. There was still one she had no knowledge of if Moe hadn't mentioned my translation out on the road. I was pretty confident she had no idea; at least, she'd never brought it up. One thing Moe did was respect everyone's privacy within reason. And there was no reason for her to tell Amaia because as far as she was concerned, I had never posed a true threat. I'd learned to value that part of our friendship.

It wasn't that I wanted to keep secrets. There were just some things about me that came with questions. Not every question in life needed an answer.

"Armas abajo. Alexiares es un amigo," Lola ordered, the others surrounding us disarmed. One by one they melted back into their hidden locations and Lola guided us back through the hidden door.

If Amaia was impressed by the outside of this place, the inside would make her jaw drop. Lola and her group had built an elaborate array of tree houses spanning the entirety of the park. They were connected by wooden carved bridges leading to the conservatory and zoo they now cared for. The place was beautiful for sure. First impressions could be deceiving though, especially when it came to the *brujas*. Civilized actions and thoughtful design had not been kept in mind in its establishment.

I found myself dog-piled by children rushing to greet me in appreciation. A thank you for what I had done for them. For sparing their lives.

They scattered at the snap of Lola's fingers with the exception of an older boy. He had to be about eighteen now. Green, catlike eyes stared back at me. We stood there for a moment, saying nothing before he offered a tense nod, tapped my shoulder and walked off. There were no words he could say that would amount to what I had lost because of him; he was just thankful to still be here.

"What the hell was that about?" Amaia asked impatiently, clearly fed up by all the confusion she'd experienced over the last fifteen minutes.

"Lola and the other *brujas* don't sell people, Amaia," I offered, trying to decide what was and was not okay to share. Lola offered no help, so I continued, "They help them. This is a haven for those who escaped violence or were hunted, then they are trained. When Lola gives the go ahead, they're made into weapons of their own. To protect themselves, and then others. That's why they think it's the black market; they extend their services for a … fee."

Lola glared at Amaia for the negative implication in her question. "¿Vender personas? Eso es lo que ella pensaba. ¿Quién es esta mujer?"

"A friend," Amaia snapped, not appreciating neither Lola's tone nor her insinuation, "like he said."

I whipped in her direction, an even mix of shock at her understanding and pleading with her to refrain from instigating a fight we stood no chance of winning. Fear of a motorcycle on an open road, check. Fear of a witch with unknown powers, not on her radar.

"You speak Spanish?" Lola asked her directly, sounding slightly impressed. She glanced over at me for confirmation.

I shrugged, not having an answer to give her. "First I've heard of it."

"No, ma'am, I do not." Amaia smiled at her, the tension between the two easing. "I do, however, understand."

A smile crept onto Lola's face and she moved to grab Amaia's hand, guiding us to the largest treehouse. Her home.

An older woman, with fierce features and harsh lines on her face appeared. Despite her tough exterior, kindness seeped from her as she placed two cups down in front of us.

"Horchata," she said, proud of her concoction.

Tiago had made it for us during the few holidays we'd been able to spend together. While his remained alcohol free, María's was not. She'd gotten me fucked up on more than one occasion. At the time, I'd been grateful, needing the relief from my travel, but now, there was one person here who didn't need such a distraction.

I scooted the drink away from Amaia toward me, careful not to insult her. "Ella está bien, María, gracias. Tomaré su ración."

Her nose scrunched as she scrutinized the denial of food before noticing the tapping of Amaia's leg. Understanding washed over her, and as quickly as she had entered, María disappeared into the semi-functional kitchen Lola had in the back.

"What is this about, Alexiares?" Lola asked, always one to get straight to the point. "I heard you fled The Expanse eight months ago. I did not expect your return so soon."

"It's a long story," I mumbled, not sure where to start.

"Lucky us, it'll be dark soon. We have all night to cover it."

I grabbed her hand, squeezing it and grateful for what she considered an invitation to stay. Then, I told her everything. From the moment I returned from my last trip here, to dropping off the boy who had greeted me earlier. Jensen and his father had been the reason I had fled, unable to complete that last mission for Finley. I recalled how I'd ended up in Monterey, and how that had led me back to The Expanse, to Duluth. Amaia glared at me in warning, but I knew I could trust Lola. She was one of the last people in the world whom I did trust, and she trusted me all the same. Our relationship depended on it.

María had returned with some Fresca for Amaia, followed by two large plates of rice and beans for us both. Amaia scarfed it down, noting how delicious it was, which brought a smug grin to both our hosts' faces. I wasn't sure what María was to Lola, only knew she was always present. Always taking care of her, making sure she was fed and remained sane. María was Lola's Riley at first glance, but I caught the looks they stole toward each other and couldn't help but wonder if there was more to it.

"That explains why we've had people snooping around lately," Lola muttered. More to herself than to the rest of us at the round wooden table.

I nodded my regretful agreement, "She found out where Jensen and his father went from one of the others in the area. I'm sorry if it's caused you trouble."

"The only trouble comes from those who live to tell the tale."

Amaia grinned at her in response. "I like her."

"Igualmente," Lola said, sliding the extra bowl of rice and beans María had brought her toward her.

Amaia turned to me, it was her turn to ask questions. "You brought the people here you were meant to kill?"

"In the latter part of my time at St. Cloud, yes." I had zero regrets about any of it, regardless of how it made my situation end up. "Mostly children, adults too if they really didn't deserve it or weren't total dickheads. The people Sloan talked about, some of them were good people. Others were nightmares personified, I was doing the world a favor."

Lola's head tilted, a motion I'd learned to recognize as coming before a subtle taunt when it came from her. "Yes, your boyfriend here found himself on the other side of one of my death spells when he'd realized what we had here. Lucky for him, the stars aligned that night and I was in a rather merciful mood for his pitiful looking face. We made a deal: he brings any children that woman orders dead to me, I won't kill him."

"He's not my boyfriend."

"She's not my girlfriend," we echoed at the same time, both whipping our heads around to stare each other down.

Lola smiled knowingly. "Claro."

"Why would Finley want children dead?" Amaia asked, clearly mortified.

I wasn't sure why. Nothing she'd seen or heard of Finley had indicated that the woman had any redeeming qualities. Maybe the fact that I had married her had led her to believe that there had to be *something*. The thing was, there wasn't. I was blinded by beauty, and desperate for any ounce of affection. Finley had recognized that and made me her prey.

"Because she's Finley," I said definitively, my voice rough at the thought of her, "and a threat to her gaining power doesn't have an age. A threat is a threat."

"My children are promising. Since they developed their gifts early on in life, they had an easier time adapting than most adults. The older they got, the more powerful they became, and to that woman, knowledge *is* power." Lola added proudly.

To her, they were all her children. Well, the ones who had no parents left, and even then, she became a surrogate mom for some, a second mom for others. I'd never known a true mother's touch; for as long as I could remember, I *was* my mother's protector. It should have been the other way around, and these kids were damn lucky to have someone who cared enough to be that for them.

I loved my mother as much as the next guy, but I deserved someone to protect me as a kid. Yet, I had always missed out. At least my brother Evander had me; some of these kids had no one. No one but Lola and, now, each other.

"So they aren't elementals or *Umbras*?" Amaia asked, slowly putting the pieces of the puzzle together.

Lola and I shook our heads at the same time, but she was the one who answered. "Tinkerers and Scholars as you all say in Monterey."

"How did you know where I came from?" Amaia's eyes narrowed and her hand reached toward her weapons still strapped to her hip.

None of anything she carried would do us any good here. By the hesitancy in her movements, she knew that. Still, she was skeptical though Lola had posed no true threat to us yet. We'd caught her on one of her better days, but I understood Amaia's reluctance to trust someone who clearly knew more about her than either of us had divulged.

"I know more than you think, General."

"You've heard of me." The absence of a menacing look on Lola and María's face calmed her suspicions. "Does that mean you'll help us?"

"Help is already on the way." Lola grinned mischievously.

Amaia's grin fell from her face before it had a chance to fully form. "And the cost of your help is …"

"Consider this an act of good faith. I'm sure our paths will cross again in the future."

THERE WERE FIFTEEN IN LOLA'S COVEN, AND ONLY HALF OF THEM could leave their little compound for it to remain safe against any threats that may make their way here. The numbers dwindled when we realized that some would have to follow close behind Reina and Tomoe on their emissary tour. The remaining others would work through Duluth's population, then spread out throughout the allied territories. It was fair enough. We were just thankful for the ease of which Lola was willing to help. I thought it would have taken far longer to convince her, but she had her own *Scholar* here who was able to see the same daunting future Moe had seen.

She noted that there were other covens she knew spread around what was left of the continental United States. Lola would get the word out and hopefully, others would be inclined to help. She remained hopeful—that had to mean something. Tomoe hadn't sent the spell with us for obvious reasons; Lola's people would have to get it when they arrived at Duluth in a few days. From there they would relay the message to Lola, and Lola to the others.

As we lay on the lumpy mattress of straw and feathers Lola had crafted, I lay awake that night listening to the soft snores of Amaia. She tossed and turned in her sleep, her curls soaked with sweat of whatever nightmare she was having before she finally settled. She inched closer to me, tucking her body against mine.

I curved to meet her position, my arm spanning across her waist, and I pulled her closer. The sweet scent of her hair made me relax instantly. A taste of home no matter the distance I was from Monterey.

The thought kept me awake longer than I wanted to be. I hoped we would live to see the end of this, because I wanted nothing more than to experience my new home with her by my side every night for the rest of my life.

CHAPTER FOURTEEN

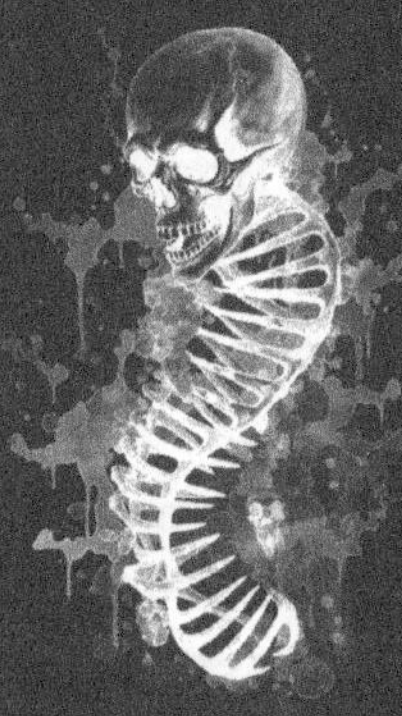

REINA

In the last few weeks, I hadn't had a moment of boredom, but I found myself to be quite antsy since Amaia left. I sat on the floor, ripping apart the God-awful clothing this place had and creating something new. You would think they would have some vague sense of style here. It'd probably make living here a heck of a lot better. I mean, layering up made the fashion possibilities endless, it was such a waste.

When things got better again, I'd ask Amaia if I could come spend some time up here. Someone would have to show them that part of getting to a new normal was acting as though some of the smaller things, like how they presented themselves, mattered.

A hurried knock against the door startled the life out of me, making me jump. Tomoe never bothered to knock back home, plus she knew how to pick these crappy locks easily. Alexi and

Amaia were still gone; as far as I knew, they weren't due back for another day, maybe longer. It could be Abel, though he hadn't stopped by the room without being invited yet. I grabbed the knife Alexi had given me and tucked it into my trousers.

Sloan blocked most of the door frame, an oddly serene visage on her face that I hadn't seen since the last time I'd visited her in The Before. She tried to push her way through, but I shifted into her path, wanting to know why she was here before letting her into my last place of peace.

"I think it's about time we had a talk," she said calmly.

I glanced over her, shocked to see the older woman with strawberry blonde hair in her wake. "Auntie," I gulped out.

It wasn't a surprise that she was in Duluth. At my door, however, was unexpected. Sloan had rejected each of my requests to see her. I guess with my brother's nonsense, Sloan couldn't be too sure I wouldn't hurt her.

"Reina." She flew into my arms, hugging me tightly.

My body tensed.

It'd been a long time since I'd let someone hug me. Well, a long time in my book. Okay, perhaps only a few weeks, since before Seth left me behind.

"You want to know about Uncle Harris," I said, pulling her back from the embrace. They offered rigid nods in response. "Come in."

"Was going to do that anyway since I own the entire place." The cold in Sloan's voice slipped through again.

My auntie wasn't having any of her crappy attitude. She grabbed her shoulder in warning. "Sloan Victoria Moore."

"Sorry," Sloan, shrugged at me half apologetically.

They moved across the small living room and took a seat on the couch. I forced myself to sit across from them on the coffee table, the guilt already creeping back up in my heart.

Taking a few meditating breaths, I spilled it all: how I'd caught Hunter and Uncle Harris arguing, about what, I wasn't sure. He had shot my brother in the back of the head when he'd turned away, ready to leave whatever they had argued about behind them. It was so typical of Hunter, he hated confrontation.

Though Seth and he were twins, they had always differed in that way. Hunter was a giant teddy bear; he wanted nothing more than for everyone to live harmoniously, to spread love. I had screamed in shock, which had caused Sloan's father, my uncle, to turn his attention toward me.

I ran for my life as he shouted after me, running into my father's arms. Quickly, knowing he was right on my tail, I'd explained what I could. When Uncle Harris approached, my father unloaded. I spared Sloan and her mom the gory details and the absence of emotion my father had presented when he'd done so.

That wouldn't help anyone move on, which is why they were here. *Right?* My father had told me not to tell Momma what had happened, to blame it on the Pansies. Then one grabbed my father, dragging him into the pond he stood around. He'd been bitten.

The word 'father' burned my tongue. He was no father; he was the antichrist. The more I sat back and thought things through, the more I'd become determined to stop at nothing to end him.

I paused, trying to calm myself after recalling such horrid memories. They waited patiently for me to continue, and when I felt strong enough, the rest of the story unfolded. My father had ordered me to kill him, thinking he would turn.

We hadn't known any better, no one did. At least not out in Montana. I missed, my hands shaking too much at something I'd never imagined I would have to do. Even as death lingered, my father had consoled me, told me it was okay and he would take care of it. His instructions were simple, to find my mother then blame it all on the undead. So I did.

Panic seized me. I ran off, never getting a chance to learn what had become of him. The gunfire had drawn attention to our ranch and my home had gone under attack. Seth and I had fled within an hour of it all happening, my momma succumbing to the Pansies in our defense. That was the day I learned a shotgun meant nothing against a herd. You needed more than that, an array of skills and an armory to back you up.

"Shit, Reina …"

"What, Sloan?" I said defensively, expecting the worst to come from her.

Her words were gentle, "You are braver than I could ever be."

I sat there for a moment, questioning everything. *Brave? Am I supposed to be proud of what I did to survive?* Because I wasn't. I missed my brother, wanted him back. I would do anything to rewind time and try to do things better.

Sloan leaned forward, her freckled hands taking one of mine. Her thumb circled the base of my hand, my cousin, the one I had admired my entire life, was now facing me with earnest blue eyes. "I am so sorry."

"For which part?" I asked. There was a lot she'd done the last few weeks, most of the things had dug deeper into a wound already formed by family. Sloan had hurt me in a way only family could.

"For all of it. My behavior since you all arrived. For trying to have you all killed, for having Seth betray you under false pretenses. My father … I'm so damn sorry for it all."

"Yeah," I chuckled, though it was absent of any real humor. "Guess we both got fathers we can't be proud of."

My auntie sat there, a display of shell shock in her once vibrant hazel eyes.

"Auntie?" I asked softly.

Her wispy hair fell in front of her pale face as she peered up at me slowly. "I knew about his past, what he did out in Montana before their parents sent him to the military. I thought he could change … thought he did change."

Seth had found old newspapers in Sloan's attic of a string of murders around town in the '80s that went unsolved. My uncle had left for the military shortly after, never to return again. Until one day, Sloan's momma had kicked him out, and he'd come to stay with us. Then the bombs dropped, the rest history.

"Momma? What the hell!" Sloan's lips curled in disgust.

"It's all my fault," she offered, "Oh God. I'm an enabler. I just thought … I thought I wasn't strong enough to raise you on my own. I had no degree, never worked a day in my life. I got pregnant with you right after high school. Met him at a bar visiting one of my childhood girlfriends. We'd snuck ourselves in. I didn't think I had any options. Oh Sloan, what have I done?" Hopeless tears streamed down her face at the confession.

Sloan moved to comfort her, dropping my hand in the process. "No, Momma. This isn't on you. This is on *him* and only *him*. He was a monster. Guess it's a signature Moore trait."

"It's not. Don't say that. Sloan, we are not the people who fathered us." That was something I was sure of. I may be his daughter, but Ronan Moore was no longer my father. "We can be better than them, I know it."

"Easier to say when you don't have blood on your hands, cousin. Seth and I, unfortunately, we have a lot."

"You and her are one in the same, ya know?" I said, the realization bringing me a sense of comfort in the oddest of ways. I suddenly found myself glad they had found each other in The Before, like God had put them directly on a path leading up to this moment in The After.

Her auburn brows furrowed at the indication. "Who?" Sloan asked.

"Amaia. I know you two were friends in The Before, so you had to have something in common. At first, I couldn't see it, but now, I reckon you have even more similarities. She didn't want this either; she reminds us of it every day too."

Sloan released a dry laugh, her fingers twiddled with the hem of her sweater. Probably itching to spark a cigarette if I had to guess. "Yeah, well, for someone who doesn't want it, she does a damn good job at it."

"She isn't without her own failures on her way to being who she is now," I said, unsure if I was still mad at her or trying to come to her defense. "Amaia made mistakes, people died because of them. Seth left because of it."

"Sweetie, you can't put that on her. Seth left because that's who he is. I know you love your brother, but he has always walked in your father's shadow. His departure was inevitable."

She was right, but that didn't make the words easier to digest.

I must've appeared lost in my thoughts as Sloan abruptly added, "You think he's gonna come back, don't you?"

More silence, what could I say? I wasn't ready to give up on my brother completely; if I did, that would only prove him right. My love for him was stronger than anything, and though I didn't justify his actions, I understood. He had acted for the love of his family, even if at some point I had stopped being included in that. The only difference between the two of our actions was that mine had always kept my number one in mind: him. But his number one was different from mine. Our father.

"Reina ..." my auntie hesitated, not sure how to finish the sentence.

My voice came out in a shout, "I know! I don't need a whole speech. Alexiares already gave me one. But my brother wouldn't leave me here. He's going to come back; we just have to figure out what angle he's working."

Nothing but sympathy lingered in their eyes. My auntie grabbed my hand, placing her other hand on Sloan's back. "We Moore women have a hell of a path ahead of us."

We all had a laugh at that. Just a few women who carried our last name like a freaking burden. Sloan rose to her feet, taking a step closer to me before pulling me into a tender hug.

"I am glad that you're here, even despite the circumstances," she said in a hushed tone.

"I'm going to have to leave soon—"

That caught her attention. She pulled back to meet my stare, "Abel's intel?"

"You should cut him some slack," I snapped, defensive over him. Admittedly, we were becoming fast friends.

Sometimes my family's energy had a damper to it. Being around Abel felt good, natural. I was glad to finally have someone who knew how to find humor and fun in the horrible world we lived in. I wanted him to stay with our pack forever, I would not budge on that.

"He's a traitor."

"He won't be," I said sternly, "not when he comes with us."

"Like hell—"

Sloan's momma popped her in the back of the head for both her language and tone. At least someone served as a check and balance around here for her. I was getting seriously concerned.

"Ow," Sloan said, rubbing the back of her head.

"Amaia's not going to leave him here with you. He's Riley's family. You don't know Riley, but he's part of my new family, that makes Abel family by default." I loved my cousin, but there was only one option in this world for a discovered spy. "And you could be, too, one day, Sloan, Auntie. I have to leave soon, and Amaia and Alexiares will stay. If you care about your people as much as I think you do, you'll get off your high horse and stop fighting back. She's made some mistakes, some more forgivable than others. I'm sure you learned over the years that her plans have an annoying way of always working out."

"And you trust this Alexiares?" my auntie asked warily.

Sloan's lip curled up in disgust at his name. *"Bloodhound,"* she corrected her.

"Stop calling him that, he doesn't like it. I don't know what he did before I met him, or even why he did what he did, and I don't care. *Alexi* is as much of my brother as Seth is. So, yes, I trust him. He's a bit rough around the edges, but his heart is good. I can sense it. That's all that matters to me."

They both gawked at me, ultimately deciding it wasn't worth the fight.

Sloan relented, taking a deep sigh. "I don't know what it is about that man that makes otherwise reasonable women defend him, but if you trust him, then I trust you. I'll … rein back the insults."

"And?" I egged on.

"And I'll stop pushing Amaia. I'll start listening and stop demanding."

I smiled at that, satisfied by even the small win. "She has a lot to teach you."

"Yada yada, cousin."

Sloan squeezed the three of us into another hug, and for a moment, all was right in the world.

"I think this goes without saying, but what the fuck?" Tomoe said, causing my eyes to dart up at the now open door to the lab.

"Holy moly …" I mumbled.

Amaia's hair was knotted around her heart-shaped face, her large brown eyes scanned the room. Her clothes were painted by splotches of deep red blood, the long coat she sported tattered. Alexiares' stare pierced beyond the doorway behind her. His dark brown hair was completely grown on the side and tousled. A deep frown formed on his usual pissed off face; he had no coat and what was left of his sweater underneath was burned at the sleeves.

"You guys look like shit." Sloan laughed, my gaze shot toward her unappeased, "Sorry."

"Umm," I said, taking a step closer to the two Pansies Amaia had chained to her waist.

The other end of the metal chains was wrapped around their torsos, and a makeshift muzzle was melded around their mouths. No biting would take place here. Then it dawned on me, maybe they'd been bitten in the process. I rushed over to her before realizing I couldn't get much closer to check her.

I skirted around them, deciding to check on Alexiares first. Pushing his sleeves up, I examined his arms and sent my gifts out to search throughout the rest of his and Amaia's bodies. Nothing. When I was sure they weren't harmed, I yanked his sleeves down and glared up at him.

"Don't look at me," he grumbled with displeasure. "Look at your general."

There was an audible shift in the room as everyone turned to Amaia. A stupid, fat grin pulled at her features. Nothing but chaos buzzed behind her eyes.

"I figured since we're running tests, we might as well have some test samples." Amaia said proudly, genuinely confused why we were confused.

Abel shuffled through some drawers and cabinets before pulling additional chains out. For what purpose? Only God knew. "Here, I'll go get some nails or … something. Honestly, I'm not sure what will hold them."

If the wheels weren't churning in my mind, I would have laughed. He had so much to get used to; I think I would enjoy watching him immerse in the mayhem. *If* we survived this war, that is.

"Yeah, you go do that." Amaia grinned at him. "Get some meat too, help with their appetite. I think they're hungry."

"Seriously, what is your problem?" Alexiares ground out.

He was growing impatient with the havoc she caused. I felt it. Strangely enough, I had no desire to tame it because honestly, I knew there were at least two other people behind me that were too.

Sloan huffed a hoarse laugh. "Don't know why you're surprised, *Bloodhound,* you should have realized long ago to expect the unexpected from your girl."

Amaia turned her head slightly, awkwardly meeting Alexiares eye at the *'your girl'* portion of Sloan's loaded statement. Neither of them offered any corrections. Amaia ungracefully took a side step away from him only to be pushed back over by the Pansies snapping through the muzzles.

"Okay, I'm going to pretend like I haven't seen through the bullshit and let you announce your idiotic plan to the rest of these agreeable fools," Tomoe deadpanned.

Sloan uncrossed her arms, moving to grab her cigarette from the ashtray on the table. "This should be good," she mumbled, lighting the tip and taking a deep inhale.

I laughed maniacally, understanding exactly what my sister wanted from me. "She wants to play their game."

Heads swiveled from Amaia to me, then back at Amaia, as they awaited an explanation. The only one she offered was a simple shrug and a head toss toward my test equipment in the corner of the lab.

"You know, Amaia, that is absolutely ridiculous, and I applaud you for it," I said, clasping her on the shoulder before jumping back at the snapping heads to my right. "She wants me to test them against each other, learn how my father manipulates our DNA even further."

"Correct," she confirmed, explaining her thought process further. "If she can figure that out, we might be able to use that to our advantage. Michael and Logan gained extra powers, why can't we?"

"This is a terrible idea." Tomoe groaned, her cheeks resting against her fists.

Amaia gave her a leveled-stare of dismissal. "Says the devil on my shoulder."

"You've got a replacement for that now," Tomoe slammed, throwing a finger at Alexiares. We both knew from the obvious disapproval in his body language that he had protested every way. Be that as it may, it was still fun to point the finger at the new guy.

"Don't you dare blame me. I tried to stop her. You know how she gets."

"Stop her?" I said excitedly, "Why would you? She's right."

That earned a few moments of stunned silence.

Sloan choked on smoke at the turn of events, "Reina …"

"Don't *Reina* me, she's right. You all want me to stop waiting for Seth to come back, save us with some master plan. Okay, I don't believe it anymore." It pained me to say, but the words felt bitterly right leaving my lips. "And I will stop at nothing to make sure he and my father don't succeed in their plan. If that's what y'all really want, then we have no choice other than to play their silly little game."

"Welp, that took significantly less convincing than I had planned, so I guess, I rest my case." Amaia took a mocking curtsy as the door behind them flew back open.

Abel strode through, a few large, industrial sized nails in hand. "Sent someone out for some raw meat." He glanced around the room, taking in the various expressions on each of our faces, "What'd I miss?"

"Chaos. You missed the absolute chaos of these two maniacal women you want to call your new family," Sloan bit out, only half-joking.

She was still mad, and I would be too, but he was hardly her problem now. She needed to get over it. Fast, before I lost what little patience I had remaining. Alexiares detailed the game plan with a few brief sentences.

"Okay, so what? Say Reina figures it out, what next?" Abel threw a questioning look at the both of us.

"Then we test it," Amaia and I said at the same time.

A soft smile exchanged between us two, and I was glad to finally be back on even ground with her. I missed our connection, missed the feeling of being on the same side. I knew we always were, but some days it was harder to believe that than others.

"I'm sorry, what?" If Alexiares had a drink in his mouth, I was one hundred percent certain he would have spit it out.

Even Sloan practically stuttered over her words. "On who?"

Tomoe's eyes glazed over before coming back into focus. "On her," she said, her finger now pointed at Amaia.

My heart sank to my butt, head shaking from side to side. "I won't agree to that. No."

"The whole point of doing what we're doing here is to keep it from affecting our people. What do you want us to do?" Amaia argued, "Put out a sign-up sheet and ask people to volunteer for testing? What if we're wrong?"

"We could use the prisoners," Sloan offered. That earned her a glare from everyone in the room, Abel, a now prospective prisoner included.

"No, Sloan. We aren't going to commit war crimes on our own people." Amaia rolled her eyes at what she viewed as an obscene suggestion.

Sloan shrugged. "You *are* our people. At least these fuckers deserve it."

"Doubt you'd take advice from a *bloodhound*," Alexiares tried, "but testing out on prisoners that abandoned their post because they were scared does *not* qualify as deserving."

"When people fail to protect our home, they no longer count as *my* people." Sloan scolded, then after a few breaths relented,

"Whatever though, you're right. That would make me no better than you."

"You're going to let her go through with this, Alexiares?" Tomoe tossed at him, like she had seen he was the only one who would be able to cancel what she deemed a neurotic plan.

"Let her?" he nearly shouted, even Sloan took a step back at the pure edge in his voice, "I don't let this girl do anything. She just does, and frankly, I'm getting fucking sick of the self-sacrificial bullshit." Alexiares turned to her, his light brown eyes darkened under the intensity of his gaze. His face was completely red. I could taste the rage seeping off him.

"We all are," I said, though that didn't change the fact that all of our options sucked. I didn't want to test my family, but I also didn't want to be responsible for potentially killing an innocent person, either.

A heavy knock sounded on the door, silencing the room once more. A young girl stood on the other side, the grave expression on her face aging her up a few years. She walked past Alexiares and skirted around Amaia and the Pansies, aiming for the table beside her instead.

Amaia's thick curls fell down her shoulders as she threw her head back, releasing a sinister laugh. She smacked the note down on the table, "Doesn't matter what any of you want right now. We're doing this, because our time is officially fucking up."

I grabbed the note, it was from Riley and Prescott. If I had Amaia's and Alexiares' gifts, I would light it in flame. But I didn't, so both knees buckled when waves of anger and pain crept from me and I worked to rein it back in. Guess we were doing this someway somehow, because my father and brother were sick in the dang head. Evil didn't begin to cover them.

Concentration camps. He was using the citizens he considered less valued, working them near death, creating weapons, and mining coal for some reason. When they had nothing left to give, he turned them into the created Pansies. The poor souls were from both his territory, and the people from settlements around the country that refused to answer his demands. Settlements like those from Duluth.

"Oh my fucking—" Sloan's words trailed off, reading over my shoulder.

Tomoe snatched the note from me, shoving Sloan out the way. "Guess we're leaving a lot sooner than expected."

"This doesn't change anything, Amaia." I stood my ground. "I won't experiment on you, and you can't make me."

That sent her over, and hell broke loose. "And when exactly in the last month have you cared about my wellbeing, Reina? You've done nothing but push me away. If memory serves me right, you and Tomoe shut me out every chance you got. I needed you both, and you left me out to dry. What I've done has made me the devil in your eyes, meanwhile you're off prancing after Seth. The person who caused this all. So, yes, I'll do this, and if I die, then you keep trying and you keep going until you get it right. You didn't care about how I was doing thirty minutes ago, don't start now on my account."

Tears welled up in my eyes, a thick, painful lump formed in the length of my throat. Her words burned because they were right. I had my own rightful reasons for my actions, reasons she clearly pranced over every chance she got. Abel and Sloan tucked into the shadows of the room, tension simmered between us as Alexiares and Tomoe took a step back, letting us fight this one out.

"I saw the look you and Sloan exchanged." She added fuel to the flames. "Something changed before I got back. From where I'm standing, it's as if everyone deserves your forgiveness, except me."

"The difference between Moe and you, between Sloan and you, is they know when to apologize," I said, fury lingering in each of my words.

"I *did* apologize, Reina," she challenged. "You just weren't ready to receive it."

I took a second to think about my next words. I didn't want to fight with her anymore. In fact, I was all fought out. The family I had left was all that mattered to me now, my fight with all of them was over. "I … I am now."

"Well, it's too late." She dropped the chains, Abel rushed over to drag the Pansies to the other side of the lab where he'd placed the nails.

"I think that we should take a beat, find a moment to think this all—" Alexiares tried to reason, but didn't have a chance to finish.

"Shut up!" Again, we were both in sync as we silenced him.

Abel let out a low whistle. "Sheesh."

The thing was, Amaia did apologize. She had tried to make peace several times, had practically begged for it, and I'd slammed the door in her face. Both metaphorically and literally, it had felt great at the time. Powerful even, but now, I felt terrible about it. I knew I owed her an apology, I just didn't know where to begin. Alexiares was right—we'd all done terrible things that led us here. We both had a lot of healing to do, but maybe, we could start now.

Tomoe released herself from her stance against the center table and strode over toward us, remorse all over her pale, delicately freckled face. I sensed it roll off her body too.

"I love you both," she said, a rare moment of vulnerability. "You are *both* the only family I have left. We're only as strong as we are unified. Now, if we're all done being sorry, it's time to move on and stop hurting each other. We don't know how much time we all have left."

That statement drew everyone's attention—a question we all wanted to ask, but knew she would never tell the answer to.

The problem with making peace was that it only worked if everyone was willing to oblige. Though I knew Amaia wanted to, she needed to remain a general right now, not a friend. Definitely not a sister. She had every right to because, unlike the rest of us, Amaia had millions of lives in her hands, and she was doing her best to balance it all. The least we could do was our part in helping her succeed.

"This will work," Amaia said. "I'm trying to save us all. Ensure that we can *all* have the happy ending we deserve. We're fighting for our home, for our family. Nothing worth it comes without risk, and I won't risk *anyone* else's life when I don't have to. Not even prisoners."

"That's a hopeful outlook if I ever heard one," Sloan mumbled to no one but herself.

Amaia shot her attention to her fiery-haired friend from another life. "Hope is everything. Can't you all see that?"

"I see someone who wants to believe that hope is everything, but hope is not enough," Tomoe said poetically.

Amaia's stare rested on me, and I nodded in understanding. As much as it pained me, I knew I had no choice but to agree, even if no one else in this room understood. We didn't have the right to bring anyone else into this mess we had created who weren't already entangled. We could not play God, but we could act against the devil.

"Let me know when you're ready." Amaia said, grabbing hold of my shoulder and squeezing in familiar comfort. The next instant she was gone, leaving the rest of us in shocked silence in her wake.

"I'll take care of this," Alexiares spoke after a few moments, breaking the tension in the air.

Tomoe had already seen every version of this; it was up to the rest of us to determine how it would all pan out. "You have less than forty-eight hours before Reina figures this out."

"I said, I'll take care of this." His words were fierce, a man determined. "Worry about what happens here, I'll worry about the rest."

CHAPTER
FIFTEEN

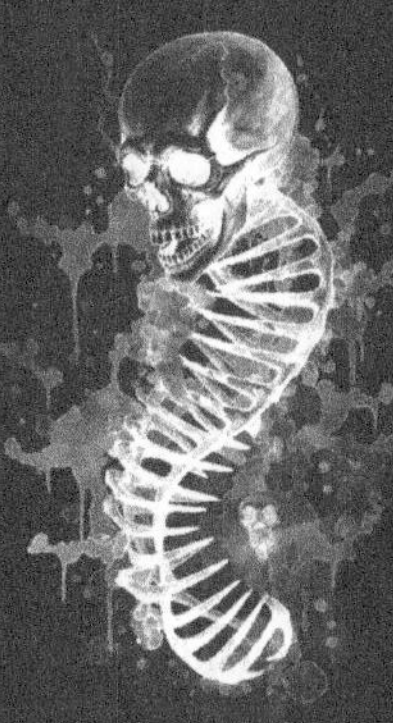

AMAIA

The best way to act as if something isn't happening is to play dumb and pretend that you can't feel it encroaching on your personal space. For me, that something was actually a someone, and his name was Alexiares.

I turned the lock to my door swiftly, closing it in his face as quickly as I had opened it. He slammed it open, and it rebounded off the wall, barely missing my head by a few inches. His rough hand closed over my wrist and he tugged me back to face him.

"I suggest you take your hands off me before you find yourself on the other end of my magic. It's been boiling right underneath my skin for days now," I said, straightening my posture to try to meet him eye to eye.

"I've heard that threat before," he snarled, "it means jack shit to me at this point."

Oof, he was angry. I shrugged him off, deciding the easiest path forward was to act unfazed.

"What? You get your magic under control and think you can take me?" I took a step closer, my fingers trailing up his chest playfully, "Oh. You do think that. Can you, Alexi? Take me?"

He didn't take the bait, slapping my hand off him. "Are you having another mental breakdown or something? What the actual fuck is wrong with you?"

"I'm growing tired of people asking me that."

"Then stop acting like a maniac." He backed me into a corner, my head pressed against the wall. "This has to stop. Experimenting, pushing the limits. At some point, Amaia, you have to question where the line is between you and them. And don't give me some bullshit about your intentions, because intentions don't stop the worst from happening."

"I'm not testing this out on some random, innocent person. That already makes me ten times better than them." I smirked, still not ready to give away the fact that I truly was panicking on the inside.

The consequences of my actions were never lost on me; I simply embraced them while others shied away.

"What we're doing here, Amaia, this isn't some game. This isn't one of your silly little books. This is war. This is real fucking life."

"You think I don't know that?" I challenged. "Need I remind you that I have been through this before."

I ducked underneath the arm he had extended over my head; he should know his intimidation tactics didn't work on me. They hadn't the day I met him, and they wouldn't now.

Moving around him, I let out a wicked chuckle. "You wouldn't understand a damn thing about walking in my shoes. What it means to send soldiers you know by name to their death. You may know what it's like to take a life, Alexiares, but you will never understand sending a group of people to an uncertain death. And death, that's easy."

I whirled on him, taking strides to put him in the same position he'd placed me only moments before. See how he liked it with his back against the wall. "Death is if you're lucky. I'm thinking of the people who will be captured, tortured, and then turned. People who will have agonizing, bed-ridden injuries, or, hell, PTSD. I'm thinking of the people who will never be able to hear a bottle pop in the back of the tavern without taking cover. So no. I know it's not a silly fucking book. I know this is real life. I'm the one who will have to answer for my sins, because where people like me go, to face and meet their maker, there are consequences."

He glared at me, and I knew my words were harsher than I'd intended. But part of me hoped that if I pissed him off enough, he would back down and not get any stupid ideas of his own. I knew him at this point. Riley wasn't here, but I had a new shadow that would watch my every move, not to mention put themselves between me and any danger. I decided weeks ago that I wouldn't let that happen, so harsh it was.

"Fine," he relented, "but you won't be doing any of this alone."

Damn it.

He left me standing there wondering how the hell I, of all people in this big-ass world, had become responsible for so much.

Almost forty-eight hours on the dot, Reina figured it all out. The eyes of the OG Pansies and the upgraded versions were different because one was lab-made and the other was of "natural source." For the upgraded versions, they had become something that nature had never intended for them, at least not from their DNA. But we knew that already.

What Tomoe and Abel were able to powershare and put together from Reina's discovery was the heart-breaking part. The

Pansies were conscious … all of them. They were trapped behind a mental wall, and they would never be saved. We could not help them, no one could, not if we wanted a chance at staying alive. Every Scholar with seeing capabilities in Duluth had powershared, determined to find a cure.

None existed in any version of history, only many, many deaths during the lengths it took to try to find one. It had gone beyond science now.

It was a hard hit for everyone, but at least they all had someone to lean on. Not me, though—I had pushed or scared everyone whom I'd cared about away. The consequence of that? I would spend tomorrow alone.

My birthday.

Twenty-eight and I had nothing to show for it. Not unless you counted years of trauma, guilt, and a desire to make sure if it were my last, that those twenty-eight years would not be in vain. That time would give me the wisdom and guidance to make the right decisions, no matter who didn't understand them.

I lay in bed, staring up at the ceiling. Xavier had known I had killed him. He had pleaded with me, those dark brown eyes coming back to life briefly, hoping I would recognize him, and I did not. Instead, I had chosen myself over him, ending his life in order to spare mine.

Tomorrow, I would have one last day of freedom before the rest of the plan moved forward at full speed. Reina was working on the last bit, trying to figure out how to perfectly extract what we needed for the experiment, and then, only fate could decide. Tomoe had seen different outcomes, some prettier than others. Until Reina injected me, until the sample mixed with my DNA, only time would tell which outcome would win.

Alexiares had avoided me since our argument. I couldn't tell if it made me sad or not. Maybe he would be mad enough to change his mind, and then it would only be me whose life would be at risk.

I doubted as much, he was as stubborn as I was. And while there were times that I admired that trait of his, moments like these made me want to curse him at every stolen glance.

His ears must've been burning at my thoughts. A knock sounded at my door. It was his, I knew the weight of his fist against the door at this point. He would wait there, hoping I would open the door for him. Most nights I did, other nights he waited a moment before leaving, giving me a chance to reconsider. Tonight would not be one of those nights; I could tell he wasn't going anywhere.

I kicked my feet over the side of the bed and pulled on my oversized hoodie I'd stolen from Sloan's closet. She'd assured me it wasn't Morgan's, which was a relief, I guess. He stood there, sulking a few steps away from the door frame, eyes pointed toward the ground.

I waited for him to speak; I sure as hell wouldn't be breaking the ice. I'd done nothing wrong, and the sooner they all accepted that, the easier it would be for us all.

He cleared his throat, then met my gaze warily. "I've found it … hard to sleep without your presence."

After a few baiting seconds, I scooted out of the way to let him in. As much as I hated to admit it, I'd grown accustomed to his presence at night too.

"This means nothing," I said dryly before heading back to bed.

The lock sounded behind me followed by thudding steps. He kicked his shoes off, then scooted in on the other side of the bed. "I know."

There was as much distance between us as a queen bed would allow. The fire in the corner lit the room dimly and our eyes met. For a few painfully long minutes, we laid there in silence, staring at each other in the near darkness. His eyes glowing gold from the flames. Before I could stop myself, my fingers traced the outline of his jaw. He was beautiful, and I wanted to remember him exactly how he was in this moment.

No one talked about it, but the option besides death in this experiment was that I could become like them, the Pansies. Trapped behind a wall, where no one would ever touch me again, let alone, let me touch them.

He grabbed my hand, stopping it in motion and brought it to his lips. They were soft as they gently kissed the palm of my hand. "Don't … don't touch me like that if you don't intend to follow through."

I backed away, not ready to commit. I hadn't been with someone since Jax, and while I wasn't a stranger to sex, part of me wasn't sure I was ready to know what it would feel with someone else.

With Alexiares, if it happened, it would mean something. What it would mean, I wasn't yet sure, just knew there would be no going back. No stopping what was happening between us.

"I'm sorry," I whispered, not sure what else there was to say as I drew my hand back to my side.

He rolled over. "Sorry or selfish?"

A pang stormed through my heart. His words weren't harsh; they were not intended to hurt me. They were rather an expression of the hurt I'd placed upon him with my teasing and indecisiveness. Alexiares was not speaking of being physically intimate, but instead the lack of emotional intimacy I provided. After a mere few weeks of the obvious tension, things had gone from simmering between us to a full-on mage flame.

An hour passed, his breaths turned shallow, and I knew he'd fallen asleep. I turned onto my back, wishing the burn of a strong drink was seeping into the pits of my soul. That was the shitty thing about the truth, it usually fucking hurt.

CHAPTER
SIXTEEN

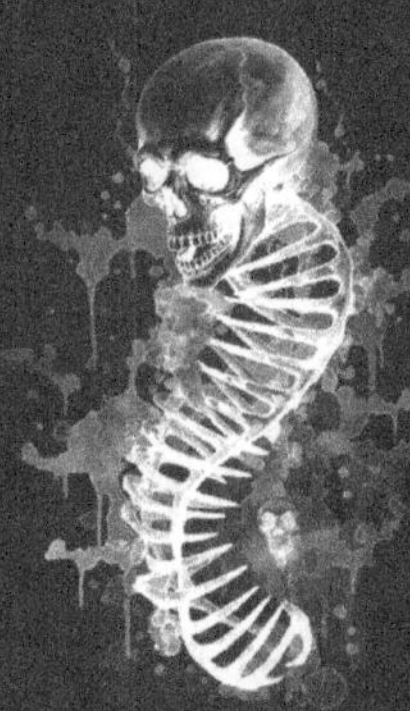

ALEXIARES

Her breathing was soft, even, deep. Still asleep, *perfect*. The last few days hadn't gone according to plan. We'd both said things we wish we could take back. I had at least. Who knows what went through her mind? She always found a way to let me in, but not too much.

It didn't matter; nothing wasn't going to stop me from executing the plan for today. I slid out of bed carefully. She was a light sleeper, and I wanted every moment of today to be a surprise. To see some of that light slip back into her eyes. I was no Riley, but I was something, damn it.

Reina, Tomoe, Abel, and hell, even Sloan had given me the go ahead on first dibs of the birthday girl. She wasn't as uncared for as she believed herself to be. Yeah, she got on everyone's damn nerves, but they all still loved her with a passion. And if I wasn't careful with my thoughts, I was starting to think maybe I did, too.

The door betrayed me as I tip-toed back in from the kitchen. Her eyelids fluttered, and she shifted her weight in the bed.

"Good morning," I whispered gently as I shook her awake.

She let out a half groan, half growl. "Is it? Because the sun isn't even up yet."

I chuckled. "Yeah? How would you know? You haven't even fully opened your eyes yet. It is, by the way, just tucked behind the impending storm. Which is why you need to get up *now*," I insisted.

"Why?" she asked, tossing a pillow at my face playfully. "What happened now?"

"It's December 16th, your birthday."

That caught her attention, and she sat up in the bed, "I never told you—"

"Besides your incredibly Sagiterrorist behavior, Reina's been gushing about it all week. But *I* get first dibs. Come on, let's go."

A faint smile fought to claim her beautiful lips. "You called dibs on me?"

"Yeah ... who wouldn't?" I shifted in place, slightly uncomfortable with this rare moment of vulnerability. "Is that ... okay with you?"

The smile won, her big doe eyes crinkled around the sides. "Yes. Yes, it is."

I sat in the living room waiting for her to get dressed, my knee shaking as I tapped my foot against the floor. I'd never in my life done something special for anyone's birthday, except for Evander. And that had been in secret. Our father wasn't a fan of celebrations. Our own mother never acknowledged the day in fear of what that might mean for us. In the immediate After, in my life before my Monterey family, to say it had never been the time or place to celebrate such was an understatement.

Finley had barely acknowledged her own birthday, let alone mine. This was different though. A possible turning point in what little time we had left.

I glanced down at the thermos full of coffee I had prepared while she was asleep and at the sad sack of sandwich wrapped in cloth. *This is stupid,* I thought, reaching out to swipe it and hide them somewhere. I didn't get the chance. She emerged from the bedroom. Her usual cargo pants and fitted turtleneck hugged her figure. She looked delectable. I tore my gaze from her curves, not wanting to make her uneasy with my lingering eyes.

I stood up, walking over toward her with my crappy version of a gift, "Three cubes of brown sugar and a splash of milk. Sorry, they don't have the fancy shit you like."

"You know my coffee order …" Her cheeks went flush at the gesture.

"I mean," I stammered out, "I've only been around you for a few months at this point. Kind of hard not to. Anyway, it's not a blueberry muffin, but I'm hoping the blueberry jam will make up for it. Reina made it for you. She's pissed she couldn't give it to you herself, but she'd only slow down our plans for the day with her birthday obsession."

That got a true laugh out of her. I had only seen the anguish in Reina's eyes when we spent her birthday on the run a few months back. The real birthday monster had come alive this last week with all the planning. A fact about her that Amaia was clearly aware of.

"Thank you," she said. "I don't know what to say."

I shrugged it off. "Don't worry about it."

"What do you mean plans for the day?" she asked, thinking back to what I'd mentioned briefly.

"Put your coat on and find out, princess."

I walked over to the couch, grabbing the puffer coat I had picked out for her. Today would be a cold one and I wanted her warm enough to enjoy herself. Holding it open for her, she slid her arms in slowly, glancing up at me in shock at my gentleman behavior.

Winking, I grinned back at her. I was just getting started.

She zipped her coat up, and I leaned in close, my voice coming out barely above the octave of a whisper. "You look exquisite by the way."

"Oh, stop with the bullshit. I just woke up."

Her way of saying thank you, I'd take it. Grabbing her hand, I led the way for a birthday celebration that may be our last.

"The motorcycle," she gasped as we rounded the corner to the tunnel. "How'd you get it back here?"

We'd left it about fifteen miles out in order to bring back her test-lab rat Pansies. I'd spent the better part of yesterday freezing my ass off to bring it back.

I glanced up at the sky impatiently. We were wasting time, and I didn't want it to snow before we got there. "Doesn't matter, let's go."

"Fine," she said, crossing her arms and pretending to throw a fit. "But so you're aware, riding this bike is a terrible way to celebrate the birthday of someone who is fucking terrified of being on the back of one."

"Oh, shut up and get on."

A short while later, we arrived at where we'd practiced my magic on the lake only weeks ago. There were logs set up in the fashion of a small campfire, two chairs lined up on one side, and a cooler half-buried in the snow. I peered down at my fingers, happy to not need Finley's stupid rings anymore. The logs lit up with my magic and I smiled, proud of myself for beating the snow before it could ruin my plans.

Amaia hopped off the back of the bike like it would bite her, taking a few steps toward the fire. "For me?"

"Who else would it be for?" I teased. "We're the only ones here."

She gave me the finger. An ear-to-ear grin pulled over her face before dropping. A tear fell down her face, and I panicked.

I inched closer to her. "Hey, wait, no. I'm sorry. You hate it, don't you?"

"No, it's not that. It's just," a soft laugh escaped her now red lips, "when I think about my birthday last year, the people I spent it with, things are so different now. I will never spend it with some of those people again. They're stuck inside my memories."

I couldn't argue with that. There were things Amaia and I would never relate to, this being one of them.

Tenderly, I wrapped my arms around her, pulling her into a tight hug. "Then let's make new memories."

She sniffled at the reassurance in my words but gazed up at me with curious eyes. I bent down, pulling the supplies out of my bag. A small pot, some water, and some chocolate. Pushing them aside, I emptied the rest, the small pan and some butchering knives purely for cooking. *Not* slaughtering, Sloan teased.

Amaia took a seat in one of the chairs, watching me intently. Something about this whole moment felt so fucking right. I couldn't explain it. My heart quickened in pace, each beat louder and more pronounced than the next. Even in her silence, she filled every space with her presence. It was intoxicating.

I opened the cooler, brought out the fish and the cutting board Reina had arranged at my request. Of course, she had put it in some fancy display, little lemons and a cup of herbs tucked into the cutout on the side.

"Holy crap!" she exclaimed, jumping to her feet at the sight. "Get the fuck out, fish? No way!"

We hadn't had fish since before St. Cloud, and Amaia had been sucking it up as best she could. She ate what meat was offered for the sole purpose of protein, but gagged at every bite.

"Sloan established a small fish farm right after Finley decided on AquaXelium."

Her brows furrowed. It was obvious that no one had explained to her what had happened here. Even when she'd asked me why Finley didn't rely on the river to feed St. Cloud all those months ago, taking the time to go over the history of it hadn't been my top priority.

"I forgot you all might not have heard the news out in Monterey." I offered, ready to tell her anything she wanted. Her wish was my command, "Yeah, AquaXelium was one of Finley's experiments gone wrong. Oddly enough, it had been her attempt to do some good and help feed our people, but it backfired. AquaXelium is a synthetic compound she created. I don't know the ins and outs of it, but she wanted to temporarily alter the laws of physics, governing the water molecules within a certain radius of St. Cloud. She fucked it up somehow. It caused a chain reaction and ruined every aquatic environment east of St. Cloud for about a hundred miles. Mostly marine life mutations from the toxic taint on the bodies of water. It didn't completely wipe out Lake Superior, but did enough damage that Duluth took it upon themselves to try to build the fish population back up in farms. Sloan said not to be mad by the way. No one has had any fish in months, they were due to release them back into the water but then, well, war. She never officially rolled it out."

"How thoughtful of the two of you to make me the test dummy," she teased.

I grinned at that, my fingers pulling off her beanie and ruffling her curls underneath. "Just another day in your life."

While the fish cooked, I made the coco and poured it into a couple of camping mugs. We sipped it down, feasting on the fish once it was ready. After a few hours of chatting around the fire, we sat in comfortable silence, taking in the scenery.

"Thank you," she said, breaking the silence.

I blinked at her, perplexed at what exactly I'd done that had warranted such a pleasantry from my sharp-tongued girl. "For what?"

"For making today special. I … I know I'm confusing and, yes, I can be selfish at times. I've earned that right." The pain in her eyes as she recalled my words last night was enough to bring me to my knees, "But, Alexiares, you give me this weird warm and fuzzy feeling that fucking terrifies me. And I just want to keep you safe. It sucks knowing it's not up to me. And, I think, I don't want to fight it anymore. I think I want to let it happen. I think I want to accept what you're trying to give me. I want to make you feel special in return. I'm learning, and I'm trying. Please, be patient with me."

I swallowed hard, cursing myself for the accusation I'd placed upon her last night.

"One day at a time, princess, one day at a time." I kissed her hand, pulling her close as I moved to her forehead, down to her cheeks, into the curve of her neck. Bringing my face level with her, I stopped short, hovering right over her mouth. "Make no mistake, one of these days, those lips will be mine."

THE RIDE BACK TO DULUTH WAS QUIET, BUT NOT IN A BAD WAY. I could tell we were both lost in our thoughts on how things had shifted permanently between us. I didn't have much experience with relationships.

Finley had been my first real girlfriend. Even that didn't last long. She quickly had become my wife under my own presumption that our bullshit love was the real thing. Then she'd ripped off the bandaid and showed her true colors, slowly stripping down the man I was in an effort to make me be her match. In a way, I guess I was. That didn't mean I wanted to be that man forever.

With Amaia, things weren't like that. The best thing about being with her was that I could be myself without shame. She saw all the horrible in me, yet sought out the little good that remained. Amaia made me want to be better, to do better.

So I ran with that. Whatever she had to offer me, I would happily take. That was something we could figure out along the way. I just knew I wanted it to work, to whatever end.

When I glanced behind me during the ride, her eyes were tightly closed, but there was a sense of peace that appeared across her face. It flickered in and out over the minutes and scenery that passed and I knew that the fleeting pain that sucked away the peace had nothing to do with me.

Reina had been upset over the last week in between her excitement at birthday planning. She remained enough in her right mind to mention that Seth's was a week after Amaia's, right before Christmas. Amaia and Seth had a three-year tradition of doing something together to celebrate, whether it was to spend the day out riding and being free, or playing in the waves near Monterey Bay. What had mattered to them both was to spend that time celebrating together, then they would have a joint party with their family at the tavern later that night. Which is exactly why I had warned against Reina's idea of how to spend her birthday today. I had no idea how she would react when she opened that door to her place.

She gave me a gentle hug as she hopped off the back of my bike and made her way to her room. I lingered behind her, hoping for the best but fully expecting the worst.

"Shit—" she yelped, flames fully encompassing both hands.

A room full of terrified faces yelled out a unified, "Surprise!"

Reina had truly gone all out. She'd decorated the room in forgotten birthday pieces she collected around Duluth and from an abandoned Party City she'd found near the outer ends of the settlement. Faded streamers hung from the ceiling, with half bobbing balloons randomly placed around the apartment. A sorry-looking

Happy Birthday hung over the window in the living room with the 'I' in the birthday missing.

"Oh my … you guys." Tears pooled in her dark brown eyes and I stepped closer, not sure if they were happy tears or sad ones.

Reina skipped over, studying her face with a sincere look of concern, and pulled her into a hug. "Happy birthday, Maia," she said, her chin resting atop Amaia's head.

"Happy birthday, sister." Tomoe stood behind the both of them, a meek grin on her face that didn't match her haze-filled eyes.

Reina reached back, grabbing Moe's hand and pulling her into a group hug.

Sloan sat atop the kitchen counter, a birthday kazoo hanging out the corner of her mouth and she blew it sarcastically. "Always was my favorite day of the year. Happy birthday to my truest friend." An actual honest smile brightening up her freckled face.

"Your only friend if we're honest," Abel added quietly.

That earned him a stern glare from Sloan. "Don't push your luck, you're already on thin ice."

Abel grinned in knowledge of his protection in Amaia's presence. "To many, many more. Reina and I made a cake!" He rushed over to the center island and pointed to a sad, un-iced loaf that sat atop the counter with a singular candle.

My hand fell to the small of her back, pushing her forward, still watching her reaction in case I needed to kick everyone out. Myself included. She deserved at least a little privacy on her own day.

The tears fell down her face, and I sighed a relief at what were evidently happy ones.

"I love you guys so much, thank you," she said. "This is more than I could have asked for."

"Please, this isn't even half of the crap Reina pulls back home," Moe offered, as if all the time and effort they'd put in making this day special for her, was nothing worth noting.

Reina released a giggle. "Can't say it's my best work, but if you like it, I love it! Come on, let's do cake!"

"It's perfect. Let me go wash up, I'll be back and we can cut it," Amaia said warmly, and they all believed her.

I, however, was no fool. I knew what she had stashed underneath that bed. My eyes narrowed as she stepped toward her door, but Moe blocked her path entirely.

"Here, before you go." Tomoe handed her a piece of tan paper folded in card format. "You might have to wash your face from the tears after but I think you should have this."

Amaia thanked her, a crease forming on her forehead as she took a quick glance at the contents inside and entered her bedroom. The door clicked softly behind her, and four smug sets of eyes turned toward me.

"So, how was it?" Reina beamed, her brows bouncing up and down suggestively.

Still suspicious of what Amaia was up to, I responded, half-interested in the conversation before me, "It was good."

"Good? That's all we get?" Tomoe pushed, reaching for her coat on the couch.

My eyes trailed her, wondering why she was ready to leave when Amaia said she would be right back.

"Yeah, you steal her more than half of the day and you can't even give us any details, *blood*—" Sloan cleared her throat. "Alexiares."

Her correction caught me off guard, my eyes going from Tomoe to scanning over the redhead's face. She'd been oddly pleasant toward me lately, and I wasn't sure why. Well, as pleasant as she could get, which wasn't saying much.

"Let the man have *some* privacy. Everyone's entitled to some," Abel said in my defense, eyeing the cake.

I shrugged them all off. "Thank you, Abel. It was good. We had a great time. There's nothing else for me to say."

"Yet," Reina said, tapping me on the chest in a giddy manner, but her eyes were focused on the cake behind me.

"It's about to get better," Sloan said, hopping off the counter. "Let's go to the bonfires tonight."

"Bonfires?" I asked, not knowing what the hell she was talking about.

Reina, however, needed no further clarification in order to have a good time. "Sounds fun!"

"You don't even know what it is." Tomoe voiced exactly what I was thinking. Reina circled back to her, resting her cheek on Moe's shoulder. The tension released from Moe's body at the comfort of her sister's touch.

"They are pretty fun!" Abel vibrated with the same energy as Reina. "Sloan actually started them a few months back, way to raise morale. We have them most nights around the city, but on the weekend, they get rowdy. Some drinking, some dancing, people roast anything they find on a hunt and want to share. It's a good time."

The two of them back at The Compound were sure to get on my last fucking nerve in the way only siblings could. Or how I would expect normal siblings to behave. Evander had never been able to interact with me in such a brotherly manner. With these two, it was hard to pretend I wasn't growing more open to the idea.

"A good time? Here? Seriously?" I retorted, not thinking Sloan was capable of anything fun. Let alone letting her people experience some of it under such trivial conditions.

"Yeah, believe it or not, buddy boy." Sloan strolled up to me as if reading my thoughts. "We do know how to have *some* fun here. It's not totally depressing."

I threw a mocking face in her direction followed by an obscene gesture. "I'm sure you know how to have *tons* of fun, Sloan. Whatever, I'll let her know."

"We'll meet you there," Moe said, a knowing glimmer in her eyes, and she ushered people out.

She was up to something; I just couldn't tell what. The odd urgency in her herding left me confused, but I chalked it up to the awkwardness of us all being in the same room with positive intentions again.

"Center of the city!" Sloan shouted over her shoulder on the way out.

I opened the bedroom door, sniffles funneled out from the bathroom. A crunch of paper sounded from beneath my steps. Crouching down, I lifted up Tomoe's card halfway tucked under the bed.

It was honestly none of my business, but then again, I had never once minded my business in the past. Why start now?

Happy birthday to the sister I never knew to ask for, but I'm glad the universe decided I needed. You continue to amaze me more than anyone I've had the honor of meeting in this lifetime. No matter where this life takes us, I will always love you and I think you need to know that you are capable of loving and being loved. So here's a small glimpse of your future. It breaks all your rules, but I think we both know I rarely follow them anyway.

Your happiness is possible and not far off. I see many futures and though nothing is definitive. You and Alexiares are a match made in hell, and it should scare the shit out of everyone — except you.

For the times I had with Seth, my future had presented many outcomes. I will never regret knowing his love. I don't wish you our ending, but I do wish you the happiness and all encasing feeling of being head over heels for someone that will love you unconditionally.

I've seen it, embrace it. Cherish it. There's a future for us all out there, one where we're all together again, even Seth. It's possible, we just have to keep faith.

I struggled with deciding whether you should know this or not, but who am I to keep it from you. I heard from Seth this morning, briefly, he said happy birthday to the one who believed the best in him, when he presented the worst.

I love you, Maia. We love you. All of us. Happy birthday.

PS: He came to me in my dreams. My guard was down for a second. Sue me. Oh wait, you can't.

Moe

That explained why Reina couldn't seem to keep her hands off her. Reaching out in small touches, trying to help. Amaia was not crying in that bathroom because of me, because of them. She was crying because Seth was not here but had still remembered. I think that made it worse than if he had forgotten. It would be easier if he had. If he had completely cut ties.

I pushed the door open without knocking, not wanting to give her a chance to hide herself from me. She stood leaning over the sink, tears streamed down her now reddened brown cheeks. A bottle was at risk of breaking from the death grip in her hand, teetering between pouring its contents out and back down to the bottom of the bottle.

Saying nothing, I grabbed the bottle from her and pointed the neck of it down the drain. Amaia did not look up as I dragged her down to the ground, pulling her into my arms and cradled her against my chest. Her body shook, and no tears were left. Just sadness, her body empty from the piece of her heart that was missing.

"I won't let you do this to yourself again," I said, more to myself than to her. "Enough is enough."

There was no way she could carry on this way. Amaia would bring the destruction of herself if she tried. Addiction was a terrible thing, a disease. As with many diseases, you cannot help someone unless they want to help themselves. You can't force someone to seek treatment at a doctor, can't force a cancer patient into chemo.

You can't force an alcoholic to quit the bottle when their body is conditioned to reach for it. They were diseases of different magnitudes, but alcoholism was still that.

"I don't want to do it to myself either."

The magic words I'd spent more time wishing to hear than I could have counted on every finger, toe and limb as I laid in her bed at night, pretending I didn't smell it coming from her. Sloan had been an unknowing enabler in the whole thing. Providing her a coping mechanism as they met at night while she escaped in her own kind of way.

The two would destroy each other if no one stopped them. Not from malice, or intentionally, but because neither one of them had been strong enough to tell the other that it was time to stop. And then held the other accountable in the wake of.

"It's okay, Amaia," I cooed. "You are not alone. Not before, not now, not ever again. I'm here. You helped me. Now let me return the favor."

Her head nodded in the cusp of my neck. After a few moments, she leaned back and kissed my cheek. Bringing herself to her feet, she moved toward the mirror. Amaia splashed her face in the water basin next to the sink and studied her reflection. A deep laugh erupted from her chest and she didn't stop. I stood, making my way behind her, trying to see what she saw.

"What are you laughing at?" I asked.

"Myself," Amaia said, in between rough gasps for air. "What's a birthday without some dramatic birthday girl tears? I'm a fucking mess."

Grabbing onto her waist, I pulled her around to face me. "My mess." I meant it too. She was stronger than she realized, but a mess she fucking was.

She smiled at that. "Maybe, maybe not."

"Come on, we're not done with the birthday girl."

"The cake!" she exclaimed in a panic. "Oh shit."

I pushed her dark curls out of her face. "Don't worry, they already left."

The apartment was silent. A birthday bomb had gone off in here. We stepped into the living room and took in the already sorry-looking cake now half eaten on the counter. There were crumbs everywhere and a fist-sized hole in the middle of the cake.

"Fucking Reina," Amaia said behind a hand covered giggle.

I couldn't help but join in. "That girl is something else."

It was getting dark and there weren't many people left out on the street. The citizens had either made their way to guard duty, their homes, or likely the bonfires if they were as fun as Abel and Sloan had said. The sky was still dark, though the snow had held off throughout the day. The lack of stars in the sky made the walk through the city eerie. Only street lamps lit the world around us, creating elongated shadows as we passed each building.

Snow mushed underneath our boots that had been missed during the last street clearing. Despite the surrounding darkness, the mood between us appeared to be rising.

Amaia glanced up at me, grabbing my hand with a smile and I swear my heart fucking stopped. Every moment of affection between us had been done in private this far. This display of PDA caught me off guard.

I squeezed her hand in response. "You didn't ask where we were going."

"Don't care where," she replied, "as long as it's not sequestered into that dark, dingy room. Plus, I'm with you. It can't be anywhere too boring."

Folk music blared out as we rounded the corner. Large pockets of flame lined the main street and echoes of claps and stomps vibrated off the buildings. Arms and legs intertwined as people swung each other around in laughter, dancing and enjoying the strings of a banjo and guitar.

It wasn't my usual taste in music, but the sight alone brought energy back into my body that it hadn't possessed in a while. I glanced down at Amaia, her eyes wide with amusement as they landed on her family, *our* family, a few feet away. Reina, to no one's surprise, was off dancing with a random group of girls, her large laugh ringing out even feet away.

Sloan ushered us over and I found myself on the other end of a tug. Amaia pulled me over to where Sloan, Abel, and Moe stood, drinks in hand. She glanced down at Sloan's cup, who extended it out to her for a sip.

"No, thank you," she said.

Sloan opened her mouth to argue, only to be met with the glare of the bloodhound. She nodded her head once in acceptance and focused back on the cigarette lit behind her ear.

"You should consider putting the cancer stick down," I said, not sure why I even bothered.

She leaned close to my ear, taking a deep drag in and blew it out in my face. "No thank you. I enjoy the things that piss you off the most."

Amaia's head turned slightly and I knew she had heard it but chose not to engage. Instead, she grabbed both of us and brought us into a circle to dance near Reina, Tomoe, and Abel followed in our shadow.

We danced to the music, following the movements of the other citizens and Abel's instructions until we got the hang of it. It was *essentially line dancing, with more looseness in the movements*, he explained. As awkward as the movements were for my rhythmless body, I could admit I was having a great time watching her let loose. Realization hit me that someone was missing.

I scanned the crowd, eyes falling upon Reina, who now hung off to the side. A small smile pulled at her lips and I reminded myself to check in with her soon. She had been straddling the extremely thin line between being okay and borderline insanity these last few weeks. While I doubted I was the only one that noticed, I was the one least affected by Seth's departure that had the mental capacity to take a step back and see how dangerous her behavior had become. Reina was in a dangerous spiral. Despite appearing to come out of it on her own slowly, I worried. She put her cup in the air in silent cheers and tossed the drink back. Her brown, mousy hair cascaded down her fur coat as she chugged.

Seth's absence had taken a toll on them all, and I wished he would have had the decency to not check back in. Just disappeared. But I would make sure that fool would get his one day. For now, however, all I cared about was having fun. A rare, blissful moment of pure fun. I motioned Reina over with my head. She smiled, squeezing through the crowd over to our group.

Abel grabbed her hand instantly, twirling her around, their movements completely free. Even Sloan and Tomoe had seemed to call a brief truce. They danced around each other mumbling the words of some song that I'd never heard. Amaia wrapped her arms around my neck, standing on the tips of her toes, and I hoisted her onto the top of my boots to bridge the gap. Her body swayed against mine, her head tossed back, enjoying herself and fully immersed in the moment. Reina bellowed another loud laugh at the dip Abel had placed her in. Even without her magic, without trying, her joy was contagious as I watched it seep into Amaia.

Maybe this little family of mine did stand a chance after all.

CHAPTER
SEVENTEEN

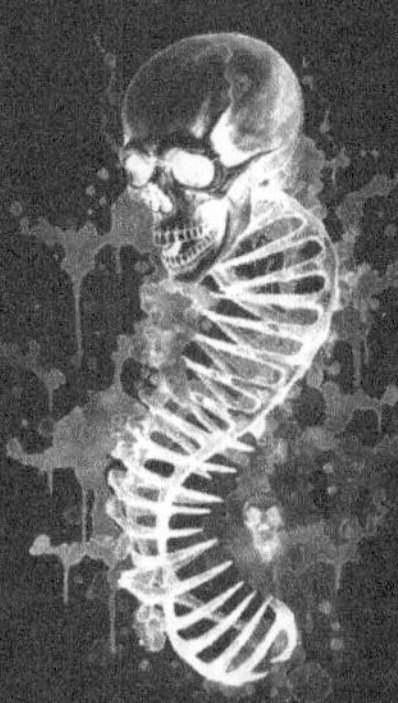

AMAIA

Today was the day. The day that could be my last.

I was grateful for that last day of fun my family had offered me, what Alexiares had set up. So grateful that I couldn't let him do this. Reina was right about me. The lines between want and need were confusing to me. I found myself not caring to seek clarity over which was right or wrong anymore. To hell with that when it came to keeping people I cared for safe.

Alexiares' deep slumber made it all the easier to sneak out of the apartment this morning and barricade him behind it. He would be furious, probably hate me. And I would have to be okay with it, even if it broke what remained of my heart.

I saw how he looked at me yesterday, how he had watched our little family. Alexiares had finally found his place in the world.

Happiness radiated off him despite our shitty circumstances. I'd be damned to be the one who took that from him.

The rest of the crew sat waiting for me in Reina's makeshift lab. Sloan's eyes narrowed at the absence of Alexiares at my side, but she said nothing. Tomoe, on the other hand, was not afraid to chew my head off with questions.

"Where is he?" Tomoe said the second I opened the door.

I feigned ignorance. "Where is who?"

"Okay," she huffed, eyes narrowing, "back to being difficult. Understood."

"Someone's got to make the tough decisions around here, Tomoe. I thought you understood that." I sighed, pretending to study my fingernails.

Tomoe, per usual, was quick in her response, "Tough, or reckless?"

"Ooh, I know the word you're searchin' for: selfish!" Reina exclaimed, a mischievous grin on her face, as she egged Tomoe on.

Sloan rummaged through Reina's belongings, letting out a huff of boredom. "Are we doing this or not?"

"Don't you care that she's about to make a life altering decision?" Abel said quietly, head low.

"Oh I care, spy," Sloan ground out before meeting my eye. "It appears I'm the only one here who knows her enough that nothing anyone says here will change her mind. Yesterday was fun and all, but you two need to leave here soon, and this is the last thing we're waiting on." She tossed her head in the direction of Reina and Tomoe with impatience.

I scanned her over with a sense of appreciation, my thumb extended in reference. "Thank you."

"Don't thank her," Reina mumbled low. "Your death will weigh on her just the same if this kills you."

"I thought you were on my side here," I countered, pushing myself up to sit on top of the table. I crossed my legs awaiting further instructions, my gaze set on the Pansie strapped in at the neck in the corner of the room.

Reina shrugged, her hands flowing up, surrendering. "I am. Just sayin'."

"Next time, say less, and let's get this over with."

Reina took a deep inhale. Her long legs strolled over to the Pansie and motioned me over. I hopped down at her summons, trying to put on a display of confidence, but my shaky hands and the crack of my voice betrayed me.

"He can't get out," she said, her finger teasing in front of his face and he snapped at her, "Since Alexiares isn't here for us to have options, I think it's best we do our initial test from the source. Let's keep him away from any major arteries, but I'm here to heal you up right after."

"What happens if he doesn't let go?" Abel asked, his fingers pressed into the side of his face.

"Then we kill him."

I flinched at the voice, slowly turning on my heels to face a surely enraged man. Alexiares loomed in the doorway, still dressed in the gray sweatpants he'd slept in the night before. His dark long coat sat on top of the black hoodie now pulled over his disheveled hair.

"How did you—" I stammered.

He shoved past me and I fought the urge not to grab my now bruised shoulder. "Get out after you stockpiled every piece of furniture in front of the bedroom door and then melted the door handle and lock into the door frame? Quite fucking easily, with the help of my rage."

I bit the inside of my cheek and glanced down at the ground. There weren't any words I could offer that talked him down, and frankly, I was a bit pissed off myself. What other sign could a girl give to show that his presence wasn't wanted here? Not that I wouldn't have tried to break my way out if I were in his position.

Honestly, I would have climbed out the window and scaled my way down, but that was me.

"Sheesh, don't fucking bark if you can't bite, Amaia," Sloan taunted, her tongue skimming her teeth as she laughed at my sheepish display.

I rolled my eyes at her but decided against responding to either of them.

A hand grabbed my chin roughly and I found myself staring into pretty, angry, brown eyes. "Let me make one thing clear, Amaia, if you go down, then *we* go down together."

It was hard trying to force myself to look away. One glance at him, his rage, the pain that lay behind his expression, had me wanting to drop to my knees and grovel for his forgiveness. Then I remembered how much I'd protested for him to stay out of this and found my own fury all over again, thinking better of it. Instead, I simply nodded my head and jerked away from his grip.

"Aw, how stinkin' cute!" Reina chimed from the corner of the room. "I can't wait to see how this love affair turns out after whatever monstrous fight happens later ... if you survive. Which I hope you both do, by the way, but if we want to get the results before we leave in a few days, we gotta do this soon. Plus, I think Frankie is getting a wee bit restless over there."

"Who the hell is Frankie?" Tomoe asked, even though the answer was obvious.

Reina pointed in the upgraded Pansies face again, giggling as she noted she was still out of its reach. "He's like my own personal little Frankenstein."

"Frankenstein was the doctor, Reina"— I sighed, clasping my hands in front of my face —"not the monster."

"Not surprised you know that!" Reina sang out. "Anywho, Frankie has both earth and air magic. It's a fifty-fifty chance you'll get one of the two. Any questions before we begin?"

Abel, ever curious, asked the question that loomed over us all, "How long is this going to take?"

Reina shrugged nonchalantly. "As long as it takes infection to set in. This technically isn't a virus or bacteria; it's a bit of both in a way from what I've analyzed. Judging by Michael and Logan, I'd say anywhere between twenty-four and seventy-two hours. There is one thing we need to discuss."

"Of course there is, let's hear it," I said, willing her to just spit it all out at once.

"One of you will need to be the control group, and the other a variable. We're short on time, so I need to be sure the others can replicate my work once I'm gone. If there're any differences between incubation and overall results, I need to be able to instruct them further through my notes." Reina brought her hair to the side and braided it back to stay out of her face for the duration of the experiment.

Abel wore the same expression as the rest of the room, utter confusion. "That's a lot of words to mean things no one else understands," he said for us all.

Reina moved to shake his shoulders playfully. "It means, only one of them will be bit—"

"And she'll inject the other from those tubes," I said, pointing to the assortment on her lab table, "attached to the agitator thingy I'm guessing."

She nodded in confirmation. "My father, based on Moe's vision, is injecting people, but as we know, bites appear to be effective too. We need to figure out the difference or if it's only a matter of convenience."

"Isn't your father injecting people and having them turn to zombies?" Sloan asked, a peek of interest lingering in her icy eyes.

"Uh, yes," Reina replied with less confidence than I would have preferred at the moment. "But I was able to adjust what I think, for lack of a better word, the recipe was. I don't think that would happen here. At least I hope not."

"Which one is the most dangerous?" Alexiares questioned, the demand obvious in his voice, and I bit down on my lip, knowing exactly where he was headed in his line of thought.

I mumbled honestly, no point in hiding it. "Whatever's in those tubes."

"Great, I'll take that option then."

Of course he would, because that's exactly what I would have done, and he knew it.

"No," I said firmly.

"This isn't up for discussion." He closed in on me but I held my ground. "You got your wish. You're going through with it, now let me have mine."

"Cute," Sloan mocked. "Arguing over who gets to die first."

"Sloan!" Reina said in an attempt to silence her.

"Just saying," Sloan replied, not missing a chance to add insult to injury. "I hope it's him."

I ignored her, the beef she had with Alexiares growing tired by the day. "Let's get this over with."

Moe stepped forward, cutting off our path to where Reina had set everything up. "I have to ask one more time. Are you both sure? Infection is no joke. You're going to feel like you're dying before you're better. And that's because you technically are, your body has to fight off the rest. Reina won't be able to heal it away."

I thought about it for a few seconds to satisfy her, then pulled her in for a tight hug. A goodbye, just in case. "I'm sure. And thank you, for caring."

An array of, "Love you's," sounded around the room. Each of my family and friends said the words in their own way.

A tense silence followed before Sloan broke it with another tease, "I'll light one for you while we await whatever disaster comes next."

"If there was any question on how we were friends before, I see none being asked now." I gave her a soft kiss on the cheek, my hand falling upon her cheek, praying to whoever would listen to guide her if I no longer could. She squeezed my hand, and I made my way over to the Pansie, sliding my sleeve up to make room for the bite.

"Ready?" I asked, turning my head toward Alexiares, now seated next to me at Reina's station.

Reina wrapped a band tight around his arm and he grimaced. She gave it a few taps, searching for a healthy vein then tapped against the needle, an ooze of liquid seeping out.

"Together," he said, not taking his eyes off me.

"Together."

REINA HEALED THE CHUNK OF SKIN FRANKIE HAD CHOMPED OUT OF my upper arm, but the trauma of it remained. I'd been bit once before—by Xavier. This was different though; it wasn't nearly as terrifying, instead, I found it sickly nostalgic. I mean, if I was going to go out, hell of a way to do it, going out the same way it all started for me.

The peace that came with that had caught me off guard. I didn't want to die, not anymore. People were counting on me. By the time the panic of the possibility set in, my portion of the experiment was done, and Alexiares' had commenced.

Staying calm was the only thing I could do as the light faded from his eyes. The syringe emptied into his veins, and those fierce brown eyes kept their focus on me. Then, his body went limp.

Reina's mouth hung open. The syringe bounced across the floor, rolling away from her as she stared over him, unsure what to do. Abel leaped into action, untying the band wrapped around his arm, massaging the injection site.

"Reina, water," he ushered softly, encouraging her to remember her training.

She blinked twice before coming out of it, guiding small drops of water over his face. When that changed nothing, she released a gallon's worth, but still, he didn't stir. Abel slapped across his face, trying hard to get a reaction. A sign of life. Anything.

"Is he … is he dead?" I sputtered.

Sloan rallied at my side, pulling me under her wing, hand rubbing against my shoulder. The others said nothing. Moe sat in the corner, pale as a ghost, her eyes glazed over, searching for an answer.

Reina lowered her head to his chest. "He's not breathin'," she gasped.

Pushing her back to give him space, Abel moved his hands down to Alexiares' neck. "He has a pulse, but it's weak."

I let out a whimper, pushing off Sloan and moving to the ground. *My fault, this is all my fault.* Brushing my hand against his cheek, the room went silent for agonizing seconds as Abel and Reina toggled over what to do.

"Don't touch him," Moe snapped, coming out of her vision.

Reina jumped back from her position, her hands clasped together, ready to pump life back into him. A gasp from beneath me pried my attention back down and away from Moe. Alexiares shot up, a confused expression on his face.

"What … what's going on? Where am I? What happened?" he asked, rubbing the reddening injection site on his arm.

"Oh no. Oh man, oh no. I messed up real bad, guys," Reina said in horror.

My heart sank. I peered up, looking to Moe for answers only to find a morbid smirk on her face. "This is funny to you? He's lost his memory!"

"I don't know, it's kind of funny," Sloan said. "Maybe he'll be a better person with a second chance."

She may have cracked a joke at his expense, but the display of genuine concern on her face said otherwise. Abel rolled his eyes, his arms crossed over his chest as he bit down a smile. I narrowed my eyes at him, *what on earth is going on?*

"This would be my third chance, Sloan, but I doubt I'll take advantage of that," Alexiares said, pushing himself off the ground.

I pinched his arm, right over the bruising skin that had been the cause of it all. "This is not a joke, Alexiares. You scared the crap out of me."

"Yeah! Me too, that wasn't nice." Reina pouted, hands on her hips. They were still shaking from the pressure.

"Come on, it was too good a joke to play out. I mean did you see the worry lines on Sloan's forehead? One hundred percent worth it."

Sloan leaned forward, smacking him in the chest in response, "We aren't here to play games, Bloodhound. If you died, then we'd have to do this all over again. I personally didn't want to volunteer to go next."

"Alright, alright. I'm sorry. But seriously, what happened? My arm feels like you hacksawed it. One minute I'm waiting for Reina to finish the injection, the next you're all circling me …"

His words became muffled background noise. Losing him had been my fear, and it had almost come true.

I wasn't sure how to move forward with my day, pretending that my heart hadn't stopped in utter fear that his had taken its last beat. I found his irritation to match my own as he stalked behind me on the way back to our rooms to rest. *Doctor's orders,* Reina had chided.

Our experiences had not been the same. There was still no change in my veins now that the adrenaline had worn off, just tired. He had almost died, his system shocked from the invasion.

My fingers trembled as I stared down at them. I stumbled in my steps a bit, my head spinning, body shaking. Focusing on taking deep inhales, I grounded myself in the cold.

"Get off," I grumbled, shrugging him off. "I'm fine."

"Yeah, okay," he bit out, his voice was hoarse, likely a side effect from almost fucking dying.

I kept walking, my back still to him. "This isn't from the damn bite."

"Oh really?"

"Yes, really," I said, "It's called a panic attack, and it's your fault!"

A tense laugh erupted behind me, his distaste clear. "My fault? Oh, princess, on a long list of things that may be my fault, this isn't one of them."

"Leave me alone," I pressed.

"Gladly."

He didn't leave me alone, though. His stupid presence hulked behind me the entire way up the steps. The walls rattled as I slammed my door in his face. After waiting there for a moment, I glanced around the messy room. The couch was tipped over near the kitchen island, the coffee table on its side, the contents that sat atop it scattered around the room.

When I heard nothing, I walked over to the bedroom door, taking a minute to heat the hinges back into place. I leaned against the door frame, my fingers massaged my temples, trying to relieve the stress headache he so happily provided.

The front door burst open, rebounding off the wall where a small hole from the doorknob that had rammed into it one too many times now formed. I jumped to my feet in defense. Clearly, he didn't understand what a door closed in your face meant.

"Get out!" I yelled as viciously as possible, but my voice betrayed me. The welling of tears building up in the center of my throat.

"Make me," he ground out. Alexiares stood in the door frame, rage radiated off him. His face had completely reddened and his brown eyes were nearly black. I glanced down, watching his fingers open and close as he tried to calm himself by squeezing a fist.

I stalked toward him, ready to fight him out if I had to. "Gladly."

My right arm pulled back in preparation to punch him in the jaw, break it if I had to. I was sick of his two-cents. Two-cents obviously didn't translate to common sense, because if he had any, he wouldn't be here right now.

Blocking my hit, he grabbed me by the throat and pushed my back against the wall.

"I didn't ask you to do that." I gasped out, trying to knee him in the stomach without success, "Didn't ask you to risk your life, to almost die! If I remember correctly, I'm not only insane, or lack the mental capacity to separate fact from fantasy, but I'm also selfish. Why the *hell* would you decide to follow in my path toward destruction?"

He released me from his grasp, sulking away until he was across the room. I rubbed my throat as I watched him, his head low and shoulders heaving up and down with heavy breaths.

His back remained to me as he leaned up against the window, "Yeah, Amaia, you *are* the most selfish woman I have ever known."

Ouch. That fucking hurt given that Finley was his wife. "Excuse me?"

"You're excused." He turned around, eyes meeting mine with such anger and something else I couldn't quite put my finger on. *Desperation maybe, passion?* He kept his eyes on mine, slowly stalking toward me. "Selfish, but the most selfless."

Alexiares voice went from hard to tender and my mind wandered back to that day at the little blue house in Monterey. The day I'd met Suckerpunch, the place where I'd first gotten a glimpse of his life and his past. The parallel to now at the forefront of my thoughts.

His eyes darkened, "The most selfish, insane, infuriating, woman I have ever met." With each word he took another step forward. I took a step back without realizing it until I was pressed up against the wall. Both his arms found their way beside my head, caging me in with nowhere left to go. "Selfish as in, you are so focused on keeping the people you love safe and protected that you selfishly close out the ones trying to do the same for you."

Tearing my eyes away from him, they burned with tears from the hard truth, "I'm … I'm sorry. I—"

"Look at me, Amaia. I'm not finished." His words weren't harsh, but commanding. I let out a soft whimper, forcing myself to face him. "You, Amaia, my girl, my princess, are fucking insane, and *that* drives me insane."

Alexiares' lips hovered, grazing mine with each word spoken. He paused, stopping to kiss both sides of my cheeks, my forehead, then the tip of my nose. My resistance melted away with every passing second, bringing me a moment closer to the inevitable.

"Let me go before I set you, and this entire place, on fire," I said, a feeble last attempt to maintain my control.

The charge between us was palpable, something neither of us could deny any longer. Our connection had extended beyond physical attraction—we were two fucked up souls mixed up in a complicated history of animosity and new affection. I bared my neck to him, a small submission I'd never granted anyone in my life.

Challenging me, he dipped his head until his lips grazed my ear. "Stop bluffing and do it for once."

Our gazes locked, his eyes burned dark with a mix of desire and defiance. A small, condescending smirk formed. He knew I was done for. I smashed my lips into his, instantly met with desperation that matched my own. He lifted me up, pressing me hard into the wall.

Alexiares paused for a moment, studying me. My fingers found the strands of his hair in an effort to bring him back to me and deepen our kiss. Every barrier that stood between us crumbled as we surrendered ourselves to the magnetic pull that had drawn us together for months now. I groaned out in pleasure, my lips parting to grant him access.

Alexiares nibbled at my bottom lip, pulling back gently before intertwining his tongue with mine. His lips were softer than I imagined; he was gentler than I'd assumed, too, but rough enough to my liking. My lips brushed against his, softly, teasingly.

I leaned my head back against the wall, wanting to take in the beautiful, sharp angles of his face. A hoarse laugh escaped me as I studied him. His hair was tousled from my grasp, his lips plump and red from our kiss. A rush of emotions flashed over his face as he watched me, uncertainty crossing his features at the lines now blurred. I didn't let those thoughts spiral for a minute longer, I wanted him. Wanted him more than anything I could imagine wanting in my life.

My fingers skimmed the crevice of his neck, and I whispered into his ear, "Am I yours yet?"

"Not yet," he growled back, carrying me into my room and tossing me onto the bed.

Another moment of hesitation passed over his face, seeking my consent on furthering where things were headed. I sat up, pulling him closer and wordlessly granting him access to my heart, my soul, and anything else he desired.

Craving, *needing*, the warmth of his body against mine, I tore his shirt off. His bare skin revealed a collection of ink and scars. So many scars. I'd forgotten the wounds I'd discovered down on the river over a month ago when he'd nearly bled out.

My fingers traced each one of them gently, he studied my reaction. Starting at the crook of his neck, I took my time kissing each and every scar making sure he got the message. What he saw as damaged, I saw as a beautiful story that spoke to his strength. When I pressed my final kiss against the largest scar near his hip, I took my time scanning back up his body. Shame fell upon him, years of pain trying not to break through.

"Who did this to you?" I demanded, anger feeding the flame beneath my skin.

Alexiares said nothing, his body tensed under my touch.

Kissing the scar along his hip again, I mumbled, "I will kill them for hurting you." And I meant it. I would set them ablaze and watch them burn, melt, turn to ash with my power for even touching him.

"He's already dead," he said, his accent echoing his voice.

"Then I hope he burns for eternity." I grasped his jaw, forcing him to meet my eye. "You're beautiful."

One hand found its way across my throat, the other reaching to tuck one of my curls behind my ear. The moment was so tender and soft compared to our usual ruggedness. His eyes darkened, the once gentle grip around my throat tightened intensely. That was the last warning I got before his lips collided with my own.

He pulled my sweater over my head and tossed it across the room. "Not as beautiful as you," he mumbled as he kissed the space between my bra, removing it without effort.

Warm, rough hands cupped my breasts. His fingers tracing all the right places. Slowly, he licked his way down my stomach, stopping only to nibble on the skin above my hips. He bit down until I was sure he would draw blood. I moaned at the pain, embracing it as he licked and kneaded the spot until he soothed the pain. I laid flat on the bed, my nipples forming into stiff peaks and my head swimming with both pleasure and pain.

Tenderly, he left his mark down the entirety of my body and I was honored to wear each one. A shiver went down my spine, gratitude encasing me and I wanted nothing more than to show him how much he was cared for.

I flipped him over and a deep chuckle released from his perfect mouth. I mirrored his actions, kissing each scar again until I reached the point of no return. Straddling him, I leaned back, a moan released at my shift in weight against the one part of his body I couldn't wait to release.

Smiling at my achievement, I unbuckled his pants, releasing the tension of his dick against his pants, grabbing hold. My face flushed at the realization I'd need more than one hand to satisfy him. He stopped me, and I laughed at the will of both of our stubbornness to be the first to give the other pleasure. Alexiares moved swiftly, tossing me on my back. He removed my pants, then my panties at a tortuously slow pace.

"Not yet, princess. I want to take my time with this." He smirked, a finger tracing down the center of my body, pulling me free of my remaining pieces of clothing.

Alexiares studied every inch of my now naked body. My cheeks flushed under the scrutiny of it all. He leaned over me, no words left between us as he stared into my eyes. His fingers traced up the inside of my thigh, stopping abruptly to trail the outside of my mouth. I opened to his silent command, my mouth closing around him before he slowly pulled them out, not breaking my gaze as he drove two fingers inside me.

I squirmed at the building pressure from the curve of his fingers pumping in and out. My eyes traveled to his neck. I wrapped my arms around him, pulling his body flush with mine. I'd been bitten many times today, but he bore no marks. It was time for that to change.

Pleasure and pain were one and the same, I knew that was a fact we could agree on. He hissed out in agony, but a smile remained on his face. One second my hands were around his body, the next they were pinned above me on the bed. He kissed back down my body and dropped to his knees at the end of the bed. My legs now rested on his shoulder, with his gaze holding mine, he placed a light kiss on my left inner thigh, then the right.

Alexiares smirked before he devoured me whole. With every stroke of his tongue, I was left questioning where the hell he'd been my entire fucking life. Each moan encouraged him as he figured out exactly what I liked. My eyes fluttered closed as I reached my climax, his hand reaching up to muffle the moans of ecstasy escaping me. I propped myself up, forcing my eyes open to watch as he destroyed my entire being.

His eyes went wild with desire as he caught me, one last flick of the tongue and I was his.

I was out of breath, but I wasn't done with him. If he thought he would have total control over me, then he didn't know me well at all. I pushed him off me and he rose to his feet, towering over me he positioned himself right at my entrance. Sitting up, I slid to the edge of the bed and pulled him inside me. He groaned, stopping for a moment to adjust as he let out a soft, shaky exhale. The sound of it alone only encouraged me and I shifted my weight against the bed, slamming myself into him repeatedly.

He watched me intently, awe falling upon him before he took control. He flipped me to my knees, not breaking us apart, and I tossed him a look back, letting him know the movement was *too* smooth. It made me want to kill every girl that had a piece of my man before me. Alexiares grinned, knowing exactly what I was thinking, and he brought his hand down hard against my ass, his nails drawing blood as they slid down the back of my legs.

It stung. I yelped out, his name escaping my lips, begging him to continue. He obliged me, moving inside me slowly in and out, quickly getting to a faster pace. A single glance in his direction and realization crossed over him, remembering that neither one of us were the slow and sweet type.

One hand pulled a fistful of my curls back, the other intent on leaving a handprint where only he could see. He hit deeper, his dick bruising against my cervix. Each stroke pulsed inside me. I moaned as his thrusts got shorter, harder.

His hand squeezed the spot on my hip that drove me wild as he rammed into me, pressing my stomach to the mattress. He lowered his head near mine, a pleasurable grin encompassing his face.

Proud of what my body was doing to him, I met him with the same force, arching my back and throwing my hips back in a circular movement. I wiggled my hand under me, grabbing him where it mattered the most and teasing gently.

I squeezed his balls, and the movement sent him over the edge. He groaned in my ear, biting the space between my shoulder and neck.

"Say my name again," he commanded.

"Make me."

He gave me a humorless laugh as his grip on my hair got tighter and he pounded into me with an unforgiving force. All it took was him applying more pressure with the hand circling my core and it left as nothing but a whisper, "Alexiares."

"Good girl."

I lost it at that, and so did he. He twitched inside of me with a raspy moan, warmth filled me and I smiled as he had claimed me in every way possible.

He released my hair and the weight of Alexiares slammed into my body. He guided us back down to the bed and pulled me close, kissing the side of my face with quick, tender kisses.

I felt whole in a way that I never had before. Being with him felt right in every way. Alexiares had surrendered himself to me with raw intensity, in the only way he knew how, and I had enjoyed every moment of it. The room spun blissfully around me, the delicate symphony of our mingled breaths being the only sound.

There had been no conquest in our actions, it had been even, a healing of the wounds of our past in order to build something new together. A delicate dance of trust and respect, but animalistic at its core. Every touch and caress spoke volumes in a way our words hadn't yet learned to do.

I fell asleep in his arms, not knowing where this was headed, but willing to enjoy the ride.

CHAPTER
EIGHTEEN

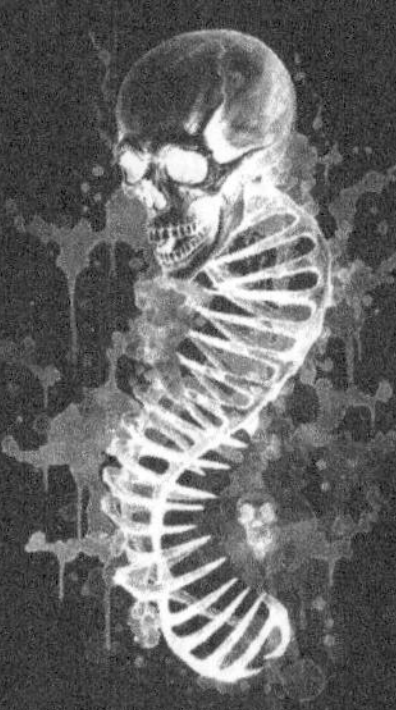

TOMOE

Walls are thin, and my night was about as restless as the one Amaia and Alexiares were having. At least *they* were enjoying their time awake. I, however, was not.

I hate the word jealousy, because I don't think that was the correct way to describe how I felt. I was happy for them. It was about damn time, and honestly, maybe Amaia would finally get her act together now that she wasn't as wound up. But damn, did I miss my man.

Seth contacting me brought me back to square one. Just as I was finally processing it all, ready to move on the second I left this place and could stop seeing his face on Sloan's body, he'd ruined it. I'd lied to Amaia earlier, my guard hadn't slipped an ounce. There'd been a tug at something from deep in my chest, a prodding sensation. He was begging for my attention, and when

I hadn't graced him with it, he demanded it instead. Seth had grown stronger in his absence. I wasn't sure which was more terrifying, that or the possibility he'd always been that strong and I'd let something as stupid as love blind me.

There had been no apology, no sense of regret, not even a real acknowledgment of the person he'd claimed to love and left behind. Just a half-assed happy birthday that had a chance of sending Amaia back into another spiral. I mean what the hell was that?

Maybe that's what he had wanted. Maybe I was still ignorantly in love and had played into his hand. At the end of the day, none of that mattered because I was done keeping secrets, done hiding things *especially* when it came to Seth fucking Moore. So I told her.

Knowing that Alexiares would be there to pick up the pieces had aided in my decision. It certainly made it easier knowing that she would recover as best as she could even after hearing the news. I half expected her to come out in a rage, demanding me to tell her what other secrets I had kept and why I hadn't immediately made her aware Seth had contacted me. She still could, it had only been twenty-four hours and my sister had a habit of bringing up old news. The future had not favored that version of our reality, at least not yet. Instead, Alexiares had found the right words and managed to get her out of that bathroom and into celebration.

A one and a million chance out of all the alternatives to the horrendous endings to that day that I'd seen. They both seriously needed help when it came to expressing themselves. Between the fighting and making eyes at each other, there was a 99.9 percent chance they'd fuck it out by the end of our stay here. It was only a matter of time.

At least they had each other now. I had Reina, but Reina also had Abel and now Sloan and thus went my distraction. In a self-serving way, I'd been excited when Abel had made us aware that we'd have to set out to convince the other settlements to join our cause. My sister and I out on the open road, doing our part in this war. It would be a successful mission, just as Abel had seen, though not one without its own complications. What I hadn't realized at that point, or seen, was that Abel himself would be joining us.

I didn't have a problem with the guy. In fact, I barely knew him. He'd left not too long before I'd arrived, and by then, he was little more than a memory to Reina and Seth. Amaia and Riley barely spoke of him and now I knew why. The situation he'd been placed in or rather *he* himself had been the one real disagreement they'd ever had. And now Amaia would be bringing him back to join our little family and I was back to being lonely.

The presence of one specific person would solve that, and it turned out he was an egotistical asshole with daddy issues. Which tracked, given my type from The Before. Shit, I don't even know if I ever really knew him, at least not in the way I'd let him know me.

How could you know someone who kept such a big part of them hidden? His true motivations in life never to be brought to light until it was too damn late. It wasn't just the fact that he had valued reuniting his family. I could understand that, sympathize with it. But in honor of reuniting his family, he had abandoned the one that we built. Disposed of us, and the blood he claimed to care so much about. A distraction until he could have what he truly wanted. That was not just hiding a part of himself, it was a definitive rift in our core values.

He had been right in the fact that I would go to great lengths to get my birth family back if I had found out that they were still alive. Seth was wrong, however, about one thing—I would never betray my found family for the sake of reuniting with the one that I lost. There would be no reason to, because I knew, despite everything, that I could trust Amaia. Trust my family to help me when I needed them the most.

Reina said it best time and time again: while we may not understand the choice Amaia made, her decisions always had a funny way of working out in her favor. She was too damn smart for her own good. If I had learned anything at all the last few months, is that the Universe would do whatever it could to make sure Amaia got what Amaia wanted. The singular condition to her desires being answered was that she kept the wellbeing of others forefront in her mind. If he had only trusted Amaia, allowed her to come up with a way to help, he could have had it all.

That wasn't true though. He would have been able to have what he thought he was seeking until he got here and found out the truth. Then he still would have left without looking back.

Truth be told, I felt helpless. The girl who could see the future, except when it mattered most.

I knew I wouldn't be able to see that part of the future even if I wanted to though. It was dependent upon information he had no knowledge of, that his father was in charge of the entire damn Covert Province. I couldn't see anything pertaining to them regardless because of whatever voodoo, magic blocking bullshit powers they had in place.

In the end, every possible outcome I considered came down to one final conclusion. Seth would still leave, and for that choice, Seth would die.

I didn't need visions to read the fucking room. Every person I surrounded myself with, hell walked past in this settlement and surely Monterey Compound once they caught wind, would want him dead, with the exception of Reina.

The only indefinite thing in this moment was by whose hand?

CHAPTER
NINETEEN

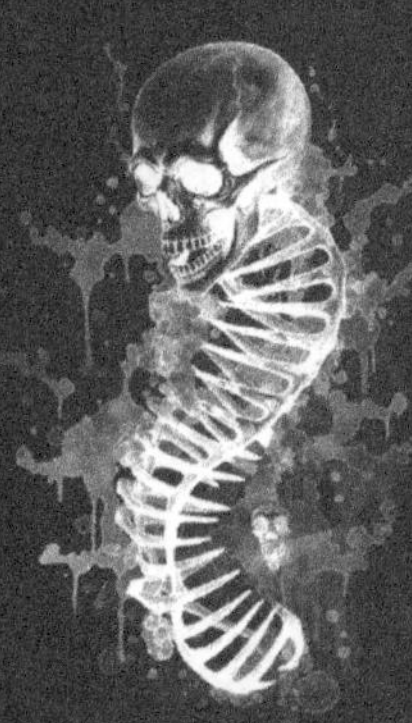

SETH

I guess I'm the villain in everybody's story at this point.

Strolling through the pristine streets of Covert Providence capitol, I sucked in the crisp winter air. Moe's resistance to block me out in her damn sleep had sent me over the edge. Without space to ride, this was the only way I could clear my head. I'd never stop being enamored with that woman's utter determination. Don't get me wrong, it was hard as hell to walk away from her. Walking away from them all was the hardest thing I've ever done in my life.

That was before my dad had helped me realize that the hardest things in life are often the most rewarding. He'd listened intently, met with me as much as possible to help me adjust to what was to become my life.

Men and women passed by me. Some in suits, others in business casual type clothing. I stuck out like a sore thumb here. My Levi's and boots didn't exactly blend in with their uniformed way of dressing. Add in my cowboy hat and I got a lot of stares. It took me a while to realize why. Factor in that there weren't too many *Supras* roaming around here and I guess I truly was a spectacle. An anomaly in their oddly mundane society. Most of the ones I'd seen were military and even then, there weren't many of us.

I was starting to think there wasn't a place out there meant for people like me.

It was my dad who centered me, brought me back down to reality. Really helped me channel my anger and confusion into something productive. The more I thought about my decision to leave 'em all behind, the more my role in this world became clear. Everything I loved about Monterey had become a blur. Since my time here in Richmond, Virginia, I'd come to realize that not everyone was meant to save the world.

In this world, it was rare that someone had Amaia's heart, Riley's loyalty, Tomoe's determination, or my sister's overall desire to do good. Some of us were meant to destroy the world, to rebuild it in a better, more worthy light. I'd reckon Alexiares was more like me than he was willin' to admit, but only time would tell. I didn't need to wonder around his filthy mind to see what he was capable of.

He was no less a monster than I was. The only difference was he'd make it into Amaia's bed before Finley got her claws back in him. A woman's touch could do that to a man, make 'em wanna do better. Be better. Moe had that effect on me for a while until I'd snapped out of it. There were bigger things in this life to be accomplished than settling down and making some lousy settlement a home.

That's what Monterey was—lousy as hell compared to what Covert Province had to offer.

I stopped at a crosswalk, waiting for the light to turn to walk. We didn't have enough traffic like this back home to bother with such things, so it had taken me a few days to figure out why those around me gawked in fear as I jaywalked. It wasn't until a man my age passed me on the sidewalk one day that things had become clear. He offered a simple warning, *follow the rules and your life will be good*. So follow the rules I did, taking social cues from the others, doing my best to blend in.

My dad had done his best to show me the ropes the moment I got here, finally proud to slap my shoulder and call me his son. It felt good, felt right. The work he was doing here would rebuild this country the way it should have remained. Led by the strong on the backs of the weak.

That's how things were meant to work, how they had always been done since the origins of man-kind. This wasn't Monterey, and the rest of the world would never *be* Monterey. I'd tried things their way. While it wasn't bad, it wasn't sustainable. Not on a bigger scale.

Amaia would get it one day, when I came back for them. She understood history, how things worked; I'd always respected that about her. They needed to see things through the right lens, and I could help with that. Moe could help with that. If I could get them to understand where my father was coming from, we could all be a family again.

All would be right in the world.

But the only way I could do that is if I worked on the inside. Saw what this was all about, then tell them the truth that no one that had left Covert had been willin' to tell.

The ones that had fled had been the weak ones. They weren't worthy of understanding our ideals, not ready to work for the bigger than themselves.

With Amaia on our side, there wouldn't be a need for a war. People trusted her, listened to her judgment. She had a way of getting people to believe. I just needed my dad to come around to that fact. There didn't need to be two sides to this, only one.

She and Prescott had made a name for Monterey Compound, and they could do great things with my dad and our people. Between what we had there, and what Covert Province really was, we could make this country what it should be. Make it great.

I rounded the corner, a newspaper stand in front of my building had my face plastered on the front standing next to my dad. *Odd, I don't remember taking that.* A teenage girl with raven hair and gaunt cheeks met my eyes from behind the stand, her gaze shot toward the ground as I approached and remained there. Something I'd observed all the women did here when speaking to a man.

It honestly kinda bothered me, and perhaps it was something Amaia could help with once she got here. My mom, Reina, they'd never been submissive women. While my dad adored them growing up, I'd always noticed it wasn't a particular quality he appreciated. In the end, his word was always law.

Monterey had its pitfalls I suppose, but Amaia and Tomoe had helped me see the world through fresh eyes. There was nothing to fear with powerful women, other than being on the other end of their rage. It would be in my father's best interest to embrace that. After all, that's what his vision of the world had always been—elevating those who possessed a certain level of greatness.

"Hi, Miranda." I nodded in my approach.

She shifted on her feet. "Want a copy, sir? It's about you today," she said.

I took it, glancing down at the headline.

Ronan Moore is Hopeful About the Future

After years apart, Ronan Moore has reunited with his son, Seth Moore, previously deemed a traitor of Covert Province. Covert Times sat down to interview our fearless leader on how the reunion has been and what we can look forward to in the future.

"It was tough, I thought I lost both my kids," Moore said, pausing to reflect on the years passed. "I was devastated when I went to search for them at our family home in Minnesota. There wasn't a soul in sight in that neighborhood. It took everything in me to carry on to Covert Province, the only thought in the back of my mind was, how can I make my children proud? How can I give others the life I'd always promised them? Then, God granted me a second chance at being a father. I've loved every second of it. My boy Seth is one of the strong ones. I raised him well."

We at Covert Times are thrilled to have this addition to our leadership. As we spoke with Ronan, we uncovered some of the guiding standards he held himself to over his rise to power since the war. While his viewpoints have certainly evolved over the years, he states the standards he has for members of society have remained the same as they always have.

I scanned the rest of the bullshit article, rolling my eyes. He loved talking about himself every chance he got, so it was no surprise he used my return for a moment of publicity. In The Before, dad had always been lost in his own mind in some fashion or another. The bite only exasperated the hyper-fixation: he'd become enthralled with the *what if*. When he made it out to Richmond, it was like God had answered every one of his prayers. After the war between territories, my father had climbed his way up the power ladder. How he'd managed to convince a city full of former government agents into trusting him to run a third of the country was still a mystery I hadn't gotten any closer to solving.

Turning the page, my heart stopped. A photo of my sister, Amaia, and the woman my heart ached for were plastered front and center.

> A recent skirmish outside enemy territory in Duluth has resulted in the death of several troops. The death count is unclear. We'll be sure to keep you updated as Ronan Moore receives more information. Daughter, Reina Moore, remains harbored by Sloan Moore inside Duluth's city walls with Tomoe Sato and rebel leader Amaia Bennett. They are expected to flee soon though their next movements have not been determined at this time. A reward is being offered to those with information. Any individual living in the Outskirts who would like to volunteer for search and capture efforts, please report to the capitol. The incentive of an elevation of status awaits the successful capture of all three women.

I slammed the paper down on the stand, and Miranda jumped back with a yelp. Mumbling my apologies, I entered the high-rise apartment complex dad had me cooped up in.

Before dad even had a say around this place, they'd already been placed into different factions. I mean, if you thought about it, it was the best way forward. For humanity to truly survive, the strong needed to make it out every time. It's basic science.

From an outsider's perspective, I could see how it looked like everybody else was just collateral. That wasn't true though; their efforts weren't overlooked in the slightest. We valued it, truly. It was just important they didn't get the wrong idea, which is why it was better to keep things separate.

The hierarchy was simple, and I wasn't sure why people complained. This was all luck of the draw, for now. It wasn't as though *we* had all been genetically engineered and created people to lead a lower life. We weren't monsters, and it wasn't our fault that higher powers had bigger plans for us all. Until my dad's testing could be confirmed in a few years.

They needed to wait it out, give my dad a chance. He was trying here, and eventually, we'd be a society filled with greatness. What we could achieve together would be the beginning of a new order in history.

The lobby was filled with Elite assholes. I shuffled between them, pushing my way into the full elevator. The capital had such a stuffy, know-it-all aura to it and this fancy building didn't help tone it down. But I guess that was the point; people that had a tangible value for society deserved to be awarded for their efforts. Work hard, play hard and all.

Scholars, Tinkerers, and the Umbra Mortis all resided here, the forefront of greatness. We possessed advanced powers that led the way for innovation and progress. *We* were the ones that would leave humanity better than we the world we had been born into.

People like Miranda resided in the outskirts of the capital, and were often placed throughout the outlier states. The *Elementa Manipulatus* helped bring the Elite's ideas to fruition.

Elemental magic was no small thing when you had a vast amount of power. They were treated right, had a decent living. Especially if they knew all the right people. Fire elementals were what kept us in business, honestly. Between their skilled forgery and engineering, there wasn't much we could accomplish without them.

Turning on the shower inside my apartment, I stepped in, grateful for our aqueduct engineers. They were the reason the entire territory had access to fresh water for whatever needs they saw fit, not to mention the healing aspects many of them were able to provide. There were more healers here than in Salem and The Expanse combined. Unlike my sister, they had the ability to heal many at once too. Reina would have a field day if she saw the hospital here.

Imagine my surprise when my dad had alerted me to their fully operational Navy. Okay, maybe calling them a Navy was generous, but they were ramping up for war. It was mostly fisherman and general border protection, but still, impressive.

There was a great reason most people didn't make it out of Covert Province, and the ones who did were too traumatized to speak on what they encountered. The airborne reconnaissance here was lethal. The phrase "word travels fast" was true as the sky was blue. Their Air elementals could track those through the wind in more ways than one, not to mention the way they could influence airflow as a whole.

Air Elementals mixed with the Geokinetic Trackers from Earth elementals, and I found that I'd never leave this place without my dad's permission even if I did have any regrets. Which I didn't.

Either way, they'd hunt me down before I made it anywhere near a border. They were the ones who found me and brought me home the moment I crossed it.

Did I feel sorry for the Outsiders? Kinda, but not really. It wasn't my fault they drew the short end of the stick power-wise. Maybe their kids would luck out and be more powerful than them, or, hell, maybe they'd be granted more than one power. But good luck making their way out of the outskirts of the territory. The cities out there were decimated from either bombs, radiation, the after-effects of the apocalypse, or all of the above.

We'd crossed through some on my way to Richmond, and it wasn't pretty. That was life though; it couldn't all be rainbows and flowers.

THERE WAS A KNOCK ON THE DOOR OF MY APARTMENT. I PAUSED THE movie playing on the wall from the projector above my couch. I sighed, walking over to open it, but already knowing who was likely on the other side. Malachai, one of my father's self-proclaimed "guardians." He was an ugly fella, in his forties, clearly had it tougher in life in The Before. Wouldn't be surprised if hard drugs had been part of his daily habit by the craters in his skin.

We didn't get along, him and I. Hadn't since the day I arrived. He didn't trust me, and I found that I didn't trust him much either. He was such a simpleton, in his secret service ass suit.

"Malachai," I said, waiting for him to tell me what displeasure brought him to my door.

He placed his hand on his ear piece, the other moving directly in my face, silencing me like he wasn't the one who disturbed *my* peace. I cleared my throat impatiently and he glared, motioning me to follow him.

Rolling my eyes, I slammed the door in his face. Striding across the room to pull my boots on and strap in my weapons. A small smile pulled at my lips and I fought to shake it off. Moe had given one of the pistols to me, *blessed it for protection* she'd claimed. Whatever the hell that meant. Malachai's fist throttled into the door, shaking the room.

"Chill the fuck out," I yelled, knowing it would only sour his mood but reveling in the idea of it.

I yanked the door back open, sliding past him without a word. His heavy steps sounded at my rear and he let out a low grumble as if it would make me tremble in my boots. He was at least a foot shorter than me, and he didn't look like he'd ever fought a day in his life. There was nothing to fear here as far as I was concerned.

He mumbled in between whatever conversation he was listening to in his ear, "Your father would like to see you."

"Figured you wouldn't be here bothering me if that weren't the case."

I hopped into the passenger seat of the blacked-out SUV; it was still a weird thing for me. They still lived a life of luxury in these parts. Cars, electricity, air conditioning, hell, even smart homes if you were important enough. If I didn't know any better, I'd never have known bombs went off anywhere in the vicinity of this place.

Malachai grumbled to himself as he pulled off. Ten minutes later, I stood in front of the old capitol building. It looked like a knock off version of the White House. Of course my dad had claimed it as his own.

I smirked—power always belonged to those who took it. Nothing new under the sun.

Dad was gifted, as were Reina and I. Her brains, my brawn, but better. It didn't take long for him to worm his way to the top of the food chain, especially when he'd begun the experiments. His work with eugenics was all theoretical as far as I knew, but his work on the Pansies … that had brought him some notoriety. His own bite had inspired him when he'd failed to turn. Then people of power around him dropped faster than flies, the only answer as far as the Elite were concerned, was him.

The halls were decorated with classical bullshit. Not exactly my taste, but, hey, it wasn't my mansion. Reina would love it when she got here though; she'd get to be the little princess she'd always dreamed of being. After this was all over, I'd go back to the outskirts, find myself a ranch to settle down on. Moe would come around eventually. We could be happy there. All we needed was each other—she'd said so herself.

I followed Malachai down the narrow hallway, a chill passing over my body, still not accustomed to the feeling of A/C on my skin again. The door opened to a room full of people surrounding several surveillance screens, maps were pulled up on the smaller ones scattered around them. There were red dots littered over a few settlements I recognized, a large X placed over the place I once called home.

Dad glanced up, his freckled weathered face pulled into a grin, and the room cleared out. The men stared me down as they left, measuring me up like I posed a great danger to them all. Insults rolled off their tongues quietly, addressed toward each other but meant for my sensitive ears to hear. And I suppose I could be a threat to them all, if I wanted to. I kept my face hard, not wanting to show any signs of weakness. They would eat that shit up here and toss me out to the dogs.

His head tilted to the side, taking me in as though he still couldn't believe I was here. He glided across the room gracefully, his rough hands cupping my face gently. "My boy, I'm glad you're here."

There was excitement in his voice, but I rolled my eyes in response. "It's not like I had a choice," I grumbled, throwing a choice look of disgruntle in Malachai's direction.

He yanked my face back toward him. "Don't disrespect your elders, Seth. If you want people's approval, you'll have to establish a relationship with those surrounding you, *supporting* you. Tell me, are you not up to the task? Arrangements can be made if that's the case."

"No, dad," I replied, making sure my eyes remained on him. "I apologize, no disrespect intended, Malachai."

Malachai's only response was a grunt and the click of the door. He hadn't gone far; I could hear his labored breathing outside the door. My father's first line of defense indeed. The thing about Malachai was he didn't appear threatening, but his power was lethal. Nothing Amaia couldn't take out if it came down to it, but for around here, powerful enough. The best of the best were placed where it mattered, preparing the troops.

"We're leaving here when arrangements have been finalized," Dad said, his words interrupting my thoughts. "We'll be heading west. It appears your sister and her friends have initiated preparation for war and have warned other settlements in the area. Our test squadron was compromised within days. I thought you said Duluth's military was a mess."

I cleared my throat. "They are. Or were, but as I already made you aware, Amaia would be focused on training them—"

"Ah, yes. Made me aware, same way you made me aware of the supposed battle tactics she would use. You were right, for the most part," he cut me off, moving toward the screen and zooming in a few miles outside of Duluth. "*For the most part*, Seth, didn't spare many lives. Lucky for us, they were Outsider grunts attempting to move up with the promise of cross-breeding with more successful members of society. Not a real loss, we learned enough. What I can't seem to understand is why you didn't tell me they could improvise against our higher tech."

My brows pulled in confusion, not understanding what he was getting at. He spared me from having to ask, the screen now showing a picture from one of the scouts. There was snow piled high and wide as I stood tall. Our weapons had barely made a dent.

That wasn't Amaia's planning—she knew nothing of defense in the snow. I knew that much. I also knew exactly who had assisted her in laying her little valley of death out, but that was information that need not be disclosed. For now.

Shrugging, I looked at him like I was none the wiser. "There's a lot of people there. Just because their military sucked, doesn't mean Amaia wasn't capable of inspiring innovation. I told you, she has that effect on people."

"Which is exactly why Salem Territory is our main target. They managed to get some settlements on their side, but others remain hesitant. Monterey Compound is our main priority. That little bitch Amaia has to go. I will not be made a fool of."

I fought to keep my heart beat steady, fully aware my dad would be able to detect any changes. Moe had done her best to keep me out of her mind, but I was there long enough to know a general idea of what they had planned. Knew enough to keep them all as safe as I could. I didn't give a rat's ass about Monterey. Riley could take care of himself as long as Amaia was nowhere nearby. But the others, they would go out fighting with the people of Monterey. Hell, Amaia would go down for *any* place she passed through, left her mark on. And if Amaia went down, that meant my idiotic sister would too. If she did, then Moe would.

The only person who had a chance of getting them all out, even against their wishes but for his own selfish purposes, was Alexiares. I saw the way he watched Amaia. He was my best hope, which is why his name would be left out of things for as long as I could hold out.

"Devil's advocate here, hear me out, sir." I forced my gaze to meet his level stare. When he said nothing, I took it as my cue to continue. "We should take a beat to consider the repercussions of directly breaking the treaty. It's not just one territory we're talkin' bout here anymore. It's three. That's how many it would take to cross over and get to Monterey—"

The way he straightened his posture made me stop talking. I knew that stance. "Son, if treaties were abided by then the world would have never fallen to nuclear war. Treaties are for losers, for those who lost. A victor makes a treaty in pity of the loser. No one benefits but those who win. That treaty was made with Salem in mind, which is why life over there is a step out of the ring of hell The Expanse calls home. Now it may surprise you, but I want Monterey for that exact reason. The strong live out there, and that's why I want them here."

"They aren't in Monterey, clearly." I said nervously.

He offered me a look of disapproval, my omitted truth obvious. "I think we both know it's not for long. Even if she isn't there, taking Monterey Compound out would be a hit against everyone's morale. Effectively dissuading the others from trying to defend themselves. It'd be easier to take them all over. We'll take what we can along the way, but Monterey Compound is cutting the head from the chicken."

"What about Reina? Sloan?" I pressed, hoping that maybe he would at least care about them. They were blood, something he claimed was important to him, with only one other thing being top of his list of priorities. "They're powerful. You know this."

"Watch yourself, son, lying doesn't bode well for you. Sloan is about as powerful as she is an effective leader. If your sister and your cousin want to be on the wrong side of history, that's up to them. If they want to join the cause, then they are welcome to. If not, they go down with your pathetic General." He paused for a moment, considering his options. "Though it would be nice to breed your sister, Amaia, and that girl you spoke of. Too much power needs to be nipped in the bud. Too much power leads to rebellion."

"Dad, please, consider the—"

He struck me, my hat flew across the room at the impact, my cheek flushed with heat and stinging in pain. I resisted the urge to raise my own fist in response. It took every ounce of control in my body to not flinch at the same hand that slapped me. My father reached out, attempting to soothe the very spot he intended to bruise.

"Son," he said soothingly, "I'm proud of you for coming here. Don't make me regret it."

He left me standing there, the faces of my friends now displayed across each of the screens. I gulped down the desire to scream at the picture of Elie down in the corner. A child, she was just a child and had no part in any of this. But she would hurt Amaia, as would Prescott displayed right above her.

In my nearly thirty years on this earth, I had never felt so out of control. So helpless. I bit down on my lip and bent down to grab my hat off the floor, placing it back on my head. I studied my reflection on the screen before me, my face was there too.

I took it for what it was, a warning if I didn't comply. The only thing I could do to save them all was try to get them to understand and take our side. If not our side, my side. The side of the brother now lost to them but who still cared.

CHAPTER TWENTY

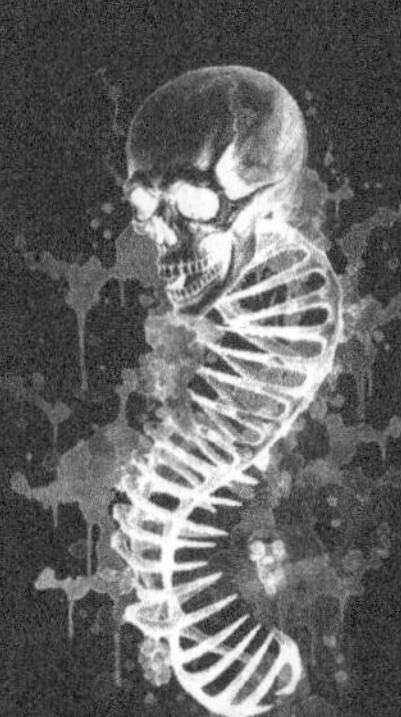

AMAIA

Soft lips kissed the crevice between my shoulders, and Alexiares' warm breath tickled the back of my neck. I smiled to myself, not wanting to separate from him, but the warmth in the room had become oddly intolerable.

"Unless you're trying to be someone's father …" I teased, knowing it would get any sane person to take a moment to pause and reflect. It was a fifty-fifty shot given that this man of mine was the furthest thing from sane I'd ever known.

His body stiffened, the beads of sweat dripping from my back as he pulled back, reassessing his actions. "Fuck, I'm so sorry—"

"Shh," I said, turning over to kiss him, gently flicking the tip of his nose. "I'm only kidding. Ironically enough, I had a ten-year IUD put in before shit hit the fan. It'll be another four before I make Reina figure out a way to get it out of me."

His exhales were still ragged, but Alexiares' facial expression eased. I, too, would not be comfortable bringing another life into this shitshow. No offense taken. My eyes narrowed, his face had turned a tinge green.

I reached out to place my palm against his forehead. "You're hot."

"Hell yeah, I am," he joked. "I figured that's half the reason I ended up in bed with you."

Shaking my head, I moved my hand to his cheeks, double checking it wasn't an ill assessment on my end. "No, Alexiares, you're burning up. How are you feeling?"

Before he could answer, a wave of queasiness twisted in my stomach. The tendrils moving up my throat and the sour taste of regret clung to my senses, pleading for relief. I leaned over the side of the bed, bile working its way onto the floor.

His hand rested on my back soothingly. "I'll go get—"

"No need to get us, we're already here!" Reina's voice boomed from the living room.

I mustered the energy to climb out of the bed, careful to avoid the waste now piled near the edge as I pulled Alexiares' T-shirt over my head. Opening the door to my room, my hand found its way to my stomach for support. I was greeted with the sight of Reina lounged on the couch, resting on Moe's lap, a knowing smirk on both their faces.

"How long have you been here?" I asked, trying to force myself upright, the movement making me queasy all over again.

Moe's hands moved to rest behind her head, a smug expression crossing over her face. "If you're wondering how much we heard, the answer is, the walls are thin."

"In other words, everything. All night." Reina nodded, twirling her hair around her fingers.

Abel cleared his throat, startling me from the other side of the room. "And morning. Were you guys even trying to have privacy?"

He added, sitting on the counter. He'd helped himself to the mason jar of peanut butter, spoon hanging from his mouth.

"It's about damn time, honestly." Sloan said, closing the front door behind her. A pot of coffee in one hand, a teakettle in the other.

"Fantastic, gangs all here," I groaned. "At least we're decent."

"Morally?" Sloan mocked. "Absolutely not. But sure, he has clothes on, so that's a win I guess."

Alexiares came up behind me, hand rested on my shoulder, intent on ignoring his least favorite person in Duluth. "Moe …"

"What?" she asked innocently. "The alternative was you seizing up on the floor and Amaia passing out before she could make it out the front door to get help. Told you, infection is a bitch."

"Here," Reina offered, shaking a tumbler in her hands before passing it over to me. "It's a tonic. Will help keep the fever down, thus, limited passing out and no seizures."

"Tastes like rat poison," Abel said, a kiddish grin tugging at his lips.

"How do you even—" I began to question, then decided I didn't have it in me to care. "You know what? Never mind. I'm going to put more than just a shirt on."

"Wouldn't do that if I were you," Moe warned.

I turned around. Clearly, she knew something that I did not and was enjoying every second of it. "Why might I ask?"

"Because you're going to throw up in three, two …"

The contents of my stomach threatened to come back up. Moe's cackling mocked me from the living room as I sprinted toward the bathroom, the others joining in on their laughter in between heaves.

"There's a wet cloth with your name on it when you're ready! Keep sipping the tonic until you're able to keep it all down, should help with retaining fluids in a few minutes," Reina yelled, having a blast with the guessing game of the future that her and Moe were playing.

A loud thud sounded against the hard floor and Moe called for Abel.

Abel's steps crossed from the kitchen near the door of the bedroom. "On it!"

I glanced over from the bucket I was leaning over, somehow placed in my bathroom without either of us knowing. Likely in the few minutes we'd fallen into a brief slumber before one of us teased the other back awake. Abel dropped Alexiares back on the bed like he was nothing more than a mannequin. If how I felt was any indication, I probably appeared to be in just as bad a state, if not worse.

"Here's the cloth bucket," Abel said, strolling into the bathroom, sheepishly taking me in. "Reina said place it on the back of your neck to help keep you cool until you can keep the tonic down. In hindsight, it would've been best to conserve your energy for other purposes. We'll be out in the living room until you two come to again."

His shy behavior fooled everyone but me. I remembered how much of a jokester he was when under Riley's care, and I doubted that went away with a few years of distance. "Which is when, Abel?"

"Moe won't tell anyone, because she and Sloan have a bet placed." He leaned in close, whispering my reprieve in my ear, "But I've been practicing, and I've seen it. Give it a few hours, you'll be better than new."

He gave my shoulder a squeeze and walked out, leaving me to suffer on my own.

GIVEN THE POSITION OF THE BLAZING SUN NOW BEAMING INTO THE room, a few hours had passed since I fell into a fever-hazed sleep.

My body was heavy, the sight of my bite throbbed angrily. The skin surrounding it had turned crimson and swollen. Every gasp of air I took was a fight toward life. The sheets stuck to my skin having stripped in the hazy moments between naps.

Abel was either more than optimistic than Reina or he had a skewed idea on what *better than new* meant.

Groaning, I turned over in bed. Alexiares was awake, staring up blankly at the ceiling. If I had the energy, I would have laughed at the look of regret itching to take over his very being.

"Told you that you didn't have to do this," I struggled to say, my throat still sore from throwing up.

His thick brows rose slightly, the only other movement on his face coming from his lips. "Do you really think now is the time for 'I told you so?'"

"If not now, then when."

"I liked it better when you were asleep." He pulled the pillow from beneath my head and brought it down over his face. "The light is giving me a fucking migraine."

"Here," I said, using what little movement my body provided to reach for the curtains. Half my body on the bed, the other half struggling to maintain my balance.

I got halfway there before the curtain moved on its own. My breath caught, body paused in its tracks, and I swore I was seeing shit. "Ummm, did you?"

"Hear you still talking after I told you I have a migraine. A migraine I only have because you forced me to volunteer to kill myself? Yes," Alexiares ground out.

"No, you imbecile," I said. "The curtain moved on its own."

The pillow lifted off his face slightly, concern taking over. "What?"

"I think … I think I got air magic."

He reached his hand out toward the curtain, then frowned when nothing happened. "Either Reina's injection is going to kill me or the incubation period will take longer than we thought."

If Reina's frame wasn't so delicate, I would have sworn she possessed her brother's *Supra* senses. She opened the door, a smile that didn't meet her eyes welcoming us awake. "Or —"

"Reina, you have zero boundaries," I hissed, yanking the sheets over my naked body.

She shrugged. "Nothing I haven't seen before. Though some parts I find less pleasant to look at than others."

Reina glanced down at Alexiares who had also stripped down from his fever to nothing. He pulled at the sheets, begrudgingly covering himself in its warmth.

"Here, try to do something with this," she said, offering up the pot of soil in her left hand.

Alexiares squinted in confusion. "With dirt?"

Reina turned to me for confirmation. "I was speaking English, right? Or do I need to try one of the other three languages you know?"

Taken aback, I faced him, unaware of the remaining language he had yet to disclose. I'd only been aware of three: English, Greek, and now Spanish.

"You're speaking English fine, Reina," he chided. "I just don't know what you're asking of me."

"It's soil; the other magic Frankie possessed was Earth. If she has air and you don't, then that means my cousin is not as much of a genius as she claims to be and has decided to do us all a favor by killing you instead." Reina shot her cousin a glare over her shoulder,

"Or you have earth magic now running through your veins," Sloan corrected, leaning in the door frame.

"Oh, he has it alright," Moe insisted, sounding to be still lounged out on the couch.

Alexiares prodded for more information. "Fantastic. Any pointers would be useful considering my brain cells were fried as of a few hours ago."

"If I told you everything that happened in the future, then the future would never be the same. You know this," Moe protested, her tone tinged with amusement.

He groaned in frustration, hand hovering over the pot. Pity was never my thing, but in the moment I felt sorry for him. Alexiares had spent the last month trying to master the gifts that had brought him nothing but pain for years, shortly followed by training our Steamfire. Now this. It had to be frustrating, and I knew he hated the idea of appearing weak. I was proud of him though; he'd learned a lot in the last few weeks. That was no easy feat.

Minutes passed. Slowly, a tiny sprout formed in the soil. I wasn't clear on what the hell it was, but it was something. Proof that we needed to stay motivated.

"Still a genius," Reina said, tossing her hair over her shoulders. She threw her cousin a devious glare as she sauntered out.

"See you in the morning," Moe called from the other room.

I watched as Reina and Abel trailed her out, Sloan remained in the door frame to Alexiares' displeasure.

"Shouldn't you be anywhere else but here?" he bit out.

She gave him a sinister smirk. "Nowhere I'd rather be than here. Keeping at least one of you alive. Sorry, both of you. Doctor's orders."

Sloan closed the door behind her, the couch groaned under her weight as she took a seat. I rolled over in bed, nestling up under him. Silence followed, but an apology fought its way to my lips.

"I shouldn't have let you do this," I said apologetically, "I admit, there is a tinge of regret for being a total dumbass now that I'm facing the consequences."

He shifted his body, face tilted down toward me with a twinkle in his eye, "An apology and a reflection that your actions do, in fact, have consequences. Must be my lucky day."

"You don't believe in luck," I snarked.

"Never had it my whole life, why would I now?"

Huffing a laugh, I offered a gentle reminder that us being alive was truly a gift. "Because you're here. We're here. Alive against the odds."

He paused thoughtfully, undoubtedly considering how fair my assessment was. "Michael and Logan did fine defying said odds," Alexiares said at last.

"That's not what I meant," I countered, my voice no more than a whisper.

He pulled me closer, tucking me into his side. "I know."

I was about to tease him about how the only way I could get any closer to him was to be inside his skin, when gentle breaths whistled in my ear. We needed our rest and his body appeared to be having a tougher time adjusting than mine, so I let him take as much time as his body required. The only way to get through this infection was to let our immune systems fight it out, to win the war waged within our bodies.

When sleep evaded me, I crept from the bed, pulling his shirt back over me. Desperate to find something to please my stomach, I ventured into the living room. Sloan peered up from her notebook, her wavy red hair tucked behind her ears. With a warm smile, she dropped her pencil, deciding whatever she was doing was no longer worth it, and made room for me on the couch.

I sat next to her, pouring myself a cup of tea. Opting to not have the coffee further upset my stomach. She watched me as I forced half a roll into my mouth, savoring the taste and overall feeling of something in my stomach.

Sloan watched me warily. "There's still peanut butter and jam in the cabinet," she said.

"Honestly, the thought of anything sweet right now might send me back to the bucket."

That earned me a rare, true laugh. One that I missed hearing. Over the years, I'd learned the only thing I liked more than hearing my best friend, Sammy from The Before, laugh was having her and Sloan's laughter fill the room together. They had both brought so much joy to my life for different reasons, them getting along had been a pleasant surprise. Sammy was sweet, an old soul, where Sloan was rambunctious, always challenging the status quo. I had been so nervous bringing them around each other, fearing that Sloan would push all the wrong buttons for someone that only knew kind words. Sammy, however, had found Sloan oddly endearing.

Maybe I was a fool for thinking I could have that here again, with the family I'd become embedded in. She was Reina's cousin, but their relationship was strained. The Sloan I'd spent so much time with was now hidden deep into the mind of an emerging leader. I wasn't even sure she was fighting to get out. Actually, I was almost certain Sloan kept her tucked away, protected.

"You'll be leaving soon," she said, startling me from my thoughts.

I debated how to approach this subject with her; it had been years since we'd had a heart to heart. But it pained me to know she'd be left here on her own, fending for herself, and lost in her own mind. "As will your cousin."

Sloan nodded in response. "The *brujas* arrived today, that's where she and the other one went."

"The other one has a name you know." I sighed, knowing exactly where this conversation was now headed. More defense mechanisms.

"I know," she mumbled, "but she doesn't like me much. She's a bitter woman, that's for sure. Not sure how you tolerate her, or him."

In every friendship there are times when you have to know when to shut the fuck up. This was one of those times. I didn't offer a retort in their defense because the pain behind Sloan's eyes was telling enough. Being disliked had never sat well with her. She pretended like it didn't matter, that she couldn't care less. But I knew the truth: Sloan had always been a people pleaser, much like Reina. So this, being in charge and Moe's reaction to her, had surely offered a lot of pain.

"You're a spitting image of him," I said carefully.

"Who?"

A curl fell in front of my face as I gave her a hard stare, making it clear she knew exactly who I was speaking of.

"They were in love," I explained. "I'd be a fool to think that she didn't still love him, and he left her like all that time spent together meant nothing. She saw forever with him, and that means a hell of a lot when your magic grants you the access to see forever."

Sloan sat there, her body stiff on the couch taking in my words. We hadn't had an actual conversation about Seth since his departure, only what his departure had meant. Speaking of his character, of the cousin she grew up with, what he meant to everyone else, this was new territory for us both. Part of me felt silly never having put two and two together for years. It wasn't as though Seth and Reina spoke of her or the family they left behind. Now I knew why, because Reina had carefully avoided the topic. But Sloan had spoken of them both many times in college, of the other brothers too.

This world is big, and names are fleeting. Still, I should have known.

"He killed Jax." The words were painful leaving my lips, the first time I'd said them aloud. "And that might have been a worse sin for her than had he simply up and left."

"Your boyfriend?" She shifted her weight uncomfortably at the topic. I hadn't spoken to her of Jax either, not what he had meant to me. Sloan knew *of* him, that was all.

Jax was as known throughout these parts as I was, but of our relationship, that was something kept close to home and for good reason. When you love someone, and people know about it, they can be used against you.

"My fiancé," I corrected. "Few people knew outside of Monterey. But yes. They were close. If anyone knew Jax as well as I did, it would be her. Every morning at The Compound, they would spar together then head to breakfast. He never discussed the extent of their conversations with me. I can say with full confidence that they opened up to each other at a level that I envied. I knew Jax inside out, but some things, I don't think he shared with anyone but her. Not on purpose, not to keep me out. There are some thoughts you only share with certain people, you know? We're all family, but he filled in that sibling void in her life that she had lost. Jax was kind, warm," I smiled to myself.

"One of those people you meet that you can tell had a hard life but fought to make something of themselves, not letting the past burden them. He had this way about him that made everyone feel understood, and the man she loved took the other man she loved from her. That's a hard hit, and I wasn't there for her when it happened. I made her grieve through that alone, but Seth stepped up to the plate. Comforted her under false pretenses. I don't blame her for not being able to get over that, for not being able to see your face without seeing him. I see it, too, when I look at you."

Sloan sat back, tracing the outline of her hand against her thigh. "How do you go from a man like that to the man who's lying in your bed?"

She was talking about Jax in comparison to Alexiares now, not Seth. I didn't need to ask for clarification to make the distinction between her tone when she spoke of Alexiares versus the other people that had wronged her in life. This was a grudge I didn't ever foresee her moving past, and I wouldn't ask her to.

"You don't know him, Sloan."

"No, Amaia. *You* don't know him," she countered. "You know what he's allowed you to see. It's what he does: he blends into his surroundings, and then he strikes when you least expect it. That's what they all do at St. Cloud—pretend to be helpless, like they need support. That's been their MO since the war; I doubt time has changed that."

I could see that now, the feigning of helplessness Finley liked to put on. Knowing what I did now, that fact was clear as day. St. Cloud was the way it was because of the leadership they chose, not for any reason aside from that. Finley used the absence of resources for her benefit, to make people rely on her. They were far from a helpless crowd of people. Men like Alexiares didn't come from the helpless; they came from lions pretending to be sheep.

It wasn't my place to convince her what type of man I laid with, nor was it her place to press how I'd gone from one end of the spectrum to the next. Sloan only knew a small part of the woman I was now. I couldn't help but be a bit guarded over him, because if Sloan hated Alexiares, then she'd probably hate me too. She could add herself to the list of people to hate for she was no better than either of us. She just didn't realize it yet.

War gives you few options, being in charge during times of conflict presents one with even fewer. *How could you?* quickly becomes, *What if I did?* which only gives way to, *What have I become?*

"I understand where you're coming from," I offered a small token of acknowledgment. For that's all I could do. One day, she would understand. "I respect it, it's a fair assessment. Alexiares has had a rough life and led one that is certainly … questionable. But I don't question who he is now, the person he wants to be. I've done things too, Sloan, things you'd probably disown me over. Nobody is perfect in this life anymore, it's just not possible if you want to get things done. The only difference is what side you play for. He's played the wrong side, admitted to being lost. He owns that. Now he wants to play for the right side, and when history has its eyes on you, that is all you can ask for."

Sloan scoffed, "How many scars are you going to justify just because you love the man holding the knife? If everyone forgave as easily as you did, there would be no line between good and evil."

"Being against evil doesn't make any of us good, Sloan, it just makes us human."

"You always did see the good in people, my friend," she said, moving to grab hold of my hand. "I love that about you, but I've always been able to see the truth."

I leaned my head against her shoulder, taking in possibly the last moment of comfort from an old friend. "I know, Sloan, and that's why it pains me to have to leave you here on your own. I want you to come with us."

"Me too," she echoed.

"Then come," I insisted. "After this is all over, you, your mom, Violet, you'll always have a home out in Monterey."

"Not all of us are destined to survive this, Maia, I think you know that," Sloan said with such definitiveness that I was afraid to ask where the confidence in that statement came from. *Who* it had come from.

"Don't speak that way."

Her head rested atop mine, fiery hair blurring my vision already filled with tears. "I really do thank you. You've given a lot, and I know I don't show my gratitude as much as I should, but I'm incredibly thankful to have had a friend like you in this life."

"My offer will always stand—when this is over, I'll send someone out to Duluth, and I'm going to bring you home." I prayed it would come true, but the truth was I didn't even know if I would be there to greet her if she came.

"I'll be waiting."

CHAPTER

TWENTY-ONE

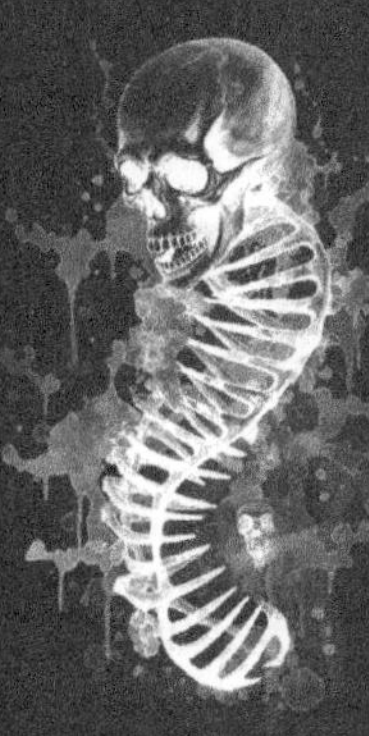

AMAIA

Rain pebbled against the large center window in Sloan's study. My family gathered around her desk, a map of what had once been the continental United States spread across with smaller ones of individual territories on the side.

Sloan moved one of the chess pieces covering St. Cloud on the map, a Black Rook. "If we take Finley out, what are the chances we can get St. Cloud on our side?" she asked, eyes boring into Alexiares' soul.

"Don't know why you're staring at me. I'm not the one with the visions," Alexiares replied, voice sharp.

Moe interjected, sparing us all the back and forth. "Because it's going to come down to you."

"What do you want me to say?" he asked, annoyance lingering in his tone. "It's not like I can go up there and take over myself.

They don't trust me and even if they did, I don't consider any of them worth my time."

"It's not about where you would be happy to live at, let me be that friendly reminder for you," Sloan said, knocking the chess piece over in emphasis of her point.

Alexiares' patience was wearing thin today. We'd only recovered from infection mere hours before. "You sure you want me in charge, Sloan? If I did, the first place I'd set on the path of destruction is here."

"Alexiares," I warned, a headache still pulling at the tendrils of my mind.

"Whatever." He bit out, "We don't need them. We hold all three remaining settlements in Minnesota."

He was incredibly touchy when it came to Finley or St. Cloud. I understood. She and the settlement had brought him a lot of pain, but if he couldn't pull it together in my war room, then he needed to leave. This wasn't the appropriate time to let emotions take over our thoughts, not when millions of lives were at stake.

Abel saved me the exasperation. "It's less about that, than it is about the influence Finley holds over some of the others."

"I thought she claimed to be ill-connected," I said, admittedly slightly confused about what connections such a bitch of a person could hold.

That wasn't how relationships worked in The After. There needed to be some semblance of a reciprocal relationship to stay connected to other territories. This life didn't offer a free pass to anyone, and her sharp tongue and piss poor behavior didn't count as an incentive as far as I was concerned.

"Wolves dressed as sheep ..." Sloan tsked in reference to the conversation we'd had only a night prior.

"Fear of Finley's reaction is what will keep South Dakota from our side," Abel explained. "She will also be the deciding factor in the split over Iowa. Both of which are pivotal in holding the line considering Kansas and Wisconsin are lost causes."

Riley would be damn proud of him right now. The sudden urge to tear up over how much of a man I'd seen him grow into in such a short time overtook me. Maybe Riley was right, maybe he had been old enough to seek a life of his own. I just hoped I could buy Elie a few more years so she wouldn't be as inclined to lead the same kind of life. While I was proud of Abel, I didn't want this for Elie. He'd been at this since he was around her age and had only recently matured into the role and his gifts at the age of twenty.

"What do you mean, Wisconsin?" I questioned him, pausing over the map instead of placing a Black Rook over them as well. This was news to me. "Madison has already sent confirmation that they await our orders."

"Madison is on our side, but Kenosha, Milwaukee and Green Bay have already sent correspondence to Covert that they intend to fight against us." Abel faced me with earnest eyes, knowing the information had the possibility of sending me off on a tangent from the last war.

Of course, they did, those weak sons of bitches. They'd barely been a benefit to us in the last war, claiming they didn't have enough people to feed themselves, let alone loan us soldiers for the war. A sorry excuse for a group of settlements and an even sorrier alliance to hold. They weren't much of a loss, but every soldier gained was a benefit I couldn't deny.

"Sorry to them then." I refrained on the extra commentary, but damn, it was hard to not shit talk those fuckers.

Reina snorted in disbelief. "So what? We leave all the innocent people in Madison to die? They're not gonna go down without a fight, you know how Everhart is."

It was true, Isabella Everhart was a fierce general. One of the few other female generals out there—we were a rare breed. A woman to be respected and even feared, but she would not be able to resist when she was surrounded by people dedicated to a cause other than our own. Isabella was wise enough to know to keep her head down and wait to see if an opening presented itself to keep her people safe.

"We have no other option, Reina. They're three against one," I said, sympathizing with her concerns but knowing sympathy wouldn't win us this war. "It would be a waste of time to send you up there and a waste of resources to redirect troops to cut off their lines of communication."

"Casualty of war," Sloan muttered, a Black King in hand.

She placed four of them over each settlement. The sight was unsettling, but not a real game changer. I doubted they'd do anything but pledge their allegiance and put lackluster soldiers along the borders. They weren't a true threat to us unless they decided to cross over into one of our allied borders, which was hard to imagine with their history.

"It will never get any easier, Reina, which is a good thing. Means you have a good heart." I wanted to console my sister, make her understand her intentions were good, that she shouldn't abandon her kind soul just because we were in the middle of civil unrest. "The best we can do for them is to hope war never makes it out their way. On the off chance that it does, have faith they can hold their own long enough for us to do what we must."

Alexiares cleared his throat, taking the tension away from one situation and placing it on another. "Lola will handle St. Paul. They're too scared of her to say no. Any that do, well, they won't be a problem for much longer."

I nodded in confirmation, studying the map. The White Queen symbolized Salem Territory, reflecting our reputation for welcoming those who sought refuge, diplomacy, and the instrumental role we played in maintaining the peace. Transient Nation was captured as The White Bishop due to its uncanny fluidity. The mystery of where they stood in all of this was unsettling.

The Expanse, this vast and unforgiving realm, was our Black Rook. Things out here were straight forward, much like the piece itself in the game of chess. The people here were gritty and un-yielding, essential players represented by their relentless struggle for survival. Then there was Covert Province, the Black King on our board of real-life chess. That was self-explanatory. If we didn't make the right moves, they would dominate.

And right now, looking at the maps in front of me, there was a real chance that could happen. There were too many of them on our board. If Reina was unsuccessful and we didn't do something about Finley, we were in for some serious shit. Shit, that would cost us many lives.

"Salt Lake would side with us," he added on, reminding us of what he'd explained on our journey here. "They don't like out-siders, much less assholes like the guys running Covert Province. We don't need to stop there. If we send word, they'll take care of Provo, Ogden, and Sandy for us."

"You're sure?" I asked.

The question was for him, but I checked with Abel and Moe for confirmation. Both of them offered nothing but a tense, un-sure nod.

"Positive," Alexiares said with as much confidence as I could ask for.

I moved several more black rooks in place. "Where does that leave us then?"

"Cheyenne and Casper up in Wyoming. Montana is split in half. Billings and Missoula are solid ins, Bozeman is a hard no, Great Falls undecided." Abel explained, the states of Wyoming and Montana a jumbled mess of black and white.

In Reina's defense, the words she offered were poised, un-wavering. "On it," she said, but the creases in her face let me know returning to her home state would be nothing short of nerve-wrecking.

"What else?" I pushed, trying to gain a full picture of what we were working with before sending my family out into the field.

Moe placed more rooks down over North Dakota, a small but important group of settlements for keeping the border intact. "Bismarck is being difficult, but Fargo and Grand Forks have it under control."

"Then it's decided then. You three will head out to Wyoming and Montana." I didn't like my orders, much less felt confident in saying them. The results of me not trusting Abel in this could be catastrophic. I mean, what was being a good leader without trust in my soldiers?

Reina closed her eyes for a moment, opening them after taking a deep inhale in, then out. "Do we have time to go to both and make it back home?"

"We will if we take the horses," Abel said, tentatively glancing toward Sloan. "Word has spread. As long as we skirt around St. Cloud, we shouldn't face any issues with the treaty. I've already sent word out to connections to secure safe passage."

I gripped the edge of the desk, leaning over the maps and tossing a demanding glare in Sloan's direction. She met me with a pleading look.

"Seriously? Our calvary is already under-manned; we can't afford to lose any horses." Sloan swore under her smoke-stanched breath.

"You can and you will," I commanded. "Your cavalry is also under-prepared. They won't be on your front line, only serve as scouts."

"You're the General," Sloan muttered in response.

I gave her a smug grin, letting her know that sarcasm would only lead to me asking for more if she kept it up. "I am."

"And you'll take care of Finley?" Moe asked, redirecting the conversation back at Alexiares.

"Sure, if it comes to that." He grumbled, hands pushing through his gelled back hair.

I bit down on my lip, fighting off the urge to run my fingers through them myself. I hated having to deal with his difficult behavior from the standpoint of his general, but from a girlfriend's point of view, his arrogance was sexy as hell. Not to mention the thought of him putting an end to Finley once and for all.

He gave me a once over, pupils dilating in a way that let me know he was reading my thoughts. The corner of his mouth twitched in response. *Girlfriend?* The word lingered in his heavy gaze and I wondered if I'd said the words aloud. We certainly hadn't stopped to have *that* conversation in the past twenty-four hours. Surely, I was reading into the imaginary situation unfolding before my eyes.

Sloan cleared her throat, and I apologetically took in the uncomfortable energy now filling the room.

"Should we be afraid of what *sure* entails?" Sloan mocked.

Alexiares waited for the seconds to pass, making her wait and think the worst of whatever he planned to say next. "Do you really care as long as the mission is achieved?"

Silence was her only answer.

"That's what I thought," he said in jest.

Well, only I knew he was kidding. *I think.*

I reassured them all that I was still the one in charge, regardless of the relationship building between us. "I'll be the deciding factor in that once we get to Lola's."

And it was true. At the end of the day, I would do what was best for everyone. Compound first, after all. If that meant working with the queen of hell, then so be it. Though I wouldn't stop him from throwing in a few hits or two first. Probably a few of my own slashes to her skin if I had the chance. Payback was a bitch, but revenge was even sweeter.

"That you will, my sister, that you will," Moe said, a small, almost imperceptible smile tugging at the corners of her lips, a silent acknowledgment of a shared secret.

There was one lingering question remaining. One that everyone had made sure to avoid until we had no other option.

"What's Transient Nations' role in all this?" I asked.

Abel sighed. "It's fifty-fifty either way. They do what's best for them out there. Whoever brings them the best deal will determine where the people go."

"That can be arranged." I surmised, "I imagine we have far more to offer than Covert."

"They value freedom there more than anything." Moe confirmed, then paused thoughtfully before adding, "Covert knows that, though. They'll offer to let them keep their freedom to stay out of the war until they control the rest of us."

I had full faith in her assessment. She knew the people of Transient Nation better than us all, having lived there for some time before finding Monterey. My sister had been pretty fucked up in the head when she arrived. If her tense perception of humanity was any indication, getting them to join our cause wouldn't come easy.

"Then let's make sure they're aware of what's at stake," I replied, thinking of what we had to offer.

It wasn't much, given they had the ability to obtain everything they wanted. It wasn't like they were trapped there. They chose that life. Enjoyed the freedoms that came with it. Life at Monterey Compound or even anywhere within Salem would hardly be enticing, considering there was nothing stopping them from joining us in the first place.

Moe's eyes glazed over. Her balance became nonexistent. Alexiares reached out in time to catch her before she hit the ground. The others remained quiet, watching her, waiting to see where her vision would take her and what we could learn.

She was back by the time I pulled up the chair behind Sloan's desk to place her in.

Moe squeezed the sides of the leather seat, grounding herself back in the present. "We'll need to be aggressive in our offer. You can't go in with kindness. They'll take it as a negotiation. If you allow it, Your Majesty." She sneered at Sloan, then continued, "I'll need to get a messenger out to an old friend. She's in Texas at the moment, but not for long. She'll make sure word will spread. They'll have to decide individually where they want to end up. It'll be a waste zone if we win."

Reina whimpered at the thought of more loss, "Thousands of people will lose their homes."

"They have no home, that's the point," Moe said, a bit harsher than I'm sure she intended. Nevertheless, it was the truth.

"Reina, you need to understand that this is not like the last war we fought," I interjected. It was essential she fully grasped the severity of where this was all headed.

"This will be a fight that ends in many deaths, the innocent included. A fight over freedom and autonomy, not just borders or land. You're not a healer or a medic anymore, you're in this as a major player. There's a strong chance that something you do, a settlement you play a role in securing, can end up in the death of your father or brother or even people you don't intend to hurt. By the end of this, if everything goes according to plan, we don't plan on taking survivors of their leadership. If that's too much for you, that's okay. No one will hold it over you. You can go back to healing, to making people feel better about what's going to take place. But I need you to say the word and let us know."

Her face hardened, the blue storm in her eyes raging. "When should we leave?"

Abel, whose visions were not as intense as Moe's, eyes rolled to the back of his head in response. Moe watched on proudly, knowing she'd been working with him on strengthening his gifts to prepare him for the trip. The unsaid being, in the case of her untimely demise.

It was a smart play. I hated referring to it as such, but it was important we had a backup, especially out on the road. I'd hate for Reina or even Abel to be left out there defenseless. Which, technically, they were. At least it felt like it with my absence. I reminded myself that it wasn't true. Both of these women were strong, and had fended for themselves in one fashion or another before arriving at The Compound. The world was different now. Oddly enough, more dangerous than it was years ago.

"Night after next," Abel said, voice cracking a bit.

His tone made Reina uneasy. "You want us to leave at night?" she asked.

"The path of least resistance in this case happens to be the one no one expects." A mix of confidence and jest emerged back in his voice.

Reina groaned, "Oh God, you sound just like Moe."

He beamed at the words, turning to face his new mentor, who simply stared at him with a blank face then turned away. His smile only grew wider at that, knowing that was as close to a thumbs up that she would ever give.

"We'll be right behind you by a few weeks," I said, trying to maintain my composure. "By the time you make it to Monterey, we should only be about a week out from return."

"I know." Abel grinned decisively.

Moe studied my worried demeanor. "You'll be fine without us. We'll see you at home."

My facade nearly faltered, a ball thick in the center of my throat. "You and I both know that's not a promise you can make," I murmured.

"No, but if you two behave, it's as close to a promise as I can get."

How do you prepare yourself to send the last remaining family you have out into a world that is designed to kill them? We were a family who had been broken, beaten down when we were at our lowest, then mended itself into something stronger. Indestructible. I had to have faith in that, because there was nothing else I could do.

Moe spent the rest of her time here training the *brujas* Lola had generously donated to the cause. She had only presented us with one condition: they stay here, safe within the walls of Duluth, until Reina received confirmation that their mission was complete. It made sense, though it would slow down our plans.

Lola didn't want *her* family to be held hostage, used as a bargaining chip, if the settlements we sought to bring on our side chose the more difficult route of dealing with us. There was no option other than to oblige her request. After training with Moe, they would set out on their own journey to perform the ritual on other troops within our alliance. They would not make it to each settlement, but would have a set list of instrumental ones, ones that held a solid number of soldiers and power.

That had been my decision. Did it make me the same as Reina's father, the asshole reigning over Covert Province? Maybe. Tough calls had to be made for the benefit of the greater population. It was better to put our limited resources into those who already held an immense amount of power, make them *stronger*, than to focus on those who would never see the front lines.

I oversaw the initial effort at Duluth, watched as Moe guided them through their practice with specific instructions. Deviating from them was something we couldn't afford. I would stay here with the soldiers they worked through for the next two weeks, training them to master their newfound gifts. The key to that was patience and good temperament. It was a fine line between rushing something that had no business being rushed and working off borrowed time. Because that's what this was—borrowed time from our show of ingenuity in our little valley of death weeks ago.

It gave Covert pause on how to engage with us. They say not to kill the messenger, but I'd made sure some of Sloan's more skilled soldiers doubled back and killed all but two. It had caught them off guard, being hunted down like the animals they were weeks after they'd fled the scene. They'd felt safe, out of dodge, ready to send word to Covert on exactly what we were capable of. That was until the soldiers had shown up with a message to deliver. Killing the messengers also sends a message, and the terrified accounts of the survivors had clearly done so. My instructions to the soldiers had been clear.

Show no mercy.

Alexiares had given specific, detailed directions on how to do so. And I'd be lying if I said it didn't bring a sick sense of joy to watch him in his element. Where Sloan saw the devil, I saw the Hades to my Persephone. My king of this hell of a world.

Power is attracted to power, and that man of mine possessed so much of it. More than he gave himself credit for.

"You ready for this?" I asked, helping Moe secure her extra pack on the back of her horse.

She scoffed, "Did alright on my own the few years before I met you, can handle myself out there just fine."

"You're so brave, Moe. I want to be just like you when I grow up," I said, a broad grin on my face.

Moe playfully bumped against my shoulder. "Look who's talking."

I turned, setting my eyes on Reina, now saying a tearful good-bye to Sloan and her aunt. I was happy she'd gotten this bit of closure after she'd lost so much. But just as that bit of closure had come, she was back out on the road, this time, for the first time, without her brother at her side.

"I'm worried about her," I mumbled, knowing Moe had heard every word.

She sighed in response. "Yeah, me too."

I faced the sister next to me, the black layers drowning her out while allowing her to blend in with the night and remain warm. "I'm worried about you, too."

The surrounding darkness hid it to an extent, but her nose crinkled in response. "I know what I have to do. You shouldn't worry."

"I always will," I said, making sure she not only understood, but knew the gravity of my words. "No matter how far the war takes us from each other."

Her mouth twitched, giving me a half smile. "How many times do you want me to tell you that you shouldn't worry?"

"How much time do you got?" I teased, "Not gonna tell me you're worried about me too?"

"You're annoying, not dumb."

Moe winked, her dark eyes glistening in the moonlight above. We stood there, taking each other in for possibly the last time. I studied every inch of her, from her long dark hair pulled off her pointed, sporadically freckled face. The thick socks creviced over her wool lined boots, her long legs covered by thermo pants and gloves covered her small hands. My sister, my beautiful little demon on my shoulder.

"I don't have to worry about you anymore," she said, her voice gentle as she gestured over toward Alexiares. "You have him. He's good for you."

"Sloan doesn't think that," I snapped. In my defense, I had said I could understand where her concerns rooted from, not that her judgment on him had brushed off me.

Alexiares stood off to the side, engaging in a stern conversation with Abel. Then his features relaxed. Abel reached out offering him a handshake. He looked at it for a moment before pulling him into a hug. I fought the smile from my lips, noticing how comfortable he'd gotten to displaying affection since he'd arrived in Monterey what felt like ages ago. Abel tensed, his face leaning heavenward, and he blinked in quick succession, fighting off the tears that threatened to fall.

He was certainly entitled to being emotional over leaving this place, but the sadness taking over him hadn't been expected. I watched him, realizing this place had become another home to him for the last two and half years.

"Sloan doesn't seem to think about a lot of things," Moe paused, "but that doesn't mean she's not a good friend. I didn't see that before, and I'm sorry for that. I see it clearly now, though. She'd do anything for you. Rough around the edges, but a solid person. Take your time with your goodbyes."

My gaze fell on Moe, studying her for a moment. She would not say more than that. It had already taken all the maturity in her body to say those words. I nodded, pulling her into a tight hug.

"I love you. Be safe," I said.

Her body shuddered against mine. "Always. I love you too, sister. Until fate decides to intervene again."

"Whenever destiny chooses to meddle once more."

She pulled away, walking over in the direction of Alexiares. Moe gave Sloan a tense up down, a quick nod of respect as she passed by, to which Sloan gave her a similar one back.

I moved toward Reina, now leaned over her pack, checking it one last time before she tossed it over her back. She turned at my footsteps, tears immediately coming to the surface. I was in her arms within seconds, the smell of vanilla and something tangy coming from her usual fur coat.

"I … I don't think I've been without you since we met," Reina said in between shaky breaths. She nuzzled her head on the top of my head as if she was trying to remember my scent.

I laughed her off. "That's not true. I've been on plenty of missions where you stayed back."

"I know, but not for this long." She rebutted, "It's weird, like a part of my soul is being left behind."

"Likewise, my sister, likewise." It took everything in me to keep it together. If I fell apart, then she would too, and I needed her to remain confident in herself.

"I'm gonna make you proud, I promise," Reina replied, reading the words right out of my mind.

"You've already made me proud, Reina. There is nothing you need to prove." I reassured her. "You are strong, you are capable, you are more than enough. But you are also kind, don't lose that. Not on my account."

"I will do whatever needs to be done to protect my home. I'm a soldier now, Maia, *your* soldier."

The nickname passing through her lips brought a smile to my face. I took her in, deciding carefully over my next words. Ultimately deciding there was nothing else to say that had been left unsaid. Then I noticed something different for the first time.

"Your hair ..." I said, my fingers reaching for the side of her head.

She beamed at the recognition. "I chopped it. Didn't make much sense to keep it too long. Can be used against me in a fight."

Her long, wavy brown hair was now hovering inches above her shoulders. She pulled it into two tight braids on either side— my battle hair. I swallowed down the words I wanted to say, landing on words of reassurance instead.

"It's beautiful," I offered in compliment instead. It was true, her hair was beautiful; it just wasn't Reina.

"I've got this," she said, her tone strong and unwavering. "I'm going to win us this war, I know it."

Without question, I believed she was capable of fulfilling her role in this. In fact, it had never been a question from the moment

Abel revealed what needed to take place. Something told me she was trying to convince herself more than anyone else.

"Reina, you are a fucking warrior. There's no doubt in my mind." A prideful look crossed over her pale face, confidence exhibiting through her posture. It almost made me halt my next words, but I couldn't do that. She needed to hear this, needed to know she wasn't alone. "It's okay to not be okay … It's okay to not be fine."

Her brows furrowed in confusion. She stepped back nervously. I tucked a stray strand behind her ear with a smile. "What I'm trying to say is, none of us are okay. None of us are fine. And that's okay … In this world we live in, that is okay."

She studied me for a beat, slowly nodding her head. A hint of color found its way back in her cheeks. "This ain't goodbye, ya know? It's a see you later."

I ran my hand down the side of her face, wiping the tears that fell. "We don't say goodbye in this family. Keep your eyes peeled and your head high. I'll see you when I get home."

Our next embrace was tighter than the last, a grip that left no room for words. My body shook in unison with hers as I bit back my tears, to no avail. In a moment of clarity, I slipped an envelope into the side of her coat.

"For Prescott and Riley's eyes only. You can't open it."

Her braids slid across the sides of my face in acknowledgment. Abel and Moe could have no knowledge of this. It could change the course of the war. I could trust Reina to keep this secret, for she knew the threat her brother posed if he learned what lay inside. I loved Moe, but after my birthday, I knew the only mind I could trust to keep him out was my own.

Abel strolled over, hands in the pockets of his puffer coat. "We need to go now or we'll miss our window."

Reina and I separated. She hopped onto her horse. The image staring back at me reminding me of myself almost four years ago.

For she was broken, but not lost. She was now finding her own path ahead and stronger for it. A woman to be feared, a woman much stronger than I would ever be. Her heart and soul would help change this world, I was sure of it.

I faced Abel, a reflection of Riley now meeting me head on. His expression was stern, but I saw right past the bullshit. There was a scared little boy in there, one who was becoming a man before my eyes.

"Riley is going to be beyond fucking happy to see you." I said, "I'm amazed by the man you are, Abel. Thank you for holding down the fort."

There was one final hug I needed to give out. I pulled him taut with my body, whispering into his ear so only he could hear it. "Remember who you are, remember what you're capable of."

His soft words brushed against my ear. "A wise woman once told me to 'fear the quiet ones.'"

I leaned back, grabbing onto the side of his face, meeting his eye even though somehow, over the years, doing so now required me to look up instead of straight on. "I'm never wrong," I said smugly, kissing him gently on the cheek.

"Catch you on the flip side, General." He laughed, humor absent in the words.

Abel finished tying his pack into place, and I watched part of my heart ride off into the night. Three figures of death, on their way to preserve what was left of light and life.

Sloan led her now inconsolable mother away, mourning the loss of their last remaining bloodline. Seth and his father had no longer been considered as such from the moment they chose sides. As they passed, Sloan's features turned tense, a weak smile pulling at the side of her round lips.

Footsteps sounded to my right, and I turned to face the owner of them.

"I saw that," Alexiares said, now at my side.

I brought an innocent visage to my wide eyes. "Don't know what you're talking about, Alexi." A half-assed attempt of a childish grin formed on my face, knowing the name alone had the potential to throw him off.

Strong hands found my waist, and he pulled me close. "Nothing slips by me unnoticed, princess. And distractions only work until they don't," he said, his voice turning deviously low.

A fire burned at my core at the challenge. His touch ignited something in me, though the thoughts inside my mind remained sad. I turned to face him, my fingers grazing the top of his lips before I offered him a gentle kiss.

"How long do I have before the 'until they don't' takes place?" I said, grabbing at the front of his pants. His body greeted me, a slight bulge forming at my touch.

A sinister chuckle escaped his perfect mouth. "Not long at all. Let me know when you're ready to ... how did you say it all those months ago? *Share with the crowd* what was inside that letter."

He left me standing there in the night, cursing the wind for his resistance and praying to all that answered for the safety of those I loved now lost to the darkness.

CHAPTER
TWENTY-TWO

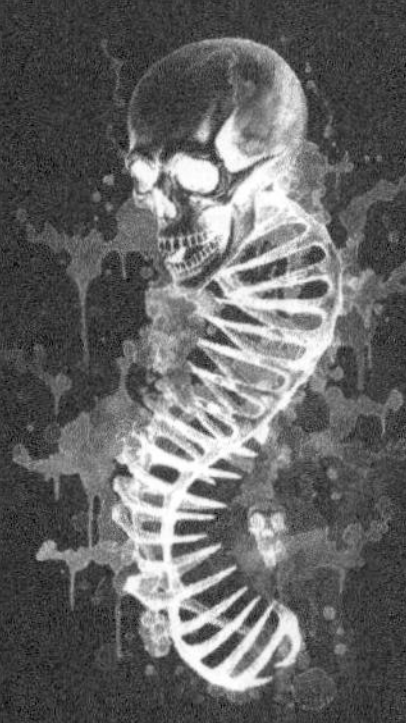

REINA

The sooner we reached Great Falls, the better. I was ready to get back to Monterey. My fingers were about to freeze off from holding the reins, and I was growing so stinkin' tired of the cold. In my mind, if we made it back home, I could pretend for at least a week that everything was okay. It would be too easy to convince myself that my brother was off with Amaia securing our borders, doing routine work, having her back and what not. But then, my sister would make it back home without him, my new brother in tow, and I would be reminded of the truth.

Going back to Montana was haunting. Like I was chasing ghosts or something. The way down to Casper would be worse. We'd just miss passing our ranch right outside Billings. Two weeks on the road would not be preparation enough for the gravity of emotions attacking my psyche. Big Horn County had been home for a long time, a home I'd wanted nothing more than to escape. And I had, against all odds and crumby circumstances, I'd survived. Now I was stuck with that feeling all over again.

Part of me wanted to check on the ranch, see if my home had succumbed to the flames Seth had ordered me to ignite. I wondered if some kind stranger had laid Momma and Hunter's bones to rest. Visiting James' grave would probably do me some good too, a nice healing exercise. At this point, I was convinced inner peace was a bunch of mumbo jumbo until this whole, stupid war was over. What would be the point if I was just going to break all over again?

Passing through Minnesota was not nearly as stimulating as it was on the way to Duluth. With Abel's guidance and connections, we remained unscathed. Between him and Moe, we were able to avoid pretty much every herd of Pansies in our path. Every urban area was the same as Duluth. Brown, dull, and boring as heck. I silently begged for some semblance of action. I understood Amaia now, why she thrived in chaos. Having all this anger inside my body and no outlet for it left me physically itching for a good fight.

Moe, to my great displeasure, had picked up on far too much from my brother when it came to riding. Every time I rallied Bimbo, my lovely lady horse, to ride on ahead, she caught up, sensing what I was up to. Abel trailed behind more times than not. He didn't appear to be mad about it, and I appreciated that about him. Instead, he watched me in understanding. Heck, maybe that was why he'd come up to Duluth on his own in the first place. Something told me his desire to thrive in solitude was not a decision he had taken lightly. Everyone ran from something in their past, eventually.

By the time we hit North Dakota a couple of days later, the flat grasslands made us relatively vulnerable. Something I welcomed. Let them come for us, let them answer to my call of magic. No fight came, however, North Dakota had sided with us. Even Bismarck didn't give two craps once we crossed into their territory. They'd been outnumbered, Fargo and Grand Forks ensuring they stayed in check.

Before I knew it, I was home sweet home. As we approached their natural barriers of rivers and hillsides, my nerves took over at the sight of the makeshift wall. It was a mixture of various woods, metal, and a touch of concrete where it mattered most. A good portion of their community remained outside the walls, the ranching lifestyle not lost on its population. Aside from the animals though, most of those structures had been abandoned in preparation for what was to come.

I bit down on my lip, cursing myself for not asking Amaia more about the inner workings of Great Falls. The knowledge I held of their military or their government was a blank slate. Being unprepared was as good as being dead. Amaia's words, not mine. Shaking off my thoughts, I inhaled deep.

If Amaia hadn't bothered to brief me, it meant she had full confidence my abilities would be more than enough. My sister didn't often make oversights in her judgment during times of war. This had been her plan all along. I just needed to decide which persona I'd have to put on today.

The closer we got to what I presumed to be the front entrance, soldiers lined the outer wall, the thickest bunch gathered directly at the gate. Three hundred feet out, they cleared out in the center and a lone woman took their stead.

"Let me do the talking," I said.

Abel and Moe pulled back on their reins, their horses falling in line behind me. With no objections from the two who had likely seen every outcome of how this could play out, I tossed my ruffled hair and licked at my lips. The arrogant smile I'd seen Amaia put on one too many times took over my features. It was showtime.

"Hi, darling." I gave a flirtatious wave, my smile pretty. "I'd introduce us, but by the weapons now raised in our face, I'd say y'all know exactly who we are."

A woman around my age kept a stern face, unimpressed by my gesture. Her long blonde hair cascaded down her back, tucked under a brown cowboy hat that reminded me of my brothers. Her green eyes bore into mine and it took everything in me not to wince.

She gave a small nod of the head, fingers tucked into the pocket of her blue jeans. I glanced down at her wrist, resting on her holstered pistol. "If we wanted you to pay us a visit, we woulda made that known, *darling*."

"Is the boss around, or should I leave a message at the gate?" To be completely honest, I wasn't sure what I should say.

In the past, our relationships had already been fairly established on my emissary visits. That made it a hundred times easier to do my job, knowing I'd have to knock someone on the wrong side of the head to mess things up. Now, I was walking in unknown territory, literally.

My comment earned me no favors, she remained unimpressed. "You're talkin' to her."

Well crud.

I shrugged nonchalantly. "Didn't realize it. Don't hear much from out your way."

"Interestin' perspective given you're here at our gates," she said.

I kept a blank stare; she still hadn't called me by name, which meant there was a good chance she only knew where we were from and not us individually. My magic spread itself among as many soldiers that were within its grasp. *Fear.* I sensed nothing but fear. They were scared, even though they didn't know who we were.

Pushing deeper, I tried to pick up on anything else that would be helpful. Their fear was powerful, too strong for an armed group of people to be of three young people strolling up on some horses. I was wrong—they weren't scared of us per se, they were scared of what lay ahead in the near future.

"Sure we are!" I exclaimed, a mischievous smile pulled at my lips, knowing I was about to ruin their day. "But the real question is, are we here to warn you or make you bend the knee?"

"Warn us?" The woman gestured to the wall and the group of people surrounding her. "We appear unprepared to you?"

I gave a slight nod, Moe rode up next to me joining her hand into my now extended one. She closed her eyes, focusing on the scene she wanted to unravel, my gaze steady on the intense green eyes ahead. I didn't need to close my eyes to see the vision Moe unleashed, none of us did.

Carnage, death, rotted corpses lined the wall. Decapitated heads staked in a walkway straight to their front gate. Our magic mingled together, intensifying their fear, turning it into desperation. Some of the men at her side fell on all fours, grasping the air in front of them, seeing their loved ones' shattered bodies instead of the green pasture. A wave of sadness cascaded through their being, one by one, I focused my energy on them. Preying on whatever weakness I could find, determined to heighten the worst of their most prevalent emotions.

When Moe released my hand, I was met with a look of horror. The green eyes on the woman at the gate lightened with a welling of tears. She straightened her composure, the tan in her skin returning from the ghostly pale it had faded to.

Slowly, she forced a warm smile. Her hand shot into the air, and the gate behind her opened at her command. "Come right on in."

"That's one thing I love about being home, Moe," I said with charm, "you can always expect some real hospitality."

The gate creaked open, we hopped off our horses leaving them to an older woman with frizzy gray hair and bronze skin. We followed the blonde-haired girl into what resembled a western front town during the time of expansion west. I remembered what Seth had taught me since we were kids along with what Amaia had enforced during our journey to Duluth. Staying vigilant of our surroundings was key to getting out of a sticky situation. *And a sticky situation this is.*

It was a dizzying task, checking for the exits and taking note of the elevated watchtowers lining their wall. Not only did I have to focus on the essential infrastructure checkpoints, but I also had to keep my eye on the disgruntled citizens grumbling under their breath at our presence as we walked through their town.

Carefully, I sent my powers out to the scariest, broodiest ones of the bunch, calming their nerves. Whether it was for their sake or mine, I wasn't quite sure. All I knew was that if they received us well, their disgruntled leader would be more inclined to work with us. I wouldn't touch her with my gifts, not yet, not now that she expected them. Something about her overall demeanor made me wary. Overlooking their outer appearance, she reminded me of Jessa. Cunning and smart, a woman who knew her way through the world.

I had missed her throughout the journey to Duluth. In between getting chased through the woods and tortured in a random basement and all. She was as wild as I was, never one to be held down by another. I valued our relationship, and for a long time, the freedom it provided. Then I remembered what had happened the morning I'd left.

When I thought about it, I couldn't exactly remember when she'd even arrived. One day I'd been talking up Elie at the coffee counter and she'd flirted her way into taking my cup, forcing me to wait on the new one to brew. Then I began seeing her around

The Compound. Frequenting the places I loved, it seemed like a fairytale. Fairytales aren't real though, she made that very clear.

The blonde woman led us into a cabin-like building at the center of their town, the jolt of the door against the wall bringing me back to focus. It was a simple layout, one large room. Near the back sat a dark oak desk. She took a seat, motioning for us to do the same. Moe and Abel sat in the two plush chairs that flanked the one directly across from the woman.

I glanced around at the decor, "Cozy place, could probably use a woman's touch."

A terrifying smile formed on her plump lips, "It has the only woman's touch that matters," her voice was cold.

"My apologies, Ms. …"

She scanned over my body, briefly halting at the outline of my breasts exposed from my unbuttoned coat. "Millie," she said, offering no other information.

"Ah, yes, Millie. The animal heads mounted to the wall and overwhelming amount of plaid made me think we were borrowing someone's office."

Something was off, I just couldn't put my finger on it.

Millie said nothing, just stared at me with hardened eyes. After a moment of tense silence, she smiled again. "You all parched? Can I offer you something to drink? Coffee, tea, a good ole bourbon?"

"Waters fine," I parlayed. "Thank you."

She raised her hand again, the man standing guard at the door brought over a pitcher and four cups. He filled hers to the brim, stopping halfway with ours while holding my eye, a snarl forming in lieu of a smile.

I glanced away, studying Millie, trying to find an in. No matter which way I pried, she offered no additional information. I didn't know much of Great Falls, well, really nothing at all. I did, however, know that Amaia knew every woman in power throughout our network, a network Great Falls had once been in. There was something off here, and I couldn't quite place my finger on it.

A silver band rested along her ring finger. Pointing to it, I asked, "There a Mr. somewhere around here?"

Millie frowned, a solemn look gracing her pretty features. "There *was* a Mrs. Are you here to talk business, or do you plan on keeping up with the misogynistic bullshit you've been leading with?"

Abel coughed a laugh, finding humor in the way I was butchering things. I clenched my jaw, maybe I was coming off too strong. But now, I knew I had an opening.

I gave her a kind-hearted grin, "You're right. Let's start over. I'm Reina, this is Moe and Abel. We're here to let you know it's in your best interest to follow in Billings and Missoula's stead. Courtesy General Bennett of Monterey Compound, of course."

"Just Monterey?" Millie's nose scrunched quizzically, "Last I heard she's got her claws in all of Salem Territory and most of The Expanse."

The mention of my sister's power warmed my heart. Dang right she had her claws in half the continental US. Rightfully so too, the reliance on her had not been an unearned decision. These people were lucky she cared enough to include them in her plans. I wanted so badly to let her know we could leave them to be damned like Madison, but we weren't. They were blessed when others would lose everything.

"What can I say? Don't you love a woman in power? I know I do." I smirked at her, bringing my eyes slowly up every graceful line in her body visible from her seat. Flipping my hair to the side, I leaned forward, bringing her face to face.

She shifted in her seat, head tilting in curiosity. "As a matter of fact, I do. So on with it, tell me why me and my people should join your cause."

The door behind us flew open, a slender man walked in, though his size did nothing to diminish the aura of power he possessed. His hair was a brighter blond than hers tucked neatly behind his ears underneath a matching cowboy hat. He pulled his leather gloves off slowly, first taking my family and me in, then tracing over the woman behind the desk.

Millie jumped up, her tan face flushing under the scrutiny. "Father! You're back early."

Confusion pressed my brows together, not understanding what was happening. Shock seeped from her and my initial suspicions were confirmed.

"I am," he said sternly. "Imagine my confusion finding out a group of Monterey arrived before I did."

"Sir," I responded, offering him a tense nod as I rose to my feet.

Moe and Abel shot up at my side. Moe's hand moved behind her back. Abel brushed it away, pretending to be off balance in his step.

"Millie, please show our guests suitable arrangements for the evening." Though his face remained kind, the command behind his words was clear. "It just so happens, I'm willing to entertain whatever this Moore," his long fingers outstretched pointing directly in my face, "is here to spew. I'd like to settle in, my time beyond the walls was … exhausting. We'll discuss it over dinner."

Millie nodded, throwing an uncomfortable glance in my direction before gesturing for us to follow. We made it a few steps outside before Moe opened her mouth. For as long as I knew her, she had never been one to resist the urge to taunt someone that was already knocked far off their high horse.

"A woman in power, indeed," Moe said, smirking to herself.

SIMILAR TO MONTEREY, THE HOMES DID NOT HAVE INDIVIDUAL ROOMS to wash up, but rather conjoined bathing houses shared between a few homes. Moe and I shared one bathing pool while Abel lingered in one on the other side. His eyes flitted between the both of us, throwing a flirtatious smile and wave. I sent my magic over, splashing him completely, and water dripped from the small tight curls that had grown out during our travels.

"Hey! Just making sure everyone's okay," he exclaimed.

Moe waved him off, "We're just fine, you would know if we weren't."

I was glad he was here, valued the new perspective he brought. At times, I wondered if he was brought into my life to remind me of who I was. I could finally understand what Amaia meant when she said Moe was to keep her honest and I was to keep her good. Maybe that was why she'd sent me off with them both.

When we made it back to our shared room, two dresses were laid out on one bed, a pair of slacks and a polo on the other. *My kind of place*, I grinned, running my fingers down the beautiful long black dress. The slit at the side and the thigh high cowboy boots to pair.

Moe grumbled at her similar apparel, not impressed by what it had to offer. Hers was gray, her least favorite shade to put on, and her boots were white. I'd offer to trade, but that would mean I'd have to sacrifice the outfit that brought the essence of home.

We got dressed, following a note on the door on the way out. It directed us to stop at the house at the furthest point in town, we'd be dining at Millie and her father's home. A private location for what we'd planned to discuss. I didn't know if that excited me or not. On one hand, that meant no audience and, thus, no need to hold back on our end. But that also meant the same for them, they could dispose of us with little resistance. It would be as if we never arrived, despite the few people who had watched our entrance.

They lived in a humble home, resembling the ranch styled abode I'd grown up in. I fought off tears that threatened to form in my eyes. The floral couch at the center of the living room was nearly identical to the one passed on from my grandparents to my father. The one my momma had begged him to get rid of to no avail. She was desperate to bring a small remnant of her coastal lifestyle into our home.

The second we took our seats at the long, candle lit dining table, her father cleared his throat, calling our attention to him. "I've welcomed you into my home. Clothed you, now I'm feeding you. Here is your chance to convince me to not make my kindness come with a price," he said, hazel eyes trained on me.

Millie's gaze bored into my own as I nervously peered around. There was pleading behind her stare, like there was something she wanted me to refrain from divulging. She fumbled with the silverware surrounding the empty plates, her hands trembling with her own nerves. I couldn't figure out what, I hardly knew her to have even an inkling on what she needed. But the way she looked at me, it became obvious that she would be the key to securing this alliance.

Reaching for the diced potatoes at the center of the table, I helped myself to the food when no one else dared. I cleared my throat, "Thank you for your hospitality, a nice dinner is quite the treat after our time out on the road. I'm famished."

Moe followed my lead, reaching for the corn in front of her. Abel sat there, staring down at his lap unmoving. He felt my stare, reluctantly he grabbed the glass of red wine, taking a timid sip.

"Please, help yourselves," he said, gesturing to the spread of food before us. "I'm sure my daughter made it clear that is our main prerogative here."

I tilted my head, narrowing my eyes at him skeptically, "I'm not sure I follow."

"Helping ourselves," the man doubled-down. "That's what we do best, that's how we've survived this long, and we intend to keep it that way."

"What do you think we do out in Monterey?" Moe reached for the roasted chicken at the same time as him, pulling it toward herself without breaking her stare.

He gave her a polite grin, motioning for her to *help herself* as an example. "Help everyone *but* yourselves, from what we've heard."

"Then you've heard wrong," Moe countered, biting into a leg then offering him the scraps in challenge.

Millie coughed, drawing the attention to her. "Care to elaborate?" she asked, eyes set on me.

"I'm assuming you mean General Bennett?" I concluded, scrunching my nose at the bitterness of the wine. "If you've heard of The Compound, then I'm sure you've also heard how hard her and Prescott have worked to make it a welcoming place. Type of place where people can do exactly as you say, help themselves to the life they desire."

"At a sacrifice to their own wellbeing, I'm sure," Millie's dad countered without skipping a beat.

"I don't think I caught your name yet, what should I address you as? Surely, it's not Millie's father," I extended my hand with a mocking grin.

Millie snickered under her breath, silenced by the glare of her father. "Nash is fine," he said, taking my hand with a tight squeeze.

"What a lovely name, Nash." I batted my eyelashes, letting him see me as the naive girl he believed me to be. "You see, a good leader knows that a sacrifice to themselves often benefits their people. While my general and her counterparts may be subjectively self-sacrificial, our people thrive. The people within our network *thrive*. After all, a helping hand is a benefit to us all. Something I'm sure you remember during the last war."

Nash shifted uncomfortably in his seat, his knuckles tightened around the knife he used to dig into his chicken. "We did not fight in the last war."

Abel jumped in, sparing me a response, "Oh, we know, Nash. That doesn't matter; while you all sat back idly and watched the world around you fall into turmoil, the few people here still gained from all of our loss. We're not gonna let that happen a second time."

I squinted my eyes, nearly missing the flickering of his eyes as he spoke. *Holy moly. Go, Abel.* I sensed that there was more to Abel and his gifts than him or Amaia had let on.

"Excuse me?" Nash thundered, his fist pounded the top of the table at the mild threat.

"It's not a threat," Moe said with a thin smile. "It's a warning, as we said we were here to offer. You side with Covert, then you'll understand what a *real* threat is."

Nash focused on me, eyes narrowing with accusation. He raised his knife, scoffing as he pointed it across the table in my face.

"You're Reina Moore, your *father* is the threat," Nash scoffed. "Yet here you stand, on the other side."

I shrugged, deciding to bring up the obvious. "Shouldn't that tell you enough? If his daughter fights against him, why would you want to be on his side?"

"Your brother stands by him," Millie said, her plate remaining untouched, hands in her lap.

"I thought you understood women in power." I snapped my attention toward her. "Why would a woman align herself with misogynistic, prejudiced men?"

Millie's mouth tightened, her eyes darted away from me and over to her father.

"So, that's your final argument?" Nash sneered, unimpressed. "That is a foolish reason to get us to fight on your side."

Millie put her hand out, timidly silencing her father. "Who said we even wanted to fight at all?"

"To not fight," Abel said calmly, "to not choose a side *is* choosing a side."

"You think you can do what you did in the last war, but you're wrong. That vision we showed you, that was not our own projections. That was the true outcome for your people if you don't fight with us," Moe insisted, nothing but honesty in her eyes.

I'd had little control over the vision portion of our power sharing. Truthfully, I hadn't even stopped to think if what we'd shown them had been real.

"What is she talking about?" Nash whipped around to face his daughter, daggers flying from his glare.

"They showed us a vision when they arrived at the gates," Millie stopped, trying to recall what she saw. "I thought it was a trick of the mind—"

Nash shoved himself free from the confines of the table, pacing around his seat. "What kind of vision?"

"It was so vivid, like nothing before," Millie recalled, tucking her hair behind her large, pointed ear. "How did you do that? My own rest inside my mind, unable to be shared and only described."

Seer *and Supra*. We hadn't realized she was either, let alone both.

She had a powerful build that I'd attributed to riding. Most of the girls I'd grown up knowing had a similar frame. Riding had never interested me much outside a contender in my array of hobbies, so I hadn't been as blessed in the thigh area as them.

Moe offered a cunning smirk. "A secret we only disclose to those we trust."

"If you aren't ready to trust us, then you should walk right back through those gates," Nash taunted us, walking his fingers around the air.

"Father," Millie's lips pulled into a thin line.

Nash slapped the wall, silencing her for a split second. "Quiet, Millie."

"No, Father," Millie commanded, rising to her feet in defiance. Genuine concern scattered her simple features. "You be quiet. We need to hear them out. What they showed us, we'll be destroyed."

He said nothing, only stared at her with the promise of punishment later. I feared for her, the anger spewing from his flesh was overwhelming. I'd witnessed the other end of anger like that before.

"You think you can trust Covert Province, my father, my brother, but you can't," I said, taking my cue from the floor to speak Millie had given me. "They will take what they need from your people. And the woman you speak so poorly of … she will wipe you from this land you call home and show no mercy. General Bennett is kind, welcoming, she cares for her own. All kindness has its limits. If you get in her way, there will be no *you* left to look out for."

Nash's brows quivered. He stopped pacing, forcing an unbothered countenance back over his demeanor. "Sure, that's why you're here then. Because the powerful need help from the powerless?"

"No, we're here because we request your help to make things easier on our soldiers, our resources. As I said, we care for our own. The fewer the casualties, the better," I reasoned, patting a napkin on the corners of my mouth from the delicious meal accompanying this show. "Make no mistake about our intentions, declining this offer may save your lives for a few months. But when war comes this way, because it will, darlin'. You can bet on it. We won't be taking any prisoners."

"Such a sweet and innocent looking girl. You're a fool, a weak fool that thinks she has power, that she can control things, but you can't. You show up at my gates making idle threats disguised as a warning with two half-assed Seers showing us the worst-case scenario." Nash leaned against the table, scoffing as he scanned Abel and Moe up and down, "See, in our meeting with Covert, I wondered, what would make a father abandon his little girl. I couldn't bring myself to come to terms with the idea of family turning against each other."

He took a seat back in his chair, Millie following suit. Her gaze was a laser, eyes narrowing in on him in disbelief. Nash ignored her, keeping his focus on me. "I found your father to be a bit ruthless, in my opinion, but I see now what he saw. A lost little puppy that jumps to the command of her owner. You can pretend all you want over in Monterey that kindness and empathy get you far, out here on the battlefield, your general proves otherwise. Many of the people that lie here within our border were *victims* of her misjudgment in the last war. Came here when they had nothing else left after the idiots in Billings did Bennett's bidding out in Yellowstone. Covert has offered us a pardon, to leave our people unscathed in a fight that is not our own. All we have to do is follow their rules, rules that don't matter when you are thousands of miles away. Rules that don't matter if you have a seat at their table."

Moe banged her glass down on the table, forcing Abel to leap back with a loud screech of the chair. I reached my hand out to them, calming one's anger and the other's nerves. Millie's eyes landed on me, watching me in awe.

"I'm the fool?" I laughed, fixating on Nash. "You can't even see what's going on around you in your own home. When we first arrived, it very much appeared like everyone here had Millie's back. But I couldn't help but notice that they cowered at your presence."

"Do you have a point?" Nash's glass shattered, cutting the flesh in the corner of his palm.

"My gifts," I explained, taking note of his lack of reaction to the trauma on his hand. "They sense primitive emotions. Things like fear, happiness, lust, *anger*."

"And my people are angry?" He scoffed in disbelief, wiping his bleeding hand on the table cloth like a barbarian.

"While there were a mix of emotions here, my best advice to you would be to let someone like my general, someone like your daughter"—I nodded my head toward Millie—"have a say. While fear certainly makes the wolf appear bigger, after a while, a wolf can lose its pack. And no one fears a lone wolf, instead, they seek to put the nuisance down."

I finished my class of wine, leaving both my plate and glass clear. Slowly, I folded the napkin from my lap and placed it down on the table.

Moe and Abel rose at my side, waiting for me at the door as I glanced between Millie and Nash, grinning sweetly at Millie. "We'll take our leave come first light. Thank you for your hospitality."

"That went well," Moe grumbled as she kicked the gravel from the center town road.

I clenched my fists, fighting the urge to make a less than pretty face at her. "It would have helped if everyone around me wasn't just leaving it up to my own volition on how to handle this."

"Reina, please," Moe scoffed, disregarding my complaints.

"No, I'm serious. Y'all act like I'm supposed to know how to handle things simply because I made sure a few settlements would share some science and mend a few relationships over the years. I'm not a war mastermind. I'm not Amaia, I'm not Seth …" I let out a frustrated huff, gaze fixated on the starry night sky. Time stretched as I collected my thoughts and tailored my emotions. "I don't know what the heck I'm doing, and it would be nice if I could get some support."

"You're doing fine, Reina," Moe reassured me, but her tone lacked authentic kindness. "There's nothing we could have done in there to change how it would have turned out."

I don't know when Tomoe became such a Negative Nancy in my life, but at the moment I found myself lacking the patience for it. Abel cleared his throat, trying to disrupt some of the tension between us. When no apology came from either of them, I stormed off ahead of them, wishing I could be anywhere but here.

Abel jogged up next to me, his presence lingering like a parasitic nuisance at my side. The last thing I wanted to take on right now was some more angst, and he reeked of it.

"Buzz off, Abel," I muttered.

"I'm not leaving you to be alone right now," he said, hand falling upon my upper back. "I can be your silent buddy. You're right, everybody needs some support."

I shook him off, not telling him to go away again.

The room remained silent when we got back. Each of us prepared for bed, no one wanting to be the first to speak, to apologize. I had no intention of apologizing for my outburst, and I'm pretty sure Tomoe felt the same dang way. Abel shot us concerned glances periodically, trying to figure out how to approach the mood now looming over us. Ultimately, he landed on the idea that shutting the heck up would be best for him and fell asleep, mouth open and snores blaring.

Tomoe drifted off soon after, leaving me awake with my thoughts at her side. A slight tap sounded at the door, so light I swore I was hearing things. The knock came again, this time harder yet still muted. I slid from the bed, tugging my nightgown further down to limit my exposure.

I cracked the door open, Millie stood there in front of me, face blank and mouth unmoving. "What do you want? I don't need another blow to my ego tonight, spare me," I whispered roughly.

"I think we both know we're not the same as our fathers," she replied like her presence alone wasn't an inconvenience to my night. "Come with me."

I gave her a quick once over then closed the door in her face. Tip-toeing across the room, I dressed myself in my thermo leggings and heavy coat, leaving my boots for last when I got outside.

Millie sat on the first step to the house, a literal jump scare when I opened the door and I bit down my yelp.

She took off the second my boots were laced up, leading the way outside the gate. I kept quiet, interested in where she was taking me against my better judgment. But truly, who listens to their better judgment these days? Not anyone I knew, that's for sure.

"Mind telling me where you're taking me?" I asked as she tossed the saddle over one of the horses tied up near the gate.

"Somewhere where we can talk … in private." She hopped on, extending me a hand.

I pretended to consider my options, knowing deep down, I wanted to be anywhere *but* here. Ignoring her hand, I pulled myself up, refusing to hold on to her for support.

It was nearly pitch black, the only source of light the stars in the cold night sky. That didn't hinder Millie one bit. We arrived at a set of stable buildings my family and I had passed on our way in about a mile from Great Falls' walls.

Millie hopped off, this time not offering me any assistance. "No one's been here since we got word of what was comin'. We're safe to talk," she said, pushing the creaking red door open.

I followed close behind, "Well, you've got me here. I'm all ears."

She lit a few candles around the room. The stable office was less than impressive. Everything in here was made of wood and covered in cobwebs. I brushed some off as I took a seat.

Millie smiled at me, one that let me know she had more than a singular motivation for bringing me out here. "I like you, you're adorable."

I crossed my legs, lowering a brow at the suggestive undertone. "What happened to your wife?" I deadpanned, not beating around the bush.

"Dead," she replied, her tone unattached from the statement. "Died in that first week, turned into one of those zombie shits."

Millie fiddled with the ring, sliding it off and placing it in the top drawer of the desk she leaned against. "I keep it on to keep those assholes from messing with me. No one tries a grieving widow."

I smirked, thinking of Amaia and how that was *so* not true with my new brother. He didn't care one bit, I could tell. The fight at the river had solidified it. I could see right then and there how he would die for her. Didn't know a single man in her life who wouldn't. But Alexiares would do more than just die for her, he would kill for her too. I missed them, wished they were here. She was a lot better at this strategy mess than I was.

"What are you smilin' about?" she asked, eyes curiously lit in the dim candlelight.

"My friend," I said, and it was true. "But how that is a load of horse crap with her man."

"You mean your general and the Bloodhound?"

Feathering through my hair, I tugged at the ends as I observed her warily. I'd said nothing of Alexiares, and as far as I knew, no one but Finley and those at The Compound knew he had acquainted himself with us, much less knew he traveled with us to Duluth. "So you know more than you let on," I hissed.

"I knew enough to be comfortable inviting you in, my father cleared up the rest," she countered.

I leaned back in my seat, letting the room fall mute. I wasn't really sure why, just knew I'd seen Amaia make people squirm in her silence when she commanded power. Seth had said something one time about how whoever spoke first after a moment of silence lost, so I guess that's what I would do now. Millie had dragged me here after all, it was time she came out with what she had to say.

She tsked, pressing herself off the desk and pulling a flask from the pocket of her coat. Her back turned to me as she strode across the room, returning with two glass cups in hand. Millie handed me one, and I accepted, watching her with narrowed eyes as she poured me a shot.

We sipped in silence, Millie studied me, a smoldering look on her tan freckled face. I knew exactly what she wanted, could feel it. Scratch that, I could practically taste it, the lust simmering off her was strong.

"I'm inclined to be on your side, Reina," she said once the silence had gone on for too long. "There's not many people up here like you and I, and if there are, they're still stuck in more … traditional ways of living. My father's a bigot, if you haven't noticed. Makes people uncomfortable."

I tapped my fingers against the arm of the chair. "I understand; my father was the same way."

"It's funny, you know, how they claim to love us still. Yet somehow, they can't love *all* of us. We're their perfect little girls, 'except.'" A humorless laugh left her heart-shaped lips.

I knew exactly what she meant; it was part of the reason I wanted to leave Montana behind. My brother assumed it was the ranch, but it was really the entirety of life out here in general. There was a place out there that was better for me, I'd always known that.

Venturing out into the city, where no one knew me, where I knew no one, that was the dream. Sure, my mother and brothers had accepted me, but my father, some of the comments he'd made at my expense had been cruel. None of them came to my defense. No one wanted to be on the other side of his remarks, but even still, I'd come to their aid, shifting attention from them to myself. They rarely did the same. Only in private had they offered me their support, and what was done in the dark in one Moore room, didn't dare be brought to light in whichever one my father occupied.

"I wouldn't trade my life out here for a thing though," Millie continued. "I love it, the freedom, the fresh air. My horses. It's why I never left, why I stayed even when the apocalypse came for us all."

I shrugged, not knowing where she was going with this or what she expected me to say. "I get what you mean."

"But you didn't stay, did you? You ran."

"I had no home to go back to," I snickered, "burned it down to the ground."

There was no benefit in telling her why, letting her know it was at my brother's request, that it hadn't been something I'd done willingly. I certainly didn't reveal that in the end, I hadn't been the one to fire off that flame wielding arrow, hadn't had the stomach to. My brother had though, the same way he destroyed everything he touched that kept holding him back, including me.

"Of course you did," Millie laughed, offering me another over-poured shot on bitter liquid. "I wish I could be as brave as you."

Another person awarding me for unearned bravery. The girl who was deemed brave for simply existing, for playing her part at someone else's command. I wished they would open their eyes and see it was wrong, I was only surviving, much like the rest of them.

"You can be too," I pushed, "if you do what's right."

She downed her drink, watching me, awaiting me to do the same. I paused for a moment, taking a quip of air before downing what was in my cup and holding it out for her to refill. Millie did no such thing, instead, she took a long swig from the flask.

"Is she as great as they say?" she asked earnestly.

"Depends on what you've heard," I shrugged. "I often find that she's better than what they say."

Millie sighed, pulling her long hair back behind her shoulders. "I want that, for my people. For this place. There're families here, children that could have a real future ahead of 'em. This place ain't much, but it's better than whatever the hell they'd be facing out there. Certainly better than whatever your father has to offer."

I uncrossed my legs, giving a slight nod. "Don't think your father see things that way."

"My father is a moron," she mumbled, taking another swig.

Now she has my attention. "Well, hands up if you have daddy problems." I laughed hoarsely.

In unison, we threw both of our hands up, painful belly laughs filled the air. Nothing was funny about that statement, not even remotely, but the fact that I had someone to relate to, under such cruddy circumstances, was. I mean hey, if you don't laugh, you'll cry, and I was so stinkin' sick of crying.

"Is that why you asked me here?" I pressed for more information, "To talk about how much we hate our fathers?"

"No," she said impatiently. "I asked you here because I agree with you. This place needs a woman's touch, and I've decided it's time to make that happen."

"How do you mean?" I extended my cup out, quickly chucking back the shot as soon as it entered my glass.

The room was spinning now. I didn't want drinking to become one of the many coping mechanisms at my disposal. I'd seen the way it had torn Amaia apart, limited her logical thinking. Though my sister had come back stronger, I was just fine learning my lessons through her mistakes. Funny as life would have it, the moment I was in right now, it felt good to let go. To relax.

"How else does any woman come to power?" Millie chided, rubbing the nape of her neck. "On the backs of weak, broken men."

"You plan to overthrow your father and you want our help?"

"I plan to kill my father, and I don't need anyone's help." Her pupils dilated, swallowing her emerald eyes, the hand grasping the flask trembled. "I figured that was something you'd understand given you'd do the same if you could, right?"

I gulped. *Could I? Would I?* The answer was yes, *I think.* No, *I know.* That didn't make the idea any easier, I hadn't exactly pulled it off the first go round.

"Right." I reasoned, "I understand why my father needs to die, but why would you kill yours? Surely you don't need to kill him to overthrow him."

Her lips turned down, contemplation encasing her soft features. "That fear you sensed, the mix of emotions … you're barely touching the surface of it. My father is not a kind man, never has been, never will be. There is no changing a man like him. If he has a seat at your father's table the way he claims, it will only get worse around these parts. Worse for everyone. He's been small-minded since I was a child. Cruel men do not become good when the world falls to shit. Things will only get worse once your father gets involved. My home will become a mini-Covert, and that is something I can not allow. There's good people here, some that support him, the assholes I speak about, but the rest … they're just honest people who want a home. A place filled with peace. A place like Salem, like Monterey Compound. And if we're going to get absorbed into another way of living, another territory, I'd rather it be on the right one. The good one."

I jeered at that, recalling words I'd heard not too long ago. "There is no good and evil in war; there is one wrong side, and the one that's slightly better."

"Did your general tell you that?" she asked, adjusting the cuffs of her coat, refusing to meet my eye.

I nodded. She didn't look up, but I saw her take me in from the corner of her eye.

"That's exactly why I choose her." Millie said, "What I need from you is whatever secrets y'all are keeping that allow you and Tomoe to play that trick of the mind. That's not a God-given power. I'm not the smartest woman around, but I'm smart enough to know that's not something anyone else out there can do."

"That comes with time, and not from either of us. When you're ready," I gave her an empathetic stare, insinuating the death of her father, not wanting to say the words aloud. "We'll send a team out, they'll take care of the rest."

Millie said nothing, just poured what was left of the alcohol into both our glasses. She clinked her glass against mine, and we tossed the contents back.

"So be it," she said with a nod of the head. "Give me a few weeks. I'll send word when it's done."

"You don't have a few weeks; we can give you one."

I didn't know how much time we had, only that we didn't have long. The more urgency I placed on this, the better Amaia's reinforcements would be. That was all that mattered, that I was able to get that chess piece filled map to be set up exactly the way she wanted. The way she needed it to be to protect us all.

Millie grinned slyly. "And where should I send this messenger, Reina."

She leaned forward, eyes trailing every inch of my body. A thrill of excitement tingled down my spine.

"Duluth," I whispered, my breath intertwining with hers.

"Consider this the start of something new then. Should we seal the contract with a kiss?"

Millie pushed herself to the edge of the desk, bringing her closer to my face, her eyes landing on my mouth. I peered up, meeting her intense stare, weighing the pros and cons of the option now laid at my feet.

There was a brief moment of hesitation, where my thoughts and all the logic in my body surfaced. Everything in my life right now was wrong, a freaking miserable mess with no real hope of being set right. Even at the end of this war, I would have a broken family, one less brother to call my home his. One less brother to call a brother. Possibly more depending on if the boys made it out to see the other side of this.

People were counting on me, their lives were now in my hands, and I understood Amaia. Understood exactly why she constantly wanted to run for the hills and abandon all her responsibilities, say screw it and just be normal. Just exist in whatever remnants of the world remained. Then it dawned on me why she stuck around—you could not run from your responsibilities, you could only avoid them. And you can only avoid the weight of the world on you for so long before it comes crashing down on you, suffocating any life in you that you had left.

But there were choices in this life of duty and obligations, choices that helped you forget, even for a moment, the pain that threatened to do you in. And Millie was giving me a choice. One that could make or break this alliance. Millie would still side with us, I knew that, but it would be easier if she was … more inclined to bend to my sister's will.

Or mine.

Long blonde hair tickled my mouth as she hovered over me, awaiting permission. I granted it to her, tilting my head up my lips becoming flush with hers. Millie's fingers caressed the strands of my hair pulling me closer to her. I grabbed her waist, bringing her down onto my lap, straddling my waist. Her mouth opened, granting my tongue access to her mouth. There was no passion here, just need. Desire.

I bit at her bottom lip, her grin pulling them tight. "Take this off," I commanded.

She complied, releasing me from her grasp as she slid her coat off. Her sweater was next, revealing the lack of bra underneath. Round, full breasts welcomed me, urging me to reach out and touch the peak of her nipples. With her hands clasped against my cheeks she stroked her thumb against my lips, my teeth grazing over it as I took it into my mouth and sucked.

"You next," Millie whimpered.

The order brought me pure joy. I yanked my clothes off quickly, baring myself to her and surrendering myself to the moment.

Pulling her back onto my lap, I placed her nipple in between my teeth, taking turns in an attempt to discover which one I favored the most. Gently massaging them, my tongue flicking, circling, craving the sweet taste of her skin. She released a moan, her hair falling down her back. It tickled my skin, light as a whisper, gently kissing over where my nails dug into her.

Her hips bucked against me demanding I redirect my attention to getting the tight pants off her curved hips and down her thick thighs. Thighs meant for riding, I smirked. *My favorite.*

Millie stood, dancing out of her panties, and dragged me down onto the ground. The moment my head touched the floor she kneeled over my shoulders, her ass brushing against my now exposed nipples. My tongue teased against her most sensitive spot. She begged me to slow down.

I did no such thing.

I had thought her skin was sweet, but the juices falling from her were sweeter than cherry pie. She pulsated on my face, her legs squeezing against the side of my head, wetness from her dripping down into my mouth. There was no air left for me to breathe, and I welcomed the lack of oxygen. She let out a scream. I pushed her up, sliding out from beneath her.

"What are you doing?" she asked panting for air.

I brought my hand over her mouth, closing in directly behind her, using my other hand to guide the back of her to a tilt. Dragging my tongue right up her center, I didn't stop until I reached the crevice of her ass then made my way back down. Over and over again as I worked around the spots that made her wiggle the most.

Millie let out a gasp, as I pumped two fingers inside her. Moving my body in cue with my fingers, I pulled at the lengths of her hair. Her pleasure became my own.

When she had enough, she turned over, kneeling directly in front of me. Her eyes locked on mine, lust seeping right off her. She grinned as I indulged, reveling in her lust and letting it encase me. It was my favorite part of sex, all the emotions that I could take on. It fed me, brought me toward my climax in a way that people without my gifts could not.

She moved closer, our knees intertwining, forcing our bodies to touch. Millie grinded against my thigh, I returned her efforts. Slowly, our bodies moved together, my mouth found hers. I let out a soft moan that drove her wild and she sped up.

I pushed my desire outward, letting it feed into her soul, careful not to invade her self-will. Always leaving the option for her to stop but also keeping watch for an invitation. One I accepted once she realized what I was doing. She gave into the cravings and I wiped away all aspects of her pain. Neither of us would benefit from the emotion.

Blissful, precious minutes passed. When we were done, she pulled me into a spooning position, resting her chin atop my shoulder. She kissed it gently, then the nape of my neck, and finally, the back of my head. Sadness seeped from her, not from our act, but from what she knew she'd have to do, what she would have to plan when she left here.

I took it away, accepting her pain and her sadness as my own.

And when she fell victim to the slumber I placed on her, I fought off my tears. Pushing them back down to the depths of my soul. I bit down on my lip, inviting physical pain to subtract from the open, raw, empty feeling that remained left in me.

For this had solved nothing. It was a temporary distraction on this journey to hell my brother and father had forced upon me. Since I was already headed in that direction, it only made sense to finish the job.

CHAPTER
TWENTY-THREE

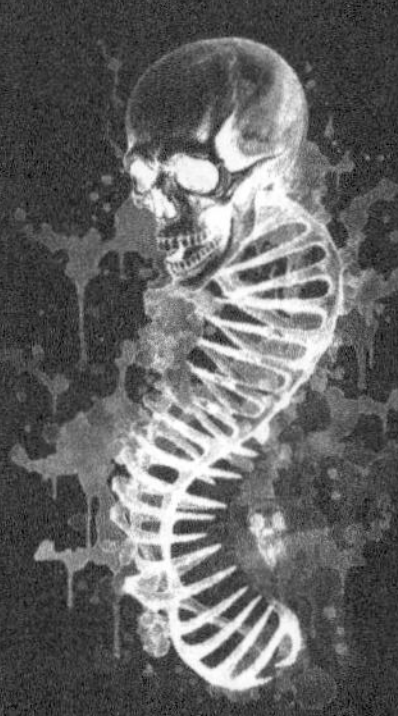

TOMOE

My eyes snapped open the moment she entered the room. Reina halted in the doorway, hands placed behind her back. Her fierce blue eyes remained trained on the ground. She granted me a light smile in recognition that my attention had fallen on her, a smile I didn't buy for one fucking second.

I knew what she had just finished doing, had known what she would do the moment she decided to 'sneak out' of the room last night. My sister had made her decision, and now we would have to run so Millie could clean up her mess.

"Why?" I asked as I slid out of the bed.

Knowing we'd likely have to flee before first light, I'd taken the liberty of packing my clothes last night. I had tossed Abel's belongings into his bags as he snored, ignorant to what was taking place during the hours he slept. He began to stir in his bed, eyes creaking open at the noise.

Reina stepped into the room, the door still open behind her. "So she wouldn't have to," she mumbled.

I sighed, nodding in understanding, still not finding the right words to say.

"What's going on?" Abel asked, his voice hoarse.

My sister walked over to his side, prodding him up, pretending nothing was wrong. "It's time to go."

He groaned, pushing himself up at the urgency in her voice. "The sky's still dark. We have another hour."

"We have to go now, Abel. You can sleep when you're dead," I said definitively. "That wasn't a statement up for debate."

Abel studied us both, shrugging at the lack of information either of us offered. "Women."

I rolled my eyes at the comment. Of course, he would think it was some hormonal bullshit. Guess I couldn't blame him, given our spat last night.

"You know where the horses are?" I strapped Wrath onto my back, awaiting Reina's response.

She still refused to meet my eye, but I caught the slight tilt of her head. *I'll take that as a yes then.*

Tossing Abel his shit, "Good, let's go," I muttered.

They followed me out of the room, sticking close behind me as I kept to the shadows the remaining darkness provided. There was a corner in the settlement I'd noticed remained relatively unguarded. Reina focused on the one's a few hundred yards away. They yawned, stretching their arms out before their heads bobbled off to the side.

When the coast was clear, we scaled over the wall and made our way to the horses. A chill went down my bones at the feeling of being watched. I turned my head, catching the figure of a woman atop a horse's back near the portion of the wall we'd just come from. She sat there, watching us load up and saddle in.

Reina's curiosity got the best of her. She guided her horse in the direction of my focus, a lost expression in her eyes. The sun peeked over the horizon, and I recognized the woman as Millie. She offered Reina a tense nod. My sister moved her horse, Bimbo, back around, presumably southeast. Her fingers clasped with a steady grip on the reins. She shifted her weight forward, with a gentle nudge of her heels, Bimbo took off across the horizon. Abel and I fell behind, riding into the sunrise at a silent gallop.

We rode for hours, always at Reina and Bimbo's heels, but never next to them. Reina wouldn't allow it and I had decided long ago into this trip not to push. She seemed to know where she was going, which was enough for me to let her take control. It was hard being atop a horse, riding where Seth had ridden for years in The Before. We were going to pass their home on the way to Billings, a home every indication in Reina's body language let me know we would not stray too close to.

Part of me wished he would be here with us, pretending he was riding at my side. It was stupid. I was stupid for longing for him. Chasing the ghost of a man who I wasn't sure ever existed. At least not the man he allowed me to get to know.

Reina slowed at the Missouri River, stopping for the horses to rest and get a drink. She stayed on, gaze focused out in the distance. My sister hadn't said a word since we'd departed Great Falls.

I rode up next to her. "Here, I took the towel from Great Falls. You should rinse yourself off."

Reina glanced down at her body, eyes wide. A whimper escaped her lips. Trembling, she brought her hands up toward her face. She absentmindedly ran her fingers through her butchered hair, breaths rapid.

In the light of day, the blood covering her coat down to her pants was evident. I pressed my lips together, trying my best to not to turn away from her when she needed me the most. The blood had smeared across her pale skin.

It was a sight I never expected to see. She had slit Nash's throat, causing his blood to splatter all over her. Given my preferred method of killing, I knew the mess that came with such an action. Reina was a healer, not a killer. Of course, she hadn't known any better.

That wasn't entirely true. Not really. She may have not known the mess it would cause, but slitting someone's throat was far from a quick death. It was slow. He would have died choking on his own blood. Reina was no stranger to basic anatomy. The gore was what was fucking her up, and now, with the evidence of what she had done, guilt.

She went mute, focusing on moving one foot in front of the other as she entered the freezing water, a whirlpool forming around her. I swallowed my tears. Watching her was painful. Reina clutched at her chest. The second the blood reddened the water, her deep breaths shifted to hyperventilating. Abel came up behind me, removing his outer layers to help calm her. I put my hand out, signaling for him to come to a halt.

"I've got this," I said, yanking off each item of clothing that I couldn't spare to get wet.

I ran into the water, the sensation stealing the air from my lungs, but I pushed forward. The brisk air paired with the shrill water could kill me, but I didn't care.

Wading over to her, I grabbed her shoulders, making her face me. Her icy eyes searched mine, and I hoped she found a sense of peace within them. I gave a slight nod of my head, a tense smile pulling at my lips. Without a word, I guided water up the length of her body, making sure I didn't miss a spot. When she was rid of all the blood, she stared at the reddened water around us.

"I had to," Reina whispered, "I couldn't let her end up like me … like Maia. This isn't her war to fight; it's mine. My brother's. My father's."

I hated hearing those words. That wasn't true. It was everyone's war. There would always be evil in this world. If it wasn't her father, it would simply be someone else. It sucked that her family had guilted her into feeling responsible. Fuck that, it more than sucked. It infuriated me. They would pay for this, I'd make sure of it.

My love for Seth would always be there. The kind of love that we shared didn't disappear overnight. But I refused to let that cloud my judgment ever again. Fool me once, shame on you. Fool me twice … Well, I would never let that happen. There was no need to even finish that line of thought.

"Shh," I said soothingly, "It's okay, Reina. I believe you. It's okay."

"I'm a monster," she mumbled, throwing herself down into the current.

I watched as she floated on her back. Peace took over her kind features. Her brown hair formed a halo around her head. It was fleeting. Her nose crinkled and her cheeks went red. The water masked her tears flowing into the quickening current.

"If you're a monster, then we are all damned."

Fighting to keep upright, I pulled her into me, cradling her until her tears stopped. The current slowed, and Reina abandoned floating, coming back to her feet. Her eyes opened, and she faced the sky, void of all emotion, a new mask taking over. Reina's features had hardened. My sister was gone.

"Come on," I said, grabbing her hand to guide us back to shore. "We need to make it to Billings before nightfall. We'll be safe to set up camp along their borders. No need to go inside the town and see anyone you may know."

She chuckled in response. "I don't care much if I see them. I bet they'd hardly recognize me anyway."

I examined her, not liking the sound of that. Shaking off where my thoughts were headed, I continued rifling through her bag, searching for some clean clothes for her to dress in. Abel watched on from the horses, an expression marked by worry. He turned away when Reina caught him, punishing him with a glare. His jaw ticked, and he redirected his attention out into the distance, continuing his surveillance over the perimeter.

Abel and I worked on setting up the tent for the night. Reina sat near the fire, poking it with a stick. She hadn't spoken a word since we left the river, which was fine by me because I wasn't sure what to say. Comforting someone had never been my strong suit, not in The Before and not in The After. That was Reina's job.

I suddenly found myself in the same position as I had when Jax died. What do you do when the strong friend falls apart? Amaia was strong for us all, making the decisions we couldn't and bearing the weight of it. Reina was strong in a different way. She shouldered our emotions when we couldn't.

How the hell was I supposed to help someone who could take away our pain when the only thing I could offer was a pat on the back and false statements about how everything would be okay? Everything would not be okay. Nothing would ever be the same again.

Seth's words echoed in my mind. *I'll come back for you too.* Words that I heard every fucking night on replay before I fell asleep.

We nibbled on the deer Reina had caught at the precepts of sunset. With the fire now out to avoid detection, inside the tent was the warmest place. Abel snored the second his head hit the ground. Reina took it upon herself to take first watch, hanging near the flap of the tent. So I laid there, staring up into pitch black. My head spun, eyelids drooping low. I let the vision take over.

I'm … I'm Seth. A chill went down my spine. He had called for me, forced me into his mind from a distance against my will. He scanned a room full of screens and other electronics. Electricity? Shit. I mean, Duluth had power for lights and things, but this, wherever he was, had remained untouched from The Before. His tan, calloused hands fiddled with items, picking them up and placing them directly into his line of sight.

Seth was showing me something, something he wanted me to know. I had told him of the vision my sister had offered before her death. He was making sure I took in every inch of his surroundings, so I knew what we were up against. But why?

He glanced back at the wall of screens. My family's portraits lined them. The words 'Kill Order' atop each of our heads. He stopped on mine. 'Scholar - Seer' was written in my description. Seth turned away, back to one of the devices he'd held in his hands the first few glimpses of the vision.

My line of sight was now on a keyboard. He began typing … 'VeilSight Disruptor.' What the hell … Seth stared back at the screen in front of him and clicked on a file. The details popped up on the fucking screen.

This device, disruptor or whatever the fuck it was, blocked out facial recognition to limit the exposure of Coverts spies, but it was more than that. He scrolled down. It emitted a low-level electromagnetic field that emitted pulses throughout the continental United States. It was why people who fled Covert Province had never been able to recall the details of their life there once they crossed through the borders. The second component was to attack memory, letting them only recall certain things.

Seth scrolled again, clicking into a subfile marked classified. If what he had shown me was declassified information, what the flying fuck did these assholes consider classified? With horror, I fought to maintain our wavering connection. I was losing strength from this. It was too vivid, too detailed.

Only approved individuals were granted the ability to walk through specific checkpoints with their memory intact.

Fuck, fuck, fuck. Shit. What Seth was showing me was the answer to every problem I'd encountered these last few months when it came to my abilities. My visions. These assholes had been limiting my ability, every Seer's ability, to see anything that went on within Covert Province. They were specifically targeting Seers' minds, using the pulses to aim for brain waves that our minds patterned. It replaced detailed images with vague impressions and shifting shadows, making it difficult for us to gain any meaningful insights.

The vision faded, the already blurry images turning into tv static. Seth moved the mouse over to the corner of the screen, it hovered on a button, "OFF." He clicked it back on, picking the device up and moving it a gemstone over toward its center. Before he could place it there, a loud thud sounded behind him.

He jumped at the noise, dropping the device. A tall man identical to Seth swayed into the room, his face red with anger. He grabbed Seth by his shirt, plowing him into the wall. Seth gasped out for air, cut off by a stocky older man whose hands now gripped around his neck.

His father searched through the clutter for the gemstone. Seth's fingers reached out for a pen now scattered on the floor. The man tried to snatch it from him, but Seth resisted, stabbing him in the hand. When the man jumped back, Seth scrambled for a piece of paper.

The gemstone was returned and the world around him went to black, but not before his message was received.

Monterey. Coming 4 u now.

ONE OF THE SHITTIEST THINGS I'VE EVER HAD TO DO IN THIS LIFE WAS look my family in the eye and pretend nothing was wrong. It was not easier the second time. In the days it took us to arrive at Casper, I had to put on a face of concealment. Pretending to be none the wiser that the closer we got to home, the closer we were to meeting our fate. I wasn't sure if that fate would bring us doom or not. I spent most of my time trying *not* to know, actually.

Maybe it was a fool's choice, but I couldn't face the sight of watching my family stumble toward their deaths. I'd done it prior to arriving at Monterey, and I'd be damned to subject myself to that again. I couldn't bear it. No one should have to watch their family die twice. Four times if you were me. Twice within visions, and twice when it played out in real time.

Abel watched me, like he knew what I had seen. If he did, I knew him well enough to know he wouldn't bite his tongue. Instead, he assumed something was off. I wasn't sure if it was something Amaia and Riley had taught him, or if it was something he'd learned on his own the hard way, but there was a benefit in not asking questions. Especially if you knew something was amiss. Sometimes, with our gifts, not knowing was a gift in itself.

It was Reina who suggested we leave the horses a few miles back in the trees. Somewhere along this quiet leg of our travels, she'd decided walking up to them was our best bet. I'd be a damn liar if I said she caught me off guard. Everything about her demeanor suggested she was up to no good. I found myself not giving a fuck. I would've, had I known exactly how she intended to handle things.

Never could I have prepared myself for what my sister unleashed on the unsuspecting guards of Casper.

We arrived, weapons tucked, arms in the air, showing we posed no threat. It meant nothing to the guards who waved their guns in our face. It also meant nothing to Reina, who walked right through them, head held high and arms spread wide.

One by one, they fell to their knees in her wake.

Each man and woman we passed displayed a different emotion. Fear, anger, pure panic, terror, grief, hopelessness. Outrage. None at us, though, at least not yet, not until she released her grip on them. Reina reached back, finding hold on my arm and dragging me to her side. Without asking, she shot hope through me, forcing me to down my barriers and let her in. Our magic swept through them as she guided the visions, redirecting their emotions toward the entity of their choosing.

By the cries and whimpers, I could tell they were weighing the cons of aligning with Covert Province. They cursed them, wished them ill. Some shouted at the sky for mercy. I wasn't helping my sister do this. This was all her. Reina had taken control of our shared magic. I knew she was powerful, but to this extent … holy hell.

"Reina, what the fuck are you doing?" I hissed, stopping in my tracks to try to help some of the people I passed back to their feet.

Reina ground her jaw, annoyance rolling off her tongue. "My job."

"This is going to cause problems," Abel muttered.

I turned to face him. Fear lingered behind his brown eyes. For the first time since he'd joined our family, he saw what Reina was capable of. Abel had finally realized what many at Duluth had already known, Amaia and Alexiares were not the only two people he should fear.

Welcome to the family.

"Obviously," I mumbled, glaring back at him, irritated with his unhelpful words.

"Not now," he said, eyes glazing over. "If she keeps on this path, this is going to make some of the soldiers flee. We have to do something."

Well, shit.

I clasped my free hand around Reina's, trying to get her to stop to regroup. She shook me off without glancing back. Before I could take another step, a ruthless shot of misery knocked into me. It took every ounce of strength that I had to stay on my feet. *That bitch.* She'd channeled the emotions I'd been keeping tight, close to my heart these last few months and directed them back at me full blast. Never once had I expected her to use my own sorrows against me.

Reina was out of fucking control and I could not stop her.

Abel came up behind me, hands falling to the pits of my arms to offer me support. "We need to help her, she can't go on this way," he said, training his eyes on her, worried she would direct whatever she felt at him next.

"I had a vision the other night," I divulged, deciding at least one other person needed to beware. I could trust him to keep this between us. "As much as I hate to say it, she's going to need to carry on like this for as long as she can. It's going to be the only thing that keeps her going."

He faced me, quizzically searching me for an explanation. When no words came, I took his hands, deciding that showing him would be best. It wasn't power sharing in the way we'd been working through at Duluth, but how others with Seer capabilities could channel each other. It allowed us to share visions, use each other's gifts to direct our energy to a certain point in time, and dive deeper. I just wasn't entirely sure how it would work, since it had been a vision sent to me with Seth's powers intertwined with mine.

"Alright." Abel nodded absentmindedly. Hopelessness replaced his fear. "If you think that's best, then I'm down to do whatever I can to help."

"Good."

REINA DID NOT GIVE THE PEOPLE OF CASPER A CHANCE TO MAKE ANY decision about their future for themselves. She used every ounce of magic that she had to make sure we came to agreeable terms. By agreeable, I mean, every item on what she determined was on Amaia's list of demands was checked off by the time we descended through the gates and back to our horses. There was no need for us to stay the night, or even sit for a meal with the speed she worked her magic. The people of Casper were defenseless. Everyone was when it came to Reina's powers, but their citizens didn't even get a chance to acknowledge who she was or what she was capable of.

We'd spread out our belongings, running through a quick check of all our materials and what we were running low on. Reina had said two sentences; we do not need to stay at another settlement again. Not if we could help it.

As we settled in, my thoughts drifted off to our next stop: Cheyenne. While my sister needed to keep this facade for her own sanity, the people of Cheyenne would end up better off siding with us in this war. Something had to give.

If it didn't, Reina would never find the power to forgive herself for doing what was necessary. Her actions were brutal. There was a fat chance many, many people would never forgive her. But it was important that she left room inside her to forgive herself.

That night, during the full moon while Reina slept, I surrendered another piece of my soul. For magic like this always demanded a price.

My sweetening spell wouldn't do much, but it would make her more tolerable for Cheyenne and the rest of our journey back home. If Reina continued on with this lack of empathy and emotion, two things she was known for, people were going to compare her to her father and brother. That fact alone would destroy her when this was all said and done.

Reina would never be the sweet Reina she once was. I knew that. Despised Seth for taking that from her. But I would do everything I could to preserve what little of it she had left.

It was risky, given the fact that Reina could feel every emotion Abel, and I had. Most of our energy throughout the day and while we waited for her to fall asleep had been spent trying to keep a level head. I needed to make sure this spell stayed buried deep down, where Reina could not feel it, but it would still affect her in small ways until she was ready to heal. Only then would it restore what remained.

I pulled out my small vial made from ethereal glass. It was a gift I carried with me everywhere. My sister June and I had used it to make our mom more ... susceptible to letting us do things we pleased. I'd kept it put away for so long, holding it in my fingers now was odd, as if it was brand new. When we first left Monterey, I wasn't sure why I had packed it, something had told me I would need it one day soon. That time was now.

Ethereal glass was an integral part of the spell, enchanted to hold and release emotions in a controlled manner. Abel handed me a silver spoon he'd stolen from Casper. I'd told him to disappear into the shadows the moment eyes were off him. Much like Riley, he was damn good at doing so. Hey, they always said it's the quiet ones you need to watch out for.

He handed me the Indian Paintbrush flower from their greenhouse next. I dropped in some water from the river, pausing briefly, making sure I was sure I wanted to go this route. My options were nonexistent. After a quick moment of meditation, I placed in the last ingredient, prairie agate, to ground the spell in my intentions.

"Vicus, affectus dormiunt, intra hanc phialam, secreta sua custodiunt. Lenis lunae tactus, fluvii fluxus, sana ac renoua, cum crescunt parati."

I grabbed Reina's bag from Abel's lap, cutting a sliver in the side and placing the vial inside. Quietly, in order to not disturb her, I sewed it back up, leaving it there until it sensed her desire to heal. When the time came, it would awaken what remained within.

"This is so freaking dope," Abel said with excitement.

I brought my finger to my lips. "Shh." Against my will, a small smile snuck across my lips at the comment.

Abel was the first one besides my sister June to call what I did *cool* and not fear it. I brushed Reina's hair out of her face, dropping low to kiss her cheek. She tossed restlessly, mumbling to herself. We both shot down into our sleeping bags. When Reina stilled, Abel moved to the front of the tent to keep watch.

I fell asleep cuddled up next to her, finding serenity in her signature lavender scent. A small, consistent part of my sister that I had left.

There would be hell to pay for what Seth had stolen from our family, from Reina, for all of this.

CHAPTER
TWENTY-FOUR

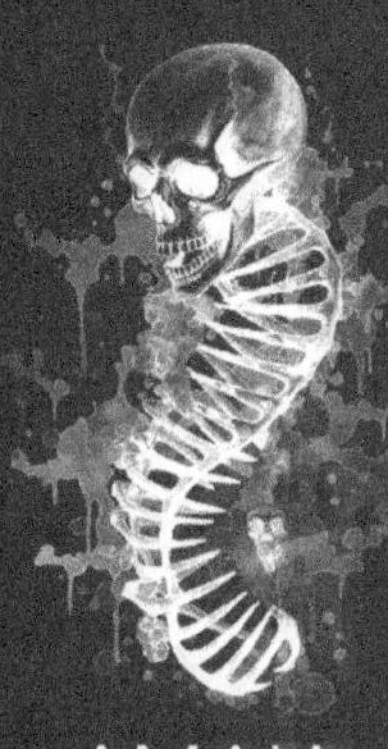

AMAIA

Two weeks came and went, but it would never be enough time. Even with the help of the *brujas,* my confidence in Duluth's abilities to hold strong had barely increased to a decent chance of survival. Only once they were presented to the face of danger and time would tell how they would prevail at the end of this all.

I had to worry about my own people now. Preparing them for the war to come was my number one priority. The idea that troops would mobilize and we could meet Covert Province on the battle-field was fun and all, but I knew better than that. I had an inkling that we would be met at our front doors before any of us had the chance to deploy to common ground. Covert had been silent since meeting my valley of death.

Silence was never a good thing in war. It meant they were plotting, preparing, adjusting. Surrender was the goal, not silence.

"I still don't think they're ready," Sloan said.

She'd stepped up to the plate, grown into her role. I was sure she was ready, even if her people were not. Sloan had spent every waking moment using me as a sounding board. Running her own ideas by me but also stopping to take in all the advice and knowledge I had to offer. If she kept her time with Morgan front of mind, combined with all that I had taught her during our almost two-month stay, she would be just fine in a leadership role.

I'd made my own threats to their new general. They were less incompetent than the former one; I'd selected them personally after all. Still, the threat lingered. Sloan dies, they die. Violet and Sloan's mother perish, so does he. Simple enough. I'd crafted a playbook specifically for their resources and troops they had written at a level a child could understand. In the end, that would matter little. Their ability to pivot on their feet in the chaos of war would determine everyone's fate.

I pushed Sloan's wild red hair behind her ear, studying her freckled face wanting to remember it forever. "Pretty sure you're saying that to keep me here longer," I teased.

"You always did know me best." Sloan smiled.

Her breath was no longer marked by the stench of tobacco and smoke. She had always been better than I when it came to kicking bad habits. She was stronger in that way.

Alexiares grumbled unpleasantries, ready to leave this place behind him.

"Quiet, *Bloodhound*," Sloan spat. "Dare I say I might miss winding you up."

His lips pulled to meet the tip of his now scrunched up nose, "Ew. I think I hate you being nice to me more than hearing your smart-ass remarks."

Sloan smirked, lacing her fingers through his shaggy hair, ruffling it up in disregard to the careful pattern he'd gelled it back in. "You're not as bad as I thought." She paused thoughtfully, "that's a lie, you're actually worse, but I suppose it's easier to digest when you're on our side."

Alexiares eyes widened in horror. "Never say another nice word to me again or I'll throw up." Those two would never be able to have a decent conversation, but he gave her a weak smile before walking over to his bike.

I watched him as he strapped in his pack, making sure there was still room for me on the back. He admired it with a smug grin, happy for another ride. A long one at that.

"A sight I never thought I would see," I said.

Sloan's head tilted, and she blew on her hands, rubbing them together to provide extra warmth on the chilly January day. "What is?"

"You giving him a backhanded compliment," I coaxed, "and him being glad to take it."

"I remember when the idea of your man and your best friend getting along made your entire day," Sloan suggested, winking dramatically.

Heat flushed my cheeks at the words, *your man*, and hoped it would pass off as being a reaction to the cold. Bringing my gloved hands to my face, I patted gently in an attempt to cover my ass.

"Oh my God!" she exclaimed, a finger wagging in my face. "You love him, don't you?"

Smacking her finger down, I shushed her, begging her to lower her voice. "I don't know if I'd go that far."

"It's okay to care again, Amaia, open yourself up." Sloan said gently, "I hate to say it, but I was wrong. He's good for you. You've … settled into yourself with him around. Like you're not hiding who you are, not a single part of you."

"Okay, I'm with him. Your niceties are making me queasy," I groaned, tossing my head back to wrap my curls into a bun.

Sloan playfully shoved my shoulder. "I'm being serious. When you first got here, when my cousin did what he did, everything about you said you were defeated. Like you were struggling with a reason to keep moving forward, to stay alive. We both were."

I shook my head, not ready to accept any of what the word *love* entailed. "When he looks at me, Sloan, it's like he sees something worth looking at." I turned back to face her, keeping my words hushed and between us. "I know what that means. So many people give me that look, but two of them had love in their eyes while they gave it to me. And now, I think there may be a third. That scares the crap out of me."

"*Something* in this world needs to scare you. I'd say that's healthy, considering not much else does." Sloan said, her signature Moore eyes boring into my damn soul.

I offered her a loose smile that gave way to a small pout. "Tell your momma I said it was nice to finally meet her. I left a map to Lola's home in case you want to bring Violet and some of the younger kids there before all hell breaks loose. We'll let her know to be on the lookout for some fiery red hair once we get there."

Sloan was fiercely protective of Violet. I'd seen her once in the two months that we'd been here. She kept her away, off with her mother and a few of the other leadership kids. I understood, told myself to take no offense to it. If there wasn't a face to put to the name, then her little girl could have a chance of dodging the fray. Kids were not off limits in war, at least not with enemies. Especially a child of someone in charge. If you kept them alive and they were old enough, they would grow up with vengeance to pay.

While Sloan had nothing to worry about with me, I knew she would never fully trust the rest of the group, not even her cousin. It had been one of her cousins, after all, who had betrayed them all. So off Violet stayed, away from anyone who could identify her upon capture.

Still, it melted my heart to hear *Auntie Maia* just that one time. Something we had spoken so much about in The Before. When we thought there was a chance of our kids growing up alongside each other. Now, I wasn't even sure if I even wanted children, not if I could help it. To bring someone into a world that was full of uncertainties would be cruel.

"Thank you, I'll consider it," she said, words ringing with a hint of truth. "Though me and the other mommas here will probably sleep best knowing our babies are okay by a short walk over to the shelter."

"Remember, don't stop until you hit forty feet. From there, all the Earth elementals you can spare need to put their energy into building the shelter out, and quickly. It should be enough to keep them safe from the worst of it. Oh! Don't forget, you need a code that changes to let anyone—"

Sloan's hand reached out to cover my mouth, my words lost to muffles. "Maia! Okay, okay. We went through this twice already. We'll be okay. It's time for y'all to go if you want to make it to the *brujas* before dark. I had a few people go out to clear the road enough for the two of you to get through to St. Paul on his bike."

"Thank you." I pulled Sloan in, hugging her tightly. "I meant what I said. When you're ready, there's space for you at Monterey Compound, all three of you. Anyone else that wants to come too, we'll make room."

Her only response was to turn me around with a slap to my ass. "Goodbye, my forever friend, goodbye."

I swung my leg over the other side of Alexiares' damn motorcycle. He pretended to crank it obnoxiously a few times, earning a scowl from Sloan, whose hands now crossed against her chest in dismay. Clutching onto him for dear life, I watched my only remaining friend from The Before disappear into the distance.

With a flash of my power, I tossed a small flame into the sky. One final goodbye.

THE DESIRE TO RUN INTO FINLEY WAS NONEXISTENT FOR THE BOTH OF us. Cutting through St. Paul was the smarter route rather than risking getting caught skirting around St. Cloud again. We made it about thirty miles outside the city before hitting a roadblock.

I'd grown relatively comfortable on the bike now, well, as comfortable as I could get. Resting my head on Alexiares' shoulder was an added benefit. Every negative parcel of energy in my body was sucked away, dissolved from his mere presence.

That was something I had missed in the months since Jax's death. Except this was different. Where Jax would take my troubles on as his own and help me shed them, Alexiares made me forget about them completely ... to an extent. It was hard to forget you were on the back of a death-mobile. But when the wind was whipping past your skin and the idiot driving it went out of his way to swerve to make your heart jump, it was very possible.

Alexiares slowed to a stop. I squeezed tight against his waist thinking he was about to pull some bullshit to piss me off.

"Why are we stopping?" I asked.

He chuckled, prying my hands from him, and took a deep breath. "If you opened your eyes for a few seconds, princess, you'd see that the road is blocked off."

My heart dropped into my ass and my eyes shot open. I peered over at the road sign falling over toward the right, White Bear Lake. This was wrong, I felt it in my gut.

"That's weird," I mumbled. "Sloan said she had them clear a direct path here."

"It's Sloan. Did you really expect her to have full insight on the ins and outs of her orders? They probably stopped here and turned back before they'd have to close in on St. Paul," Alexiares said, irritation heavy in his voice, his accent pulling through the way it always did when he got a bit ruffled. It was sexy as hell, made me want to take things a step further and piss him off more.

"Be nice," I teased. "Believe it or not, she's grown rather fond of you in her own weird way."

"I'll be sure to send her an invite to the wedding," Alexiares grumbled, kicking the stand down on the bike and hopping off. He grabbed his pack, tossing it over his shoulder, brows wiggling with acknowledgment that he was privy to the game I was playing.

My heart skipped a few beats. *He's trying to fuck with you*, I told myself. Forcing myself to recover with humor, I glared at him mockingly, leaning back on the bike as if I were comfortable on it. "Quit mouthing off and help me see if there's a way around."

He shrugged, taking off to the right. I sighed, grabbing my bag and taking a look around. The placement of it all struck me as oddly intentional. A big rig blocked off the road, the wheels popping on all sides, making it immovable even if we were able to get the engine going by chance. I peered around it. Cars lined the perimeter and filled within a maze pattern. We could try to drag the bike through, but that would take time and the sun was already getting low in the sky. If we could find a more direct way around, it would make things a lot easier.

With this many vehicles blocking our way, it was highly probable that Alexiares was right. Or Sloan's people had done all that they could, stopping here when it became more work than it was worth. We were close enough to St. Paul that there was room for reasonable assumption that we could navigate the rest without assistance.

A wide path sat to my left, probably used for park rangers or emergency vehicles in The Before. It wasn't too overgrown and there was enough room for his bike to get through. That said, there was a lot of tree cover that would make visibility when it came to Pansies an issue. My thoughts were damning. Two of them emerged the moment the entrance to the path came out of sight.

It was harder killing them now that I knew I had been right all along. There were still people trapped back there, but if the dried blood on their clothes was any indication, it was still very much an us versus them situation. Choosing us, choosing life would forever be my decision, no matter how hard it was to do so. I had a lot of regrets in this life, but protecting the living would never be one.

My knives flew in secession, one finding each of their skulls. They flopped down before they had the chance to gain more than a few feet on me. I pried my blades from their skulls, the sick, wet slush echoing in my mind.

"Find peace," I mumbled over their bodies, stepping over them to continue down the path.

We would have to decide whether we wanted to take the risk with the noise of motorcycle attracting however many more lingered in these woods. Continuing on without the bike was also an option if Alexiares didn't find an alternate route wherever he'd gone off to.

An explosion sounded back from the main road. I was flying through the trees before the flames finished spiking above the tree line.

"Alexiares?" I screamed, in full panic mode. "Alexi!"

Right before I hit the clearing, a flash of blonde hair took up space in my peripheral. I hit the ground. Nails pried into my face as I scanned my surroundings trying to figure out what the fuck just happened. Grabbing at the hair, I kept my eyes closed, protecting them against the claws that would aim for them if given the chance. Throwing them off to the side, I rolled over, jumping back to my feet.

"Finley," I growled.

"In the fle—"

"Oh shut up, you wicked bitch," I cut her off, not needing a repeat of her villain tagline.

She tossed her hair over her shoulder. I charged, throwing a right jab out, finishing with a kick to her ribs. Finley caught it lifting me up, tossing me onto the ground. I landed flat on my back, the wind knocked from me. A shot of pain shot down my spine.

Gasping for air, my hand reflectively reached out to my back. With my breathing constricted, the edges of my sight narrowed, my attention solely on Finley. A surge of adrenaline coursed through my veins, senses sharp to a razor-like clarity.

My movements became visceral, primal, a storm of blows and counterattacks fueled by a singular desire; destroying this motherfucker.

I tried for my flames but they flickered in the palm of my hand. Frowning, I made another attempt. They flickered a beautiful blue then orange before going out for good.

A wicked grin crept across Finley's face. "Aw, poor little General. Forced to fight like a woman, no magic to back her up." She waved a needle-laced glove in my face, wiggling her fingers.

It dawned on me then, where most of the pain had come from in my back, now crawling down my leg. I inspected a blood stain seeping into my pants.

"I don't need magic to kick your ass," I vowed, reaching for my knives. Instead of throwing them, I kept them steady in my hands. "I'm going to enjoy this."

Finley grinned, charging me again. I sliced at her arm with her first reach. She hissed back in pain, then threw out a kick aimed at my jaw. It connected but only because I allowed it to do so. On my way down, I sliced into her leg grabbing onto her hair as she recoiled, cutting through her dry ass strands.

I cackled at my work. "You look like that fucking doll from Rugrats."

"Bringing knives to a fist fight, oh how the mighty have fallen," Finley said, pushing herself off the ground, face red. She froze, mouth agape and eyes wide when she noticed her hair sprawled around my lap.

"Fine," I agreed, tossing the knives to the side. "No knives, no magic. Just my fists against your flesh and my arm around your throat."

We were both on our feet now, circling each other. Finley tossed out another shameful kick, I reached to grab it. My mistake on that one. She used the momentum of my hold to grab hold of my neck, kneeing me directly in the nose. A loud crunch sounded, blood gushing, and I saw fucking red.

Enough games.

Anger roared an inferno within. My strikes became swift and precise, every hit, kick, knee or slap fueled by the intensity of my red-hot rage. I latched onto her arm, aiming a punch for her chest followed by a kick to the head. Finley ducked when I expected her to, my leg swinging over her head. I grabbed onto her waist, pulling her onto the ground, straddling her the way she had pinned me in that filthy basement months ago. She was on her stomach, face in the dirt, and I put that bitch into a headlock.

Finley gulped for air like a fish out of water. A maniacal laugh sounded from me in an out of body experience. Killing someone was never easy. Often necessary, but never easy. With Finley, I never wanted to kill someone so much in my life. For what she did to my family when she held us captive, but most importantly, for what she did to Alexiares over the years.

She had molded someone who already held onto an unfathomable amount of pain and further twisted him into someone who now deemed himself unworthy of love. Unworthy of happiness.

Her thin fingers found one of my knives before I could stop her. Finley reached back swiftly, weakly jabbing it into my thigh, not having enough oxygen to go deep but enough to make me release my hold. I yelped out in shock, the pain following short-ly after.

"Amaia!" Alexiares shouted, not too far in the distance.

Like a lovesick fool, the pain in his voice caught my atten-tion. He sounded injured. The distraction cost me. Finley maneu-vered around, graceful as a cat, slinking up behind me, knife to my throat.

Alexiares pushed through some brush coming into view. His eyes met mine, wide with fear. They scanned the scene, taking in the puddles of blood then landed on Finley, the cause of it all. Vines slithered up Finley's ankles, crawling up her body and wrap-ping around her neck.

"Let her go, Finley," he growled. "Your men are dead. There is no one else here to help you." Alexiares' eyes narrowed on her, marking her as a target. It was precisely that exact moment when I understood why they called him *bloodhound*.

Blood covered his face, his teeth, his hands, the entirety of the clothes he wore, but there wasn't a single scratch on him. It wasn't his blood. Right now, the man in front of me was biting down the urge, poised to snap this woman's neck. Every ounce of him seethed with the threat of violence. He cracked his neck, hand on his gun. Alexiares watched Finley, staring her down like prey.

"Pity, I rather enjoyed the company they kept me in bed." She teased, "I bet you enjoyed pulling Joey to pieces after the rather compromising position you found us in. Then there was the way he proudly pistol whipped your bitch in that field. That is what you did, didn't you? Ripped him apart, limb from body, finger from hand? It is your signature after all. Creepy but no one ever laid it down the way you did, so I dismissed it. I miss that."

I tossed my head back into her face, shattering her nose, re-turning the favor. Finley laughed through the pain, pressing the knife further into my jugular. A trickle of blood ran down my neck.

"Aw, you didn't like that one did you," Finley mocked. "I sense that the two of you have taken your relationship to the next level. Don't worry, he knows I don't mind sharing."

Alexiares cocked his gun, aiming it right for the center of her head. "Touch her again, and I'll take my time slicing you up then feed you to your fucking corpse."

"Whatever happened to hey? How are you? *More, Finny?*" Finley chided, unimpressed.

"Get fucked," I said, there was a special place in any version of hell for her.

"Gladly. All you two needed to do was ask." I could hear the smirk on her face and I wanted to smack it right off. She paused, releasing a sigh before she continued, her grip loosening a bit. "First, I think you'll want to hear what I have to say."

I swiveled my head, aiming for her hand. I chomped down, drawing blood as she pulled back, giving me a chance to push myself away. Knocking the knife out of Finley's hand, I spit out a chunk of her skin, blood trailing down my lips.

"If you wanted to talk, then maybe don't start by attacking me. Might be more inclined to listen," I said, voice throaty from the fight. Groaning from the pain, I set my nose back in place wanting the aching to stop so I could focus.

Alexiares' gun stayed trained on Finley, his vines tightening. "Or set your sick fucks on me," he added.

Finley cackled, "You think I would miss the opportunity to hit a bitch? Especially her? Never that."

"You're losing my interest, Finley," Alexiares sighed impatiently, "that's never a safe place to be."

She bared her teeth at him, snapping her jaw. This was a fucking joke to her. I almost pitied her ignorance to the world around her. Almost, but not quite.

Alexiares fired a shot over her head, "Next one goes through the pearly whites, choose your next course of action carefully."

"Urgh, no one likes the hero, Alexi." Finley groaned, "Put it to rest, this one can clearly save herself."

I looked at him, he studied my face before I gave him a nod and he lowered his gun.

"Ohhh. You always did do best working underneath a woman." She winked at him. "I blocked the road off because I knew you'd never cross back through St. Cloud. You'd need to stop for the night, the best place for you to do that is with Lola and the other witch bitches."

"Get to the point," I commanded, already tiring of listening to the shrill of her voice. There was no need to ask how she knew that, Alexiares had already warned she had people watching the city.

She huffed in frustration. "Fuckers up there in Covert stole my invention, and I don't like thieves."

"Torturing people, cool. Stealing, bad. What invention?" Alexiares prodded, trying to push the point from her instead of letting her drag it out the way he knew she so enjoyed. "You tend to have a new one every other day."

"More importantly why should we give a shit?" I questioned, leaning up against the bark of one of the trees.

"Because it affects you and that other girl too. The one with the visions. Affects all of us."

Alexiares' eyes darted to meet mine. I squinted, begging him to keep his mouth shut. We needed to let her speak. As much as I hated playing nice, she had information that concerned the people I love, which left us at her fucking mercy.

I closed in on her, smirking at the small flinch she tried to hide. "What is it that you think you know, *Finny?*"

Apparently, Finley and her network of spies had been busy since we attempted to burn their place to the ground. She'd discovered Covert Province had stolen an unfinished invention from her and maximized its potential. Where she had spent the last few years struggling to get it working as a one woman show, Covert had used their best to get it working.

She'd tried and failed to create a tool that could block out visions from Scholars with Seer abilities for years. Her goal had been to target Seers within specific settlements that she determined were a threat, aiming to halt their technological advancements. They were still functioning as far as I knew. How often it actually ran as intended however, was up for debate. Covert, in turn, had stolen her blueprints, improvised, and created a tool that now emitted electromagnetic pulses throughout the remains of our fallen country.

"That's what you get for playing mad scientist." Alexiares snickered, "Sucks to get the short end of the shit stick, don't it?"

I reclined my head, peering up at the tree tops. "That's why Moe wasn't able to look into you when you first got to The Compound. We both thought it was because she was frazzled with everything going on, didn't think twice about it to be honest. Figured she was simply overworked."

Alexiares' thick brows raised, eyes dancing between me and Finley, "You guys did what?" He scoffed, "Can't say I'm surprised."

"What does *that* mean?" I challenged; as far as I was concerned, I had every right to.

What he failed to remember time and time again was that I was a general first, a person with emotions and empathy second. Caring about minute things such as privacy was further down on my list of priorities. About as far down as it could get to be honest.

"Means trust is an obscure illusion to—"

I cut him off, "I'm sorry. Were you or were you not a suspect in an act of terrorism when you arrived?" Pushing off the tree, I fought off a wince at the sharp pain shooting up my leg, storming up to him with my chin held high. I remained unblinking in an attempt to hold his infuriated gaze.

He ground his jaw but said nothing further on the topic. I took it for what it was, a win for this battle, but knew an all-out war awaited me as soon as we were without an audience.

"That's what I thought." I said assertively, "I don't apologize for protecting my people, but I do apologize for not disclosing it after the fact."

His expression softened, then hardened again, something in my words triggering him once more. "Does that mean you're ready to tell me about the letter you sent out with Reina?"

"Do you seriously think now is the time to share that information with your crazy ex-wife present? Classy." I could not believe he was doing this here of all places.

There was a time and place for everything, something he lacked awareness of. Or didn't care about.

The vine around her neck tightened with a sparkle in his eye. "Dead bodies don't talk."

"Ex-wife?" Finley gasped, focusing on the wrong thing. "I still have a ring on my finger last time I checked."

She removed her glove, waving a finger in my face. My gaze trickled down; she did indeed have an ugly ass bronze ring on her finger. My eyes drew upward, involuntarily locking onto Alexiares to my side. I grimaced, trying to rein in the intrusive thoughts.

A tinge of jealousy rooted in me, a sudden twist in the pit of my stomach that I couldn't ignore even if I damn tried. I dug my nails into my arms as a last-ditch attempt to win against my subconscious. *Nope. Fuck that.* I swung on Finley. She spit the blood out her mouth, glaring at me with murder in her eyes. A tooth landed into her disgusting saliva, and I grinned with pleasure.

"I don't," Alexiares said, hand out to keep me from landing another hit to match the other side of her now bruised face. "Kind of hard to get a divorce in the middle of an apocalypse. Scratch that, it's hard to get a divorce when a marriage is never official.

You put a ring on my finger in my sleep and called me your husband, get a fucking grip."

I turned away from them, kicking into the ground. "As much as I'm enjoying this awkward-ass conversation, I don't understand why any of this is relevant."

"The settlements all around The Expanse are voting every day whose side they want to be on. Just because Sloan *says* people are with you, doesn't mean they actually are." Finley yawned, twitching her jaw left then right. "She never had the pull Morgan did. With her people and those outside the walls. Word on the street is Kansas and Wisconsin are still holding out."

Alexiares cleared his throat, the sound stealing my will power forcing me to meet his gaze as he tried to pass unspoken words between us. My bottom lip jutted out, forehead scrunching together, and I nodded.

"If you two look at each other that way in my face again, I'm going to turn feral." Finley huffed in a childlike fashion, "Anyway, lucky for you all, Kansas and Wisconsin happen to fear the repercussions of pissing me off on the wrong day more than they fear facing Covert Province. Unless of course ..."

"Why do you give a shit?" I pressed, genuinely fucking confused on what she had to protect in all of this. "Seems to me your morals align more with Covert than they do us. You hate our way of living, or did you forget your whole villain speech from when you *tortured* us."

"He tortured you too, let's not forget that important detail," she said, swirling my knife in her hands before tossing it back to me. "To answer your question, I have no interest in working for pieces of shit who steal my work and would have me stuffed in a lab if they had the chance. I rather like my position and intend to keep it. Autonomy suits me well. I bet you understand that, huh, General. You and I aren't that different in the end. Even have the same taste in men." The latter came out in a snarl.

I let out a long, deep breath, *typical*. As much as I hated to say it, I see where she could draw the parallel between us. In the midst of all this drama, here we were, two stupid girls having a pissing match over a fucking guy.

"We don't need your help, Finley. Even without Kansas and Wisconsin, we have things under control." Although I said the words, I didn't believe them. Not with every fiber of my being, which was pretty essential when you were in charge. My mind wandered back to the war room with Sloan's suggestion. She hated Finley and her people, still, she had recognized the need to work with them, and I'd shot her down.

"The enemy of my enemy is my friend," Finley sang, her shrill voice piercing my ears. "I have things that you need and you have the manpower to support my cause."

"One, we aren't supporting shit for you. Two, we aren't your friends," Alexiares snapped.

"We this, we that. We, we, we. Real cute. Problem is, I don't care about being your friend." Finley turned her entire body to face me, like addressing me woman to woman would make her more likely to get what she wanted, "You may be a lot of things, sweetie, but you're not dumb enough to deny my help."

I shifted uncomfortably. "What are you offering?"

"I know you've been struggling to recreate my work up in Duluth. Perhaps I'd be willing to turn a blind eye to that considering they've had a poor replication of some of that shit in the works for some time now."

"How do you know what's going on there or in Covert, Finley?" Alexiares' eyes turned lethal, the light in them completely gone and replaced with black. "We can't trust her."

"I wouldn't trust me either. Sucks for you since you have to if you want my help. And spies. My love, you know how I work, ignorance doesn't flatter you." Finley pulled out his vines, strolling up to him, his gun now resting on her forehead. She grinned, taking his lack of reaction for permission and grazed her hand on his chest.

He smacked her hand away, jumping back in repulsion. If I didn't say something now, this conversation would end with a bullet in her brain. Considering the circumstances this war had placed us in, I couldn't have that, at least not today.

I stepped in between them. "Seems like you have more to gain from our help than we do by any sort of relationship here."

"Or maybe you just have more to lose." The way Finley said it, like it was concrete. Something that everyone knew. "I've taken the liberty of sending enough shields down to Monterey that will cover the main gates of your little sanctuary. One hundred pounds of my gas too."

"I'm listening."

"Maia ..." Alexiares warned.

I raised my hand, something he hated but every other soldier I worked with had learned to accept as my one and only warning to shut the fuck up. The general was speaking, and I was not to be interrupted, didn't matter who it was.

He took another step back, pretending to bow to his *princess.* I would never tell him that his submission brought me pure fucking joy.

Finley smirked, the blood around her mouth and face crusting. "Hmm, good boy, Alexi."

"Shut the fuck up and watch your mouth." I spat venomously, "I'm listening, but your five minutes are coming to an end."

Alexiares released a throaty, sarcastic laugh, obviously pleased with my choice of words. He waved his gun at her, a reminder and a promise.

"I can have the same resources sent up to Duluth by tomorrow morning. More to other allies if you'd like," Finley offered.

"Oh, I'd like," I said. "I need the *exact* recipe sent to each and every one of the settlements within Salem *and* The Expanse."

She tilted her head, the stray strands of her hair sticking to her face. "Can't do that, champ."

"And why not?"

"Top secret." Her response was short and sweet. "What I can do, however, is send a fraction of what I'm offering you; if they figure it out on their own, I won't kill them for it. I promise. See, don't even have my fingers crossed."

"It might be in our best interest too; you don't want the ones that were forced to join us knowing information they can take right back to Covert," Alexiares warned.

My eyes stayed trained on Finley, making her wiggle under my silence for a few moments before conceding, "Fine. You expect me to believe the only thing you want out of this arrangement is what? Your freedom? Finding it hard to sit with that."

"Not asking you to believe it," she said, "but the cost of freedom is high. I'd rather not pay for it with my life, which is exactly what Covert would have to take from me if they ever forced me to work under them, to take my city from me."

"You mean the way you took it from your father?" Alexiares' voice broke and I turned to look at him briefly. Pain was written all over his face. "He was a good man."

I knew it had hurt him, learning of Cal's death. We hadn't spoken of it in detail, he'd refused to. Alexiares had never known a father's love, and while Finley's dad had been the farthest thing from a fatherly figure in his life, he had shown him kindness. Kindness no one aside from Tiago, had ever displayed when it came to him. For that reason alone, he believed he owed him a life debt. Had Alexiares stayed, he would have died by his own hand, but Cal had offered him freedom, a chance to run. The unsaid words in Alexiares' confession one night had been his guilt for leaving, the fear that Cal had traded Alexiares' life for his.

"His death was quick." Finley's wicked smile returned. "Besides, if I told you I didn't kill him, I doubt you'd believe me."

"Did you?" The question left as a hushed whisper, forgotten to the wind.

"Yes."

Alexiares faltered, his boots grinding into the ground. Finley had held on to that, waited to use it as ammo to wound him for good.

I scoffed. "You disgust me. This conversation is over. When we get to Lola's, I'll have a list of demands and settlements sent your way. If you divert from any of what we discussed, the deal is off, and your life will be threatened by more than just Covert."

Shaking my head, I turned, making my way back toward the our bike. I brushed past her, shoulder checking her on the way out. I spat at her feet, "Patch yourself up, *champ*. Your blood reeks. Wouldn't want the Pansies to come crawling for dinner."

"Toodaloo, my new friend," Finley chided. "It'll be a pleasure to work by your side."

No footsteps followed, and I paused, turning back in curiosity. Alexiares hadn't moved an inch. His chest heaved up and down. I watched as his fingers tapped against his gun, waiting to see what he would do. It would ruin things a bit, but I wouldn't fault him for whatever he wanted to do. Monterey was already a few days out of receiving our portion of the deal. I'd be okay sparing a few of her inventions to send out to the others if he wanted to pull the trigger. There were a few people in this world I wished I could have the chance to take out if ever graced with the opportunity to confront them.

Finley trembled. I know she didn't want to, was fighting against it, but she did. When faced with him alone, without me as a mediator, she was scared of the man she had molded. It was precisely then that one long-standing question I'd had was answered—Monsters weren't born, they were created.

She had made him into a weapon. The poor girl had begged for a sheep and found out she'd received a wolf instead.

I happened to like wolves, and I wasn't scared of the monsters under my bed.

He strolled up to her, less than an inch from her face, bending down to meet her where she was at. Slowly, his head tilted as he examined her, watching her in such contemplation, like he saw her so clearly for who she was now. A chill went down my spine at the image. She reached for his face, reading the situation entirely wrong. Alexiares leaned closer, there wasn't so much of a sliver of space between them. A terrifying, toothy smile took over his face. His gun pressed underneath her chin, she trembled against her will.

I watched as Finley's mouth moved, a whisper leaving what appeared to say *pull it*. He hooked his foot behind her knee, she flopped to the ground with an *oomf*, head bouncing off the dirt beneath her. She had no time to react to her injuries as he fired four shots around her head. Finley flinched with each one.

Alexiares holstered his gun, reaching into his pocket, pulling out the rings he'd abandoned weeks ago. He dropped them onto her face, stopping with a final one I hadn't given a second thought too before, a bronze one that matched Finley's. Reaching down, he lifted his pants leg, removing the twin blade they shared, the one his father had given him. With a flick of his hand, it pierced the ground, pinning her golden locks beneath it.

"Consider this our official divorce. If I ever see you again, I will kill you before you have the chance to see me coming. Not with magic, not with a blade or even a fucking gun. I will use my bare hands, and I will enjoy every second of it."

Without looking back, he walked toward me, pulling me in by the waist, he kissed me deep. Hard. My tongue intertwined with his accepting this claiming, an invitation to remove any blurred lines between us. There was nothing left to keep him from being mine completely if I so desired. He grabbed my hand, leading the way. Finley's stare followed us, the weight of it on my back until we disappeared beyond her view.

CHAPTER
TWENTY-FIVE

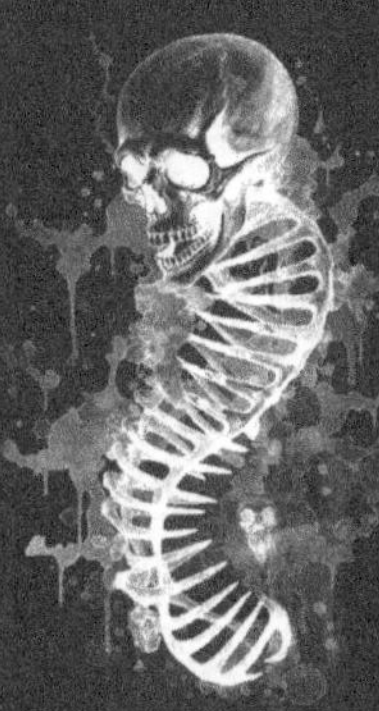

AMAIA

Apparently, Finley was new to the concept of allies. At least I hoped she was considering it was Alexiares' bike she'd blown to pieces as her little distraction. I didn't think distraught could even cover the pain etched onto his face when he'd seen what she'd done.

The woman had taken everything from him, and when he had finally made something for himself on his own, she had tried to take that from him too. Had succeeded in the smallest of ways, with something material. I understood though; it was the principle of it all that got to him.

Alexiares dropped his bags, his knees giving out, face buried in his hands. I stepped over the larger pieces that were scattered, coming up behind him in support.

"Hey," I cooed, rubbing his shoulders as he took in the scene, "it's okay. We'll get you a better bike, something faster, cooler. Like what you had in The Before."

He brushed me off, reaching down to paw through the rubble. The echo of the largest pieces he launched at the big rig sent me jumping back. An animalistic scream ran through him, one of pure agony and suffering. Standing there, I felt fucking helpless, watching as his body shook, shoulders slump, burdened by the weight of his loss. His chest heaved, gaze distant, lost in disbelief and heartbreak.

"I wanted this bike," he bit out, rising to his feet. Alexiares' fists clenched tightly, turning his knuckles a ghostly white.

I nodded in understanding, "I'll help you build another one when this is all over. I can find the pieces, we can——"

"It's not about the fucking motorcycle, Amaia."

And it wasn't, but still, I didn't know how else to help. So I did all that I could. Picking up the rubbage, I tossed shards of metal at his side, screaming when he screamed, yelling out my frustrations. The rage that had been simmering underneath the surface emerged, my own grief erupted from the depths of my soul.

This life was not fair. It was not kind. There were no breaks in the waves, because the world would always go on.

His cries reverberated through me, his grief had somehow become mine to bear too. The tears that welled up in my eyes spilled freely, dust and debris from the wreckage obscured my vision. I didn't care if anyone or anything heard us, watching us in our feral rage. The only thing I gave a damn about was letting him know that he was not alone.

When there was nothing left to throw, Alexiares took a deep inhale, turning to me. "This will never be over. I know that. You know it too."

I searched into his glassy eyes, offering a weak smile before resting my head against his chest. Alexiares wasn't talking about the bike anymore, not sure he ever was. His chin found the top of my head and we held each other, watching the sun tuck beyond the horizon.

"Come on, let's find a place to hole up in," I said, grabbing his hand.

WE FOUND SHELTER IN A SMALL, COTTAGE-STYLE HOME LESS THAN A mile away. Alexiares pulled the blinds then the curtains, in an attempt to keep Finley from lurking should she have followed us.

A death wish didn't seem to be on her list of priorities. Finley would have to be far beyond a fool to come anywhere near either of us anytime soon. Alexiares' promise of death to her was very real. If he had tattooed it on his forehead, it would merely be a souvenir for what was coming and not a reminder. I had no doubt Finley would steer clear, but if it made him comfortable, then I'd let him find peace in the smallest ways.

"Hey, this is pretty cool," I said, raising up a coffin-shaped diamond ring to one of the candles I'd lit when we arrived.

Ruffling through other people's crap never got easier. The promise of finding cool things kept me from stopping my usual snooping. Sometimes it was plain eerie, walking into homes that were still intact. It always made me wonder what happened to the owners. For this home specifically, it was clear no one had ever come back in the almost six years since the bombs went off.

A box of Cheerios was knocked over next to two rank smelling bowls of what had likely once been milk. There was a white board calendar on the fridge, listing out the soccer practice Thursday at five and gymnastics Saturday at noon. Shoes were clattered against the floor like someone had recently stepped out of them. The washer machine tucked into the closet behind me was left open, moldy clothes still sat crumpled in the dryer.

He kept his back to me, not paying me any mind. "What is?" he asked, double and triple checking all the entry points to the house.

I grabbed the matching silver band from the jewelry dish on top of the armoire near the door. Sliding them onto my fingers, I walked closer to him, waving them in his face.

"These babies. Riddle me shocked, but she didn't seem to be the type," I said, glancing at the pale, conservatively dressed woman and brown man in the picture behind the dish.

Alexiares fought off a grin, "There you go again, judging a book by its cover. Very … I don't know, untraditional, somewhat gothic. It's probably costume jewelry—maybe it was for Halloween."

Rolling my eyes, I pushed past him, placing them back where I'd found them, "Well, I think they're beautiful. And I'm not judging, just saying that it looks like something I'd have, not a soccer mom."

"You're not helping your case," he muttered, still distracted from peeking out the windows.

I groaned, plopping down onto the couch, "I'm bored and hungry. Can't believe there's nothing in the cupboards that's edible. What mom doesn't have Chef Boyardee or ramen noodles stashed away? At minimum she could have graced the house with Kraft Mac & Cheese."

Biting into a piece of jerky, I did everything in my power, not the gag. This shit would never go down easy. Damn me for thinking it would be a good idea to stock up on real food once we made it to Lola's.

He joined me on the dusted velvet green sofa with a huff, resting his head on my lap. I stared at the photos on the wall, my hands traveling through his hair, rubbing the sides of his face soothingly.

"Wanna play a game?" I asked.

Alexiares chuckled half-heartedly. "Okay, Jigsaw."

I smacked him gently and he feigned pain. "See the people in the pictures on the wall? We have to guess what their lives were like based on the photos alone. No cheating."

"How could you possibly cheat in this game?" he mumbled.

"By using the room around you, silly," I said, recalling exactly the way Jax had managed to beat me every time before. "It's not I Spy. It's people watching through photos. Use that adorably graphic imagination of yours."

It wasn't about recreating my life with Jax with him. I only wanted to use what I had learned to help Alexiares through today. Jax and I had played this game countless times while scouring through abandoned homes for anything salvageable to take back with us to The Compound. The game helped ground me in reality when everything around me spun outside my control. I wrote the story. And now Alexiares could too.

"I see, okay, umm. You go first."

"Don't try to be a gentleman now. It's far too late for that," I teased. "Fine. That lady there, the mom. She goes to restaurants and complains about things she could have known if she had read the menu. *Excuse me, ma'am, I asked for a cheeseburger plain. This burger has cheese on it.*" I cackled, mocking the ridiculous statement I'd heard as a waitress during college.

"What makes you say that?" He released a small laugh.

"Her haircut," I said, pointing toward the short brown pixie cut with blonde highlights throughout. "It's self-explanatory."

He nodded against my lap, turning his head slightly to get a better view. "Yeah, good point. My turn, princess. Her husband spends his weekend in the yard blowing around leaves and tossing dirt to avoid the little devil kids."

"They do look pretty bad," I agreed, my voice dancing with joy. "That one in the corner has never listened to a damn thing his parents said."

"Ooh!" he exclaimed, getting into the game. "The little girl for sure gets whatever she wants, smug-ass grin. Reminds me of someone I know."

I shrugged, pretending to be dense, "Don't know who that could be."

"Someone in this room."

I glanced around the room, scanning for whoever the culprit must be. Certainly it wasn't me. He grabbed my hand playfully, prying my pointer finger up and making it turn toward my face.

Laughter exploded from me. "Too bad I'm not in the picture, that's not part of the game!"

Something changed between us, the air in the room growing tense and his body stiffened. I could see the thoughts churning behind his eyes, turning darker the way they did in the woods with Finley.

"Yeah," he shoved away from me, putting distance between us, face grim and serious. "Maybe I don't want to play anymore."

My throat bobbed as I swallowed hard. I knew what this was about, but I was hoping he wouldn't go there. Not now, not when his emotions were already running high. It wasn't as if he didn't understand where I was coming from; he had to. But with everything that happened with Finley, this was a fight he could pick with an easy target.

Part of me wanted to give that to him, the other half wanted to remain stubborn and push back. "Then what do you wanna play, *Alexi*," I said grimacing at the pain all over my body as I reached across the couch to tap playfully on the tip of his pointed nose.

He grabbed my hand roughly, holding onto it with a squeeze, "You are the only person I don't want to call me that."

"I thought it infuriated you for me to and I quote, call *you by your government name*, unquote," I said, still trying to defuse the situation.

"I'm being serious, Amaia. Keep calling me Alexiares." He refused to meet my eye, instead turning his head back to stare at the photo from the game.

"Why?"

"It sounds right when it comes from you," Alexiares declared.

I took a few breaths, my heart beating quickly inside my chest. "Only me? Not anyone else?"

Maybe this conversation wasn't headed where I thought it was, but I couldn't help but feel like it was still taking a turn I wasn't yet ready for. I felt a lot of things for Alexiares, but our relationship had been fast tracked. Intense.

Everything about us ranged from one level of intensity to the next, nothing simmered, nothing grew overtime. I was terrified. Things that burn quickly tend to burn out. I didn't want that for us. You don't get to decide how love burns though, not when your heart guides that path.

"I go by Alexi because Alexiares is too fucking close to my father's name," he declared. "Alexiares is what *he* called me."

"You want me to call you the name that someone you can't stand used to call you by? I'm confused." And I was, that didn't make sense to me. Sure, I wasn't ready for everything he appeared ready to offer me, but that didn't mean I was ready for him to hate me again, either.

"Don't be, it's simple. My mother, Evander"—his voice caught on his brother's name—"Tiago … the people who knew me the best, the people who loved me, the ones who spoke to me with kindness, they called me Alexi. So Alexi it was, for years. But with you, you make me proud to be Alexiares. You put strength and love back into my name, so for you, you call me Alexiares and don't ever stop."

I smiled at that, a sense of pride running through me. Something else too … joy. No, joy didn't cover that flutter in my stomach moving toward my heart. It was something else, something I realized maybe I was growing against my better judgment, against my wishes for myself.

My hands found the sides of his face, brushing his hair out the way. Blood still covered his mouth, the under parts of his eyes but that didn't stop me from pulling him in for a kiss. He turned his head at the last moment.

"What's wrong?" I frowned.

"I think you know that conversation from the woods isn't over."

Damn it, there goes that I guess.

"What conversation?" I said, giving him an innocent, doe-eyed blink that I knew he couldn't resist.

"Cut the shit, Amaia," Alexiares bellowed. "You know damn well what I'm talking about. You don't trust me."

An odd sense of fury washed over me, not liking the way he'd made me vulnerable before proceeding to have a tough discussion. It felt manipulative in a way. Funnily enough, I knew we had both manipulated each other during the conversation. Using the way we knew how the other felt to try to steer the outcome of the inevitable topic we now landed on. The only reason rage seared through me was because his plan had worked—I'd fallen right into his trap—and mine had not.

I slid off the couch, pacing the room as I tugged on my matted curls. I'm sure I was an unsightly creature to see at this moment. It wasn't as though he was in any better condition; we kind of looked like Pansies if I thought about it. Biting back a laugh, I focused my thoughts. His head followed me with each step, eyes hard and unforgiving as he awaited my response.

"*Didn't* trust you," I said thoughtfully. "I trust you now, you know that."

No dice. Alexiares rose a brow, not cutting me any slack. "You don't seem bothered by what Finley had to say."

"Because I'm not."

His pupils dilated, and I diverted my eyes back to the ground. "Why not?"

The question stopped me in my tracks. I honestly didn't know how to answer that question. Lying was an option, but the thing was, oddly enough, I didn't *want* to lie to him. Not anymore, not ever again. It would almost be as if I were lying to myself, but it wasn't my truth to tell. There was always the option to omit the truth, work my way around it, but it still felt a bit dirty.

"Lying through omission is still a lie," he said through his teeth, as if he had a front-row seat to my thoughts.

I crossed my arms, my stubbornness pushing to the surface. "It's not my place to say."

"I thought we were a team," Alexiares pushed.

Damn him. Damn him for trying to use that against me. He knew we were a team, knew I trusted him with things I didn't trust the others with. Confided in him with some of the darker things I was capable of that I didn't want Moe, or Reina, or even Riley to see.

"We are," I ground out.

"No, we're not." He was pissed. An unimpressed glare greeted me when I found the courage to meet his gaze once more. "Not until you stop hiding things, until then, I'm just your side-kick. Your lapdog."

CHAPTER
TWENTY-SIX

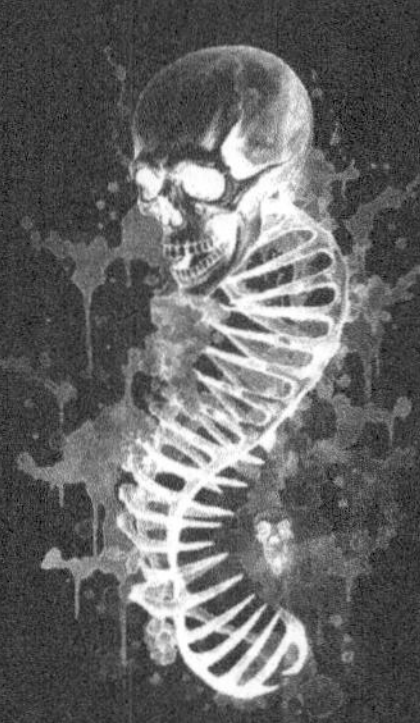

ALEXIARES

"I'm not worried about what Finley had to say, because we don't need her. Even still, she offered us something of value, anyway. It's a win as far as I'm concerned." Amaia fought to keep her tone even, but I saw right through the bullshit.

She was hiding something and the thought of that fucking hurt. Had I not proved my loyalty to her? I would do anything for this woman who had rocked my world in more ways than I could count. What was worse was that I knew better than to buy into the whole family shit they had pushed so hard for. Of course, that didn't include me. Why would it?

"Why don't we need her?" I asked, wanting her to be straight up with me. "I thought you were worried about Kansas."

Her lips pulled into a tight smile, head held high. "I was until I made plans."

"Of course you did." I scoffed, hating when she did that stupid, prideful shit. "Care to enlighten anyone else?"

A lie. I didn't hate it. I just hated it when it was directed toward me.

"Riley has it under control. He should be putting them into place by the time we get back. Don't stress over nothing."

"Right," I gave a tense nod in frustration, "Riley. What can Riley do that I can't?"

She wiped her palms against her torn pants, turning her back to me. "There you go again, with that string of jealousy. It's not cute."

"It's not jealousy, it's annoyance. What's not cute, Amaia, is you trying to use Moe to look into my past and future. How long did that go on for? Until we made it to Duluth?" I ground out.

The thing was it made sense that she had used Moe in that situation. I got it, really I did, scouts' honor or whatever. I was the new guy who had shown up in not the best of circumstances. I had been cagey when I arrived. That certainly hadn't played in my favor in hindsight. In my defense, it hadn't exactly been the most welcoming environment. In her defense, she now knew I had been there to kill her and burn Monterey Compound to the ground. Semantics.

"Oh," she muttered.

I crossed my arms in response, biting the inside of my cheek. "Oh?"

"Yeah, *oh*." Amaia sighed her haughty little sigh, matching my stance. "As in, you're still stuck on that."

Her curls bobbed around every time her head moved, attitude rolling off her. It was shocking how much insolence and stubbornness could be kept inside such a small body. Amaia was a Tasmanian devil, wild and untamed. Not able to control an ounce of her emotions the way she thought she could when it came to me. We were so similar, sometimes it was as if we brought out the worst in each other.

I kicked that thought to the door the moment it entered my mind. That wasn't true. Amaia brought out the best in me. She challenged who I was at my core and I could only hope to one day return the favor.

Swallowing the laugh that wanted to find its way free, I kept my face slack. I was pretty sure Amaia didn't want me to bring out the good in her. That wasn't what she appreciated about me and I knew it. We both took what we needed from each other. She fed her beast from mine.

I loved that about her. Loved a lot of things about her.

"Hard not to be, considering it came out an hour ago," I retorted.

Amaia inspected the dirt beneath her nails. "Hm, then you'd be even more mad if you knew why I wasn't upset when she couldn't."

My tongue slid across my teeth, biting down on the anger rising within me. I didn't want to be angry with her. Most of it wasn't even coming from what we were currently arguing about. This was just an outlet I could find relief in, a fight she might let me win. My girl did no such thing. That was how hurt people operated. We hurt each other.

"Continue," I said.

"You don't give me orders, Alexiares."

Nodding slowly, I smirked. Daring her to go on. "Continue, Amaia."

"Damn it!" she shouted, kicking at the wall. The photo of the family fell to the ground with the impact. Amaia stared at it for a moment, flames encasing her hands. She took a deep drag of air, willing them away. "Stop pushing me on this! I made him a promise. It's not up to me to reveal his secrets." The latter came out softer, adjusting from her unsuspecting anger.

I was better off solving a fucking five-hundred piece puzzle than trying to understand Amaia. Every time I thought we got closer, she pushed me further away. I didn't like it, it made me feel … lonely.

"His secrets or the secrets the two of you share?"

She went quiet, attention trained on the stupid dust coated floors again. I crossed the room, towering over her. Cautiously, I guided her chin up, forcing her to meet my stare.

"Oh … it's not just the two of you, is it?" I questioned.

Still, Amaia said nothing. Her eyes told another warring story. There was something there, something she wanted to tell me but couldn't. Somehow, that made things worse. Made me feel even more left out from what I thought I had finally found.

A mocking laugh forced its way from my lips. "Got it."

"Everything is under control," she said gently, trying to cover her tracks. "You don't need to worry either."

"Don't need to worry? If we're a team, we need to act like a team. All of us, not everyone *but* me."

There was sadness in her dark brown eyes. "It's not like that …"

"Not like what? Like all of you are a family and I'm just the new guy?" My voice broke against my will and I pushed myself away from her.

She didn't need to see me this way. *Would she still like me if I let weakness show? Why did she have to be so difficult all the damn time?*

"Yeah, Alexiares." Her words were barely a whisper. "Maybe you shouldn't be a part of this family. Maybe none of you should want to be a family with me. Matter fact, you should all let me do this all on my own. I work better that way anyway. Somehow everyone connected to me ends up hurt or dead. You're all just biding your time."

"Unbelievable," I sneered. "Open your fucking eyes, Amaia. Look around you! You have people helping you on all sides, even when they're mad at you or can't stand to be in the same space as you. Stop playing the fucking victim. It's getting old."

Her composure shattered like fragile glass. The calm facade she tried hard to put on cracked, leaving nothing but the molten anger churning beneath. Flames, fierce and unrestrained, surged to life along the edges of her skin, dancing and flickering menacingly.

My hand darted to her bag next to the door, snatching the contents out before she could muster a response. Since we were making people vulnerable … It took no more than two half-hazard movements for my fingers to graze on exactly what I was searching for. I knew it was there without having seen her place it.

A bottle of liquor. Untouched, the cap was securely in place, but that meant nothing when it came to her. Her flames doused. Out of the corner of my eye, I watched Amaia's hand near the dagger at her hip.

"You're going to stab me because you're caught making poor choices? You thought I wouldn't notice? Wouldn't smell it on you the second you took a sip? We share a bed for fuck's sake." I closed in on her, pressing her back to the door. The liquid inside the bottle splashed around the inside as I forced the bottle in her face.

What the hell were we even doing this for? I couldn't even remember how this all began. This had to stop. I needed to stop, but all the emotions I felt … I didn't even know what to do with them at this point. Anger was familiar to me. I was comfortable with it. But this, seeing this bottle in her bag, it was the ultimate betrayal, completely disregarding the words of disowning that just came out her mouth.

This felt like … heartbreak, maybe? When I left St. Cloud, it wasn't from heartbreak. Sure, Finley had been the main cause of my departure, but mostly because of the disgust over what I'd become. And anger, that had been a main motivator.

Amaia glared at me. "How many times are you going to say the word *fuck* to make your point?"

"As many as it takes to get through your thick, fucking head that this"—I shook the bottle wildly, the sloshing of it ringing through the room—"is not more important than the people around you. The people that are counting on you, that need you. That want you. I want you. I want to be a part of whatever you're a part of. Your family, your team. I just want you, Amaia. I want all of you, and I want you to trust me. And I want this to stop being a crutch you fall back on when things get hard." I let it drop to the floor, shattering into sharp fragments, the liquor seeping out into a puddle.

She lunged out, trying to catch it, but it was too late. "No … No. That wasn't for you to do! I wasn't going to drink it. It was just in case—"

"In case what?"

"In case I end up alone," she whimpered.

Mortified with a tinge of guilt, I watched on as she wiped her hands through it, bringing it to her lips. "Look at me, Alexiares," Amaia cried. "Why would you want to be a part of anything I play a role in? I couldn't even protect you. I couldn't stop Finley from hurting you again. The most powerful woman in this wasteland right now, and I couldn't even keep your property safe. How the hell am I supposed to protect my family?"

I didn't need her protection. We were a team. Teammates look out for each other. She had once told me that she didn't want a savior or a protector, and I thought she understood the same for me. What happened today with Finley, that monstrous bitch, was not on the woman standing before me who owned my heart.

Kneeling on the ground, I grabbed her hands, holding them into my palm and rubbing them gently. "This isn't about me."

"Isn't it?"

I dropped her hands, frustrated, choking out a humorless laugh. "About me? No, Amaia, it's about you. It's always been about you."

She hopped up, the woman warrior I had learned to admire, and glared back at me. Amaia's hands found both my shoulders with a hard shove. I fell onto my back, the sticky liquid beneath me seeping into my clothes, sharp glass poking into my skin. She wailed on me, coming to a rest on top of my legs, pinning me to the ground. I stopped counting the slaps when I realized they didn't hurt. They were barely a whisper against my skin.

If she wanted to hurt me, she was fully capable. Part of me thought she didn't even realize what she was doing. She needed this just as much as I needed to destroy the ashes of my only prized possession hours ago, so I let her.

"Come on! Swing, I know you want to!"

I stared at her, covered in blood and gore, but at that moment I wanted nothing more than to swoop her up and kiss her. In her fitful rage, she was the most beautiful woman I had ever laid eyes on. Amaia spent all her damn time making sure that everyone around her was built up to their fullest potential but never stopped to give herself any credit when it was due.

There was no fighting back for me. I would never do anything to hurt her, not ever again. I would do the opposite, actually. For the rest of my life, I'd do everything in my power to ensure that nothing would ever break her again.

"No," I said simply, leaning up, sliding her off me.

She shoved me again. I didn't move an inch.

"I never asked for you to care, I never asked—"

"You're scared." I suddenly realized.

It all made so much fucking sense now. She constantly pushed me away, let me in with conditions because she was scared of losing someone else. And while I sympathized with her, I would be relentless in my attempt to get as close to her as possible. There was no leaving her side for me. I knew she was scared of the inevitable, of death. But the only way my death would ever be a factor was if we were taking that last breath together, and I would be damned to let her take hers a moment too early.

"Fuck you," she growled, backing away from me slowly.

I scrambled to my feet, my heart a frantic rhythm charging the space between us. The rise and fall of her chest caught my attention and my eyes lingered on the exposed skin, trailing down the length of her body. I closed the gap between us. With the lightest touch, I urged her chin up, begging her to meet my gaze.

"It's okay to be scared, Amaia, fear is what keeps us alive. We both know that, live by it, and will probably die by it. You—You care so fucking much, but you're way too over protective." I confessed, "You're fearless and beautifully confident, but you're also arrogant and cocky. You expect nothing short of perfection, which leaves you insatiably unsatisfied. You're—"

"I can't tell if this is a hate speech or a confession," she interrupted.

God, sometimes she just needed to shut the fuck up. Let someone else do the talking.

"It's me telling you that I think I'm falling in love with you, you idiot. And I need you to trust me. I … I don't even know what love feels like, but fuck, Amaia, I think I'm falling in love with you in a way that makes me love living. I've never … I never thought I would make it this far in life, but you, you calculating little demon, make me love breathing. God dammit, Amaia." I broke our connection, pacing across the room, the emotions of it all overwhelming. "From the moment we were captured in St. Cloud, I realized how important you are to me, how much you make me care. But you won't let me help you. You do everything on your own. So yes, I push and I pry. And—"

When I turned around, she was there. Her lips were on mine, answering my plea. The kiss deepened, and I forgot the world around me. Forgot it all.

Every bad thing that ever happened to me didn't matter as long as I was here with her. With each press of her lips, every brush of her fingers gently down my face, raw emotion reverberated through every tendril of my existence.

The touch of her, the taste of her, it all felt so fucking right. Her tongue raised every goosebump on my body. I understood instantly that this woman, right here, was the beginning to my end. We were not brought together by a higher being or the universe. We were two broken souls clutching at each other in a world that had dealt us nothing but brutal blows.

It was messy, untamed, a brutal spark that defied the odds, but both of us had decided long ago that our fate would be our own in The After. Fuck everything else. And for once, in the midst of the wreckage of my life, I wholeheartedly believed I had a fighting chance to claw my way out of the darkness. The anger. The misery. With Amaia, there was a faint glimmer of hope and redemption in a life that had only shown me suffering.

"Take your clothes off," I ordered.

Her eyes lit up the fucking room, and she grinned, stripping clean of her layers. When the last piece of clothing hit the floor, I showered her with my water magic. Letting it cascade down every inch of her, removing all the dirt and grim, preparing my feast.

She was fucking otherworldly. I would worship her for the rest of what life I had left in me. I watched as she shivered, her full breasts peaking at the coolness of my water. I channeled my flames beneath her, fighting for control to make sure they recognized her as an extension of me, willing them not to harm a hair on her beautiful head.

Amaia's eyes never left mine. She smirked in recognition of the control I now possessed. "Alexiares, look at you."

"No, princess, look at you," I said. If only she could see herself through my eyes.

The water formed a small pool on the floor, not having a route to escape. I didn't give a shit as I splashed through, wanting to join her. She pulled my shirt over my head, fingers running over every hard line and ridge of my torso.

Amaia's mouth found mine again, cool drops of water finding their way through the thin space between us as her teeth caught on my bottom lip. Gently, she pulled back, nibbling in a way that she knew drove me wild.

Her hands toyed with the buckle of my pants, wildly searching for a way to relieve me from them. I groaned, ready to be inside of her but not wanting to rush her pleasure.

"I'm convinced I'll never be able to get enough of you," I said as I grabbed her throat, my mouth against the skin of her cheek.

She nuzzled against me, a small laugh sounded between her words, "Then don't."

It dawned on me then. That meant everything to her. That was as far as she would ever say, and it didn't matter to me. It would be an honor to be loved by her in any way she was willing to give.

I shifted my focus to her nipples, kissing down the center of her body then back up, my mouth toying over each one. Her curls tickled the top of my head as she glanced down to watch, a moan escaping her.

Leading her to the wall, I pressed her back against it, locking her hands down at her side with the vines of my magic. She arched with pleasure as I dropped to my knees. I teased my tongue closer to my end goal.

Amaia ripped her hands free. Inhaling sharply, she tipped her head back as I placed handcuffs made of fire around her wrists, my hands now occupied by the plumpness of her ass. I squeezed, nails digging into them, cradling the heaviness that greeted me. Her body was quickly becoming my favorite thing. Just the thought of being in her made me want to succumb to her every desire. Whatever she wanted, I'd be damn sure to provide.

I bit up the side of her left leg, leaving my mark as a guiding trail to her core. Stopping briefly to torture her with her lust before realizing I was stupidly torturing myself instead. Then, I feasted.

My tongue circled every sensitive spot at her center, making her wiggle, fighting to stay upright. Her eyes fell closed and I'm not sure why, but that pissed me off.

"Look at me," I ordered.

They whipped open, heat lingering in her gaze. Wetness gushed over my tongue and I grinned, the whisper of my small laugh driving her wild.

"Fuck," she purred, urging me on.

I didn't stop until she broke free from my flame, hands curled within my hair and she dragged me up. When met face to face, I noticed a smear of red still stuck on the side of her face.

"Missed a spot," I chuckled, my tongue running up her cheek, removing the blood.

She paused, and for a moment I thought I fucked it all up. A wicked grin formed on her face and she grabbed me, her tongue intertwined with mine. "You like that?" she asked, her voice hoarse.

Before I could answer, she was on her knees, hand reaching for something within the pile of clothes, water sloshing beneath her. Her fingers curled around the item she was feeling around for, one of her blades.

Amaia held my gaze. If I had ever known what awaited me, I would have not come to Monterey to kill her, but to worship the ground she walked on instead.

Slowly, she kissed up my body, stopping at my chest, waiting for my permission. I nodded, gripping the back of her neck. Leaning my head against the wall, I watched as she carved letters over the inkless space above my heart. My memories flickered back to the ritual, the smile I'd tried to bite down from the satisfaction the pain of the bloodletting offered me. Of course she had noticed, because she thrived in pain, too.

AMAIA

I grimaced through the ecstasy of the pain. Groaning as my dick pressed aching into my pants. I bit my lip, embracing the cold, piercing sting of the metal against my flesh. Her eyes danced when she finished, a burning heat rising to my face as she examined me through lowered lids. She twirled the knife in her hands, slamming it against me to pass the torch.

Hesitantly, I took it. Studying her, making sure she was certain. Fuck knew I wouldn't be able to stop if we went this route. One look at her pleading eyes and I was reminded how similar we were. In pain, there was pleasure, and she would always have as much pleasure as she desired.

Amaia pointed to a space near the lower part of her right hip, drawing a line across the scar that marked her death. She placed her finger on where she wanted me. This scar was the trigger of a story that led me here. The reason I both hated and loved her. She kept her eyes steady on mine, bracing herself for the kiss of the knife.

It didn't make me nervous to disrupt that perfect blemish on her skin. I'd done enough tattoos in my day. My hand was steady as I got to work.

I watched her with each letter, making sure she didn't want me to stop. She whispered moans at the white-hot pain, finding a thrill in the coursing throb of all nine letters. When I was done, I admired the beauty of my work, now sporting on the most delicious body I'd ever laid eyes on.

ALEXIARES

Dropping the knife, I grabbed her hips. Amaia pushed my head forward, applying pressure as I licked her wound like each stroke of my tongue had the power to heal her. I don't know what tasted better, her blood or her wetness.

The only way to find out would be indulging in both options. She stopped me before I got another taste, pushing me toward a lounge chair next to the couch. Leaning back, I spread my legs, resting my arms on the side. Amaia crawled over to me, finally relieving the tension from the clothes that restricted me.

She took my dick into her hands, tracing her tongue around my tip, then dove right in. Amaia took every inch as I fucked her throat, choking as my fingers laced through her curls, pushing her head down. Little moans escaping when I let her up for air, squirming at the absence of her lips around my dick. The sound was music to my ears.

At the sensation of me pulsating inside her warm mouth, Amaia pulled back a moment before I found my release, a dark smile crossing over her plump, reddened lips. I leaned forward, wiping the spit from around her mouth.

"Bend over, beautiful, that wasn't very nice, teasing me that way." I tossed her into the lounge chair, switching positions so quickly she yelped in surprise.

I stared at the curves of her body, admiring it. Questioning what the hell I'd done in life to have the privilege of ending up here with her.

She smirked back at me. "Now who's teasing?"

I broke out of my trance, slapping her on the ass, proud of the hand print I left behind. Gripping her hips, I drove into her relentlessly. I pulled her head back near my lips, wanting her to hear exactly how she was making me feel.

Her moans grew louder, a hand finding hold of my wrists, her nails digging in and drawing blood. The sight of my blood on her made me painfully hard. A new sense of agony added to all the pleasure that being with her brought me.

She was intoxicating. I got rougher the more she pleaded, begging me to keep going. *Harder. Deeper.* She screamed her climax, my hand covering her mouth, allowing her to bite down for relief. When my job was complete, I fell into her, breathing heavily for a few moments as I found my release. Every muscle in my body went tense.

It took me a minute to gather myself, finding the strength to leave her warmth but desperate to find her lips again. She rolled over, making space for me within the lounge chair, and I pulled her into my lap. Amaia leaned against me, kissing along my jaw, then placing a few soft pecks on my mouth, stopping at her favorite place, the tip of my nose.

The room grew quiet, the weight of my confession suddenly creeping back in. She turned, tossing both of her legs over the side of the chair, tracing the outlines of her name on my heart.

She kissed it gently, "Now you have a new scar, one with good memories."

I thought about her words, realizing the reason she'd wanted to put her name there outside of the obvious. My chest and back were speckled with the scars my father had given me over countless beatings I'd taken. Some on behalf of my mother or my brother, others from what I probably deserved for mouthing off. A few were given as punishment for fucking up some of his business deals, ones that I just couldn't let happen.

No one should be sold to another person, especially not women and children. There were some things in this world that I refused to turn a blind eye to, and that was one of them. I had no regrets. I would gladly take every lashing all over again. Some lines were thicker than others.

The thinner ones were from the wire hangers he'd straightened out from dry cleaning, others were from whatever stick he'd forced me to find in the yard. The thickest ones, the ones that hurt surprisingly the least, had come from his favorite leather belt. He never wore that belt. It was just his favorite because it had been the first thing he'd ever struck me with.

My father used it when he wanted to drive one point home; I would always be a lost little boy that he held an immense amount of power over. There was no escaping that, even when I'd tried as an adult and he'd sent his men out to hunt me down and drag me back to him.

The only escape had been during his death, and then I'd fallen pawn to another master. The scars she'd left were mostly hidden, with the exception of the few moments she'd turned her cruelty toward me full blast. The moments when her anger had sunken so deep that she'd lashed out at whoever was around her, who, more times than not, happened to be me.

Tattoos only covered so much. Being in the public eye had caused a lot of questions as the scars continued to appear, which served as a disservice, only angering my father more. I'd covered them the best I could. Only when you got close enough could you see the raised skin underneath. The kind that didn't come from a needle. No one noticed, because there was no one who I let get that close.

Amaia guided my face to her, resting her forehead against mine, trying to ground me back into this moment with her.

"One I'm proud to have," I whispered, pushing a curl back behind her ear.

"Those words," she stammered, "those words mean death."

I knew what she meant. She was speaking of the words I'd confessed to being on the verge of. I kissed the top of her head in acceptance. My confession had come with the knowledge of knowing she wouldn't say them back, but that didn't matter to me. I knew where she stood on the matter long before I'd grown the nerve to speak them. She'd confided as much to me long ago.

"I … I understand how you feel, Alexiares, but you deserve the world. Happiness," she said, and my heart skipped a beat. "You deserve a love that I don't think I can give you."

"Be quiet, princess. I know that I may never hear those words leave your beautiful, perfect, fucking lips. But I want you to know that I know *exactly* what I mean to you. It's in everything you do."

She nestled in close to me, placing a hand over my heart. "My heart beats for you and only you. That is all I can offer you. Take it or leave it."

I said nothing, just placed my chin atop her head, pulling her as close as possible, a fat grin all over my stupid fucking face.

CHAPTER
TWENTY-SEVEN

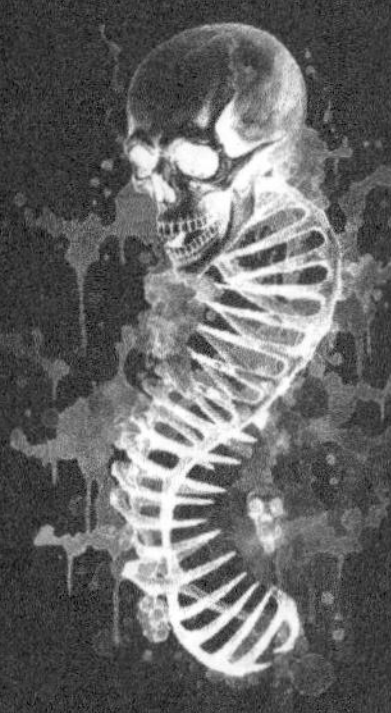

REINA

We pushed the heck out of those horses until they couldn't go anymore. I knew my way around a horse and over the last month, I'd gotten to know Bimbo pretty darn well. The others were forced to keep up, not that Moe needed much assistance in the matter. Seth had taught her enough whether he had realized it or not. Their time together had obviously rubbed off on an already quick learner.

Abel wasn't fooling anybody either. He may not have been as experienced as we were, but he made up for his shortcomings quickly. Pushing these babies from Cheyenne to Monterey should've taken less than a week. I couldn't blame Abel for the delay, or even Moe. We were simply just too dang late.

War had broken out around us.

My heart ached thinking there was a chance it had already reached the gates of our home. Salt Lake City was in absolute chaos. Alexi had been right, they would have our back in this war. That didn't mean much of nothing, though—not when the surrounding settlements caused mayhem with their fighting.

I mean seriously, I understood having traditional values and all that. There was a nice ring to it for some, I guess. To be honest, it just fed into my question on how stupid could they be to side with the people who wanted to strip them of their freedom? The math wasn't adding up on that one.

Provo and Ogden were fine. They'd have to have a death wish to ignore the demands of Salt Lake while in such proximity, but Moab had grown some balls. Trying to squeeze through their fighting unnoticed was as possible as a pig flying. Doing so atop a horse had essentially been riding with a literal target on our backs.

Saying bye to Bimbo was harder than I thought. We'd only spent a few weeks together, but she gave the comfort of a home I'd known long before my life had fallen apart. I patted her hide, saying my farewell before sending her on her way, in the opposite direction of all the riff raff.

"Come on," I said, pulling my hat down on my head.

I'd ditched the blood splattered fur and warm clothing outside of Cheyenne. We wouldn't need it anymore once we cleared Utah. Which was a feat I had wrongly assumed would take a day.

It wasn't like I was freezing my tail off. My black leather riding pants and hide-colored fringe jacket were enough for a girl used to the cold. I slid my black cowgirl hat over my hair; it did the job maintaining the warmth inside my body. After all, heat exited the body from two places—your noggin and your feet. Both of mine were solidly covered, in a cute way too, so I was good.

Abel was fine and dandy. He'd spent years up north. The brisk air down here was nothing on him. I offered him a warm smile, handing over the extra pack to toss over his newly acquired hoodie. A lady should never have to carry more than her weight when a man is around. I was fully capable, but I preferred my hands to be free for other things, like my new toys.

My sister, on the other hand, appeared to be moments away from becoming a frozen human statue. Her teeth chattered, hands rubbing against her arms to give herself some extra warmth.

"You know," she stammered, "I'm getting real fucking sick of these visions leaving out the important details."

Abel chuckled, dropping everything to remove his hoodie and toss it to her. She pulled it over the two layered, black turtlenecks, sliding her leather jacket on top. I tsked, all her layers in these conditions would slow her down in a fight.

More fight for me.

I wouldn't mind, truly. Making a kill had become easier, simpler, than the first time. At least now it wasn't on the unsuspecting, but on those who had it coming. You attack me and mine, and down you go, buddy boy.

"I told you before we left Wyoming to keep your coat. But nooo, no one listens to little ole me." I said, leading the way Alexi had drawn out on a map before we left.

Moe scoffed, "Yeah, well, Reina, it's kind of hard to make sure all my belongings are together when I'm chasing after you and whatever kills you're chasing for the day."

"Better than woman of the day," I mumbled, a smile on my face at the memories of what awaited me at home.

"*Maybe*," Abel offered, trying to simmer some peace, "if you had a system, some sense of organization, it would be easier to grab your stuff and go with full confidence."

Moe flipped him the finger, mocking his words as she worked to keep my quick pace. I shushed them, noticing the fresh tracks on the ground. Someone was here, watching us. I could sense it with my magic.

"Not many places to hide," I mumbled, scanning our surroundings.

We'd entered a deep canyon. The rugged, red rock formations would've been beautiful if I was here for a vacation. I wasn't though. I was here to make sure my family and I made it home in one piece.

There. Silly, silly soldiers, you're mine now.

Up ahead, a reflection of metal gave up the location of a few soldiers hidden behind a few of the towering mesas not too far in the distance. A river teased the other side of the land. I'm sure they thought we were the trapped ones. *Not for long.*

"Abel?" I asked calmly, meeting his quizzical gaze "How much you wanna bet I can scatter those fools with one pull of my bow and arrow?"

A sly grin pulled across his brown skin. "Hmmm. Why do I get the feeling your room is the comfiest one in The Compound?"

"Because it is," I said, pulling out a match to set an arrow aflame.

"Okay, if you miss, I get your room and you have to move in with Riley and the creep."

"That *creep* is about to be your roommate. Reina doesn't miss," Moe teased. "The real question is, what are they hiding for? They outnumber us." She scowled, peering at the world around us for an answer.

Abel grew rigid in response. "Maybe we should figure that out before we scatter them—"

"And if you lose this bet? What do I get?" I arched, ready to pull and taking a sharp snuff of air. "Never mind, I never miss."

It flew through the air before either one of them could stop me. Seconds later, my arrow hit its mark. A small blast scattered ten soldiers in the wind.

"Did you just—" Abel started.

I laughed, a defiant grin now in place. "Shoot a fiery arrow down the barrel of a gun several hundred feet away. Duh."

The tranquility of the canyon shattered. A deafening roar of energy and weapons split the air. A wave of troops emerged from different corners that I hadn't seen. My heart raced, adrenaline surging through my veins.

My training took over as I transitioned into my favorite deadly dance. With the agility of a cat, I weaved through the oncoming chaos, my movements fluent and precise. I vaulted over fallen soldiers, Abel's gun singing a sweet song past me, having my back to where I could not pay my attention.

I spun through the air, arrows flying and meeting their marks with half a thought. Moe's Katana sliced through soldiers, its movements an extension of her arm aiding her in silencing the screams as she cut them down. Their heads rolled under my feet, forever stuck in an inaudible cry for mercy.

The scene around me calmed. All the soldiers in our immediate vicinity were down. A mag clicked into a gun behind me and I turned, the wild look only the taste of violence could bring all over Abel's face. I hadn't called him on it before, but the kid never missed either. His accuracy didn't hit in the way that my arrows always met their target. I had trained for that. As easy as I made it seem, it took practice, aim, focus.

With Abel, well, there were only a few other people I knew that had such effortless accuracy, no matter the weapon, no matter the stance, no matter the distance they fired. One of them named Amaia.

"Are you going to stop toying with us, Abel, or you gonna tell us what you *really* are?" I teased.

Moe's head shot up as she wiped guts off on some poor dead soul. Her eyes bounced from me to Abel, her eyes narrowing in suspicion.

Movement caught my eye, a groan of a soldier trying to push themselves up brought me back into focus. His palm faced up, fire raging in it as a last-ditch effort to make one final kill.

"Behind you," I said with a grin.

He fired his weapon without looking, two bullets hitting the center of a now very dead man's head, "Is that necessary? My actions are obvious enough."

Before I could answer my friend, his attention darted behind me. I pivoted at the terror behind his gaze. An onslaught of more soldiers coming to avenge their fallen. I was out of arrows, but that was fine by me. I dropped my bow, freeing up some of the weight on my shoulders.

"And this," Moe said, her aggravation at the situation clear, "is why we wait to scope out a situation."

She was right, but once again what she failed to realize is that I didn't care. A fight was a fight. It was going to happen whether we passed through here untouched or not. At least this way, my father and brother had a couple dozen fewer soldiers on their side.

Moe reached out to grab hold of me, wanting to use our new magic to take these out, but I shook her off. I, for one, didn't want an easy fight. When they got closer, I realized it wouldn't work, anyway. These weren't men and women running at us. I mean they were, but they technically weren't. These were Pansies. The kind my sick-in-the-head father had created.

Oh the joy of destroying something he cares so dearly about.

I had full confidence in Abel's ability to aim, especially now with the confirmation that he was more than a Tinkerer or a Scholar with Seer capabilities, but also *Umbra Mortis*. Walking through the valley of the canyon, I stepped over corpses strewn about, a backup pistol on loan from Abel in hand.

It'd been a long time since I'd held one in my hands. The day I'd thought my father had died to be exact. This time, the trigger felt natural in my hand. I squeezed, letting the bullets flow freely, not caring where they landed. A few went down as I approached, whether they were from me or Abel I wasn't sure. Moe's eyes bore into my back, unmoving, watching the scene play out in front of her. *Whatever her problem is, I don't have time for it.* I shook off the annoyance seeping from her, like she was intentionally pushing it out toward me to make her emotions clear.

There were only two left, yet my gun was the only one I heard left firing. I reloaded, realizing the chamber was empty. Strolling up to them, I put five rounds into the one that presented as what was once a young woman, not much older than myself. Still a woman perhaps. Not one that had a fighting chance of living again though, might as well put her out of her misery.

I halted abruptly, the final one was nearly seven feet tall. Its fiery red hair snagged my attention. Cropped right about his ears, his pale, ashen face was torn, hanging off on some sides, yet the remnants of freckles speckled near his nose and under his eyes remained. Its eyes were glazed over from what I could tell, but as I got closer, blue eyes stared through me, white haze dusting atop them.

He fumbled, arms slack at his sides as he stumbled toward me. Grunts and inhumane screeches slammed toward me, and he pushed into a full-on sprint closing in on the final few feet. I held my ground, let him get close enough where his rancid breath reached my nostrils.

Then, I unloaded what was left of my magazine. His body dropped. Ten shots rang through my ears, but the only thing I felt in that moment was the pleasantry of the recoil.

I holstered Abel's Beretta, swapping it for a blade I'd been itching to use for some time. The one Alexi handed me when I'd departed Duluth.

If you find your brother, Reina, and he tries to drag you back to your father, don't you let him. Not if you don't want to. You fight like hell and you stand your ground. You're stronger than he could ever be, stronger where it matters.

Alexiares had pressed his hand over my heart, placing the blade there, waiting for me to take it. *And if he tries even once to put his traitorous hands on you, cut those fuckers off.*

I had a better idea right now, something that would grant me instant gratification. My knees touched the red soil beneath me as I hovered over the long-lost, recently dead soul. I drove my knife into his head splitting it like a cantaloupe.

Pocketing the knife, I made my way back over to my family. Abel's eyes scanned my body, hand out waiting for me to return his gun. I slide it out my holster and into his palm. He chuckled nervously, turning back to pick up his dropped magazines sprawled around him. Moe's mouth was open, and I tilted my head, trying to put feelers out there on what to expect, bracing myself for her impact. Water from the river emerged behind me, the current sweeping each of the scattered bodies and remaining weapons into the rush.

"You're acting like a psychopath," Moe snapped. "What is *wrong* with you?"

"I'm cleaning up all evidence that they were ever here. No body, no case. What is wrong with *you*, sister? Leaving the two of us to a fight could have been a disaster."

"She's right," Abel said off to the side.

I grinned at him. Although he had my back, as usual, the concern on his face was as clear as it was on Moe's.

"I'm just dandy," I grumbled. "You're one to talk, Tomoe. No one yells at you when you chop heads off and keep a big grin on your face while doing it. Mind the business that pays you."

Her features softened, she grabbed hold of my hand squeezing it in response. There was confusion, sadness, and an overall sense of despair in her. Waving my free hand against some of the cuts on her body from her own fights, I healed her wounds.

With a touch of my magic, I sent her some peace. I kept my tug small, something she wouldn't sense unless she searched for it.

She didn't need to worry about me, her grief alone was enough for us both. If she couldn't bring vengeance into her heart, I would hold enough of it for us.

"We need to move, now," Abel prodded, clarity in his deep brown eyes. He passed Moe some jerky from his pack, taking a bite out of mine before handing it to me, a sly smile on his face.

When I looked at him, I saw what others probably saw in me, youthfulness. That refreshing joy and optimism that had yet to be taken from him. I hoped one day we could have worry-free fun together. We were only going to be young once, our responsibilities shouldn't strip that youth from us, no one should.

"We're about a two-week walk from Monterey, race you there!" I said, tagging him playfully then taking off.

CHAPTER
TWENTY-EIGHT

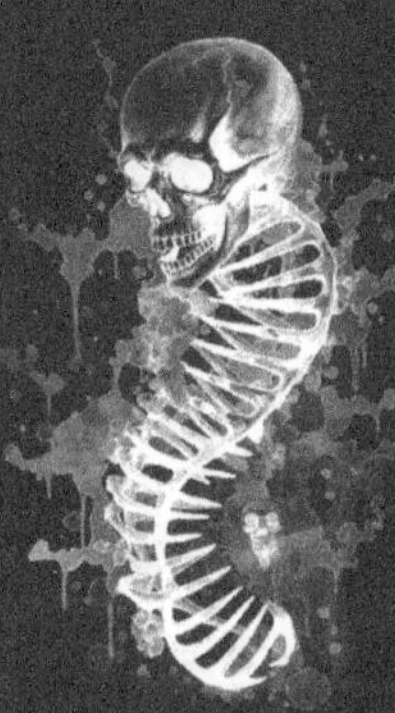

RILEY

A series of rhythmic knocks pounded against the door in the distance, stirring me from my sleep. My eyes opened, warm golden-brown skin glinted in the sunlight pouring through the window of my room. A soft chuckle sounded beside me. I squinted, looking up to the curtain of sleek black hair falling onto the pages of a book.

The knock sounded again, and I groaned, pulling a pillow over my face. I was beyond exhausted; it hurt to open my eyes completely. Without Amaia here, I'd fulfilled the role of three people. I could count the amount of people here I was comfortable confiding in on one hand. Really, a few fingers now with Amaia gone.

It didn't feel right appointing someone to fulfill the roles that now sat vacant within The Compound. Sure, my men could have helped. They had the security clearance to do so, but doing that without my sister present felt like dirty work.

"Are you going to get that, or should I fall out of this story and get it for you?"

Her voice was sweeter than honey in the most melodic way. Pulling the pillow off my head, I tossed it toward her, air magic reflecting it without a glance my way.

I rolled out of bed, kissing the soft skin on her shoulder on my way out. She smirked, a few of her teeth showing through her round lips. *Fuck me, I do not want to get out of this bed.*

"Morning," Yasmin said, skimming through the pages of one of Amaia's favorite books.

She'd left a few here during the nights we would stay up late. I found so much comfort in Amaia's presence, I'd never opened myself up to exploring another relationship that satisfied the closeness I had with my sister. Lost within the grief of Jax and Mohammed, I'd suffered alone.

Yasmin had just fit into my world. She was grieving too, Mohammed had been her forever until not so long ago. Now he was gone. The same way Jax was gone, the same way Amaia could disappear from the earth's surface in the blink of an eye without me there having her back.

Amaia and Jax had been my forever too. Not in the same way as Mohammed and Yasmin filled that role for each other. In the same breath, I could claim in full faith that I never saw life outside of the three of us.

Grief appeared to be the binder of most relationships in The After. I mean, even Before, it was that rallying concept that made you seek comfort in the similar. But somewhere in our grief, Yasmin and I had found happiness within each other. That subtle reminder that Mohammed could live on within us. I didn't expect it to make sense to everyone, but it made sense to us, and that was all that mattered.

I peered out the window, trying to determine what weather would greet me on today's adventure, "Good morning, beautiful."

The banging at the door became an obnoxious beat followed by mumbled rapping and a second, harsher knock of impatience.

"I'm coming, Eleanor," I yelled out. "Knock it off!"

The olive-green sheets pulled around Yasmin's body and she reached on the floor for one of my shirts. Teasingly, I used my magic to creep leaves of the Pothos plant on the shelf above her to tickle under her chin. Her smile had become my favorite thing in the world.

"I like that girl," Yasmin giggled, closing the book and sitting up in bed.

"Of course you do. Everyone does." I pulled some dark blue cargo pants on, splashing some water from the basin at the side of the room on my face.

She came up behind me, arms draped over my shoulders, "It's early. Off to do important things as an important person?" Yasmin asked, tension in her tone.

"Sure am," I said, keeping it short.

I watched her in the mirror, taking in her thick, long legs. She was almost my height, her tall frame allowing us to see eye to eye. Those sultry, dark eyes … *Snap out of it, Riley.* It was best not to tell her the details; there was still a sadness that lingered in her face that I had no business adding to.

She tsked, "Important things like …"

"If you say 'important' like that again, with those *kiss me* eyes, I may be inclined to tell you."

"So mysterious," she said, pulling me into a tender kiss. "Why do you never tell me the details?"

I bit back a groan, not wanting to argue with her. "Because the details make you uncomfortable, despite how much you say you want them."

"Riley Sullivan, I will never not be impressed by your ability to read a person before they read themselves." She smiled with her eyes, holding my face as she spoke. "But sometimes, it's okay to let people make decisions for themselves then face the repercussions of them."

The banging on the door was going to wake the whole General Living Quarters up if Elie didn't quit it. Part of me enjoyed her ability to be wild and free, the other part of me hated it. She was a little Amaia in the making and I wasn't sure if I was ready to have two little monsters running through The Compound.

"Of course it is, just not when I'm around," I said, not really joking.

It would be a cold day in hell before I would ever let someone I care about suffer again. For some reason, the women I'd surrounded myself with believed hard lessons to learn were the best lessons. If they wanted to do that on their own time, fine by me. But I refused to be the cause of any of their pain and knowing the dangerous details of my day, would only cause Yasmin distress.

I'd expected her to hate me after Mohammed's death. To blame me, to hold it against me for the rest of our lives. No one could blame me anymore than myself. I was the one who put him there, manning that damned gate. And she did feel all of those things, for a while at least. I hadn't let it go on for too long. I'd been determined to show her exactly how sorry I was. All of her needs had been met, whether it'd been by my soldiers or me alone.

A monarch butterfly appeared, landing on her cheek, and she laughed softly, releasing the tension in the room. I wasn't done seeing her smile. Lifting my hand out in front of her narrow, fine features, I grew a rose in my palm, placing it between my teeth and stalked toward her. Yasmin took it from my mouth, kissing me when she moved it to her hand.

"Okay," I said, "I have to go. See you later?" I gave her a gentle kiss on the forehead, tossing my shirt over my shoulders.

Racing down the steps, I threw open the door, glaring at the two imbeciles before me. Elie had a cheshire grin on her face, hands behind her back innocently.

"Long night, son?" Prescott greeted me with a mischievous smile as I pulled my shirt over my head.

"Ooo, are you in there with your girlfriend?" Elie said, trying to push past me into the house, "I wanna meet her, what's her name?"

"You already know her," I groaned, placing my hand on her forehead and pushing her out the door. She kept at it, body flailing as she tried to get around me.

"Elie …" Prescott warned, "Boundaries, little lady, boundaries."

"Thank you, an annoying habit Amaia and her have in common is the inability to respect them," I teased.

Harley and Suckerpunch shot out the door, the knocks not stirring them from their stumble but the voice of their second favorite girl instead.

Yasmin's hand fell on my shoulder drawing my attention behind me. "Hey, you almost forgot this." She handed me my water canteen I'd left on the bedside dresser. I shook it, grinning at the fact that she'd filled it for me knowing I'd forgotten when I came in late last night.

"Thanks, I'll be back around lunch. Meet you at The Kitchens," I said, kissing her cheek.

"Bye, Prescott, keep him safe." Yasmin grinned at Elie, but there was a strain behind it. I hated how much it pained her to see me leave. Compound first, though. If we lost sight of that, then we'd have nothing worth fighting for.

Prescott offered her a nod, waving as she shut the door.

"Yasmin is your girlfriend?" Elie chided, "Dude, she's hot. Way out of your league."

"Quiet, Eleanor." I snapped, the corner of my lips pulled against my will. "And I know."

"Elie," she corrected before skipping off, Suckerpunch and Harley at her heels.

Prescott grabbed my shoulder, bringing me to a halt with a wide grin. "Proud of you, you know?"

"Getting sentimental on me, old man?" I retorted.

The morning sun beamed down on my skin. There was a breeze swimming through The Compound, a welcoming aspect of the January air. Kids played throughout the streets, heading toward their weekend training, their parents watching them from their doorsteps. A few adults bustled about, focused on making it to whatever morning shift they were responsible for. I waved to a few as we made our way out of the General Living Quarters.

"Who, me?" Prescott countered, hand over his heart. "What I'm saying is, it's nice to see you with a smile on your face. I know you took it pretty hard, not having Amaia around. Two of you have always been attached at the hip."

I kept my focus on the cobblestone. It was hard talking about her, which was odd because she wasn't dead or anything. I don't think. *No, she's fine. You would feel it in your soul if she was gone.* Still, it tugged on my anxiety in a horribly painful way.

"I miss her," I said. "So much that it hurts. I want to know that she's okay."

"My sweet girl isn't exactly sweet. She can handle herself, try not to worry too much."

His words offered little reassurance. I knew he was confident in her abilities; I was too. But overconfidence never did anyone any favors. Anything could happen out there, unmatchable power or not.

"I know. It would be nice to hear from her is all. She was in denial about Seth for so long, didn't want to see it." I bit back the words left unsaid.

Had she listened to me, a lot of this could have been avoided. From the moment he'd arrived, I never really trusted Seth. I worked with him, tolerated him, even formed an odd friendship of sorts, but it was all at Amaia's request. Spending time alone together hadn't exactly been at the top of either of our to-do lists.

I remembered when he and Reina had arrived. The hate that lingered behind his eyes when she hopped off that horse and entered our gates hadn't been brotherly at all. There was an envy there that unsettled me. From that moment on, I vowed to keep an eye on him. You didn't have to trust someone to play nice, just needed to be good at pretending. Seth had been good at pretending too. Sneaky little bastard.

"But you did, and that's all that matters," he reassured me, indubitably noticing the worried frown on my face. "You were there for her and now you've stepped up while she's gone. I'm proud of you. Though that won't mean anything soon. She'll put my admiration to shame when she sees how you've handled it all. You're a true leader, Riley, someone they'll write about in history years from now. The three of you, the kids I never asked for but somehow got. I've lost one, but I pray I never lose another, not until I'm long buried in the ground."

"Which is ages from now, Pres," I said, side-eyeing him. Angling my head, I tried to find the best way to approach a question that had been eating at me for weeks now. "Do you think … Do you think she'll be mad about Yasmin?"

"Mad? No, I think she'll be happy to see you happy. You know her more than any of us, Riley, that isn't the true concern that you have. Perhaps you're wondering if she'll understand."

I rolled my eyes at both his statement and his tendency to redirect open-ended questions back at someone. Always making people ponder their own answers.

"Solid point. She's always been … less than pleasant to the women in my past. But this wasn't some rash decision. Sure, the circumstances are questionable, I understand that. I care about Yasmin, though. Mohammed would accept it, Yasmin said so herself," I started walking again, intent on catching up to Elie and the dogs. I knew I was rambling now, but I couldn't help myself.

Amaia never paid any mind to the women I'd been close with in the past. She had a way of welcoming them with open arms, yet treating them as though they would come and go, which they had. But there had been a few that I'd taken more seriously than the previous, and her disdain for them had ultimately resulted in me pushing them away.

"Sounds to me like you're questioning things on your own without Amaia around," Prescott implied. "The heart wants what the heart wants, my boy; something tells me when she gets back, there will be her own situation to discuss."

"Alexiares?" I scoffed, my nose pulling up at the thought of the two of them being anything more than enemies working together. They both used each other as a means to an end. Certainly, there was no romance there. A shiver went through my body as I shook the idea off, "No, she would never. The girl has standards if nothing else, Pres. Plus, she hates him."

Prescott released a hearty laugh, "Now who has to check themselves for understanding."

It was true. Since I'd known Amaia, it had always been Jax for her. Sure, Jax had confided in me as a brother prior to his death. Things between the two of them were fizzling out romantically, but they loved each other. I'd reassured him that it was just the stress of their positions that had chipped away at their love life. The way those two looked at each other, I had wanted that. Longed for it. There was no way there was anyone out there better for my sister; it simply wasn't possible. Jax had died less than a year ago, and I couldn't see her moving on from him so quickly. Then again, Mohammed had died months after Jax, and here Yasmin and I were ...

Prescott's laugh boomed off the alleyway as he took in my now distraught demeanor, finding amusement in me questioning my entire existence. I swallowed a gag at the thought of my sister with someone I'd learned to call a friend. He was a cool person and all, but to love him? It was just too beyond belief for Amaia to find comfort in a man like that.

YEARS WORKING ALONGSIDE AMAIA AND JAX COULD NOT HAVE PREpared me for what being in charge was truly like. So many questions that I'd already answered several times. I hated repeating myself. Amaia and Jax had never had to instruct me on something more than once. You either have it or you don't. But I get it, some people are slow learners.

It didn't dawn on me until I had to step in precisely how screwed we'd be if we let everyone do their own thing without checking in. I was practically hand-holding at this point.

We were out a little over a mile from North Gate mapping out what was soon to be a minefield. Should have already been one if it were up to me and my men, but unfortunately for everyone, I'd had to deploy them with several troops just to make sure my exceedingly specific instructions were followed. So now here we were, for the third time in a week, showing them exactly where to place the damn mines and going over the pattern needed for success.

Most of the playbook had remained the same, with minor tweaks due to Seth now being on the loose. Without Amaia here, it had been up to Prescott and I to adjust. I trusted Prescott—dude knew his shit. Me, on the other hand, my specialty had been working with smaller groups, forming plans on a smaller scale. Running a spy network was completely different from setting up Salem Territory for war. Because that's what it was—all of Salem looking to Monterey as they had time and time again.

They knew Amaia was away at this point, had already received word from her that they needed to pick a side and choose wisely. The threat of her wrath hanging in the air if they chose wrong. Still, they turned to me, knowing for a long time I'd just been an extension of her. And damn if I let them down.

In the two months Amaia had retreated to her room, locked away and spiraling in her own depression, I'd become accustomed to leadership somewhat. Then I'd acted as the first pass between Seth and whatever information was supposed to cross over the lieutenant's desk. But having your name on the dotted line, being solely responsible for it all, was stressful as hell.

Now, with each of the Arizona territories fallen and Elko and the rest of Nevada on the cusp of it, my stress had increased tenfold. Covert Province had moved quickly. I had my suspicions that they'd been moving their troops for months. There was no way they'd traveled with enough soldiers to take down several settlements and put others on high alert without raising alarm immediately.

"Eleanor, pay attention." I snapped my fingers in her line of sight; she was bent down playing with Suckerpunch and Harley who were eating up the attention. "We're lucky it's been quiet for the last few weeks. That won't last forever."

Elie was here purely so she would leave me alone about not being 'involved enough' in the preparation process. She was almost seventeen now; she had no place in the middle of a war. I'd already sent a long-lost brother out as a teenager. The years had not been kind on my regret. There was always that question in the back of mind if he'd been ready for such a big responsibility, if I'd done the right thing. He had been so eager. His gifts were immense for his age, much like Elie.

Most of the younger population had a hard time mastering the art of their gifts, but not Abel. He was strong, capable. Elie was too, but Amaia would have Moe take my head if she knew

I was doing more than letting Elie prepare to protect herself. Between her air magic and her Tinkerer abilities, it was better for her to learn how to use them to her benefit. Enable her to face this war with confidence in them. God forbid The Compound get breached.

"I know, I know. The bad guys are right around the corner," Elie sighed, making a mocking prayer hand in the process.

"Elie, tone." Prescott lectured, "It's imperative you listen up; if you want to be a soldier, you need to act as one. Following directions is important."

"I don't see what the big deal is. All the attacks have been miles away. Amaia will be back soon. Our defenses are good enough." Elie shrugged, groaning like we were bothering her.

"Good enough leaves us vulnerable," he added in a fatherly tone. "You want to be better than good enough, being average doesn't get you far."

"Amaia's return isn't guaranteed. Nothing is. Even if she comes back, that doesn't mean all our problems are solved." I grumbled and my heart hurt speaking the words. If only there was some tangible way to know she was out there on her way back to me.

"You know, Elie, Rome was not built in a day but burned in one," Prescott surmised.

Elie rolled her eyes, sighing, "No it didn't."

"So you *have* been paying attention during our lessons."

"It means that it can take a long time to build something great," I muttered, "but only one fatal mistake to kiss it all goodbye."

Most of my attention remained on the Tinkerers and the handful of soldiers tracing their steps in the field. They were painting crosses at my request so I wouldn't have to come back out here the next time they questioned mine placement.

"Correct," Prescott said, rubbing his hands along her arms and giving her a wiggle. "Now, eyes on Riley."

Elie chuckled, her light brown curls moving in the wind and with Prescott's shakes. "Okay, I'm listening. What kind of explosives are we talking about? I've read about a few. Seeing them in action is a whole different story."

She leaned against me, prying the piece of technology from my hands to examine it herself. I let her take it from me, knowing a prototype would bring her no harm.

"Well, that's not up to me," I said. "That's up to our explosives lead, who you were *supposed* to be meeting with yesterday morning."

"I overslept, man, my bad!" Elie rubbed her brow as if warding off a headache.

I grabbed her chin, turning making her read the words leaving my lips for the twentieth time. "Which wouldn't have happened had you quit The Kitchens like we agreed on."

"You're such a dad. I'm fine. Besides, I prefer to keep busy. Rex just wasn't there to wake me up."

Right, Rex. Her brother who I'd sent to be stationed off the coast of Sacramento following Seth's betrayal. He'd been a part of Seth's calvary, and now, under my command, she may never see him again. He was in our small naval fleet, used to monitor the shores from pirates who, at the moment, we couldn't tell if had joined Covert's side or were only taking advantage of our weakening settlements.

Her parents now had two kids working under me, expecting their protection. It only drove me to want to do everything I could to keep her safe. I could not control Rex—he was twenty and able to do as he pleased—but Elie, I had every say in how involved she was.

"Explosives are both our first and our last line of defense," I preached, remembering what Prescott had told us from the early days of The Compound.

Elie crossed her arm, dropping the prototype and tapping her foot. "That doesn't make any sense, simple English would be nice."

"The minefields," I said, pointing to the field around us, "will signal their arrival. We have scouts for our first warning, but scouts can be compromised."

"Or avoided," Prescott mumbled in reference to Alexiares.

He was a sneaky little prick, which was part of the reason I'd gone to bat for him with Amaia. Anyone who could get around our scouts and my spies belonged in my service and put to good use.

"Right. So if they get past our scouts or, hell, even if we receive word from the scouts, it's an advantage to know exactly when the bad guys arrive." I tried my best to explain in layman's terms. "If it's Pansies, they'll trigger them all. They won't be able to make out our pattern. If it's humans, that's worse."

"Why?" Elie asked.

She was young enough that her time outside the walls had made her crave violence. It was a part of her and every other child between the ages of six and eighteen at The Compound. Which also meant that a lot of what they knew about Pansies had been sensationalized from their memory and stories they'd heard and not pure fact.

"Because humans learn, adapt. Some quicker than others," Prescott said, pulling Elie from my side and bringing her under his huge wingspan.

"Correct." I confirmed, "There will be chaos, screams, but they'll keep coming. We'll have other defenses in place. If they get to our gates, that's when we blow them up a second time, make sure they stay down."

"And the soldiers outside, what happens to them?"

Elie was so curious. There wasn't a question that came to mind that she wouldn't ask. That wasn't a good thing when it came to her. Someone else close to me had a similar quality, and curiosity had a way of killing the cat.

"We can't worry about that. They know their job, Eleanor; many have given their lives to hold that gate, to protect us all." My mind wandered to my fallen friend. "We have measures in place. Most of them are air elementals, and they are adequately prepared to withstand a blast if they keep their wits about them."

Elie's posture went rigid and her brown eyes wide.

"Don't worry, Els," Prescott attempted to reassure her, but it sounded more like he was trying to reassure himself. "If our communication lines hold, they'll be okay. That part's up to me—it won't fail as long as I'm standing."

Elie peered up at him in admiration and I hid my grin, knowing at least that last part was true. He may have been trying to reassure the two of them, but I had full faith in everything Prescott's power and everything he had to offer.

"You know, Pres," I prodded, "we could always use you out on the field."

"I'm just an old man, I'm not worth much." Prescott sheepishly surveyed the green, overgrown field before us.

It was a lie, and he knew it. Being both *Supra* and a Scholar, he was a threat. A true force to be reckoned with. Knowledge mixed with power was deadly.

"Come on, man," I said, giving him a playful shove, "I know you've got some wicked war history stored up there. Whatever happened to *history repeats itself from those who don't learn from it?*"

"That is exactly why the old man must sit this one out," Prescott ruffled Elie's curls, earning him a few play punches to the gut.

I chucked, moving closer to the minefield in draft, opting to take a closer look at the soldiers mapping things out. An ear-piercing scream sounded to my left, and I backed up, pushing Elie directly behind me. Harley and Suckerpunch bounded over, taking up her rear, low protective growls coming deep within their chests. Harley crouched down, head pointed toward the brush lining the field. Elie's fingers grazed the top of Suckerpunch's head as he paced at her feet.

"What the hell?" Prescott asked, pulling his rifle around to the front of his body. "Stay here."

"Language, Prescott!" Elie called after him nervously. He waved her off, striding toward the tree line.

I cursed myself, unsure if the mini forest I'd ordered to be erected in preparation for creating our own lethal battlefield had damned us. The idea was to cause confusion with the enemy. I'd hoped to create a type of maze for the unsuspecting as they approached, directing them to exactly where I wanted them—the minefield.

"Eleanor," I cautioned, stroking the nape of my neck, "take Harley and Suckerpunch and go to your spot."

"Screw that," she spat.

I whirled on her, a wild snarl taking up her face, uncontrolled wind formed around her. "This isn't up for negotiation. Go, *now.*"

Harley and Suckerpunch awaited my instruction. With the snap of my fingers, they herded her to the other side of the clearing. I turned away, going to investigate the opposite of Prescott.

The air around us came alive. Tortured wails of lost souls echoed throughout the field, the bone-chilling screech of Pansies sounding seconds before they appeared. Soldiers at my six and twelve fired off a mix of weapons and fire magic. Havoc took over the previously calm field. Tinkerers scrambled, reaching for their guns, trying to remember their training. Metal clanked as it hit the ground, the workers abandoning their tasks and fleeing for safety.

"Fine," Elie grumbled, making me jump at the realization she was right behind me. Harley and Suckerpunch panted at her heels, looking up at her with a smile. "I'm not a child. This is what you're training me—"

A choked scream caught in her throat, the terror behind it rendering me frozen in place.

Slowly, I turned toward her, trying to locate the source of her horror. "What …"

My gaze settled on the tall figure stepping from the tree line. Prescott's gaze dropped to his chest, and I allowed my eyes to follow. His fingers clenched the fabric of his light gray T-shirt directly over his heart. His face paled, contorted in a mix of anguish and confusion as he fell to his knees. Blood welled at the corner of his mouth, staining his lips and chin.

A pulsing cadence pounded in my ears, a sense of disorientation took over. I'd merely glanced away for a minute, yet no obvious threat presented itself to me. The world around me had slowed to a blur, yet everything moved so fast—the people running past me, bullets flying in front of my face. I swallowed, slapping my hands against my temple, an unearthly cry spilling from me that I barely recognized as I willed myself to focus. Prescott's situation was dire, and I needed to stay calm.

Violent, ragged coughs came from Prescott, each one showcasing with a wince of pain. Blood splattered out his mouth onto the ground beneath him painting the green of the grass a dark red. The voices, footsteps, screams around me became echoes in the air. I had to focus on what was important right now, keeping Prescott alive and making sure Elie was safe.

"Prescott!" It was my voice, but it didn't feel like it was coming from me.

I sprinted over, Elie already at his side. Harley and Suckerpunch circled us, tearing into Pansies that managed to close in. A hand flailed past me. Out of the corner of my eye, Suckerpunch tore into the throat of a soldier with a green and tan uniform on. I clenched my teeth in recognition of the pouncing lion symbol on it. Covert Province would pay for this.

Harley brushed against the back of my thigh, a whimper escaping her. I wasn't sure what kind of weapon was in the now detached arm of the Covert soldier hanging from her mouth, but it had brutalized Prescott's chest. At first glance, I thought it was a gun, but the barrel of it was wider. Metal flecks appeared around the wound on Prescott, one of his ribs breaching the skin, his clothes burned around the gape in his torso.

"Get Elie out of here," Prescott groaned, hand on his pistol, ready to protect our back.

I knew it was adrenaline. In any other circumstance outside of the sheer desire to protect his people, he should be dead. But if he could keep that adrenaline going, if we could make it back to The Compound to one of the healers … Reina's mentor Henry was a surgeon in The Before, he could help.

"No," I defied him. "I won't leave you."

The world around us was lost to chaos. Any Tinkerers who survived the initial assault had bolted, making their way to safety, the soldiers assigned to them covering their ass. The acrid stench of battle filled my nostrils as I tried to figure out what to do. How to help. I felt useless, all my training, the time I spent with Amaia preparing for this exact scenario, forgotten. Running into action when someone you cared about was on the verge of dying left a distinct wound on psyche.

All of my battle experience previously had been concentrated on one thing—making sure Amaia was okay. I was supposed to have her back in the first war, but she had slipped my sight while the battle around me continued to rage on, stealing my focus. I hadn't been there when she almost died, when Jax sought out Reina to heal her, bring her back from death. But I had been there in the aftermath. Had torn myself up in the weeks that followed, swearing I would never let this happen again. Yet here I was, failing.

Protecting The Compound was so different from this. Sure, I cared about everyone here. At the end of the day, they were still just strangers who made this place my home. I didn't pray for their safety every night. Not how I did Amaia's or Prescott's and now

Elie's. Not the way I begged both God and the universe to keep Tomoe and Reina safe and protect their peace when the man they both loved betrayed them both.

Protecting out of duty was so much easier than protecting out of love. Fulfilling my responsibilities was natural, a thoughtless task, but here, now … I didn't know where to begin to prevent this end.

"On the count of three, Eleanor, help me lift him. Use your legs, put most of his support on me."

"Got it," she said, preparing herself.

I braced myself, my head constantly swiveling to check our surroundings. "One. Two. Lift."

Elie yelped, matching the grunt I released under Prescott's weight. A quavering moan betrayed the poised demeanor Prescott was intent on showing till the end.

"We only need to make it to the gate," I said, my voice remaining calm. "One foot after the other, Prescott, let's go."

"Riley—" he sputtered, his emerald eyes gone hollow. The light from them, gone.

"Shut up." I commanded, "Move your feet, that's an order from your lieutenant."

Prescott stumbled along, biting down on his lip, resisting the urge to yell out from the pain.

Harley and Suckerpunch covered us, attacking when they could. Closing my eyes, I felt for the earth around me, determined to find something useful to aid us in a safe trek back. The buzzing of a hive nearby snagged my attention, and I summoned the whole damn thing. A swarm of bees sent the few Covert soldiers that had pushed through our defense running.

Taking a deep inhale, I kept my focus, listening for the footsteps that evaded the bees. Vines emerged from the ground, my earth magic reaching for the ankles of those on our heels. I smiled at the banshee-like screams that left their dying bodies as fire ants ravaged their flesh.

Elie's uncontrolled wind bent to her desire. Where my magic was occupied and unable to help, hers stepped in. *This is what she trained for, this is why it will always be worth it.* Her air knocked bodies back, mostly Pansies as she didn't yet have the defensive abilities to push back against those also summoning elemental magic.

We fought our way through what had become a battlefield. One-quarter of a mile after the other, North Gate was finally coming into view. Prescott's steps became a struggle. Using my free hand, I shook his head, begging him to fight off that darkness that threatened to engulf him. His steps became unsteady, air wheezing from his lungs, and he stumbled, falling to his knees and clutching his chest. Blood stained his gray shirt now a red dark as the night.

Blood that dark was never good. Reina had said it enough that it was ingrained into my mind. It meant he was fucked. *No.* I'd be damned to not bring him home for his last moments.

"Come on, old man!" Elie yelled at him, tears catching in her throat. "Keep moving!"

Her determination pushed me, him too by the looks of it. Prescott willed himself to his feet as we moved toward the gate that marked our only escape.

My eyes never left Prescott. I could see the pain etched on his face, the effort it took him to keep going. The desire he had not to give up. For Elie. For me. For Amaia. The kids he had left. *Fuck.* It was unbearable watching him suffer.

"We're almost there," Elie urged, her voice trembling with a mixture of exhaustion and hope.

Any essence of hope was sucked from us the moment dozens of soldiers burst over from the cliffside. Pansies sprinted from the other direction. I spared a glance behind me, all of my surviving soldiers were ahead of us, no one on our side trailed. We were cornered and we would be out of luck here quickly.

Elie and I continued holding Prescott's weight, our arms supporting him. Prescott's mossy green eyes met mine, and I knew what he was asking. Telling.

"No," I refused, his request tugging at the tendrils of my heart.

"They can't …" Prescott panted, the words costing him energy. "They won't be able to hold the gate. I'm slowing you down. If it stays open for a minute longer … It's not built to withstand that level of attack."

He was right. I knew he was right. That didn't make reality any easier to digest. We could fight off a few strays that made it inside, but if the brunt of the attack made it to the gate, they would bombard us and who knew how long it could hold. The strength of the gate was built entirely on the premise that it remained closed, the bolts within hard to break down without significant force.

Elie faced me, distraught consuming her soft features. She squinted back-to-back, fighting off tears, "It's less than a few hundred yards away, we can make it."

"Go," Prescott prodded, "I'll hold them off."

Elie dropped his arm, turning on him, slapping him across the face, his blood splattering across my lips. I grabbed under his other arm, taking on the entirety of his weight.

"No, we don't leave family behind."

She was too stubborn. It would be impossible to convince her to go. Truth was, I didn't want to leave him either. I released a scream, the decision placed upon me one I never expected to have.

I could stay here, fight with Prescott to keep going, drag him back with Elie and the others would keep the gate open. They wouldn't leave me out here, let alone Prescott, not without my orders. Even then, they were likely to push back. Everyone here loved him so much. With Jax dead and Amaia gone, Prescott was the last tendril of hope these people had left. Then what? I run it all? I wasn't prepared for that. It was a future no one had ever thought would come to pass. The three of them had thought of everything, every protocol in the book for every situation, but never this.

There were three of them, how could it? But the impossible was about to happen and I was going to have to make the decision. Prescott would die whether I brought him inside those gates or not. It would be up to me to decide whether I would bring The Compound down with him.

"Give me his arm," Elie pushed me out of the way. "On three we go. Just like before!"

Prescott turned to Elie, "I'm sorry, Eleanor. You're too young to know violence like this."

My heart shattered in two. It was exactly what Amaia had told me he'd said to her the first time they met. When he'd saved her.

"You two are the future of this place, take care of her, she is all the two of you have left." Prescott said, and I knew he meant both Monterey and Amaia. "I love you, kid. Tell Amaia it's okay to be angry but never okay to give up."

He pulled his knife from his holster, cutting the corners of my hand, making me pull back at the sudden pain. I dropped him and he rolled to his knees, pistol out in hand, aiming at the soldiers closing in on us.

"Remember, Riley, history is written by the victors. Make sure when this ends, we're the ones left standing. The Compound must survive at all cost, lieutenant. Compound first," he yelled over his shoulder.

I stared at him, taking in those last few moments we'd share. Making sure the only father I'd ever known remained forever ingrained into my mind as the strong, selfless man I would forever love. "Compound first," I muttered before turning away.

Elie jerked away from me, dodging my reach for her arm. She put up a fight, using moves I taught her myself to keep me away from, reaching back out for Prescott. Air circled around her in a furious storm.

"Eleanor, fuck. Enough!" I yelled over the wind and commotion.

Focusing on the ground beneath her, I made it tremble, the shock of it distracting her, spilling her to the grass. Scooping her up, I tossed her over my shoulder. Elie beat into my back, her body tense with the distance placed between us and Prescott.

"No!" She cried out, "No, no, no! Put me down, we have to go back! What are you doing? Are you crazy? We can't leave him." The latter coming out as a whisper.

We fell in the confines of the wall. I dropped her, clasping my chest for air, pain radiated through me. Not from a physical injury, but for what I'd just done.

Tears fell down my face, and I shook them away, "Close the gate." I ordered.

"But, sir, Pres—" one of my soldiers started.

"I said," I forced command into my tone, making them remember who was in charge now, "close the gate."

"Sir, we can send reinforcements out. They're on the w—"

I sent vines out, yanking him from the entrance and placing one of the women from my squadron in his place. She faced me, studying my features before turning to see the incoming assault.

"Close the gate!" she yelled, hands behind her back but her posture shuddered at the order.

North Gate shut with a thud. Everyone behind the gate went quiet and flinched when they heard Prescott's painful cries, and then silence. When reinforcements got here, it would be too late.

Elie was on all fours on the ground, her head tilted, eyes glaring at me, snot and tears dripping down her sepia skin.

"Elie," I reached for her and she flinched back.

I pulled my hand back, brows furrowed as I tried to figure out what to do. My mind was racing. The path forward from this wasn't clear.

She pushed to her feet, her light brown curls wild around her face. Elie spat on the ground near me, "Amaia will never forgive you, and neither will I."

Staring over my head as she spoke, she took off into The Compound. I laid back, closing my eyes as my hands dragged down my face. When I opened them, I found myself to be the center of attention of every soldier and civilian nearby.

CHAPTER
TWENTY-NINE

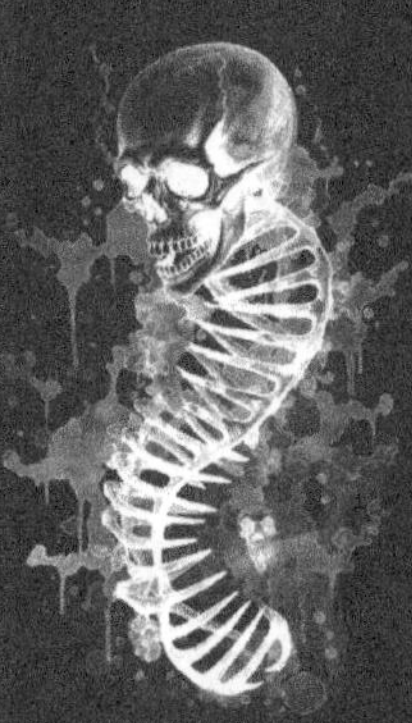

RILEY

Four hours. It took four hours before the gate was safe enough to open up again once reinforcements arrived. The night sky was pitch black, no stars to light my path out. Even the clouds had respected the need to cover up the despicable act Covert had done.

We had the men to fight back. Minutes after I'd ordered the gate closed, the soldiers had rallied up the troops that remained within our walls. Briefing them had been quick, easy. The decision to not open up our gates and fight back was the hard part. I could tell by their eyes that they understood, disagreed with my decision, but they understood why we must keep it closed.

There was no one outside our walls to fight for. Not left alive anyway. We'd be fighting back, falling right into their hands for whatever plan they'd put in place. Our fight would be just that, a fight.

Revenge was a game with no winners.

It was important to stay in defense mode right now. Being on the offense would bring about unnecessary losses from our ranks, and that was something we couldn't afford. The bigger picture was important if we wanted to do right by Prescott, by everyone here. All of Salem Territory was now counting on me to make the right move in every aspect.

Every one of our soldiers was important when it came to that final battle that inched closer by the day. There was no doubt in my mind that the attack today had intended to scatter us and weaken our troops, observe our weaknesses and strengths. If Seth had anything to do with it, which all the alarm bells in my head warned me of, it had also been done to see where we had changed defensively. He had the bare bones of our playbook, but he didn't have it all.

A weeping willow had been erected by an earth elemental three hundred feet away, aligning the center of North Gate. My eyes narrowed, trying to adjust to the darkness, only the lantern I carried and the ones of a few of my men surrounding me lighting the way. A lone figure lay propped up against the tree.

"Stay here," I ordered.

My men hung back, their whispers reaching me as I strode forward. I knew what I would find there. *Who* I would find. The screams Prescott had echoed throughout The Compound had been clear that his death had not been gentle. Soldiers lining the watchtowers along the wall had turned their heads, not wanting to watch the final moments of their leader being dragged away. Still, I needed to see what they'd done to my friend, my family, myself.

I froze mere steps away from the base of the tree. My bottom lip trembled. There wasn't enough air in this wide-open field to satisfy my need for oxygen. As my world crumbled around me, I let out a cry of agony and despair that tore through my entire being. It was a sound I didn't recognize, one I hadn't known I was capable of. A sound born from the depths of my soul, a raw and guttural wail that encapsulated all the pain, heartbreak, and, now, hopelessness that consumed me.

Prescott's hands were pinned above his head, bolted into the stump of the tree. His eyes, those eyes of wisdom and reassurance, were gone. Black holes stared back at me, nothing in their place. His shirt was gone. Instead, he now wore his skin, flailed around his torso exposing the flesh and muscle beneath. Prescott's knees were turned inward at an unnatural angle, his feet detached from his body placed below the opposite leg. The gun he'd used to cover me and Elie on our way back to the gate now shoved deep into his throat, only the handle hanging out of his broken jaw. There was a deep gash beneath the crevice of his neck, something sticking out of it in the dim light of my flame.

Slowly, my legs moved independent of my mind, and I found myself before him. My hands shook fiercely as I reached out to pull from his broken flesh. It was a folded up, bloody piece of paper. I peered up, morbid fascination wanting me to find some piece of my friend that resembled the man I knew.

My stomach churned uncontrollably. I doubled over, retching violently at the sight of him. The revulsion coursing through my veins was overwhelming, I couldn't control the wave of nausea surging up.

When the contents of my stomach were free and I had nothing left, dry heaves overtook me and I fell to the ground, desperate to crawl away. Two hands grabbed my shoulders, hoisting me up and pulling me away. I heard my men try to comfort me, some moved to pull Prescott down from the tree. I stared into the darkness, watching as a now-blanketed figure lay at my side.

When I found the strength, I unfolded the note. Crumbling it before I finished reading the last word, I tossed it to the ground in a rage.

Two down, one to go.

"Seth!" I roared, "Come out, you sick fuck. I know you're out there."

The earth rattled beneath my feet. I took off into a sprint, racing for the erected forest not far off in the distance. Footsteps sounded in my stead, the soldiers accompanying me keeping pace but respecting the distance I wanted to keep between us.

Around us, the forest came alive, responding to my influx of emotions. "When I get my hands on you, you traitorous bastard, you're going to wish Amaia was the one to find you first." I was screaming, my threat slicing through the air at the same time as my magic.

Trees slammed them to the ground as I passed them in my rage. The thuds added to the rumble beneath our feet, the cries of survivors trickled in. I slowed, not wanting to injure them anymore than they already were.

"Get healers out here for our people. Find any Covert survivors out there. Don't be gentle about it," I said.

"Yes, sir," one of my men confirmed. "Where do you want us to put them?"

I took a deep breath, willing my magic back under total control. "There is no *them*. There is one. I only need one person to question, kill the rest. Seth Moore is mine if you find him."

Seth Moore would not die by my hands today. No way he'd get off that easy. Instead, he would be a gift for my sister upon her return. *He* would have to tell her what was done to Prescott; that wasn't on me, that was on him. I'd done what I could to protect this place and would die doing whatever I needed to in order to protect her home.

Amaia had lost two of the most important people to her in less than a year, and I hadn't been able to stop the one that would destroy her the most. Jax's death was a blow to us all, but Prescott would be the stick that broke the dam. She had every right to turn her back on me when she found out. It would devastate me to no end, but I would understand.

"Help," a throaty voice called off to the side. "Please, help us."

I pulled my gun, removing the safety, finger on the trigger as I approached a large shadow and three smaller ones behind the brush. A man stared down the barrel of my gun, a look of fear on his weathered, tan face. Not of me, but for the small child he was pumping life into beneath him.

Another child sat in a fetal position, thumb in their mouth as their lip quivered at the sight of the man and little girl on the ground. The older one with wild blonde hair matted around their head stood, their own gun staring back at me. They stood firm, a menacing glare in their eyes that shot between me and those on the ground.

I moved my gun toward the child, though everything in my gut told it was wrong. You don't hurt children—children are off limits, even in times of war. And that's what they were, a child. Not a teenager, but a small frame that couldn't have been older than ten.

My hand beat against the side of my head, my locs slapping me in the face with the movement. Maybe I was hallucinating. The shock of Prescott and desperation for justice had sent me into a spiral.

It could be a trick. At this rate, I wouldn't put it past Covert Province to use children as bait.

"Emma ..." the man said in between pumps. "Put it down, we need his help."

"Why should I help you?" I spat, searching for a sign of Covert Province on their clothing and belongings, still keeping an eye on the girl in front of me.

"My name is Halden. These are my girls, Emma and Olivia. This ... this is Mason. We were on our way to see one of your people when the fighting broke out," he didn't tear his gaze from the lifeless body beneath his palms.

The girl, Emma, lowered her weapon. Her head tilted to examine me, "This was supposed to be safe. My mom sent her here because it was supposed to be safe!"

"Coming to see who? Who sent who here?"

She raised her gun back at my head, shooting eye narrowing, "He's fucking worthless dad. He won't know who Auntie Moe is. He's gonna tell others we're here to kill us too."

My arms fell to my side, for the second time tonight, I found myself speechless. "Tomoe is my friend, and help is on the way."

CHAPTER
THIRTY

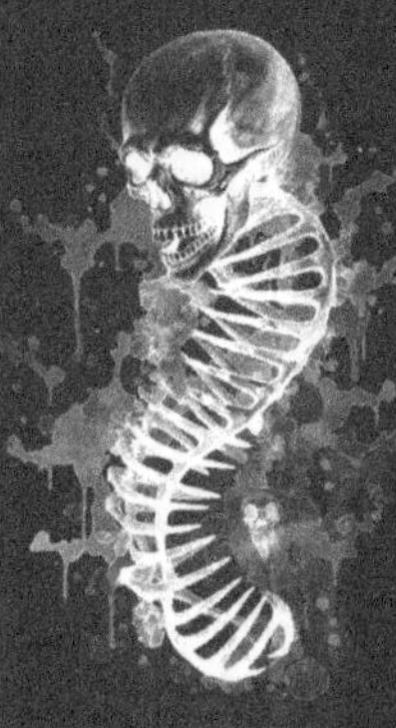

AMAIA

I was tired of death but more than anything, I was tired of saying goodbye to those lost too soon. It was my turn to keep watch. Instead of watching out on the horizon at the sun slowly rising outside the cave we rested in, I watched him.

The smooth, tan skin of his chiseled jawline leading up to the exquisite contour and perfect frame for his full, inviting lips that seemed to be molded by whatever gods watched from above. I traced the line of slight stubble on his jawline from weeks without a razor that suited his classical features up to his straight pointed nose.

Alexiares' eyes fluttered from whatever dream carried him in his deep slumber. Dark brown hair cascaded in gentle waves, partially framing his face. I brushed it back, wanting to steal a glance at the intricate tattoos that extended from the nape of his neck onto the sides of his head. His lips pulled into a soft smile at my touch.

The movement stirred him from his dream, brows furrowed, his eyes flickered open. I waited for him to pull back, the gentle touch between us oddly unnatural now that we were all in. A good portion of the time we spent together had been touched by violence and anger.

Even in our more vulnerable moments, there was this sort of tension between us, where our walls were still up ever so slightly. There had been comfort in each other's presence, yet true tenderness had gone somewhat unexplored. He studied me like he was staring into my soul. Alexiares reached up, his hand covered mine bringing it down to his mouth, kissing it before resting it on his chin.

My feelings for him hit me harder than a tidal wave. There was no confusing this with anything other than what it was. I could deny it all I wanted, but he had seen right through it. There had been no mistake in the words he'd chosen to tell me; no, Alexiares had been extremely clear. Love. He was falling in love with me, and if I was completely honest with myself, I was falling in love with him too.

I wasn't sure when it had happened. The desire to hate him had faded in St. Cloud, sure. And maybe when we'd spent time together in Duluth, I had been open to the possibility of finding companionship in the future. I'd even told him as much right before we arrived, but I hadn't thought of it as a foreseeable part of our future.

Alexiares and I made no sense. We both possessed an all-consuming fiery rage that, realistically, was dangerous as fuck to harness within an emotion as powerful as love. I did not fear us burning out. That wasn't what happened when you put fire with fire. I was scared that if we channeled those emotions toward each other, we would watch the world burn around us in favor of keeping the other safe.

That couldn't happen. I had other people to protect. Prescott and Riley were counting on me to put myself last and The Compound first. The people of The Compound, Salem Territory, The Expanse … Duluth, they all commanded my utmost focus. But when I was around Alexiares, all I wanted to do was focus on him. Alexiares had told me that I made him feel alive, that life was worth living. The funny thing was, he made me remember why I loved being alive.

Unfortunately, a life worth living wasn't based on love for so many others who were counting on us. Basing the desire to live on a fleeting emotion was foolish. Every time I loved something, someone, they were taken from me. The proof of that was all around me.

There were few people I had left in this world that I truly cared for. More than half of them had been stolen, and the rest were out there, fighting for me, for our home, outside of the realm of me helping. While I was fighting my way back to them this past month and a half on the road back from Duluth, I found myself fighting more for the person by my side.

I would not let him be taken from me, so I would not say the words because saying them meant goodbye was coming, and I was damn tired of saying goodbye.

We'd made good time on the way back home. Lola had spared one of the few horses they kept during our two-day stay and stock up with her people. It was because of her kindness that our two-month journey back was cut down nearly in half. For someone who Alexiares had built up to be all big and bad, she was a sweetheart when you dug really, really deep. I mean, yeah, she was rough around the edges, but who the hell wasn't these days.

She had a funny way of showing it, but I could tell she found my attitude endearing. The real joke of it all was that she loved Alexiares. Too young to be a motherly figure to him but too old to be a sister. Lola was the aunt who claimed she didn't want children of her own, pretended to be disgusted by their presence, but spoiled their nieces or nephews to no end.

Watching the two of them together reminded me of Prescott's and my relationship. I missed him, couldn't wait to get back to him. Riley too. They were both such an integral part of who I was that it was like missing a limb all these months without them.

I couldn't wait to tell Prescott of our journey; he'd be thrilled in the most fatherly way possible. Stern, unimpressed glares were certain to be thrown my way when I spoke of the danger, but the sights we were able to see, the places we'd stopped through, I was living out his retirement dreams of The Before. I'd made sure to burn the image of places he'd talked about seeing in my mind, ready to recount them in the most exact way I could for his ever-moving mind.

Luna had always told him every detail of her travels. I watched him sketch out what she'd relayed, admiring the freedom yet peace they offered each other in their relationship. He'd tucked them into his maps like they were photos, promising that once he handed the place over to me, he'd set out with her.

While I hoped they'd have every opportunity to do so together, I also prayed I'd never be responsible for The Compound in its entirety. I was fine being general, no need to add the stress of politics, city planning, and extra responsibilities on top of that.

The horse made things easy. That was until we reached where war had already touched down. Of all the horses we'd set free in fear of being caught, I'd hoped at least some of them were running in the wild. Surviving.

We were still making good time, even without the horses. If all was going well, Reina, Moe and Abel would be making it home any day now. If the weather held and our backup routes remained relatively battle free, we'd be right on their heels. A pit dropped in my stomach, everything was going *too* smooth.

I sipped from my water, the slushing of flesh against blade singing a sweet song in my ear. Alexiares drove his new favorite blade into the torso of a Covert soldier repeatedly. A whoosh and barely audible groan seeped from him with each stab as he clung on to the tendrils of life.

"What the hell are you doing over there, painting a picture?" I asked, handing him my canteen to sip from.

He grabbed it, taking a long swig before handing it back with a newly adorned bloody handprint and reverted his attention back to his canvas. "It's like art," Alexiares said in between knife drives, "you have to be precise on where you hit. Each organ has its own lifespan after it's nicked. If I hit the wrong one too soon, he dies quickly, or he chokes on his blood. He tried to touch you." His knife extended out toward me, red liquid dripping from the tip. "Would you really want to be with a man who made his death easy?"

It was hard to feel sorry for him, he shouldn't have tried to sneak up on me like that. He didn't have any worthwhile information on Covert's plans anyway, was just a worthless foot soldier who hadn't the slightest clue who we were.

Unlike our armies, Covert's had no women within their ranks. Instead, a caravan of women, typically in their prime, were paraded around naked to be auctioned off to the best performing soldier of each battle. Apparently, sexism and misogyny were more important to them than having the necessary bodies to defeat not one, but two territories in a full-fledged war. Not that I was complaining. As sad as it was, there wasn't a damn thing I could do about it. That kind of mindset doesn't die off with a slain leader. It would take generations to undo this damage.

Life for a woman in an apocalypse was already hard enough before all this, so I could seriously do without the constant threat of being assaulted while I used the bathroom. That was actually pretty disgusting of him.

"I'm sorry … please. Just kill me," the soldier begged.

Sighing, I glanced over at his paling skin now turning blue. "His cries for help are annoying me. Shut him up."

"What's wrong?" Alexiares asked, slitting the man's throat then wiping his knife on his shirt and leaning over for a kiss. He frowned when I pulled away instinctively. "Did you want a turn?"

I laughed, brushing up against him, letting him know I was annoyed in general and it had nothing to do with his behavior. He grinned at the slight show of affection, helping me slide my binoculars from around my neck. "Why does something have to be wrong?" I asked.

"Because you're quiet. You are never quiet," he teased.

I rolled my eyes, my lips pulling to a thin line. "That's not true, and nothing's wrong."

"Lie again."

We were on the outskirts of Montello, which no longer appeared to be an option to stop through for a solid night's rest due to the incessant gunfire erupting not far off. It wasn't a full-on battle, but there were enough Covert Province troops setting up camp in the area that made me fully aware one was in the imminent future.

A corral-shaped metal cage shimmered in the distance. Men, women, and children alike clambered atop each other, trying to gain a spot against the railing for a gasp of air. Guards posted around the sides watching the ongoing battle.

"You mean aside from being a general of not one but two territories that are counting on me, and that I'm currently cut off from all communication until we make it home? Or are you speaking of how easy this journey back has been wearing on my anxiety given the fact that *nothing* in my life the last five years has ever been easy? Oh, I know! You must be talking about the weight that knowing if I die, everyone except Covert is thoroughly fucked."

Alexiares grabbed my face, forcing me to peer up and meet his glare. "You're not dying, neither of us are."

"Yeah, well, you nor I control that, now do we?"

"Look," he said, grabbing my binoculars, he peered down into the rugged desert terrain where Montello sat in front of the little mountain. "Finley's people made it here. The gunfire you hear is going *out* of Montello. Ain't shit getting in."

I huffed, scooting forward, my feet dangling over the edge of the hillside. It brought some reassurance, but not much. "At least keeping her alive was worth something."

"Sure," Alexiares grumbled.

He wanted her dead, and I had every intention of letting that become a fact one day, just not today. She had made good on our deal, and there was no telling if we'd need her again before this war was over. But after that, once peace found our lands again, I'd let him do as he pleased, if I didn't kill her first.

I had no mercy for the people who hurt the ones I loved. To bring the people I cared for pain was to sign off on their own death.

Now was the time for my enemies to say a prayer, for them to beg for help from whatever higher power they believed in. There was no kindness left in my soul for those who crossed me. I would not hesitate to make them wish there was.

CHAPTER
THIRTY-ONE

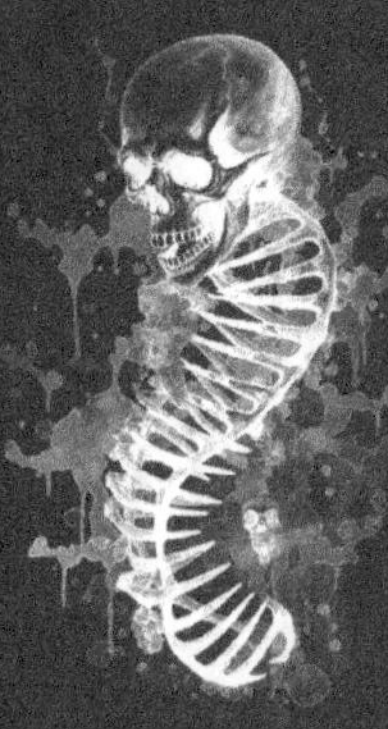

SLOAN

Someone was watching us. As soon as Amaia and the Blood-hound left, we had about twelve hours of peace before they attacked. Bright and early, the moment the sun crested over the brownstone, bullets were flying. Every day I was woken up to a headache of responsibilities, but securing our front gate was not something I conceived a possibility so soon.

We were able to hold off the first few attacks. Once the shelter was finished, I ordered all the kids, pregnant women, and old people who couldn't fight inside. As far as I was concerned, that would be their permanent home for the next few months. I'm sure it sucked not being able to get fresh air or see the sun rise, but crisp air on your cheeks wasn't worth risking your safety over.

Most of the elderly had wanted to stay and defend their homes and I'd allowed it as long as they weren't a liability. Amaia had been right about that. People wanted a chance to protect what was theirs and I had to respect 'em for it. We were under attack every other day for the last two weeks. I'm sure they'd grown to regret it.

The shelter had been sealed and it would stay that way until the signal was given to open it up. Everyone understood there was a zero chance of that happening anytime soon. Only a handful of people were given the code of entry, each differing from the other. If I fell first, then the next person in line would be responsible for getting it open and down the line it went.

Saying goodbye to Violet and my momma had been difficult. Nothing got past my momma. She knew what was up, had glared at me as the door closed in her face and I'd ordered it sealed.

"Mommy," Violet had said, clutching the stuffed unicorn she'd had since she was a baby. "I'm scared. It's too dark."

I'd pulled her into a tight hug, stroking the static down on her straight red hair. "Mommy's going to make sure you'll never be scared again. Okay, baby?"

"You pinky promise?" she'd asked.

I chuckled, rolling my eyes at how deep that Moore blood really ran. Pinky promise had been Reina's tool of manipulation growing up, making sure no one dared get one over on her. Violet reminded me so much of my cousin. They had a way of seeing the world with such optimism. I hoped that never faded.

"Pinky promise," I swore, looping my finger through hers.

Kissing my end of our connection, Violet mimicked me, giggling at the gesture. We may share the color of our hair, but she was her father's daughter without doubt.

"Okay!" she said, before darting off down the hallway.

My shoulders slumped, hand remaining in the now empty space where her little body had been as I watched her go. "I love you," I mumbled, knowing she couldn't hear me but glad I'd be able to say them, anyway.

"You shouldn't make promises you can't keep," my momma cautioned. "Children remember those things."

I kept my eyes down the dark hall, not strong enough to meet her harsh stare. "I have every intention of keeping that promise."

"She's not going to see it that way," she murmured, raising my chin to meet her scrutiny. "Promise me you'll come back to me."

"Momma ..."

She sighed, "I figured as much, then promise me something else, something you *can* keep."

"Anything," I said, my arms wrapping around my waist. Although I had all this power, all this responsibility, I still felt like a little girl.

I was doing my best to hold on to the promises I'd made to both Morgan and Amaia, but, hell, it was growing harder by the day. Truth be told, I wanted to lock myself down here with my momma and Violet. I was scared too.

"You put up the fight of your life, and you don't back down."

I nodded. That was a promise I'd made myself as well. "Always."

"Please come back to us. I love you," she said, her stare unwavering.

Biting down on my lip, I pulled her into an air depriving hug. "Love ya more, Momma. When it's safe, go to Monterey. Amaia has a home there for you both. Violet can have a life there. *You* can have the life there that you deserve."

I released her, ordering the doors shut before she had time to process what I said. The last thing I saw was her cold glare as my words hit home. Her mouth parted to respond only to be cut off by the sealing of the doors.

That was weeks ago, and it was time to make good on my promise.

Amaia's tactics had kept us safe. Divide and conquer and all that. We had our best elemental wielders dealing with the human pieces of shit intent on destroying us all. With power sharing and their individual gifts, we were giving Covert a run for their money.

Most of our troops were stationed in alignment with each entrance to our city. There were only two left operable, the others had been sealed and fortified. Controlled entry points only. She'd been explicitly clear about the fact that if our walls fell, it was game over.

The few *Umbra Mortis* soldiers we had were instructed to take our cavalry and other weapon experts to fend off any Pansies. They'd had little problems with taking down what we were used to. The ones my uncle had created, however, were fast as fuck, making them ten times harder to pin down. Still, we prevailed more times than not. Our casualties had been few and far between.

The downfall of our *Umbras* being out on mission meant our watch towers were now poised with inexperienced snipers, which were … less than effective. They were getting better by the day. Issue was, there weren't many days that we really had left.

Somehow, someway, Amaia had managed to get Wisconsin to pick our side and join the cause. Finley's *gifts* had shown up here right after she left too. I wasn't sure how she'd managed that, but I'd take it. It made our job easier. We had a singular mission from our pivotal point on the map—push Covert Province back into their territory, keep them scrambling to give the others time to prepare.

The rest would fall into place from there.

Elliot's hand clasped on my arm, bringing me back to the present. "It's time," he said.

I gave him a tense nod, letting him know I'd heard him and would follow him in a minute. Taking one last look at Duluth on the horizon, I turned my back to my city, trekking down the hilltop and onto the battlefield that awaited.

Covert Province had regrouped, pushing their way to a snowy clearing, killing every last soldier of mine in the area. They were barbaric. The things they'd done to my people … sick didn't cover the torture they'd put them through.

Our scouts had found several of them pinned to trees with missing limbs, only to find burning out campfires mere feet away. Remnants of humerus and femur bones were pitted over them, flesh removed. The thought of that made me nauseous. There was no need to eat people; while there wasn't exactly an abundance of game in the area, there was enough should their armies had run out of supply. I knew that wasn't the case either. They'd left trail mix and other food in their wake as evidence.

I strode up next to Elliot, scanning over my friend. He was Morgan's age … *was* Morgan's age when he'd died. They'd been best friends. Elliot had sworn his allegiance to me once he'd found Morgan's will. He'd aged in the last two months by a few years, the gray that had peppered his dark features not completely encasing them. The lines on his face wore his skin down, purple circles from lack of sleep under his hazel eyes.

"You've been good to me, Elliot, even when I didn't deserve it."

Our troops moved around us, getting into position, the air tense with what they knew awaited them in the imminent future. Elliot turned to me but said nothing, only a smirk on his thin lips letting me know he for sure thought there were times that I didn't deserve it. I'd been a brat at times, impulsive at others, but I'd learned from both him and Amaia. I'd become what Morgan had seen me capable of being in such a short time.

A decent amount of time had been wasted since Morgan died. I wasn't quite sure survivor's guilt was the word to cover what I went through. All I knew was that the weight of staying alive while the man I loved rotted in the ground felt crushing. It crumbled in on me when I had to condemn others to the same fate in the process of trying to balance it all. So I turned it off. Love was a weakness. I could care, but I would not love. Then Amaia had come. Without knowing it, she had shown me a new way of life.

"You know what to do. Follow Amaia's lead, send troops where she needs them. This *will* end in our favor. You just need to wait it out, give it a chance," I said, watching the people I'd grown to care for around me walk into certain death. "One day, my best friend will unite this country again. Patience will be key. Patience and time."

"For someone who has full faith that I know what to do, you sure took your time listing it out," his gravelly voice struck the brisk air. He put a cigarette to his lips, offering me one as he lit it with the tip of his finger. "You also didn't need to tell me about it. Everything you think is waiting for me up here." He ruffled my hair, walking off in the other direction.

I heard his footsteps pause behind me, and I swiveled, trying to see what gave him pause.

Elliot kept his back to me and I could tell by the rigidness of his posture he was fighting back tears. "You always deserved my help, Sloan. I just wish I could have done a better job." His words reverberated within my mind.

A painful lump formed in my throat as I watched him descend back to our city. Abel had come to me the moment he saw this all play out. As much as I'd wanted to wring his throat for spying on us for years, I knew it was because he had Duluth's best interest. He may have been spying for Monterey, but he'd grown to love the people of our city as his own.

This was how things needed to go if we wanted Duluth to still stand in the end. Our city would be devastated, but not beyond repair. Not if I did things exactly the way he instructed. He'd been clear that the future could always change, but he'd asked Tomoe to guide him through channeling his Seer abilities. Abel had grown stronger in his blessings under her mentorship, with the sole desire of keeping this place safe.

My only request to him was that he not tell Amaia. It had pained him to hold back. I knew he'd believe it to be a betrayal and I was inclined to feel that way too. But if my friend had known what I would have to do to make sure she got the outcome she was destined to have, she would have never left.

Duluth would rebuild, the entire country would heal. It would take time, years down the line and death. Many deaths of people that I'd loved over the years, but it was possible that if we kept going on the track we were gliding down, that there would be a better tomorrow.

I only hated that I would never see it for myself.

As sad as it made me, I'd been one of the lucky souls to exist on this plane. I had the pleasure of knowing love, something many people had never felt and would not have the chance to. Morgan had been my great love, something that would extend beyond this lifetime. Amaia had been my soul, a friend who saw promise in me no matter what. I'd been able to bring light into this world. Violet would survive; she would not remember her mother's love, but she would have the chance to find love of her own. She would grow up within the greatness of Monterey and live a normal life, the life I could not offer her here.

Amaia would give that to her, which made it all worth it.

I raised my hand, signaling my soldiers to be at the ready. Soldiers raised their palms filled with magic for a battle they knew they would not survive. When Covert's army came into full view, my arm swung down, and magic surged around me.

MOST OF MY SOLDIERS WERE DEAD AROUND ME. OUR SHIELDS HAD finally fallen, and magic had run its course. Where magic failed, our weapons did not, but that simple fact didn't change that we were vastly outnumbered.

It had been intentional. The brute of our forces was far off. They would take Covert on from the rear when their defenses were down. We were merely a distraction.

Reina had left me a parting gift—one prick of the needle, and I'd received my share of the power I'd always desired.

Air magic was nice; it gave one the freedom to manipulate the world around them. Water magic had its benefits too; it was adaptable, fluid, easy to bend to one's will since it was all around us. Having earth magic had a grounding, stable aspect to it. But fire magic … it was destructive, it gave one power, and it was exactly what I needed now.

How lucky I was to die knowing I could go peacefully, reconciled with both the cousin and friend I loved so dearly. The remaining soldiers under my command lined up at my side.

We faced our enemies and charged—an ear-splitting, furious yell tore from my throat. My soul blazed with determination as I focused on summoning the last reservoirs of my magic, flames flickering around my trembling fingertips.

Covert's soldiers crept forward, eyes scanning the trees for more of my snipers. They were all dead. There was no need. This was my final act, and I refused to yield. I unleashed my fiery wrath, watching as they placed a weapon I did not recognize in my eyeline, setting it alight.

As a wave of light blue fire surged closer, searing heat washed over me. I accepted my fate with a chilling calmness. I closed my eyes. "I've played my part; have mercy on my soul for this is the end."

CHAPTER
THIRTY-TWO

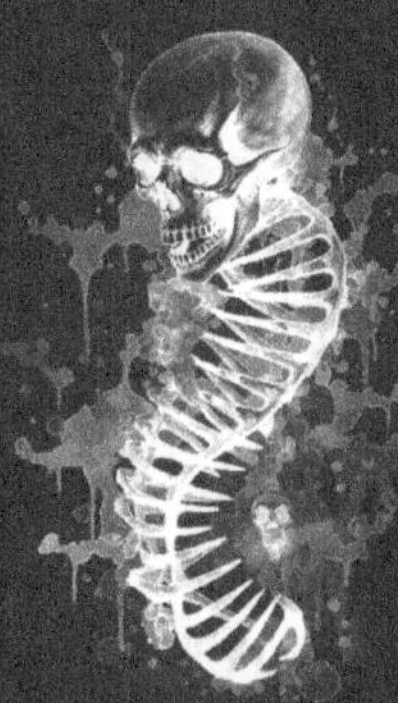

SETH

Blood is everything. Strength is sustainable. Weakness shall not thrive.

I repeated the words every time the silence in the air turned my thoughts toward the people I loved in Monterey. *The enemy.* I slapped the side of my face, reminding myself of the words Malachai had beat into me. There was a lotta silence around me these days. The struggle over controlling my thoughts was intensifying. Dad had kept me locked up after the stunt I'd pulled getting that message across to Moe.

Love is an inconvenience, he'd scolded. It was a blessing that my father had been a victim to love or I'd be dead on the side of the road. He'd excused my behavior as desperation to keep the woman I loved alive, hadn't seen it for what it truly was—a warning to them all.

If I wasn't locked away, Malachai was glued to my side, making sure I stayed out of trouble. We'd been on the road for over a month. It was February now. The incident had happened at the beginning of January, but my dad hadn't let up, intending to punish me as harshly as possible.

I deserved it. I had betrayed him.

It could be worse.

He could have stuck me in one of his labor camps. At least where I was now, I got to sleep. They didn't sleep there. The whispers around camp had been so similar, I'd come to believe them as truth. The conditions were less than favorable, but we couldn't feed everyone.

At least this way, their minds were kept busy with work and not their impending death. I'd like to think sitting and waiting for my death to come would be a far worse fate than working until you drop. On the plus side, the *outsiders* got a break and got to do the breaking. Even when we took prisoners, we didn't take them for long.

Malachai was haulin' ass toward the war tent we'd erected in between the Arizona and New Mexico border. His quick pace forced me to keep up. I tried my best not to trip over the chains around my ankles, bounding my strength and forcing it to remain at a human level. There would be no breaking free, not unless Dad wanted me to. Not except in the moments he used me to strategize against Monterey.

Prescott was dead because of me. I hadn't been the one to commit those disgusting, hell-bound acts, but my dad had ordered me to lead the way under Malachai's supervision. It was his life or mine, and I wasn't yet ready to say goodbye to this world. His death was on me.

Another death for which I would never forgive myself for.

The sun beamed down on me, the brightness of it burning my sensitive eyes. It was a rather pleasant sensation on my skin, though. I couldn't deny that I missed the heat of the west—of home. *Damn it, no, Seth, Monterey isn't home. Focus. Home is Montana. Home is Virginia. Home is where he is.*

I shook my hair out, the breeze flowing through my hair still feeling unnatural. Dad had taken my hat, said I didn't deserve it, crushing it under his heavy-ass foot, knowing it would be a blow to my soul. My hat was as much a part of me as my horses were. He'd taken that joy from me too, taunting me as they ran alongside the armored truck he traveled in.

Dark spots crossed my eyes as we entered the tent. No one was here but Dad and now Malachai and me. I stopped myself, taking him in for who he truly was. The infamous Ronan Moore. At face value, he didn't look like much, but now I understood that there was always more than meets the eye. My dad's pale skin had tanned in our travels. More freckles spotted his face, an extra wrinkle aging him from both the sun exposure and stress.

"Take a seat, son. Here's your tea." He ordered, hand motioning to one of the seats on the other end of his planning table, steaming flowed up from a metal mug. It was the only thing he let me have without earning. It was bitter, gave me migraines, made my head fuzzy, but it was something.

I sat down, glancing around at the maps on the wall. A shit ton of places were crossed off, large *Xs* over them like it was a quest map in a video game. He had stormed into Transient Nation, using his fancy trucks, cars, and his best horses to push our military across the continent faster.

Dad had set his sights on Monterey specifically but new information presented itself the closer we got. I wasn't sure if I was glad for the redirection or not. His favorite Seer had received several visions of someone causing quite the ruckus in the future. Apparently, they were aware of how Seers' gifts worked and had tailored their movements accordingly. Our Seers had no luck, too many versions of the future with no real pattern. They were erratic, always moving at random. A person with no name. At least none that we had been able to gather and none of their followers had offered it up.

They stayed in constant motion, raising a resistance as they moved through the territory. It infuriated my dad, not being able to stay ahead. He'd redirected our efforts, steaming through Transient Nation, terrorizing the good people we came across.

I had been forced to watch as he tortured people who refused to join our cause—the person of no name making it there before us, always one step ahead. Around the fifth maiming my stomach had gone weak. It wasn't right. These people were innocent. None of them had been particularly powerful, yet I found myself questioning my dad's true motivations. This wasn't the mission, at least not the one I'd presumed we'd been under. Reina had tried to protect me from this, warn me that our dad was not the man I'd grown up admiring, and I'd betrayed her.

With witnessing each inhumane act came an accompanying lesson to me: if I so even considered changing my mind on whose side I was on, that was my future too. His actions had backfired and I couldn't say I wasn't glad. Son of a bitch deserved some flack for his cruelty. Anyone who caught wind of us being in the area fled for the closest border. They didn't care where they ended up, Salem Territory or The Expanse. They were just glad to avoid us.

That meant they gained numbers though, and ours were limited enough as is. It didn't matter. I was pretty sure what my father had planned would do exactly as he intended. My father always got what he wanted in the end.

"Am I speaking to myself, Seth Moore?" he said, snapping his fingers in my face.

I cleared my throat. "No, Dad. I apologize. I'm a bit hungry is all."

Malachai grumbled something about food being for those who had their priorities straight. I glared at him. Whether I wanted to be or not, I was here, wasn't I? That had to be enough.

"If you want to earn your freedom, you have a task to complete."

That grabbed my attention for sure. "Yeah? Anything. Tell me what I need to do and consider it done."

I would do anything to get out of these chains, to have that tingle of strength course through my body again. Not to mention consume more than a few scraps of stale bread, tea, and water that tasted sour as piss.

"There is … a message I'd like you to deliver," he said, but I knew that glimmer in his eyes. Whatever deal he was offering wouldn't sit well with me. "You want to save that little bitch and your friends?"

I didn't know how to answer that. On one hand, it could be a trick, on the other, this could be the opening I needed to make sure they all made it out safely. He closed in on me and I leaned back in my chair.

"Answer the question," he commanded, huffing hot ass air into my face.

"If the opportunity presented itself, I would like the chance to save a select few, yeah."

His fists clenched and Malachai barked a laugh. *Did I answer wrong?* I was never going to recover from my fuck up. *It's fine, it was worth it.* Moe had gotten the message, but either way, I'd suffer in vain. They would never flee and leave the people of Monterey to fend for themselves. All I'd done was offer them a chance of saving their lives in exchange for mine. Even if there was a slight chance that they'd make it out with my warning, *it was worth it.*

"Very well," he concluded. "I've decided to consider your offer of not wasting good blood. You've probably gathered we're right outside Salem's borders."

I froze. Damn right I knew where we were, but I hadn't wanted him to know that. They'd placed a hood over my head during the ride back. It didn't make a difference. I knew the area from the scent alone. I'd done my best to play dumb. If he knew that I was fully aware of where we were, he might be inclined to think that I'd make a run for it.

I wouldn't.

I was smarter than that. My father would take a shot through the back of my head, waiting for the moment I thought I'd achieved freedom to pull the trigger. That was how he rolled. He would give, but he loved to take even more. The higher the hope someone had, the more my father relished in taking it from them.

He chuckled at the guilt in my eyes. "I'm sending you out during our initial approach. Get Amaia to see why surrendering can serve in her favor. If she's as solid a leader as you say, she'll take a smart deal when she sees one."

"Who said she was smart?" Malachai sneered.

I shook my head. Amaia had her own way of doing things and I was the last person she'd consider negotiating with. "She doesn't want to see me. Whatever offer you think you have isn't going to work."

"Why, son, I haven't even told you what I'm offering yet. Do this. Prove to me you were the son worth staying alive. I always thought you were the weaker one of the three. Then again, you did kill one and leave the other to die without looking back."

A pang went through my body, scratching the surface of what was now a reopened wound. That wasn't true. I hadn't left Hunter. I'd wanted to go back for him, had tried to go back for him. Anger sank into the depths of my chest. Our dad may not be the man I thought he was, but this was still Reina's fault. All of this was her fault. I hated her for putting us in this position to begin with.

My hatred for her meant nothing, though. I may have been willing to let her die when I'd thought she'd betrayed me with malice in her heart, but with distance came clarity. I knew my sister. She loved me and I'd broken her. I owed her a spared life. What she did with that spared life … I didn't care, as long as it was far as hell away from me.

So I would give this my all. I would do this last thing for her and Tomoe. I would offer Amaia this deal, give her a chance to save the people she loved as well. And if they didn't agree by their own volition, I would make them.

"Show me that I was wrong. Show me you deserve to live."

CHAPTER
THIRTY-THREE

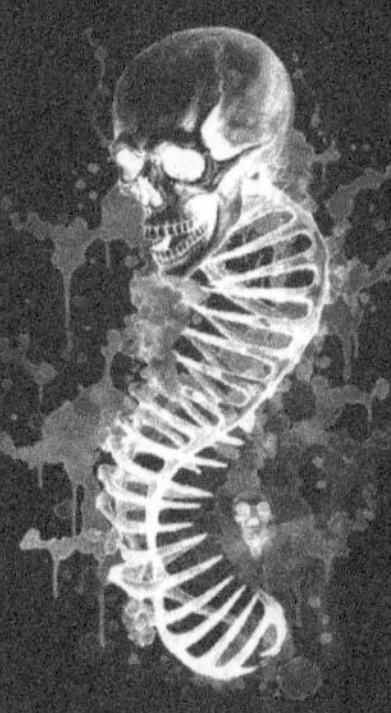

RILEY

"Sir, one of our scouts reported in. Tomoe and Reina are approaching South Gate. There appears to be an unknown adult male with them, no sign of our general or Alexiares. Should we intercept?"

I glanced up from the paperwork on Amaia's desk, one of my men offering a welcomed interruption from the mess I'd stumbled into. It wasn't right working in Prescott's office, not yet. My heart palpitated, a brief moment of relief washing over me, knowing Tomoe and Reina had made it back safe. It was short-lived as I wondered who was with them. I'd received word from a messenger weeks ago that the group had separated and that my sister and Alexiares would be arriving at a later date. But who was with them?

"No, it's fine. I'll meet them at the gate. How far out?" I asked, pushing off the desk and rising to my feet. The paperwork could wait.

He moved out of the doorway, allowing me to pass through. "Two miles, sir. They're jogging it in. Fifteen minutes out if they keep pace."

"Copy. Alert the watchtowers not to signal but standby."

"Yes, sir," he said, taking off ahead of me.

As eager as I was to be reunited, I needed to make sure it wasn't a hostage situation. I trusted Reina. She wasn't anything like her brother. There wasn't a doubt in my mind that she was bringing trouble to our gates. If they had someone with them, they were either a friend or held against their will.

I worked my way through The Compound. There was a solemn tone throughout the streets these days. We hadn't tried to hide Prescott's death. The people deserved to mourn both him and the family and friends we'd lost that day. It didn't make much sense to keep secrets from our citizens at this point. The end was fast approaching. There was no denying that. They had the right to be prepared.

It was midday, but there were no longer kids playing outside or people lounging in the greenery. School had been canceled last week indefinitely. Instead, parents chose to organize additional training sessions. We would be ready when the time came.

I would do everything I could to protect these people from the world. Unfortunately from my time in The Before and now in The After, I knew all too well how cruel it could be.

While the people here respected me, I found they feared me to some extent too. I'd kept to the shadows for a long time. They knew nothing of me other than I worked for their beloved general. Being in the public eye had never been my thing. I'd left that to Amaia, Prescott, and Jax. They had the charisma that people tended to flock to. Seth had it too. With his hulking presence, it was hard *not* to see him.

He had a way about him that made people trust him with his sly smiles and seemingly devoted relationship with Amaia and Jax. The way he reacted when Amaia or The Compound were challenged or threatened had been icing on his acting cake. What the people hadn't seen was the behind the scenes. The danger he had always posed with his anger toward the people he had sworn allegiance to.

So it didn't surprise me that the citizens of The Compound kept their eyes low, putting distance between us as I walked by. I was the unknown. The spy master who always lurked but never spoke. The protector of this place they'd never gotten to know. And now with two of their chosen leaders struck down, one gone, and the other one determined a traitor, their lives were in my hands. People feared the unknown.

But shit, wasn't terrifying people part of the gig?

The Entertainment Square was a ghost town. I stared at The Arena as I walked by. It wouldn't be abandoned for long. We had funerals in our near future. A lot more if Amaia didn't make it back soon. One of those funerals would wait for her return, though, no matter how long it took.

There'd been nothing for people to celebrate or a reason to relax for a while now. The bar and shop owners had used this time to prepare themselves for the moment they'd have to be soldiers again. Life would not go back to normal around here for some time.

The soldiers at the gate nodded, opening it with their weapons at the ready. Three figures moved at a quick pace, making their way out of the tree line. I held my hand to the sky, letting the archers at the watchtower to hold.

Excitement, the way I felt it, couldn't be held back. I broke into a sprint, meeting them halfway to the gate. Reina leaped into my arms, her long legs wrapping around my waist as I spun her in a circle.

She kissed all over my cheeks. "Riley!" Her voice broke, her tears flowing down her cheeks into mine.

They were tears of relief. Her excitement radiated off her. I let Reina pour her emotions into me, needing to experience them after everything I'd been through while they were gone. You don't know what you've got until it's gone. I hadn't realized how much I enjoyed their presence until that first night here on my own. Prescott had noticed me in The Kitchens eating alone with each meal. One morning, he'd plopped down next to me, and that was the end of my days feeling sorry for myself. They were my family too. I'd never let them in the way I'd let Amaia, but damn it, they were my sisters in every way that mattered.

"Reina," I said in a hushed tone, unable to say anything more than her name.

"Jesus, I missed you so much." Reina hopped down and I took her in.

Her hair was shorter now, barely skimming the top of her shoulders. Though happiness radiated off her, there was a sadness in her blue eyes that panged my heart. She was wearing all black, something I'd seen her do before, but this felt different.

The leather riding boots and black top were dark for the girl who'd always brought color into the world. It was more something Tomoe would wear, not her. My brow raised at the pistol holstered to her hip. Reina using a gun was unheard of, let alone carrying one at the ready. There was also an older way she carried herself, less juvenile in her gait.

"Stop staring at me or I'll think you're flirting," she chided, brushing against my shoulder.

I chuckled, granting her a sly smile as Tomoe strode over. She gave me a playful shove, which was as close to a hug as she'd ever come to giving me. I dragged her close, burying her face in my chest. I'd never hugged any of them besides Amaia when I thought about it. But life was short, and tomorrow wasn't promised. From this day on, I'd make sure the people around me knew how much I cared.

She gasped for air. "Glad to see you're still alive."

Tomoe tried her best to wiggle free from my suffocating embrace. I paid her no mind, lifting her up and giving her a whirl. She could if she truly wanted to. The girl could hold her own and had put me on my ass several times before. She wasn't slick, Tomoe could pretend she hated it as much as she liked. I knew she'd missed me too.

"Okay, release me before you lose your head," Tomoe gasped for air.

Placing her back on the ground, Reina burst into a fit of laughter. Tomoe jumped at the sound, like it had startled her and she hadn't heard it for a while. Our eyes met, and she shook her head. *Later.* I nodded, my gaze settling on the man standing behind them, suddenly remembering they'd brought company.

A ball of air caught in my throat. His eyes searched my face, waiting for my acknowledgment. It'd been nearly four long years since I'd last seen that face. He was younger then, a boy, but the essence of him remained the same. His features had matured, he'd grown taller, but there was something in those dark brown eyes of his that tugged at my memory. The familiarity in them. *Abel.*

He hesitated for a moment, unsure what to do. A slow, timid smile flickered across his face as he took a few stammered steps forward. The years apart had changed us both, but the bond of brotherhood had remained unbroken. I closed the gap between us, cupping my hand on the back of his neck and pulling his forehead against mine.

"Brother," he whispered.

I choked back tears. "Welcome home, little brother."

Reina skipped forward, pulling us into a group hug. "Yay for family!" she exclaimed, not able to hide the pain behind her statement. We were all the family she had left.

Tomoe stood off to the side as we separated, glancing over her shoulder searching for someone. "Where's Prescott? Not like him to miss a moment like this."

My eyes shot to the ground in despair. Reina read my emotions from me before I found the courage to break the news.

"No," she said, grief shooting off her.

It was a powerful wave, intensifying what I already felt. I fought to keep on my feet. Tomoe and Abel stood there, teeth clenched, used to it. That wasn't like her. I'd never known Reina to not be in control.

"You didn't see it?" I asked Tomoe.

Foolishly, selfishly, I had hoped she would have seen as much. I didn't want to have to be the one to tell any of them. It was a fool's wish. I knew Tomoe didn't watch for our deaths. It was an active decision, one I respected her for. She knew herself enough to know that if she saw it, she would try to change it, and that could have dire effects on the future.

Tomoe shook her head. "No, I didn't. What happened?"

I jutted my chin back in the direction of The Compound, signaling for them to follow me. "I'll explain inside. It's not safe to stay out here."

"I have much to tell you too," she replied ominously.

Reina leaned into Abel's side, his arm around her shoulder as they walked back toward the gate. "Here," Reina said, stopping in front of me and handing me a folded letter from her back pocket. "It's from Amaia."

I flipped it over in my hand, looking at the unbroken seal. My brows pinched as I glanced back at her. Reina always respected boundaries when asked, but keeping something like this to herself on the journey back was too long for her not to pry.

"I was told it was for your eyes only. And Prescott," she called over her shoulder.

Tomoe sniffled, grabbing the bag she'd dropped when I'd picked her up earlier. No tears fell from her eyes, just a stare filled with agony. She moved to walk past me, but I grabbed her arm, stopping her in her tracks.

"That's not all," I said, not knowing how she'd take this. I didn't want to further her pain. This was too much. Seth gone, Prescott dead, and now she'd have to face something else from her past. "There's people here for you, said they knew you from years ago. They're spooked. Put them in your room. Didn't know where else they'd be comfortable."

I knew little about Tomoe's past. She rarely offered up information and we'd never been close enough for me to get more than the passing comment about her family from The Before. Amaia had told me that bad things had happened before she'd made it here, but never clarified. It wasn't my business to know anyway, only to make sure she didn't bring any of the drama of it into The Compound.

"What?" Tomoe asked, "I don't know—"

Her words trailed off, eyes glazing over briefly, "Oh my fuck … Hal."

I nodded, and she took off, leaving Reina and Abel facing me, questioning glances thrown my way.

CHAPTER
THIRTY-FOUR

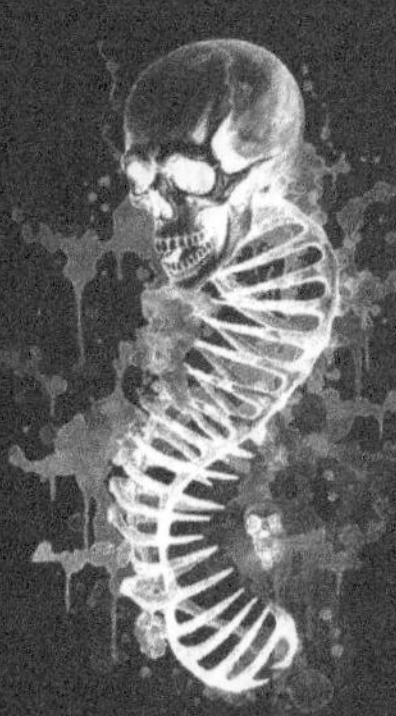

TOMOE

Coming home to my own space was something I already dreaded. Seth and I had shared it in the weeks prior to our departure. The more I thought about it, the more the space became a haunting reminder of my loss. Now it was a haunting reminder of what was stolen from me.

I ran through the corridor of the Scholar Building slowing to a walk only as I passed the Public Library. People were staring, but I didn't give a shit. That wasn't what caused me to stop. The more I focused on Laurel and the kids, the more visions flashed into my mind. Visions I could have gone my entire life without seeing.

My friend lay covering Olivia and Mason with her body. They were older than when I'd last seen them. Mason was a toddler now, shrieking as he peered up at the man who loomed over them. Laurel's blonde hair was matted with blood, falling in front of her face as she yelled at someone. Telling them her hus-band would be back any minute, that it was in their best interest to just leave.

The men in the room laughed, saying it didn't matter, they'd have to an-swer all the same. Laurel begged. My Laurel begged and pleaded, something she'd told me time and time again to never do. Never beg a man to spare you, don't ever give them the satisfaction. Laurel was fierce. In our short time to-gether, her word had become my law in The After. But with her children in the room, all she could do was ask for their mercy.

I pressed my hands along the wall, trying to pull myself out of this. Riley had said Hal and the kids were here. Not Laurel. I knew what this vision was showing me, making me suffer through. Laurel's death was about to play out in first person before me, and I didn't have enough energy left to fight it off.

"You're either with us or you're with them. Choose wisely bitch," one ordered.

He was young, younger than me even. The way he waved that ax around the room let me know his time in Covert had molded him beyond repair. My friend never took lightly to ultimatums. She would not choose, even if it meant the cost of her babies. Laurel enjoyed the freedom of The Expanse. She would never subject them to what they would have to live through if they were forced to reside in Covert Province. If there was a choice she would make, it would be to bring them here. She couldn't tell them that though. Her heart fluttered, and she glanced out the window, taking in the sun's position, trying to figure out how much time she needed to buy them until Hal got there.

The other one chuckled, a seven-inch blade slid across her cheek as he crouched low to meet her glare. "Perhaps we can convince you," a sneer pulled across his light brown skin as he jabbed the knife into her side.

Laurel cried out in pain. It was agonizing, and I endured every second of it. Olivia whimpered underneath her and Laurel bit down on her tongue.

"Be brave, baby, be brave," Laurel whispered in her ear.

The younger one walked over to them, kicking her where she bled. "Aren't mothers supposed to protect their kids? I know moms like you, had one myself. Where the pride is too big to do what's best." He kicked her again, harder this time and a crack sounded. Pain shot through her ribcage and Mason wailed, his fingers between the man's boots and Laurel's skin.

"I won't fail my kids. I'll do whatever it takes to ensure they don't end up like you," Laurel snarled.

She was so close to giving up, the pain too great, but she hung in there. Her desire to survive until Hal showed up too great to give in. Thoughts raced through her mind, she was certain if she told them she'd side with Covert they'd take them now. Olivia and Mason would never see their father or sister again. She had to hold out, just a bit longer.

They both laughed at her muffled screams as they began stabbing and hacking into her. Their cuts not going deep enough to oblige her with an instant death; no, they'd draw this out too.

The younger one swung his ax above his head, holding it there, his eyes so dark they were nearly black bore into her soul as she peered up at him. Laurel closed her eyes, knowing what was about to happen. Her only hope being that his swing would stop at her flesh. The last thing she saw before it connected was the sway of his ash brown hair.

"My mother said the same thing about my siblings right before I killed her. The weak don't have a place in Covert Province. Looks like you're no longer needed."

Pain radiated through her spine as the ax jabbed into her back and her body went numb. She felt nothing and everything at the same time, stars swarming in her eyes before it all went black.

Her eyes opened again at a loud bang. She scanned around the room for the source. Emma was there, smoke coming from the barrel of her gun as the man with light brown skin bled out in front of her, eyes unseeing. Hal's fists pounded into the flesh of the younger one; he fell before Laurel, no longer recognizable but deathly still.

"Baby," Hal said, rushing to her side.

He lifted her up, placing her into his lap as blood crept from the corners of her mouth. Hal reached over, pulling Olivia and Mason upright, scanning them for injuries. When he found none, his attention went solely on his wife.

Laurel offered him a weak smile. "It's okay my love. There's no pain. It doesn't hurt. Our babies ... they're safe."

"I'm sorry," he wept over her. "I'm sorry I wasn't here for you."

Laurel coughed, a warm feeling came over her body as she recognized Emma's light touch over her hair. "None of that. You were always there when I needed you the most." She choked, the blood in her mouth becoming too much. "Get them to Monterey. Get them to our girl. It's safe."

And all went black.

Tears poured down my face, and I pushed the door to my quarters open. They weren't safe here, but death would have to wrestle me personally for harm to come to those kids ever again.

Olivia was sprawled across the couch staring up at my cluttered shelves listening to Emma as she read from a book, Mason pulled into her lap.

"Hal ..." I whispered, stepping into my room.

Dark circles rimmed his once vibrant sky-blue eyes. His shoulder-length, ash brown hair had grayed at the roots, matching his facial hair. He rose from behind my desk, taller than I remembered, skinnier too.

Relief swarmed over me at the knowledge that they were okay. I hadn't seen anything happen to them in my vision, but the need to place eyes on them to be certain had clenched at my chest with worry.

They had been my family for a short time, but that connection to them had always remained. Their safety, the need to check in on them, was a constant in my mind. I hadn't seen this though. Laurel's death. With everything going on, my friend had shamefully slipped my thoughts.

I took in the creases of his tan face, frozen in place as I let him study me. We both looked rough as shit. Considering the circumstances, I suppose it could be worse. He had never liked me, only tolerated me for Laurel and the kids' sake.

Where Laurel saw a girl in need and a companion to have at her side, Hal had seen right through my bullshit, taking me for the threat I was. He was a good man though. Hal had taken care of me, let Laurel treat me as one of their own.

It was his decision to force me to leave after … the incident. I didn't blame him. It wasn't safe for them with me there. Fuck, it was supposed to be safer for them with me gone. They were supposed to be safe—*Laurel* was supposed to be safe. Without me there, the threat to their family was supposed to be gone.

I wondered if he realized that part of the reason he'd lost his wife was my fault too. First, I'd almost taken his children from him, and now it was my fault his wife was gone. Had I not loved the wrong man, they may have been traveling throughout Transient. They would have never sought Laurel out because of the stupid note I'd sent.

There was no confirmation that my letter of warning had doomed them, but what other reason did they have to hunt her down? She was just a mom who wanted the best for her family. I thought I was giving her that, letting her know what was coming her way. She was supposed to spread the word and get the hell out of dodge. Laurel was—

"Tomoe," Hal said, strolling toward me, shoulders slouched. I braced myself as he approached, waiting for him to punish me. It was what I deserved. Hal fell to his knees before me, head leaning onto my stomach, tears in his eyes. "Laurel … Texas …" He started.

My body stiffened, not expecting this reaction from him. "I know. I saw. You don't have to say anything, I know."

"She got your message. We did what we were asked. She got your message." I let him break.

Let him fall apart in front of me knowing he'd been strong for the kids. He needed this. And if he was here, in front of me like this, I knew deep down he didn't blame me for her death.

Only I could blame myself.

Emma shifted on the couch, placing Mason down next to Olivia gently. She was her mother's twin, her and Olivia both. Their mousy blonde hair, the specks of brown in their blue eyes. They almost passed as Hal's daughters, though I knew they weren't. None of them were, though he claimed them all as his own.

"Auntie Moe." Emma's breath caught, her fists clenched at her side as she stood. She ran forward full speed, careful not to knock into Hal as she rammed into my side. "You're here, you're safe!"

Olivia grinned meekly from her place on the couch. The girls were old enough to remember me. We'd bonded during the hours of me telling them stories as Hal and Laurel went out in search of food. It had killed me every day what I'd almost done to them, what my nightmares had willed me to do. That was part of the reason I left without a fight. Now they were here.

"Laurel wanted me to bring the girls here. It's not safe out there anymore," Hal said.

I shook my head remorsefully. "It's not safe anywhere, Hal."

His feet found the floor again as he forced me to glance up to meet his heavy gaze. "It's not. But they're safest here. If you won't have me, please, at least have them."

He must've thought me the monster he'd sent packing. Assumed I held a grudge. I inspected my study, finding the few belongings they had strewn about. They'd been sleeping out here, the clutter I'd had leaned up against the door to my bedroom still in place. I didn't belong here anymore, it was too painful.

"No, stay." I offered. "Make yourself at home. I can't promise you it will stay that way with what's coming, but my place is yours. I'll be … I'll be back. I need to take care of something."

I pried Emma off me, giving her a quick squeeze before closing the door, not giving him time to respond. My hand rested on the door handle as I stood there for a few moments trying to collect myself. I wasn't sure where I was going, just knew I was suffocating in there.

CHAPTER THIRTY-FIVE

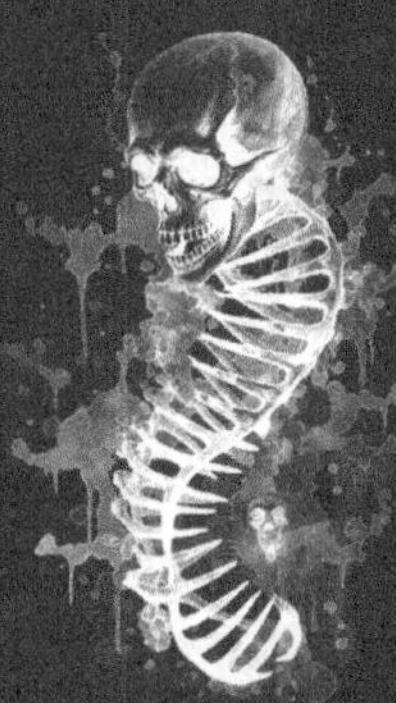

REINA

Everybody stared at me like I was the devil as I walked through The Compound. Riley glared at them, diverting their watchful gazes but it was no use. I kept my head low, eyes on the ground, not wanting to stir up any trouble. Shame filled me and I found myself searching for the confident, strong woman I'd been out on the road.

Was it fair to blame them for their mistrust? I would blame me too if I were walkin' in their shoes. That's what Momma had always told me to do, and I tried my best to keep it front of mind. My brother had betrayed them; as far as they were concerned, I was a snake in the grass too.

Only thing I could do was prove them wrong.

"I guess everyone knows," I mumbled. Riley's confirmation wasn't even needed—it was apparent.

He sighed, peering at me from the side of his eye. "It came out after Prescott died. I'm sorry."

I nodded. There was nothing else to say. *Take it to the chin, girl, take it to the chin.*

"Screw them, I know where your loyalty lies," Riley said, hand rubbing the top of my back.

I leaned into the touch. "They don't know what it's like out there. What Seth's choices made us do, what's coming our way."

He turned his head to look me over for a moment before glancing away. "They don't, but they're about to find out."

There weren't enough words to express the gratitude I had for Riley at this moment. He didn't have to be here, walking me through The Compound, yet here he was. Part of me wanted to go to my room, bury myself there, yet the other half of me wanted to remind myself what I was fighting for first.

If I went back to my room, I feared I'd be faced with memories of my life before Seth had torn it apart. The flashes of Jax dying on my bed, the clothes I'd bought for Seth that I'd forgotten to give to him, pictures of all of us gathered as a family. I'd have to walk through Unit A in The Infirmary to get there. Having to walk past the injured soldiers or my previous mentor was something I'd need to build up to.

"Did he go quick?" I found myself asking.

The answer wasn't going to make any of this better, but I had to know. Riley's sadness rolled off him and I watched as he tried to rein it back in for my sake. His mouth twisted while he struggled to land on the right words.

He shook his head, his locs brushing against my cheek, arm pulling me tighter as our steps fell into sync. "Not quick enough," Riley whispered.

It didn't take a genius to know that meant he had suffered.

Everything around here had changed in my absence. The plants that lined our beautiful cobbled streets were wilted. There were no flowers or greenery resting against the front stoops of the homes. Any children we saw were focused on a mission to be anywhere but playing on the streets as they should be.

"Reina?"

I stumbled to a halt. Fluttering surging through my stomach at the softly spoken question. Riley glanced behind us, shaking me as if I had glitched. Honestly, I think I did at that moment. Most nights on the journey back, my mind fell into thoughts of the woman back home who'd played with my heart. Now, as fate would have it, life had taken its toll on me. I wasn't sure any of that mattered to me anymore or if I even mattered to her. I mean, if she really cared for me, would she have left things the way that she did?

"Jessa," I said, swiveling around. "Hi."

Hi? That's all you have to say you bumbling idiot?

Jessa was as beautiful as ever. Her long blonde hair dangled past her waist, having grown since I last saw her. Her shimmering blue eyes matched the bright smile she gave me and I went weak in the dang knees.

She took a step toward me, a movement so subtle, so natural, yet my subconscious forced me to take a step back. Her energy was … off, though I couldn't quite put my finger on it.

Jessa frowned, deciding to stop her advance. "I heard you were back."

"She just got here, how did you hear anything?" Riley asked, suspicion lacing his gravelly voice.

I tilted my head in agreement. I'd only passed through South Gate minutes ago, barely entered The General Living Quarters. Sure, Moe had raced back to her rooms, but how on earth had she already heard? Jessa worked in the Public Library as a historian; it was possible she'd seen Moe and assumed I was here too.

Jessa cleared her throat. "Word travels fast these days. You know, end of the world and all." She shrugged.

I nodded, not sure what else to say. It wasn't that I was not happy to see her, I just needed a moment to sit with my emotions.

"Can I talk to you?" she asked. "We have a lot to catch up on."

Riley watched me, waiting to see what I wanted to do.

"Alone," Jessa added, noting he had no intention of walking away.

I scratched the side of my neck, toggling over if I was ready to talk to anyone other than my family. One look at her said if I declined, she'd just be back later, so I figured I might as well get it out of the way.

My tongue trailed over my teeth. "Sure," I ground out.

Jessa scowled at me, a questioning glimmer in her eyes as she tried to figure out where the animosity was coming from. At first glance she seemed excited to see me, and if I were the naive girl from before, I'd believe that. I knew Jessa, though; there was always more than what she let sit on the surface. Even still, her choice of words had me wondering what was left to discuss.

While she had been clingy before I left, pretty much glued to my hip, she'd rejected my question on putting a name to our relationship. It had hurt, the concept wasn't something we'd ever discussed. When she'd snuck out of my bed after the night at the tavern before my departure, I'd figured that was that. Maybe I'd misread our connection. A monogamous relationship had never been my thing, but with Jessa, I'd wondered if maybe it should have been.

"Stop by Amaia's when you're done," Riley said, giving her the death glare that said *don't fuck with my family*.

I wasn't sure when he'd become brotherly to anyone aside from Amaia but given the absence of my blood brother, it was a welcome feeling. She smiled at me, offering her arm to walk the opposite direction Riley was heading.

"How are you?" she asked timidly.

I cackled, *what kind of question was that?* "Haven't you heard? I'm evil. How are you?"

Jessa cast a sidelong glance. "That's not what I meant." Her tone softened to a hush.

"I know."

She walked at my side, fingers clenching, fighting the urge to brush against my hand. I could feel her tumbling to find the right words. We'd never had so much as a serious conversation. They were usually kept light, as was my mood. All but once. That was before, and this was now. I was not the same person she'd left.

"Reina, no one thinks you're evil. We all know you're nothing like *them*," she said, leaving my brother and fathers name from the conversation. I couldn't tell if it was intentional or not, but I appreciated the gesture. "Your loyalty runs deep. Some of us could stand to be more like you. I can't imagine what you went through out there, but I'd love to hear about it."

"What do you want, Jessa?" It came out harsher than I'd intended. I was exhausted, being tactful just wasn't in the cards for me anytime soon.

"To talk?" I could sense her confusion and a tinge of guilt. It was overwhelming. "Didn't you miss me?" Jessa braced herself, waiting for my rejection.

"Miss you." A dark laugh escaped me. "Yeah, I missed the heck out of you, didn't expect to come back with you feeling the same."

She nodded in understanding, slowing her pace as we approached a bottom floor apartment. "That's why I wanted to talk to you now. I'm sorry about Prescott. I know he was close with your family." There was real remorse in her eyes.

I said nothing, keeping my focus on fighting off the tears that desperately tried to work their way out. If I started, I knew I wouldn't be able to stop. Holding in all my grief was the only gift I could offer the people of The Compound. They didn't deserve to be consumers by the grief that I released; it was on me, all of this was on me. The least I could do for them was keep it to myself.

Jessa fumbled with the lock of the apartment. I'd never been to her place before—one of her many ways of keeping her distance while continuing to get close. I followed her inside. It was decorated with the bare minimum, and if she hadn't opened the door with a key, I would have believed it was unlived in. I don't think she'd added an ounce of decoration since she'd been here. Every inch of her space resembled what we offered people when they first moved in.

Prompting me to take a seat at a table in the corner, she continued. "Look, I don't know how to ease into this, so I'm just going to say it. I … I played both sides for a while. I'm not proud of it and it's not who I am now, not who I want to be. Because when I'm with you, I don't want to be that person anymore. You have a good heart, Reina, and I want to be good with you. Together."

"You brought me here to ramble on about which letter makes your heart sing on the LGBTQ scale? Jessa, I don't have time for this nonsense, and I sure as heck don't have time to hear about your recent hookups." My butt had barely touched the seat before I made my way to the door.

"No, Reina …" Jessa's voice trailed off. She closed her eyes for a few heartbeats. "I'm trying to tell you that I regret leaving things the way that I did, but I'm here for you, if you want me to be. I don't ever wanna leave things unsaid again."

I laughed. "You have no idea who I am anymore, and I doubt you'd want to claim me if you did."

"I don't care who you think you are now, I know what's in here." She strode toward me, hand resting on my heart. "That's all that matters to me. Isn't that all that matters with love?"

My pulse picked up, for the first time in a long time, something more than sadness creeped in. Guilt quickly swept over me on what I'd done to seal the deal with Great Falls.

"I slept with someone," I blurted out.

Jessa winced, clearly not expecting it. Pain rocked through her, but quickly absolved. "Do you … like her?" she stammered.

I pursed my lips, not sure what she wanted to hear, but decided that honesty was probably the best policy here if we were going to be starting fresh. "It was to secure an alliance that we needed; it didn't mean anything to me. She's good people, and I did something for her that will always leave us connected, but no. I don't like her, not in the way I like you."

"I wasn't exactly loyal to you either, when I tried to forget you. When I thought you'd hurt me."

My tendency to move from hookup to hook up wasn't exactly a secret in The Compound, but I'd been clear with Jessa when I'd asked her what she wanted this to be. "Why would you think I'd hurt you?"

"Because I wasn't sure you'd come back to me alive," she said, her frost-kissed eyes darting toward the side.

I stepped closer to her, pulling her in by the waist. "And what about you, Jessa … do you like her?"

"*He*'s not you," she admitted, a sly grin pulling at her perfect lips. "I couldn't like him if I tried. He was a means to an end. A face from the past. I thought about you every single day; you're impossible to forget."

"Are you gonna make me ask again or can I just assume to know the answer?" I teased, bringing my lips gently against hers.

"Reina, nothing would please me more than trying this whole monogamy thing out with you. Your burdens are my burdens. If they fuck with you, they fuck with me. You deserve some happiness in this world that tries so hard to steal your joy."

Guilt still simmered off her, intensifying as she folded into the embrace. I pulled back, eyes narrowing as she caught my drift. Her shoulders slumped, taking a step back to face me, still avoiding my gaze.

"There's … there's something else," Jessa stuttered.

She never stuttered. Was never nervous about anything since the day I'd met her, yet here she was, a whirlwind of emotions tugging forcefully against my magic.

"Yeah." It wasn't a question, more of a not-so-subtle accusation. "I bet."

"I wasn't exactly honest with you about the loyalty thing."

"For the love of all things good and holy, Jessa, stop messing with my emotions and spit it out," I prodded, my impatience growing by the minute.

"Your father sent me here to spy on both you and Seth." She glanced up at me, gauging my reaction. "I was supposed to make sure things were moving according to plan."

"What—Don't you think you should have led with that? Who cares who you slept with!"

Betraying my trust should be an Olympic sport. People were doing it enough, might as well toss in a gold medal. *I wonder if they still have the Olympics on the other side of the pond? Nah, that would be nonsense.*

"*He* is your father Reina, I never slept with anyone. Please listen to me. I never went through with it! Never did what he asked of me," she exclaimed, grabbing onto my wrists to stop me from backing away toward the door. "The moment I met you, Reina, I couldn't betray you. It didn't feel right."

"My father doesn't have women in his military," I ground out, pacing around the living room not wanting to believe her.

"Spies aren't the military, Reina," Jessa explained, "and his political viewpoints are exactly why I was the best bet."

"How could you work for him?"

"I didn't have a choice! You don't say no to Ronan Moore." Jessa grabbed at me, but I shook her off, not caring much to hear her answer. "I was already living there when the borders shut down. Things weren't so bad until he took control. It was do this or be sent to the outskirts of the territory with the outsiders. *No one wants to get sent there, Reina, it's a death sentence that happens slowly.* He has ways of making sure his orders are followed; his spies, they're everywhere. Even *I* don't know the extent of his network; he's been working toward this for over a year. Walking away and creating a new life is a risk many are scared to take. But I don't care anymore. You. This place. It's worth this risk."

I wasn't sure what an *Outsider* was or what the outskirts of the territory consisted of, but the fear coming from her told me enough. She'd had no choice, much like the rest of us in The After. Memories flashed before me of all the choices I'd made lately—some of them hadn't been as much of a choice as others may believe.

"Was it before or after Jax's death that you decided to stop working for him?" I asked, deciding that was the real damning factor in all of this.

If she had hurt him, had set out to hurt my sister, I would never forgive her. She wouldn't have to worry about Riley's rage—she would have to face my own.

Jessa shook her head. "It wasn't until your brother failed in that mission, when it was discovered Amaia walked away unscathed, that I was sent. Your brother didn't even know I was here. You don't understand how it is out there. You people have it good … it's part of why I risked my life to turn against him. He'll send someone for me, I have no doubt. Probably already has. You don't betray Ronan Moore and keep your life, especially when you know too much."

"He won't lay a hand on you, I assure you. Amaia and Riley on the other hand …"

Every part of me said I should tell Riley. I didn't want to start my first moments back keeping secrets again, but would he make her leave? *Would I be putting her life at risk even more by letting her stay and risking my father's wrath, or would Riley exiling her be a blessing in disguise?*

I don't know why I felt this protective over her—she'd betrayed me before we'd even met … Could I really blame her?

Her eyes widened. "You mean that?"

Those stupid cerulean eyes. They melted my heart against my better judgment.

"Our relationship, or whatever this is." I gestured between us and pain displayed across her face like I had struck her. "You did what was right in the end, for selfish reasons, but still, doesn't mean you deserve to die for your past mistakes."

Jessa picked at her fingernails, glancing up, worried I'd be out the door if she said anything else. "I don't know … I don't know if my replacement is already here or not. You need to close the gates, for good."

"Amaia's not back yet, we can't do that," I said stubbornly. "People will die if we don't let those who flee come in."

She nodded, knowing full well what my father's cruelty could do. "People will die if you do."

Jessa was right. But would that damn Amaia and Alexiares if we did? I doubted closing the gates would mean anything. They were both resourceful; I was sure they could make it. But what if they didn't?

"It's not up to me, it's up to Riley."

"Then help me convince him," she said as if it would be that simple.

Riley would never do anything that put Amaia's life at risk. He would always put The Compound first, but not if that meant sacrificing the one person he cared for the most. That was where he drew a cold, hard line. And I couldn't say I disagreed.

"What he does or doesn't do is none of your concern," I said, stepping away from her and heading toward the door.

"Wait—" she yelled, reaching out to prevent me from leaving.

"What, Jessa?" I hissed. "Do you have more pain to add to an already wounded heart?"

Tears welled in her eyes. "Will you be back?"

"I don't know." I paused at the door. "Give me time."

I was exhausted. Finding space in my heart to hate someone when I was losing people left and right felt like the wrong move. Time was a luxury these days, something I wasn't sure any of us had. Maybe spending what little time I had left with a glimmer of happiness wouldn't be the end of the world, but I was tired of being betrayed.

The remorse coming from Jessa was raw; it called to my magic, begging it to aid in mending that broken part of her soul. Part of the blessing of my gifts was the ability to use it as a guiding light in the perception of the world around me. If that made me weak, then so be it.

CHAPTER

THIRTY-SIX

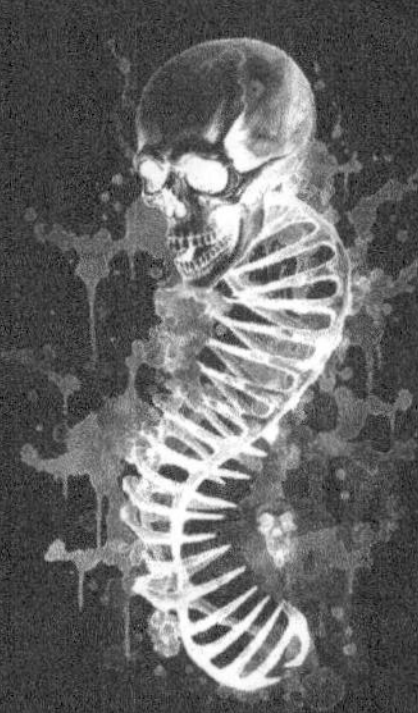

RILEY

I placed my hand against the door, waiting for my magical signature to unlock the artillery room. This one specifically had restricted access. It was important given what we kept inside. I hadn't been here in ages. My fingers trailed around the dusty gray and black artillery room. I released a quipped whistle, glancing between Amaia's note and what lay around me.

Codeword: White Moth

Plasma, Shadowstep and Chrono blades. Aqua-cannon. Soulfire Flamethrower. Acid Grenades.

The Appalachians sing, get the boys in the trees, and remember the Alamo.

PS: brother, I miss you so much my heart hurts.

To anyone but me, it would seem like a folly. A bunch of words on paper with no leading information. But I knew. Knew what she was asking of me. How dire our situation was if we were bringing these out.

Amaia had never wanted to use these. They were created as a precaution to ensure our survival. Her hope was that they'd never see the light of day.

These weapons had taken an immense amount of research from both Tinkerers and Seers alike. They were deadly, and while we only had a few, they would change the game of the war.

I grabbed the Shadowstep blade, swinging it around. It felt good in my hands. She'd created it for me, after all. Me and my men, that was. This would be fun.

Grinning, I pushed my magic into it and stepped into the shadows.

CHAPTER
THIRTY-SEVEN

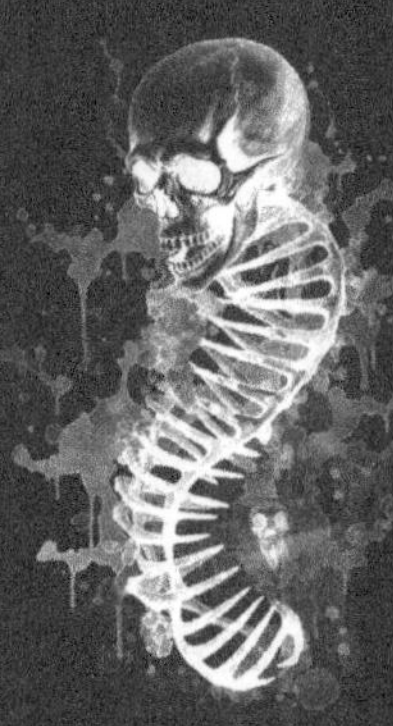

AMAIA

The center point of the borderline between San Jose and Fresno Compounds was a hellscape. It'd taken us two days to fight our way through the already camped out troops with the rest of Covert's army right on our ass. We were too late.

My heart sank at the thought that all of this was for nothing. We'd already lost. Remaining positive was a waste of energy. The truth of the matter was, Covert Province would descend on us by the end of the week.

Small flanks of their troops had kept us on the run, forcing us to skirt around and try to enter through the West Gate. Trouble called to us from every direction, leaving us low on magic. Running low usually didn't worry me, considering I'd made a point to stay trained up on my other skill sets should my magic fail me, but we were on the verge of hitting 'E'.

Powersharing was draining. We tried not to use it unless absolutely necessary, but still, through our connection, I found my fire burned with a greater intensity. With greater intensity, a deeper well of power inherently comes along with it, which only mattered if you had control. While we did, this was certainly worth noting as a risk when it came to the rest of our soldiers.

An empty tank of magic meant toggling the lines of death. To have come this far only to stare death in the eyes from something that hadn't even existed in our world six years ago was a jab in the gut.

Hiding out to catch a beat was the best bet. It would take less than half a day to replenish enough of our magic to make that final push home. We were nearly ten miles out, but I didn't want to show up after months away appearing weaker than when I had left. Not to mention I wasn't sure what we'd be walking into. If The Compound had fallen to chaos and I brought the news of Covert closing in on us, there would be little time for sleep or rest.

Alexiares and I had run out of food over a day ago and there'd been no time for him to try hunting. No time for hunting meant zero time to forage. Lucky for us, he'd managed to control enough of his water magic to satisfy our stomachs.

Filling up on water was about as unfulfilling as being 'full' could get, but it was necessary. The human body could go weeks to months without food, depending on fat reserves and other things. One glance at the both of us and my better guess would be a few weeks.

My stomach growled at the thought of the food awaiting us. I'd ask Elie to fire up some cornbread and soup, maybe some garlic noodles or veggie chili. God, what I would do for a cup of coffee right now. I smiled, knowing an evening in front of Prescott's fireplace with coffee and pie was less than a day away.

It wouldn't be the same. We'd have to spend our time discussing war and other pressing matters, but the warmth and comfort of the food and Prescott's presence was enough for me to yearn for it.

I shot up from the pile of leaves and pack I'd been lounging on, Alexiares sending a glare in my direction for startling him. "The cave!" I proclaimed.

His expression turned curious. "Now what are you talking about?"

"There's a cave about a mile from here. I had Elie set it up as a safe house of sorts. There's a few bug-out bags and supplies in case she needs to flee."

"Food?" He grinned, grabbing his pack and pushed to his feet.

I nodded. "Food *and* warmth. We can put a fire up while we rest. It faces the seaside. The flames or smoke won't give us away."

Neither one of us hesitated at the thought of a small moment of reprieve. The last week had only confirmed the suspicions I'd held about our journey being too easy. While the number of Pansies we'd encountered hadn't been outside of the norm, the enemy had only increased. At this point, I would have preferred the sight of upgraded Pansies in their stead.

The thrill of food soon filling our hollow bellies made us more than happy to jog, deciding risking exerting that last bit of energy was worth it. Half a mile out, the sound of dogs barking caught our attention. I slowed to a stop, reaching my arm out to halt Alexiares in his tracks.

My blood froze. I knew those barks—would know them if half of my senses were removed and I was forced to feel out the vibrations of them. Alexiares turned to meet my gaze, and instinctively, we broke into a full sprint.

Waves crashed into the rocks below, the sea beneath the cliffside angry. Every hair on my body stood up at the horror before me. Elie's light brown curls flew in front of her face, her arms flailed in front of her. The air around her was erratic, panic strewn across her reddened face.

Harley and Suckerpunch surrounded either side of her, trying to regain their foothold on the Pansies closing in on them where Elie's air magic failed. They were backed toward the edge of the cliff, a few steps away from taking a plunge over and into the raging water.

Alexiares sprang into action, using what may have been the last of his newly acquired earth magic to cast vines out, dragging the Pansies toward us. I went for my throwing knives, using all four to find the center of their foreheads. To our pleasant surprise, we were only faced with the slower, simple Pansies and not the new and improved versions. Few remained, now turning our direction to find the cause of the disruption of their promise of a meal.

"Fuck it," I said, finding the risk of gunfire being heard worth the safety of Elie and our precious pups.

Harley's eyes met mine, her tongue hanging out in excitement, and I almost melted. She finished a lingering one off, ripping its neck clean off its body and over the cliff behind her. Suckerpunch bounded to Alexiares' side and a cry of relief escaped him. Tears welled in my eyes, happy to see my baby was okay, but furious over the unnecessary situation she'd been brought into.

She sat at Elie's feet, tail wagging beneath her as she kept her guard, not wanting to fail at the job she believed she owned. The signal of her release sent her racing toward me. Harley pounced into my arms, allowing me to whirl her around. Her tongue swept across my face and I released the pent-up emotion, just happy to be reunited.

"Oh, my baby," I said, "Momma missed you." I kissed all over her cheeks, giggling.

"Nice to see you too," Elie said dryly, frozen in place.

Placing Harley back on all fours, I stared at her, taking her in for any injuries. Her dark-wash jeans were torn, one of my chest holsters was secured over a black T-shirt cut at the bottom. The knife I'd left her tucked into her waistband and another in the ankle holster above her boots. Elie was a mirror image of a younger version of me and, for some reason, that sent a course of fury through me.

I advanced on her with a menacing gait in my walk. Harley bound off to greet Alexiares behind me, sensing all threats had been thwarted. Elie's posture stiffened, and I stopped right before her, cupping her face between my palms. So much had changed over the last few months.

Her lips quivered under my touch. I pulled her into a tight embrace, soaking up the smell of eucalyptus and coffee from her hair, the softness of her skin.

Pulling her back, I glared at her. "Elie, what the hell are you doing out here? And without a coat, it's freezing!"

She fell back into my hug, not ready to let go. "Everyone's either dead or missing," she said, her body now trembling from the cry she tried to keep from breaking through.

My heart stopped. "What … Riley—"

"No," she cut me off before I could let my mind go there. "Everyone else I care about is gone, just not Riley. Who knows about Rex."

I hated that for her, but I hated the relief that fell through my chest more. It wasn't fair. She had lost the people she cared about, yet I found relief knowing my people weren't one of them. Her parents had always been warm toward me, welcoming me into their home, inviting me to be part of a nuclear family in the moments I missed it the most. But they weren't my people, they were hers, and though I felt sorrow for them … they weren't Prescott, they weren't Riley. They weren't *mine*.

"What are you talking about? What's going on?" I peppered her with questions, my mind spinning at all the answers I needed, that she was taking her time providing. She was young. I understood this was a lot, so I tried to slow myself down. Elie was not one of my soldiers. She was just a girl.

Alexiares' swift movement caught my attention out of the corner of my eye. I saw his hand grab his knife, but Suckerpunch intervened.

He paused, taking notice of his son's resistance. "Who the fuck are you?"

A frail, blonde child peaked her head out from the cave I'd designated as Elie's safe spot and I found myself on the defense too. Elie let out a huff, her arms crossing over her chest.

"That's Emma." Elie glared. "She followed me out here after I told her to leave me alone. She's too pussy to——"

"Am not! I killed that one over there." The girl exited the cave, closing in on Elie quick. A blue and silver Taurus waved in her small hands.

"Woah," I said, placing my hands up in between them. "Okay, everyone chill out. Elie, explain."

Elie cracked her neck, shooting a sad glance back in the direction of The Compound. "We were attacked a few weeks ago. I was out in the field with Riley and Prescott when——"

"And why were you in the field with them?" I interrupted. None of this made any fucking sense to me, and I had a creeping feeling that I'd have more questions than answers as she went on.

Her thin dark brows rose as she continued, "Because Riley said it was important for me to learn to protect myself and others. But that's not——"

"Riley said what now?" I growled.

Alexiares cut in, an amused smile pulling at my protectiveness. "Let her talk, Maia. She can't answer you if you keep interrupting."

I sighed, head tilting back and curls dusted against my shoulder from my fallen messy bun. My teeth chattered from both the chill of the *La Nina* winds on this cliff and the sense of overwhelming rage that grew the longer we were here.

"We were out mappin' the minefield when that *traitor's* people attacked us. Riley got me back safe, closed the gates, actually. What we didn't know was that the fisherman's dock was blown while we were gone. They were forced to abandon ship and row out near the beach closest to North Gate."

Her breath caught, and I gave her a few moments to process. I knew this was a lot for anyone to take in, let alone someone who'd spent most of her time within the safety of The Compound.

"The first wave of the attack hit them before we even knew they were in the area. My father was on that ship. Riley took me out to search the next day, but there's no sign of him. Only half the bodies remained on the shore. Mom refused to believe that the waves took him. She went out searching. Riley told her not to, that he'd send some of his men out to do it for her, or at least go with her. She refused, said there were better places his men were needed. Of course he listened, *Riley the All-knowing*." An aggressive chuckle left her body.

Elie had certainly changed from when we last spoke. She'd gone from the cheerful, bouncing girl who never wanted to leave my side to someone that harbored so much … resentment. She seemed furious—with Riley, with me, with the world. I couldn't blame her. It happened to the best of us, that coldness that took root within. I'd stupidly hoped it wouldn't happen to her.

"Sometimes I wish you stayed," she continued. "Sometimes I think taking responsibilities as law instead of having a heart is just dumb. Mom never came back. I … I thought maybe she came to our spot, but she's not here. Her stuff is here, but she's not."

I turned, peering past Alexiares and Emma into the cave. Her mother's belongings did, in fact, sit there. Elie would never find her mother, because her mother was lost to the sea. Woman's clothing sat folded up neatly next to a pack, a rose gold wedding band placed on top. A pair of hiking boots and socks were on the other side.

I didn't have it in me to tell her that her mother had jumped.

Something else caught my attention, Alexiares noticed, too. He walked over, lifting up the ruck packs above his head to show me. I didn't need a closer view to understand.

Guiding Elie closer to Alexiares, I attempted to refocus her on the immediate threat. "Elie, those are Covert bags. Did you check the rest of the area?"

"I'll go see if there's any of those fuckers hiding," Alexiares said, dropping them with a soft thud against the earth's floor.

"I tossed them over the cliffside before the Pansies came. They're all dead," Elie muttered, eyes on the bags, shifting between them and her mother's belongings.

"No, they aren't."

What a sweet, soft voice responsible for such ominous words. Emma's gaze remained fierce despite the attention now on her. "When I was following you, one scared me. Tried to pull me from the bushes. He's over there." She pointed, gun still in hand. "I cut his heels. They way my mom showed me, how she used to."

Alexiares smirked. "Your mother taught you how to slice an Achilles? I gotta meet her. She sounds badass."

I elbowed him in the ribs and he winced. They were kids, yet they were already racking up a body count. It wasn't admirable, it was sad.

"I don't know what that is," Emma said, biting her lip. Her brows pulled together in confusion. "You can't meet her cause she's dead. Her and Auntie Moe would do that to the bad guys who came after us without my dad there. Auntie Moe said that's what happens to pricks that hurt women and kids, that they deserve to die slow. And I think he wanted to hurt us."

My heart damn near beat out my chest. I stared her up and down, recognition creeping over me. "You know Tomoe?"

I'd never known Moe to tolerate any children outside of Elie at The Compound, and even then, she and Elie barely ever interacted. It wasn't that my sister hated children, she just tried her best not to get attached. She'd mentioned a few kids from her time before The Compound, and the pain in her voice when she spoke of them was enough for me to never pry.

Oh my fuck.

"Yeah, she used to live with us. Now we kinda live with her," Emma said.

The world around me was spinning. My hands rubbed against my temples. "Okay, I'll get to that later. Back to you, Elie: where is Rex? Where are you staying?"

"Riley sent the navy out off the coast of Sacramento. Who knows? I'm staying with him in his"—her finger lifted to Alexiares—"room. It's unnecessary, I can take care of myself. I don't need a babysitter," she grumbled.

"This is a lot to take in. Emma," I crouched down to her level. "This is my friend Alexiares. Can you show him where you left the soldier? Elie, grab your stuff and let's get you home. I'll talk to Prescott about finding you a room close to him. That way someone will be close by if you need anything until Rex gets back, but you'll have your own space too. I'll cover the costs. We'll talk more over a nice meal after we wash off."

I brought her in for another hug. The pain brought her body to a shudder, her chest shaking as she accepted the reprieve from the comfort I offered. Her whole world had shattered while I was gone and from what I could tell, she didn't believe she had anyone in her corner. I wasn't sure what had happened to her and Riley, but that wasn't anything I could get to the bottom of here and now.

Elie's hair tickled my neck as she tightened her grip on me. "Prescott doesn't say much of anything these days."

She walked off, heading after Alexiares before I could ask her what she meant. Harley pranced back over to me, nuzzling against my leg, and I dropped down low to rub her. Suckerpunch tackled me from behind and I was swarmed with puppy love, taking my mind off everything, if only for a moment.

"Riley sealed the gates off a week ago. We have to go in through here," Elie said, leading us toward the long-abandoned Pebble Beach Golf Course.

We'd left the soldier tied up for reinforcements. The kids didn't need to see what would happen to him if he felt less than inclined to walk on his own. I scanned the perimeter, nothing but tall grass and crooked signs before us. Harley circled, sitting down with a whimper around the eighteenth hole. Glancing back at Alexiares in confusion, he shrugged, the same questioning look in his eyes. His shoulders were slumped, his tan skin had paled to a greenish color. I smiled at him reassuringly, food was just beyond wherever the hell Elie was taking us.

It made sense for Riley to close off all access to The Compound. With everything going on, it was a risk to keep our gates open. I'd hate to end up in the same boat as the Titanic, but our gates were nearly impenetrable, as long as they were closed. It would take some serious firepower to get through them, and not the elemental kind, either.

Elie's hand touched the ground, and a sinkhole opened up. "You didn't think we'd leave you out here without a way to get back, did you?" She smirked. "It's *supposed* to be for emergencies and only accessed with his magic signature or yours, but he programmed it for me too, just in case."

He must've pulled some kernels of my magic from the lamp posts that littered the city. They burned with the essence of my flame.

My brows rose. "And I suppose searching for your mom all alone classifies as an emergency?"

"I wasn't alone. I had two dogs and apparently a tail," she concurred, arms crossing over her chest with attitude.

Alexiares dropped Emma off his back. The two had become fast friends the last two minutes and, if I was honest, the sight of it melted my heart. "So, how did you make it through? Riley ain't the type to do something like this without a fail-proof in place."

Emma's small lips pulled into a taunting grin. "Run fast and use your air magic to be super quiet."

Alexiares high-fived her, his eyes dancing in admiration at the rebellious attribute Emma seemed to possess. Elie scoffed disapprovingly, clearly not pleased by the antics.

"It's supposed to close within seconds after I pass through, but only if there's nobody within a few feet of me. Which there clearly was. I took off as soon as my feet hit the ground. I'm sorry," Elie said. "I could've let someone in and wouldn't have even known." She stared down, kicking dirt into the hole absentmindedly.

I placed my hand on her shoulder. "Hey, it's okay, Elie. No one's expecting you to think of these things. It's not your responsibility. And honestly, Riley should've known you would use and abuse this system, anyway."

She smiled at me, taking a step closer to the sinkhole. "Keep your hands close to your chest and, um, put your weapons away, safety's on. Don't want the air to fire them off or anything."

Elie hopped in, poised as if she were going down a slide before I had the chance to question her further. Harley and Suckerpunch went in after her. A gleeful series of howls and barks sounded through the air and I chuckled. Those two were seriously something else. It was good to be home.

Alexiares prodded Emma to go next. She double-checked the safety on her gun, then disappeared into the ground.

"After you, princess," he said, offering me a hand.

I rolled my eyes. "You're catching me off guard with your gentleman bullshit. I think I liked you better with fire under your ass."

"Who said I'm being a gentleman?" He teased, "Maybe I enjoy the view from behind you."

His hand pressed me toward the edge, slapping my ass hard before he pushed me inside. I yelled a flurry of curse-words as we went, his dark laughter filling the space behind me.

We went through the earth slide at an unnatural speed. I had no doubt Riley had worked with a Tinkerer on this, though it amazed me at the speed in which it had been completed. There was no world in which Riley existed that he would leave me out here, shit out of luck, even if I commanded it.

The narrow tunnel of earth and stone was slick with moisture and adorned with gem-resembling mineral deposits, defying the laws of physics. It twisted and turned, its walls lined with an eerie, almost otherworldly light. The ground beneath our feet hummed with the resonance of earth magic.

And then, as abruptly as it had begun, our journey through the center of the earth came to a halt. We emerged in The Gardens in a corner of produce near our little lake that wasn't yet ready for harvest. A deliberate action to avoid detection, no doubt.

My feet barely touched the ground before I sprinted through The Gardens, dashing to wherever my family may be. I didn't know where I was headed, but knew in my heart that the connection between our souls would lead me to them. Harley and Suckerpunch hounded at my heels, their huffs and doggy grins pushing me further, faster.

"Slow down!" Alexiares yelled out cheerfully, though he was more than capable of keeping up.

I heard other footsteps behind us and I smiled, knowing the girls were coming with us. Heads turned as we raced through The Compound, onlookers doing a double-take, checking if they were seeing shit or it were truly me. I slowed near Prescott's quarters but Elie found her way next to me, guiding my hand to keep going.

An odd look wavered on her face. "Not here," she said.

My lips pursed, brow furrowed, but I chalked it up to her being out of breath. I'd never worked with her on cardio in the times she trained with me. I hadn't expected her to hold pace but she was fast.

There were two possibilities at that moment, Riley and Alexiares' house or my rooms. All bets said Riley had holed himself up at my place, desperate for any excuse to be close to me during the day that he could get. It would be easier that way, anyway.

The soldiers would have better access to him, and he'd be able to oversee any training and war efforts. It was nearing the end of the day, the sun setting beyond the high walls in the distance. No chance he'd be anywhere else but pushing paperwork. With no one outside the walls except the already deployed troops, scouts, and patrol, there was no need for his presence elsewhere.

Skidding to a halt at a door I'd thought I'd never see again, I pressed my hand against the knob, pausing to steady myself. Excitement filled me as I pushed the door open. Riley had his head down at my desk, shuffling paperwork between stacks as Reina paced before him, fingers running through her hair. Movement caught my eye to the left of me as Alexiares rammed into my back. Moe sat up from her lounging position, pen wiggling in between her fingers and a notebook on her lap.

Riley's head shot up toward the door in shock and his face lit up. He pushed to his feet, hopping over the desk, sending the paperwork flying. I pounced on him, jumping into his open arms and wrapping my body around him, tears streaming down my face. *My brother. My family.* They were all safe. Losing myself to tears, I let it all out. Slobbering, messy as a fucking baby, into his chest.

Inhaling, I sniffed in his earthy scent, the sensation known to drive him mad with irritation. He set me down, pulling me in by my ear, then rubbed his knuckles against my head. Alexiares grumbled in the doorway. Reina strode over to him, not releasing him from her own tight grip.

The others entered the room, but I couldn't tear my eyes away from the one who'd left the widest gap in my heart. It had been painful to leave him behind. I loved my sisters. We'd been through a lot together, but even before all the bullshit, we'd spent enough time apart for the pain to be tolerable for the last few weeks. It wasn't the same with Riley. He never left my side for long before this, and his absence had taken a toll on my sanity.

A carefree chuckle pushed the curls against my ear, tickling them. They stuck to my skin under the wetness from his tears. He pushed me an arm's length away, hand cupping my face and searching my eyes, communicating everything yet nothing at all. My brother had missed me too, that much was clear. Riley's hands ran down my body, turning me in a circle, prodding at me for injuries.

"I'm fine," I giggled, pulling myself away. "Stop being a weirdo, Ril."

He put his hands up innocently, still staring at me as if he couldn't believe I was real. Moe strolled up to my side, her usual smug grin in place, but she pulled me into an embrace.

"I see Elie's little escapade paid off," she said, humor in her tone.

Elie gasped. "You knew?"

"She always knows," Reina and I said at the same time.

"Jinx." Reina laughed, dragging Moe and me back together for one of her famous group hugs.

I let them smother me with love, Reina's happiness pushed gently across the room. We exchanged excited chatter, the promise of catching up over a meal exciting the three of us. Reina's fingers toyed with my curls as she tsked in her usual judgment of cleaning habits, like I could help it. She muttered something about needing to run me a bath, going on about having laid out the perfect cozy, relaxation outfit out on my bed pending my return. I rolled my eyes, savoring her soothing way of taking care of us.

The conversation between us died down. Elie and Emma took Moe's place on opposite ends of the couch in silence as they observed the surrounding scene. Alexiares and Riley leaned against the desk, lost in their bro talk, playfully punching at each other.

I'd never be able to get him to admit it, but Alexiares had missed Riley. He had been his first and only friend since Tiago. It'd taken some warming up to before he'd slowly accepted the companionship Riley offered.

I watched him, studying the way his mouth curved up in a resistant smile at whatever Riley was saying. His posture had loosened up slightly, color flowing back into his face as if being back here had healed something within him.

"No fucking way," Riley said, catching me in my stare, gawking between us.

I tilted my head. "What?"

"Prescott was right," he chuckled, "I can't believe it."

"Right about what?" I asked, genuinely confused. "Where's the old man, anyway? I can't wait to see his face when he—"

Unease seared through the room, and my words fell off. The room was silent, every pair of eyes focused on the ground except for Alexiares' and mine.

"Someone fucking speak," I commanded, cold trickling down my spine. "Now!" I yelled when no one spoke up. They winced, Alexiares coming to my side, his hand falling to the small of my back.

Reina's hand trailed down my arm in her approach. A sense of calm washed over me and I accepted it, having no doubt I'd need it for whatever was about to come out. "Amaia, there's something we need to talk about. Maybe you should sit down," she cooed.

"I don't want to take a seat, *Reina*. I want to know what the hell is going on."

"She's fine where she is," Alexiares growled in my defense.

I knew then, knew from the sadness I read in his tone and the stiffness taking hold of his shoulders, that he had guessed it. Riley moved in front of me once Reina backed up. He grabbed onto my shoulders, leaning down to meet me face to face.

"Maia," he said, his voice trembling with regret. "I screwed up. I failed you. I'm so sorry. Prescott is dead."

My heart shattered into a million pieces that I no longer had the capacity to know how to put back together.

PRESCOTT. MY SAVIOR. MY HERO. MY FATHER. THE LAST OF MY great trio was gone, and Riley, the person I trusted the most in this world, had been the bearer of this news. Riley watched me, his eyes filled with sorrow. He had been my confidant, my partner through many adventures, and now he was the messenger of utter heartbreak.

Prescott rooted himself in my life as an anchor in a turbulent apocalyptic sea, and now that anchor was gone.

My tears hadn't stopped flowing, despite Reina's best efforts. "So you … you saw him? Was he …?"

Riley nodded solemnly. "Prescott thought of you till the very end, Amaia. He loved you. He said … he told me to tell you that it's okay to be angry, but never okay to give up."

It wasn't possible for my heart to ache anymore. Those words were so Prescott that I almost found it in me to laugh. Almost. Not quite.

"Prescott was brave," Alexiares said. "Must've done something right. I see the old man in you every day."

I found comfort in that. Strength. Clinging to Riley, I glanced up, his dark brown eyes, the remorse in them striking another pang through my heart. He may have claimed to not be a soldier, but he was one through and through. Duty had always come first for him and now I understood the truth, a painful one.

Riley had done what I wouldn't have had the strength to do. Prescott's last wishes. *Compound first*, Riley had said he'd taunted him with. Riley closed the gates—not out of cruelty, but out of loyalty to our leader, his *friend*, and our people.

"What do you need?" Riley asked softly.

Wiping away my tears on his shirt, I sat up. Anger and blame wouldn't bring Prescott back. This wasn't on Riley any more than it was on me. I'd chosen to leave. It was me who thought it was necessary to go to Duluth with the traitor we'd all called a brother. Had I listened to Riley at his first suspicions … *no*. I wouldn't let myself go there. Couldn't let myself go there. Right now, the only thing that mattered was getting my people through this. *That* is what Prescott would have wanted me to do at this moment, and I'd be damned sure to make him proud.

The others sat around me in a circle, hands resting on my lap in support, even Emma. She hadn't known Prescott, but there was a way about her that told me she had known pain.

"Amaia," Riley whimpered, crouching in front of me, pleading with me to stay present. "Tell me what you need and I swear on everything and everyone we love, I will do it."

"There's a soldier we have tied up. Alexiares can show you where. Get him here. Find out what he knows. Kill him, then help me kill them all." Pushing myself from the ground, I walked into my bedroom, closing the door behind me, and raged.

CHAPTER
THIRTY-EIGHT

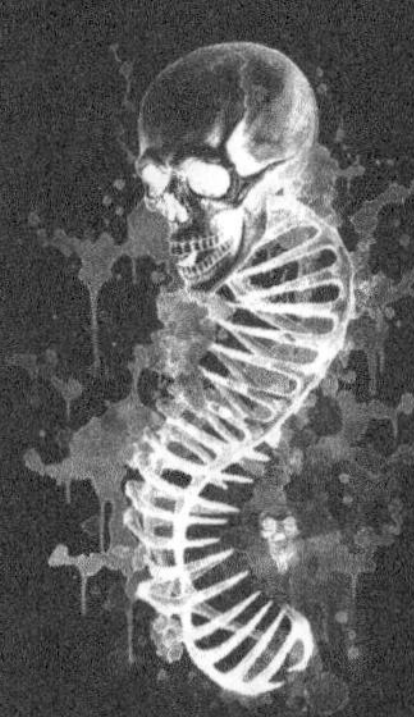

ALEXIARES

Riley was silent the entire walk to get this sack of shit back to The Compound for questioning. He kept side-eyeing me, waiting for me to damn him for what happened to Prescott. It wasn't any of my business; I barely knew the guy.

I did feel somewhat sorry that Riley blamed himself. From what I heard, he'd been following orders. Blaming yourself for loyalty was something I could relate to. Riley's case was different though. At least his blind loyalty had been for a good man.

He wasn't the type to want to open up and talk about his problems. I respected that, deciding to stroll quietly by his side. The best thing I could offer him was the peace he desired.

Emma had done a bang-up job of slicing through his ankles. My kinda kid. I'd stuffed some torn up cloth down his throat and used my earth magic to bury him in the ground to his neck. Fucker wasn't going anywhere on his own anytime soon.

I'd grabbed a sandwich from The Kitchens on the way out to help fill up my energy reserves, but my magic was damn useless. Riley, on the other hand, had more than enough to open up his little earth portal to get us there and back. The hardest part was lugging the soldier's heavy-ass body a few miles back. I was exhausted, but sleep could wait.

Riley had one of his men meet us in The Gardens when we returned to heal the guy's ankles. We'd shoved non-bloody clothes over his body and threatened to slit his throat if he made a scene as we transported him through the settlement.

We didn't have to worry about him having any elemental abilities to escape. If he did, no doubt he would have used them already. Our first stop was testing his blood in The Elemental Room and getting a scan on his head, double checking he wasn't simply tapped out, ensuring he wasn't like Seth. The guy was pure *Supra,* which served him no benefit now that he was captured.

We were in some creepy-ass interrogation room I didn't even know existed in their underground shelter. There was zero concern from Riley about him seeing the ins and outs of The Compound and telling his people about what we possessed. Motherfucker had no chance of making it out of here alive. Not that he knew that though—Riley had assured him that if he cooperated, he'd be released once the fighting was over. If the guy was smart in any capacity, he would have known that was a damn lie, but hey, here's to false hope.

I leaned against the concrete wall, arms crossed, as I watched Riley get to work. We'd start off easy. If he gave us what we wanted, I'd let Riley give him whatever death he determined he deserved. The last thing this idiot should ever hope for is for me to get my turn.

So I hung by, waiting and watching as Riley strapped him to a metal chair, head secured at an upward angle. A bucket of ice-cold water hung above his head. Riley circled him, asking him for more information as the repetitive, monotonous drops of frigid water dripped onto his forehead. I began to doubt the quality of soldiers they were building over in Covert. The utter terror in his screams after a few hours gave me a shimmer of hope. Maybe we weren't screwed after all. Still, he refused to answer any of Riley's questions.

Riley's eyes were hard. The man who brought fear to the people of Monterey Compound now before me. Sure, his tactics were more humane than what I would have chosen, but something told me he was just getting going. I was here to serve vengeance for the girl I loved, but Riley had someone to avenge.

He grumbled in frustration, tiring of the lack of information flowing. Coverts troops were closing in as each minute passed; if they weren't coming today, then they were coming tomorrow. If they weren't here tomorrow, I was certain we would not be granted a third day of peace. This soldier knew that and was simply biding his time.

I was tired and needed my rest. It had been more than twenty-four hours since I'd last slept. I needed to replenish my magic in preparation for what was to come. Getting Amaia the information she needed to make this a victory for us made me persevere. The relaxation that came from watching someone undergo torture would have to be enough.

Riley smacked the bucket down from the ceiling in a rage. "Agh! I'll be back," he said darkly, not looking over his shoulder as the door shut behind him.

The soldier rocked back and forth in his chair, the blindfold preventing him from being aware of my presence. I chuckled at his desperation. He jumped, head swiveling from side to side as if he'd be able to see through the dark cloth covering his eyes.

"Hello?" He whimpered. "Is anyone there?"

"Not anyone worth pleading to," I cautioned, taking slow, melodic steps toward him.

His movements came to an abrupt halt as the sound of my boots tapped closer to his personal space. "You don't have to do this. You can do the right thing. Set me free. I won't tell them what happened here. I won't tell them anything. You have my word."

"Buddy, we can do this the hard way, or we can do this my way. One of those choices will make this less painful for you, and let me give you a hint. It's not the latter."

He considered his options, ultimately saying nothing. Riley strode back in, a buzzing noise following him into the dimly lit room. The healer from The Gardens followed close behind, an empty stare on his pale face.

Riley never met my eye, wrestling with the better, more humane parts of him no doubt. He held his arm out, a couple dozen wasps landing on it awaiting his command. The man obliged his silent order, handing him a clear container. Riley took it, guiding the wasps inside.

"Last chance to tell us Ronan Moore's plans," Riley offered.

It was a bullshit offer. He didn't wait before slamming the man's head into the container, holding it there as the wasps went crazy. *That's the big secret then? Son of a bitch can control bugs.* I couldn't contain my laughter as the soldier screamed out in distress. Riley smirked, secretly enjoying it before wiping it off his face as quickly as it appeared.

Riley's guy came up behind the soldier, hand pressing to his face healing him. He stepped back giving Riley the space to demand answers again. When none came, he repeated the effort. On the third attempt, Riley realized we were no closer to unveiling Covert's master plan.

I walked over to Riley, whispering in his ear, "Time to reevaluate the game plan here. It's been hours. We need something more aggressive."

With a stone-cold expression, Riley nodded in agreement. He walked over to the soldier, unstrapping him and kicking the chair out from underneath his body.

"Stand!" Riley commanded.

The soldier's legs wobbled beneath him, the pain he went through not forgotten though he'd been healed. If he hadn't spoken to me before, I would have assumed he was mute. Aside from his cries of agony, he had not uttered a word. I thought this would have been easy considering the drops of water had him falling into full panic mode.

He was a tougher son of a bitch than I'd thought.

"Amaia, needs answers, and that's what I'm going to get her," Riley uttered under his breath. The earth beneath us mimicked a whirlpool and Riley pushed us back against the wall. "You will not sleep, you will not rest until I know everything I believe is worth knowing about your weird-ass cult of a territory. Is that clear?"

Still, the soldier remained silent, his feet moving in obedience. Riley's tone was always low, if you wanted to catch his words, it required you to listen close, but the soldier followed his commands. The quieter, the deadlier, everyone knew that.

I turned, studying the harshness of his usually kind features and wondered if Amaia had ever seen this side of him or if he'd kept this hidden from her. He'd always been gentle around her, caring, but a beast lay beneath the kindred spirit he presented her with. I saw right through it now, the pain that ran through his veins, recognized it as I recognized my own.

The ground moved faster, then slower, fucking up the soldier's steps. He fell, unable to keep moving. Riley calmly walked over, straddling him down on the ground. Vines locked his limbs into place as Riley dumped water over his face, crafting a gag with the guy's own shirt.

You don't make a soldier like that—they're born.

I WAS GROWING IRRITATED. IT WAS THE NEXT MORNING AFTER WE'D started this lackluster torture. We sat backs pressed against the wall, shoveling eggs and spam patties in our mouths like savages. *Fuck, I forgot how good the food was here.* I chucked some of the fruit Elie had dropped off at the door at the soldier's face, a grape bounced off him onto the ground. He scrambled for it. Riley laughed as he opened up a small piece of earth beneath it, swallowing it whole.

"Hungry?" I teased.

The soldier groaned, his legs shot from being in motion overnight. He'd fallen asleep, his body on autopilot as his eyes closed. I'd offered him some coffee of course. I suppose it only helped if it went *in* his mouth and not on his face. We'd brought in Moe's record player in the early hours, Bodies by Drowning Man played on repeat. The music reverberated off the walls, blasting at full power.

I'd left to check on Amaia only once. I didn't want to come back to her empty-handed, but it was killing me to know she was suffering alone. She'd barely glanced up from the bistro set near the window when I entered her room. One look in her eyes and I could tell she was planning, plotting, envisioning. She wasn't tumbling into the depths of her emotions, heading to another depressive spiral, at least not yet. I'd left her with a kiss to the forehead, promising the next time she saw me, I'd have what she needed.

Riley had a few more minutes of trying things his way, then I fully intended on keeping that promise.

Five minutes passed, and I pushed to my feet. The earth stopped spinning as Riley studied me curiously. I offered him a hand up, waiting as he put his food tray down, and took it, waiting for what I had to say.

"Times up," I said.

He sighed, eyes boring into the poor soul now hunched over peering at us, hoping for mercy. "Your way it is then," he agreed.

I smirked, cracking my knuckles. Walking to the metal tray on the opposite wall, I unraveled my toolkit. To some extent, it was exciting being able to use my new toys. I'd left my old kit behind in St. Cloud, but Amaia had given me permission to grab whatever I needed from the armory room. Of course, I'd had to borrow a few items from Reina's medical supplies too. She said she didn't want them back from whatever I was about to do, but they were really nice. I didn't understand why she wouldn't miss them. Oh well, her loss was my gain.

"Take a seat in the doctor's chair," I said, patting the metal chair that remained knocked over on the ground. The soldier glared at me, fear overtaking him as his body trembled. He made no movement toward me. "You can walk here on your own volition, or I can drag you here. Regardless, your ass better be sat in the next few seconds, or I'm going to be irrationally upset."

He wobbled over, pulling the chair upright while keeping his eyes on me. It wasn't as if he had a choice. I didn't ever see myself playing along in my own death, but I guess some of us had a stronger will than others.

"You made my lady sad, you know," I said, pulling two pliers in front of my face, gauging if I wanted to use the tooth puller or nail gripper first.

"*I* didn't do anything," the soldier tried to reason, sweat pouring down his face. "I'm not responsible for what that monster does."

"That's where you're wrong my friend. A soldier is nothing more than a pawn to the king, whether the soldier knows it or not, is up for debate. Nevertheless, a pawn is a pawn. Disposable." Dropping the pliers, my finger pressed to the tip of a seven-inch blade, blood pooling out. I licked it, then squeezed out some more, smearing it across his face. He grimaced under my touch. "The thing about pawns is that they do all the dirty work for the benefit of the king. Now, that may be bad news to the pawn, because I agree, they don't know *everything*, they just do as they're told. Keeping that in mind, there's so many pawns that play so many roles that it's impossible for them to not be aware of each other's actions. The moves they are making. You don't have the full picture but you have pieces of it. Pieces that I need to know to keep the Mrs. happy."

He opened his mouth to speak, but I cut him off with the blade pressed to his throat. "I know you're going to claim you know nothing again, but do know this: I used to be a pawn on two very different ends of the spectrum of evil. That's why I don't accept your non-answer answers."

"Whatever you do to me here is nothing compared to what Moore will do if he finds out I talked," he gulped out.

I laughed like a maniac in his face. "No fucking way you still think you'll ever see sunlight again, let alone outside these walls. You can't be serious." Riley joined me in my laughter and I turned to face him, thumb jabbing out as to say *can you believe this guy?*

The soldier's eyes widened, scanning the room for fucking help, finding none. "It doesn't matter. Whatever he can't do to me, he'll do it to my family instead. They'll be tortured, or killed, or worse … sent to the Outskirts. Go ahead and kill me. I'm not telling you people shit."

I didn't know what any of that meant, and I wasn't in the business of caring. "Everybody talks in the end. Guess I'll have to do my worst and see if you still feel that way."

Grabbing hold of his hair, I snapped his head back. The moment he yelped, my pliers latched onto his tooth. Yanking back, his tooth fell to the floor, the sound of it muted by his screams. By the time his bottom row was cleared out, I was growing tired of any noise other than the words I wanted to hear.

"Keep screaming and I'll give you something to scream about," I ground out.

He went silent after that, his face turning red as he fought off even a whimper. *Strong little asshole.* Lucky for him, I'd had a lot of practice over the years. Everyone had a breaking point.

I dropped the smaller pliers to the ground, fingers skimming over my next item of joy. "Change your mind? I can give you something to chew over if you need a moment?"

The soldier spat out at me, slimy blood splattered across my face. Which pissed me the fuck off. I didn't mind the blood, but I did mind the disrespect. I was doing my job, something a fellow soldier should understand, given the bullshit he was spouting.

"Ahh," I sighed, "guess not. I figured. You look famished. Let me help you out with that."

Riley tossed me the pouch from where I was sitting earlier, the contents inside jiggling. I searched his face for fear only to find encouragement in its place. Relief poured over me. I was in my element right now, but a small, hidden part of me cared about the only possible friend I had, being scared of what he saw. The monster that made the people of The Expanse lock their doors at night.

I pried the man's jaw open, dumping the glass shards inside into his mouth then shutting it closed. "Open up for the choo-choo train," I cackled, catching the bottle of water Riley threw my way next. "Thirsty? Here, something to help it go down."

His screams were harder to contain as I poured salted lemon water down his cut up throat. It burned going down, I knew first hand. Finley had done it to me the first and last time I'd been sloppy in one of the assignments. For months, the Bloodhound was a myth. Then, with a singular fuckup, came proof and a finger able to be pointed directly at St. Cloud.

Blood poured from his mouth now. He whimpered, and I pressed my ear near his face to hear what he had to say. Honestly, it was my mistake for naively trusting. With the few teeth he had left, he clamped down on my ear, tearing some of the flesh from the bottom and spitting it toward me with a cackle.

Riley lunged at him. I grabbed onto his collar holding him off. Pain didn't bother me. Not anymore. At least not the physical kind. This was nothing compared to what I could do to him. Besides, an eye for an eye and all that. Or an ear.

When both of his ears had been sliced from his face, I wiped my knife off. Sitting down next to him as I sewed them back on upside down. "Sorry about that," I whispered to him. "I go a touch too far when I'm having fun."

He was heaving now, nearing the end of the amount of pain he could take. Which was perfect considering we were now twenty-four hours in and at the end of the time we had too.

"I'm going to give you three options before I get violent, soldier." I grinned at him knowing he was about to become my prey. "We can start with your fingernails. I know, I know, that doesn't sound too bad, but I assure you, it's pretty painful. There's also my favorite pastime, a little flaying here and there, some salt in the wound. You know, old-fashioned. I'm pretty talented with a knife, tell him, Riley." I said, waving my knife in his face.

"I have to concur. He's crafty," Riley teased.

I could sense him staring at the back of my head from the corner of the room. Turning to him, I checked in on my friend once more. There was no judgment there, only the cold, hard face of respect.

"Or, or, or," I exclaimed excitedly, slicing open his pants leg. "I can cut your dick off and use my magic to cauterize the wound. Never tried that one before. I may do it right, may not. Just now getting used to this whole control thing." Shrugging, I circled him. "Up to you though. I'm always down for some experimenting. Keeps things fresh."

He jerked back and forth, glaring at me. I got my answer. Tugging the cloth on his boxers underneath, I poked at his tiny, shriveled dick, waiting for him to give in.

"Okay! Okay! I'll tell you what I know," he hollered, pleading with me to stop.

I pretended to be disappointed that my fun had been cut short, tsking in understanding. "See that's what I thought. Okay, I'm listening."

Taking a seat on the hard ground, I crossed my legs, hands resting on either side of my face. Riley closed in on him, standing behind me in support.

"We have more manpower than you. That's the least of your troubles, you have other problems to worry about than our troops being right outside your borders. The mission is far greater than you can imagine."

Riley crouched low, hand resting on the soldier's bloodied shoulder. "Tell me about this *mission* of yours."

"The general, you both care for her, right?" The soldier questioned.

I growled in response, "What about her?"

"She's our first target. Get rid of her, get rid of half our problems—"

Riley slapped him across the face, a reflex at the mention of threat to his sister. Couldn't say I blamed the guy either; if it wasn't him, it'd be me.

The soldier glared at Riley, wrongly considering him the more civilized one. "She'll have a choice when they find her. Die or join our cause."

"She would never do that," I said, knowing Amaia would choose death every time.

He chuckled at that. "She will if she cares about your people. Your general is nothing but a fish in a larger pond. They've seen it. There's a bigger threat brewing, killing your general will only halt the rebellion against us, not stop it completely. Moore may be insane, but he sees what's possible for humanity, how great we can be! Think about it—you two are powerful, I can tell. How many weak-ass people do you protect by being here with me?" The soldier paused, taking a moment to the blood pooling in his mouth. "They're nothing but dead weight, dragging down the rest of civilization. Imagine what could be achieved if you both could spend your time on more tailored tasks aimed to advance, not defend."

"I personally don't give a shit." My brows raised at Riley's candidness.

I shrugged because if he didn't care, I guess I didn't either. "Ditto."

"You should," the soldier explained. "Moore sees what you all have done here. He wants to take it, mold it into his vision of a greater tomorrow. Don't you see? We can make this country great. Ronan Moore will lead the way. His philosophy will take humanity to the next level. *That* is our mission. It doesn't have to come to blows. This can end peacefully if she surrenders."

"Do you even know what you're talking about?" I spat. Because to me, it sounded like he was repeating some rhetoric that sounded good in theory but held no real weight.

Riley refocused his attention on him, grabbing the soldier's face to stare into his eyes. "When is the attack going to happen?"

The soldier said nothing, shaking his face free. He went quiet, clearly not wanting to give us any more information.

"I'm getting tired of this," I yawned, rising to my feet.

Pulling my pistol out of my holster behind my back, I pressed it into his forehead. "Three. Two." I didn't count to one before firing.

At the last second, I pulled the gun up, aiming right off the top of his head. He flinched as it skimmed his scalp, burning a clean path down the center of his head.

"Okay! You fucking psychopath! They'll move in the night!"

Riley grinned mischievously. "Which night? We're gonna need you to be a bit more specific."

"Tomorrow," he said. "They'll make their first move tomorrow, two hours before sunrise."

"Thank you for your service," I muttered, this time not missing when I pulled the trigger. His brain matter splattered our clothes, yet Riley only appeared slightly repulsed. "I'll clean this up, get some rest. Go check on our girl, prepare her for what's coming," I offered, but not for his sake, for mine.

Riley patted my back, granting me a silent goodbye before he grabbed his shit and left. I waited for the door to close for my first tear to fall. Staring at the gore, I let them fall, not bothering to wipe them from my face.

I hated this. Hated myself for it because I was reminded about how much I fucking loved it. The thrill that it gave me seeing someone terrified of what I was capable of. It went against everything I tried so hard not to be, fought to come back from.

I didn't want to be this way, not anymore. Amaia didn't deserve this version of me.

She had only ordered us to kill him after we got the information we needed, but she had never said anything about torture. How else did she expect us to break him? Talking? A cackle released from the depths of my chest at that. Surely, she had to assume torture would be the only option when dealing with a soldier. Amaia was strong as hell; she herself wouldn't give away Compound secrets even if it meant her death. It's why I knew she was willing to die for this place if Covert got their dirty hands on her tomorrow.

Maybe she had been under the assumption that said torture would have been the kind Riley conducted. The mental kind, not what I was doing. Not the maiming and cutting.

Finley had been different. She had expected the worst behavior from me, had been drawn to anything morbid with fascination in her eyes. But my girl didn't deserve the kind of beast that I was. She didn't even heed the warnings Sloan and so many others had cautioned her about. Amaia had heard their words, but I could tell when she looked at me, she saw someone in pain who had suffered and could heal. I didn't want her to know the version of me that they all knew existed. Would she accept me if she saw it firsthand?

My girl had seen me kill but not … not this. This was the stuff I'd watched my father do to traitors, snitches, when he needed to force people into his business dealings to meet his demands. What I'd just done was my own sick creative twist I'd taken on my father's work and used in St. Cloud. But as a result of the fun I'd had, I hadn't failed her. I'd gotten Amaia the answers she desperately needed and made this sick son of bitch suffer for what had happened to Prescott. I would do this for her all over again too if she asked, even if it cost me her love.

CHAPTER
THIRTY-NINE

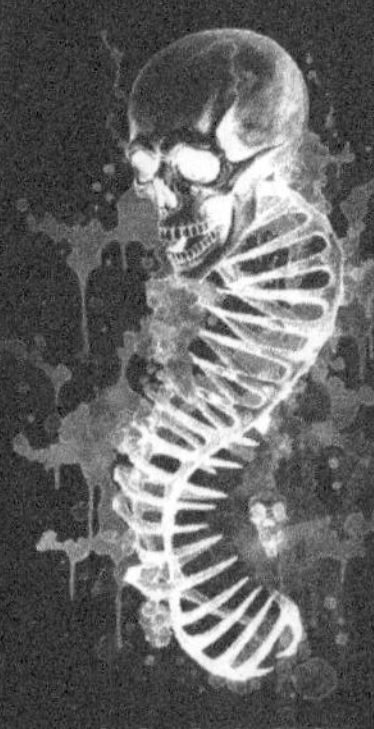

AMAIA

My fingers tapped against the desk I'd become accustomed to sitting behind over the years. If I stopped moving, stopped fidgeting, I was scared of what I would do. Falling back on old coping mechanisms would kill us all, remaining strong in this moment was the only option I had.

Harley laid across my feet, Suckerpunch at the door as I ran over my battlefield plans repeatedly, making sure everyone had their place and was accounted for. If we played our cards right, we could survive another day. That was all we could do for now. Joining all our armies as one to move on Covert Province was no longer a possibility. A shared battlefield of equal grounding would have to wait; for now, we just had to survive the night.

War was not won by a single battle, but rather the collection of strategic moves made. A battle here, a battle there. In the end there would be one winner. While I hoped we would be victorious down the line, I had to focus on my people for the moment because this battle of death was imminent.

This wouldn't be a battle to be won, but a battle to survive. I wouldn't waste the opportunity to see how dirty Covert could fight. The Prescott in me had me eager to use this as a chance for them to show us what they were made of and how exactly we could move to crush them in the future.

Survive long enough to fight tomorrow's battle.

I reached into my bottom drawer, pulling out the tattoo kit I'd forgotten about for some time. Clearing up space on my desk, I pushed the paperwork aside, lining up the pots of dark ink on the polished wood. Removing the corks with my teeth, I spit it out, dunking the needles into the alcohol in a small container within the kit. It took everything in me not to drink it.

Bracing for pain, I brought my arm to the desk, running my fingers across the *Memento Mori* text that was fading by the day. All that meant to me was that it needed a new addition. Sunlight filtered into the room, dust dancing before my face and I smiled at the angry face I'd grown to care so deeply about. His face didn't soften as he took me in, his hand absentmindedly greeting the dogs.

"Are you okay?" I asked gently.

"I was coming here to check on you, who cares how I feel?" Alexiares grumbled, eyes darting down to the mess scattered about on the desk. "Are you tattooing yourself?" Humor filled those honey brown eyes, and I sighed in relief.

"Maybe," I smirked, kicking the chair out on the other side for him to take a seat.

He huffed a laugh, reaching out to grab the needle from my hand. "Give me that and let a real artist do their job. What are we doing today, princess?"

"I didn't know you were a tattoo artist."

"One of my many, many, failures in life according to my father. It wasn't for long anyway, but you never lose the skill." His voice tightened, clearing his throat as he looked up at me, awaiting my response.

I studied him for a moment, tapping the skin where I wanted the words. *"Memento Vivere."*

He blinked, then got to work without protest. Halfway through, he paused, mumbling, "Remember you will die, so remember to live."

Nodding, I added on, "For Prescott and every other person I love who this fucking world has taken from me."

"You want to drink, don't you?" Alexiares asked, noticing the shaking of my knee that had nothing to do with the pain that I was in.

I cleared my throat. "Yes."

"Okay," he said, scooting the alcohol over to me, placing the needle down. "Go ahead."

One thing about this man was that he had no fucking problem catching me off guard, pushing me. And while I'd appreciated it in the past, I couldn't handle it right now. Especially with the temptation being so strong, I couldn't fail my people. I refused to fail Prescott.

"What …" I stammered.

"If you want to throw it all away, then go ahead. I can't stop you. I can help you, but only if you want help."

My flames threatened to coat my skin in anger. Then I considered the weight of his words. *Damn him*, he was right. I had a role to fill, one that I'd been dreading. It had always been Prescott's dream for me to fall into his position, fill his shoes when his time here on earth was up. I never thought it would come to pass, assumed I'd always be first given my line of work.

"I do," I murmured.

Alexiares smiled at me. "Okay," he said simply.

My brows pinched at how easy it was to convince him. "Okay?"

"Yeah," he replied, "okay. Now what?"

I leaned across the desk, placing a gentle kiss on his lips, licking mine after. "Now you finish this tattoo and tell me what's bothering you."

His eyes glimmered, searching across my face. He frowned, picking the needle back up. After a few punctured breaths, he spoke. "There was a time that you painted me as the villain in your story." Alexiares kept his head low. "And maybe I should have let you. It's true, you know. I'm not a good person, Amaia. You can't heal me, and you can't fix me—"

I cut him off, not liking where this was headed, "Riley already told me, Alexiares. You don't need to defend what happened in that room. Nothing you did was wrong—you did what was asked of you. You both did. That death is on me. It punctures my soul, not yours." Placing my free hand over his heart, the cold dog tag around his neck chilling my palm. I moved it up to his chin, forcing him to meet my stare.

"I don't know what Riley told you, but it can't be all of it if you still look at me like … that. Everything that happened in that room reflects on me, not you."

There was a heart-breaking amount of shame in his face, and I hated myself for it. I was no better than Finley for asking him to do my dirty work. He'd bared his soul to me, told me how much it pained him to partake in the actions of his past, and what did I do the first chance that arose? Lead him right back to it.

"I'm sorry," I said. "I should have never asked you to be a weapon at my disposal. I'll never ask you to be that again, never force you to be what you are not. You are not the man Finley knew, Alexiares. You are strong, you are caring, and you are mine."

He didn't look up from tattooing again. As much as it hurt my heart, I wouldn't press the issue. But I heard the rattled sigh he offered, and I could only hope that meant he accepted my apology. I glanced down at the new ink added to my arm. It was complete, though it didn't fill the void deep inside that had compelled me to get it in the first place.

Alexiares grumbled to himself, pushing the kit and bloody cloth from wiping the ooze from the area away. Startled, I jumped back in surprise. Large hands grabbed me by the waist, lifting my shirt. His fingers grazed under the band of my pants, hovering over the now healed cut on my right hip that spelled out his name. Something about the pride lighting his eyes as he took it in let me know that he more than forgave me.

His lips parted, ready to speak when a timid knock sounded at my door. I rose to my feet, fixing my clothes, ready to greet whoever it was. "Come in."

Alexiares retreated to the couch. To anyone who didn't know him, he'd appear poised, relaxed. But I knew better than that. He was a snake ready to strike at any moment.

"General," one of my officers greeted, ducking her head in respect, eyes drifting to Alexiares behind her. "There's news from Elko you need to see."

My hand reached out, noticing the folded paper in her hand. "What is it?" I asked, offering her a seat at my desk.

She took it, her eyes meeting mine with unrelenting fierceness. I smiled to myself, making note of the strength in her posture. It was nice to see after my prolonged absence, Riley had done well in keeping our people motivated.

"Elko has fallen," she answered, waiting for my reaction.

Shit. I opened the letter, the last words from Garcia scribbled across the paper, a smear of blood lay at the bottom of it.

"What is it?" Alexiares asked, striding over to take it from my grasp.

The soldier's strong facade faltered as he neared her, an instinctual recoil of danger driving her to react. She recovered quickly, holding her head high. "That is confidential information, General, requested for your eyes only," she spat. There was no malice in her voice, only the tone of a soldier intent on following their orders.

"It's okay," I waved her off. "Alexiares will soon have the clearance to know what I know."

She shifted her weight, uneasy, but conceded, awaiting my next command.

Fuck, fuck, fuck. This was bad, this was really fucking bad. The *brujas* hadn't made it here yet and Moe had barely recovered in time to make a dent in our soldiers. The ones she had worked on hadn't had a chance to train, let alone discover what their new powers were capable of. There was no way we could take the brunt of a full-fledged attack and make it out alive.

"Give the order for Operation Midnight Veil."

Her face paled, eyes widening. "Ma'am? Operation Midnight Veil is—"

"I know what it is," I interrupted, "and my orders remain the same. Go, now."

The soldier gave me a grim smile, nodding her head before scurrying out the door.

"What's Operation Midnight Veil?" Alexiares asked.

I took a deep sigh, trying to steady myself even though I wanted to do nothing else other than pass the fuck out. The last thirty-six hours had been fucking exhausting, and it didn't appear that I'd be getting rest anytime soon.

"The Compound is going dark," I said, leaving him in my wake as I stalked out the door to find Riley.

I BURST INTO RILEY AND ALEXIARES' HOME, ALEXIARES HOT ON MY tail. I smiled at the familiarity of it, Riley's wooden crafts decorating the place from the furniture to the paintings hanging up that we'd done as a family each Christmas. Plants adorned the entire wall leading up the steps, and I took in the freshness of it mixed with his earthy scent. It felt like home here, same as when I was at Prescott's. My own rooms hadn't been home in a while, not since Jax.

Abel shot up from the couch, a knife flying from his palm before his eyes even opened. I ducked just in time. It pierced the clay pot of Riley's favorite Pothos, shattering on the ground.

"Crap, you guys scared me! I could have killed you. Knock next time," Abel said, clutching his chest, bending over for some air.

"I live here," Alexiares grumbled. "You sleep on the couch, you knock."

Squeaking came from Riley's room. I sprinted up the steps, ready to put up a fight for whoever dared put their hands on my brother in his own home.

"I wouldn't go in there if I were you!" Abel yelled after me.

Muffled cries slid from under Riley's door. Alexiares' hand pressed in on my shoulder, trying to hold me back but I shook him off.

Kicking the door open, I barged in, fists blazing with fire as I scanned the room. Riley hopped off his bed, light brown skin rushed to pull up the sheets on his bed. My eyes narrowed, recognizing the woman beneath them.

"What the fuck. Urgh, my eyes," I screeched, the flames in my hands dimming, using them instead to block out the vision of Riley's booty buck naked body before me.

Riley chuckled, "Then close them."

"Nice, man," Alexiares chided, offering him a dap of his hand before wincing, realizing what he'd probably touched.

"You can open your eyes now," Riley said. "I have pants on."

I grabbed at my stomach. "I think I'm gonna be sick."

"Gee, thanks," Yasmin said from the bed, reaching for one of Riley's shirts on the ground. "Not that I expected you to be the slightest bit tactful," she mumbled.

Scoffing, I closed in on her, ready to smack the words from her mouth. I wasn't in the fucking mood for an attitude. "Wanna say that again? Louder this time, with your chest, I couldn't quite hear you the first time."

To her credit, she hopped to her feet, ready to go toe to toe. Riley stepped in between us, grabbing my arm and dragging me into the hallway. Alexiares wisely stayed behind, instead choosing to engage in what sounded like awkward small talk to Riley's booty call.

"Seriously, Riley," I spat. "We're a few hours out from dying and you choose to spend your time with *her*."

"*Her* name is Yasmin, and don't talk about her that way, Maia. You barely know her," he said in a hushed but soft tone.

I scoffed, "Oh, and you do? She's your dead friend's girlfriend, Riley, not to mention she fucking hates me. What are you doing with her?"

"I love her," he explained timidly. "A lot has changed since you left. Yasmin doesn't hate you. I think we can both admit she has every right to be angry with you for what happened. Just because I was easy to forgive, doesn't mean everyone else is required to do the same."

Focusing on calming my breaths, I backtracked on the first part of his sentence. "Love?" I questioned, "Riley, are you sure it's not you know … just grief and lust confusing you. I practically forced you to take a day to yourself after Mohammed, and you haven't taken time off since. Everything's been moving so fast. You should heal. You aren't thinking rationally. I mean, come on …"

Selfishly, I felt a little replaced. It wasn't fair to him, but in my absence, he'd simply filled the gap with another.

He read my mind, pulling me into a hug, my head resting against his warm brown skin. His heart beat steadily in my ear, calming me as I listened to his voice echo in his chest. "No one can replace you, Amaia. It's you and me against the world. That doesn't mean we shut everyone else out. Since Jax died, I realized there are no guarantees in this life. We have to live in the moment. We *can* die tomorrow, which is exactly why if we feel something, we gotta act on it because you never know when someone can be taken from you. You aren't fooling me. You aren't upset about what you saw in there; it's deeper than that."

I turned my head to peer up at him, knowing he was about to read me for filth.

He continued, "Jax would want you to be happy. I watched you beat yourself up over Xavier and never give yourself to Jax completely. You always kept that distance between you two until it became true. So here's the hard truth, it wasn't for a lack of Jax trying. Don't do this again, open your heart. Mohammed loved Yasmin—he'd want to see her happy. Jax would want the same for you."

"When did this become about me?" I teased, letting his advice sink into my heart and mind.

"Besides the obvious, the guy tortured someone because he loves you. He's been beating himself up about it since the moment those pliers yeeted out that guy's teeth ... Plus, Reina talks *a lot*." We laughed at that, because of course that's what she focused on when filling him in on our trip. "Now what was so important that you charged into my room at full speed?"

I took a step back, dread pulling me back to our cold reality and the reason I'd come here anyway. "It's Operation Midnight Veil, Riley."

"What?" he gasped. "Are you sure?"

Nodding against my will, I told my brother the reason I'd started to lose hope for good. "Elko has fallen. Sacramento is next.

Garcia sent word that their barriers had been burned before they could finish building the solid wall. Their horses have been slaughtered and any remaining soldiers and survivors from them both are heading here as we speak. Which sounds like goodish news but it's not. They won't make it in time, because Garcia confirmed what our captive claimed: we're the main target, and they'll be here before dawn."

I HELD MY BREATH, EYES TRAILING AROUND THE ARENA, RILEY AND Alexiares by my side. Reina, Tomoe, and Abel stood behind us, hands on my shoulders, letting me know they were with me as I spoke. Every inch of the space was filled, and the crowd spilled into The Entertainment Square.

My heart remained heavy with the burden of the role I was about to let my people decide. I'd abandoned them not once, but twice. There was a consensus that they did not blame me for going to Duluth. In fact, they deemed it a necessary action in the course of the reality unfolding around us. Even with that being true, I didn't want to be handed this position.

The people here deserved to know and choose their fate. If they were going to die, I wanted them to die knowing they'd had a say in our demise. There was no glory or heroes in war, but there was pride in dying for the life we had built together.

"I wish we could be gathered here under better circumstances, but here I stand, in the same spot I stood in months ago with nothing else to offer you than the truth. Before the sun rises, we will have to fight for the lives of the people we love." I paused, allowing the chatter and gasps to die down. "Covert Province marches on us. From the intel we've gathered, it will be a fight to the death. They want what we have. They want our homes, they want our people, they want our lives. I have no intention of letting them take that from us. They cannot take what does not belong to them, and though I live by those words, I will die for them with pride. In the last four years, you all trusted me as a soldier and then a general. I know you will follow me onto the battlefield, but I have come to ask for something else.

"In the wake of Prescott's untimely death," my voice shook at the words, still coming to terms with them. "His dying wish was that I'd step into another role, one I dread but cannot avoid any longer. Many of you know he was a father to me. Which is why I mean no disrespect when I say, though his intentions were good in this wish, they do not represent the values he stood for. I believe in the power of the people, in your wisdom and our collective strength. This is your city, your future. By placing this decision before you, it lands in more than capable hands. I will lead you into battle, but war does not stop there—there are other decisions that may cost lives that must be made. I cannot make some of them from one position alone. There is no guarantee any of us will walk away with our lives. We must trust in each other, in the brothers and sisters around you. There is no help coming, not any that give us a chance to see the sun rise. All we have are the people around us, our undying will, and our hearts. You've heard the truth of our situation, now what will it be, my friends … my family? Will you follow me into the darkness in hopes to see the light?"

I took a deep breath, eyes scanning the faces in the crowd, hoping to find support. A wave of emotion swept through The Arena. Tears welled up in the eyes of mothers, fathers, husbands, wives, siblings.

A solitary voice rang out, breaking the silence, "Compound first."

My attention focused on a teenage boy, holding the hand of his younger sister, no older than twelve. "Compound first," she echoed, both of them dropping to their knees.

"Compound first," the entire assembly repeated in perfect harmony, shuffling reverberated through the room as they all kneeled before me.

A lump rose in my throat, overwhelmed with the conflicting emotions. Prescott and Jax would be damn proud and I hated that they weren't here to see it. I would do whatever it took to honor their memory. When I couldn't face my people any longer, I descended the steps, cutting through the path made through the crowd.

A new mission had presented itself; for now, I carried all the hopes and aspirations of my settlement on my shoulders. Our trio had officially become one. The bond I had with them went beyond this lifetime. I would do right by them, that was a promise.

CHAPTER

FORTY

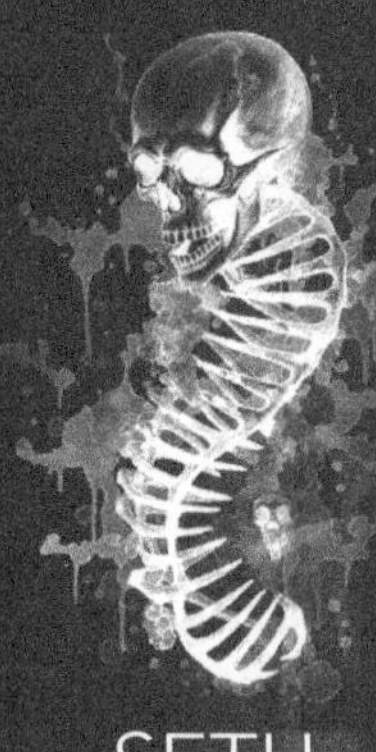

SETH

I rubbed the neck of my horse as I watched Monterey Compound out in the distance from the cliffside. My father had let me come out here on my own. Not a doubt existed in my mind that made me foolish enough to think he didn't have precautions in place to make sure I fulfilled my end of the bargain. If it weren't for the stars gracing me from above, I wouldn't even know The Compound was down there.

It had gone dark, only a few lanterns were lit on the main streets, which only meant one thing: Operation Midnight Veil. Fuck.

A sinking sentiment of dread settled in my gut as I realized the chances of me getting inside were slim to none. They knew we were coming. I had one shot at this, to convince Amaia to listen to me. Maybe I'd taken the wrong path getting here, but there was no room for me to doubt myself now. I needed her to trust me on this. Trust was hard earned with her. She wouldn't make it easy on me to force her to stop and listen. It had taken me years to gain her trust, and I'd shattered it in moments. I would never forget the pain in her eyes when the betrayal she'd refused to see as truth came to light in that cell in Duluth.

I had many regrets on how this all went down; my only hope was that she could *see* the truth of my remorse, or at least hear it in my pleas. Her life depended on it: my sister's life, Moe's life, Riley's life. Fuck, everyone's life did and maybe I fucked it all up.

Or maybe I didn't.

If I hadn't gone to Covert Province, would this opportunity even exist for them to escape with their lives? It was futile to think of the what ifs. In a twisted churn of events, the fate of The Compound now rested entirely in my hands. The gravity of it hit me harder than a sledgehammer.

As much as it was a hard pill to swallow, I missed my sister. If she had just cooperated, told me the damn truth, none of this would have ever happened. That was a lie. It would have, but The Compound's demise wouldn't have weighed as heavily on me if I'd never come to know the people inside.

That was irrelevant. Right now, there were people I cared about down there who needed me. My sister needed me. So, I would do exactly what was asked of me.

Reina would hate me, but at least she would walk away with her life. I could bear the weight of her resentment if it meant she survived. I didn't care that Moe would never see me the same way. None of that mattered much to me anymore. I wish I'd never left things with her the way that I had.

I loved her.

She wasn't just my world; she was the constellations in my sky. I'd made her feel as though none of that mattered to me because she wasn't my blood and flesh. If she heard nothing else from me again, I'd let her know that the love I held to her was unconditional. Tomoe was worthy. My entire family was.

It was three hours till dawn; the lanterns throughout The Compound trickled out leading toward the courtyard at The Pit. All but one—a singular light that sat directly in front of Amaia's room. A chill went through me. It was her magic. She was down there leading the charge even though she'd lost it all. Ronan Moore could take everything he wanted from her, but he was an idiot to think he could take her fight.

When the last light went out, I knew it was time. I placed my hat back on my head, turning my horse to make our way down to try to save the lives of the people I cared about before I was forced to take them myself.

CHAPTER
FORTY-ONE

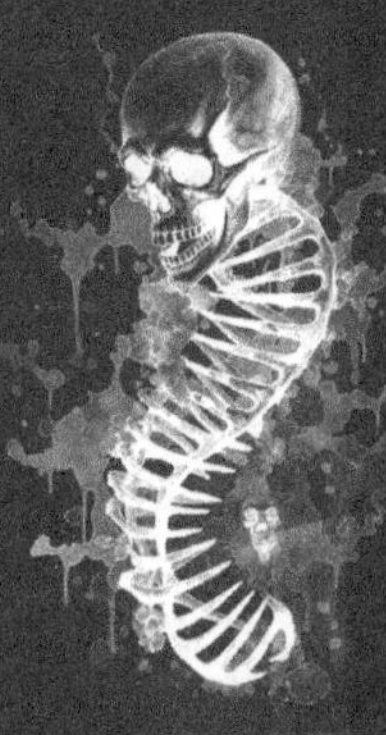

AMAIA

There comes a time in your post-apocalyptic life when you realize you've cried all the tears you have left to provide, and the only thing that remains is anger. Strolling through the darkness of The Compound in utter silence, the only sound was the footsteps of my family around me. Harley and Suckerpunch stood guard inside the shelter. It was the safest place they could be while still having a task to keep their anxious minds at bay.

The quiet didn't confuse me. I knew what awaited us beyond these walls. The force that threatened everything and everyone I loved. So much had been taken from me in such little time. That would not stop me the way Covert Province had hoped.

When you take everything from someone, you inadvertently leave them with nothing left to lose. That wasn't where I sat, at least not yet, but I was on the verge of being there. And while losing two men whom I loved dearly had fucking hurt me, it did not break me.

Nothing could break me.

Like so many women in history, I could not be broken, my fight could not be stolen. The only thing that would stop me is the ultimate price; my life. The loss of a powerful woman's life doesn't blow the flame of rebellion out. It turns it into a raging wildfire, one I now knew the people here would keep burning forever.

When I looked at my family around me, I only saw the motivation to keep going. I was never great at expressing myself. The love I had for all of them fueled me, almost as much as anger. Anger was one thing I was fucking great at. Somehow, someway, I'd become a leader of this great new part of our world. I only wished I could be better at it.

Misery emanated from Reina. She walked in tandem with me, covered head to toe in her old hunting gear. Camo cargo pants, camo long-sleeved shirt, brown combat boots. It was so … not her. Moe had braided Reina's short hair back into two tight braids, accentuating her already taut features. I grabbed her arm, bringing us all to a brief halt.

"You know what lay beyond these walls, who we might face, both of you do," I said, holding Moe's stare, who matched Reina's appearance. "No one will hold it against you if you find duties within the walls. You don't have to stay at my side."

Reina's face softened, and I moved to brush one of the stray strands behind her ear. She smiled at me, a tense one but a smile nonetheless. "We're at your side till the day you die, girl, nothing will ever change that."

Moe's morbid laugh acknowledged that day may be today, but she nodded in agreement, eyes glazing, lost in her own world. I wasn't privy to all that had happened out on the road. The evidence laid before me let me take a solid guess that it had changed

Reina to her core. There wasn't a chance in hell I'd be able to repay her.

"We have much to discuss," I said, looking around at them all. We'd had not more than a few minutes since we'd gotten back to chat and check in with each other. "I want to hear all about it, how I can help us move forward. Let's try to survive the day. After that, we have nothing but time to figure out the rest."

Abel shook my shoulders from behind, pulling both Reina and I under his wing with a cheshire cat's grin. "Let's go, team, we've got some evil ass to kick."

THE SUN TRAILED OVER THE HORIZON, MY HEART PUMMELED AGAINST my chest. I hoped this would work, hadn't allowed myself to stop and think what would come next if it didn't. Not that there'd been the time. Going dark had kept anyone who had the higher point from spying on us. Covert thought they had a leg up on us, making moves in the night. One can't prepare for what they can't see, lurking in the woods, behind our walls, out in the field. Two could play in the game of stealth.

Riley had done well. He told me he questioned the validity of setting up the additional perimeter of the forest maze before my orders had come through, but it had actually worked in our favor. Less set up and all for what would now ensue.

"Can we run through the plan one more time, please?" Reina whisper-yelled from behind a tree-stump to my right.

I brought my finger to my lips, reminding her of the volume of a normal whisper. "We defend from out here with the rest of the troops. When Alexiares gives the signal, our soldiers hidden within the walls will emerge."

Soldiers were everywhere, spanning over miles from The Compound. We'd been busy last night, though Covert wouldn't know it until they arrived. We were everywhere, hidden in plain sight from the trees, to the overgrown fields, in trenches disguised as slumps in the earth. The list could go on. While most of the troops we'd deployed wouldn't make it back in time, we had enough to defend our home.

"Remember the Alamo," Riley muttered, proud of his understanding of my wish to make adjustments to the wall.

Reina's face flushed in response. "Um, didn't the Alamo fall?"

"Yes," Moe said, a wicked smile pulling at her lips. "Not for a few days, though."

I smacked the back of Moe's head. Now wasn't the time to tease Reina's fears. "Some of them made it out, though. Ever heard of David Crockett and James Bowie? You'll be famous either way, sister. Just like you always wanted."

Reina sighed in relief. "Oh thank Jesus, Joseph, and Mary. I remember that hat! At least I'll look good when they describe me," she said, gesturing down to how she'd cropped her shirt into her bra, revealing a glimpse of her stomach. "Which ones made it out?"

"Women and children," Alexiares added deviously.

My sister nodded, feeling better about the situation. "Well, most of them are locked up tight down in the bunker, so that's good."

"Yeah," Moe deadpanned, "but we're out here."

Trickles of fear crawled over my body. I shuddered, trying to pretend I didn't see the spiders Riley channeled netting thick, sticky webs across the trees down on the path.

"We'll have a heads up. They have to break through the first layer of Finley's shields before they get anywhere close to where we're at. Inside the walls are safe. The immediate outer layer has a shield too, and so does the bunker. When they break through our first shield and the fighting commences, it'll signal the watch tower to be on the lookout for trouble. They'll be watching the battlefield. Alexiares is their commanding officer. He knows the playbook," I said, though it made my stomach churn.

The rest of my family would be fighting by my side for as long as we could, but Alexiares would be far away. Or at least it felt as though he would be. Elie and Emma had refused to go into the bunker, like flat-out put up an actual fight of both magic and force. So I'd agreed; they would have to stay within the walls, only allowing them to help our soldiers set up our Plan B should our walls be breached.

If that happened, they'd go into a designated hiding spot within The Gardens. Alexiares would be there to make sure of that. It wasn't sidelining him by any means. With Riley out here, intent on never being more than an arm span away from me, I needed someone else near the gates who I trusted with every fiber in my body. He hadn't been happy about it. Frankly, I thought he and Riley would fight it out. One look at my face and the stress they were causing me had them settle things more amicably.

Riley had been here from day one. He planned most of our outer defenses and knew them like the back of his hand. It would be easier for Alexiares to memorize a smaller playbook, an offensive one with the option for defense instead of the other way around.

A loud boom sounded off in the distance, drawing our attention toward the direction it came from. West Gate. They were targeting the area where they assumed we'd be most vulnerable, where our people resided. *Fucking Seth.*

Another one echoed, causing us to whip around entirely, East Gate, where we'd have the least amount of defense. Then North Gate, then South. We were surrounded.

"You have to go," I mumbled, not having the guts to say it louder, to say goodbye.

Alexiares was behind me, pulling me to his lips. He kissed me deeply, his reluctance to pull away telling a story we were both too scared to share. I held his face, staring into the eyes I'd thought I'd forever hate, had been desperate to get rid of. Now, I was scared to death I'd never see them again.

"Don't," I said, sensing the words that were on the tip of his tongue. Grabbing his hand, I held it tight, intertwining my fingers with his, my thumb stroking the 'hell' part of the hellbent.

He smiled at me, kissing the tip of my nose. My weakness that he'd come to know well. "I won't," Alexiares said, throwing me a mocking salute. "Until we meet again, my lethal little princess."

And then he was gone. Weaving into the trees and disappearing back to where he was needed. I reminded myself of the fact as I faced the family left standing before me. Two of whom stared at me with blank faces, unsure of where they fit into this equation. That meant little to my sisters, they were determined to fight for those who lay within the confines of our home.

"If you can still breathe, you can still fight. If we go down, we go down—"

"Together," Riley interrupted, giving my hand a squeeze.

He grabbed Abel, guiding him to where they would lie in wait. Abel turned back a few feet away. "Catch you on the flip, Gen." With a wink, he let Riley cover him in moss and vines, blending them into the trees.

"Until fate decides to intervene again," Moe led, waiting for me to finish the only departing words we'd let each other say.

"Whenever destiny chooses to meddle once more." I grinned, deciding to add to it. "And a sorry son of a bitch who ends up the victim of your Wrath."

"Let's teach these assholes a lesson about fucking with someone's home," Reina said darkly.

I met Moe's widened eyes, her expression matching my own, our jaws on the floor. Reina never cussed, but I guess some occasions called for it. She gave us a wicked grin, climbing into the tree above me, bow and arrow strapped onto her back.

WHAT DO THE AMERICAN REVOLUTION, THE CIVIL WAR, AND THE Vietnam War have in common? Guerrilla Warfare and its uncanny ability to win the damn thing. Mastering the art of stealth is commendable, but what you really need to account for is the element of surprise.

I lay in between the brush, dried leaves of the winter covering my body, making me undetectable from the camo covering me, head to toe. My fingers thumbed the pin on my grenade as I listened for the approach of our enemy. They were nearing. I forced myself to still, focusing on a life-skill my father had taught me with every hope I'd never need to use it. Four seconds in, hold for seven counts, exhale for eight. Tactical breathing was important if I wanted to shut down my fight-or-flight response and keep my cognitive well-being in check.

Well, that and the *Supras* that could be within their ranks. Last thing we needed was them detecting us before we were ready to make ourselves known. I could only hope my soldiers were doing the same.

The ground crunched underneath the footfalls of men. They mumbled to themselves, swatting at the webs tangling across their faces. Any second now, and all hell would break loose. An arrow pierced the air, flying over my head and meeting some poor soul's heart with a grunt. Another one shot past, a symphony of them dancing through the wind, some finding their marks, others planting firmly into the ground.

"What the fuck?" a soldier to my left muttered.

I kept my eyes closed, maintaining my cover with the browns and greens painted across my face. Riley had ensured our trees were tall. The soldiers would have to crane their necks up to get a glimpse of what would likely be their last memory.

Still, I waited patiently, straining my ears for the signal. Thirty seconds. A minute. Panic sounded around me. Some soldiers stumbled, crawling on their hands and knees for cover, others fled.

Boom.

An explosion sounded in the distance, followed by two more. Chaos spilled in from two forks in Riley's little maze. *Surprise bitches.*

A soldier fell inches from me. "They're in the trees!" he yelled his famous last words.

A howl echoed, bouncing from tree to tree. *That's my cue.* Springing up like the dead, my unit rose in unison, pulling pins and tossing grenades toward the center of the pack. Covert soldiers gasped in terror at the green gas that seeped from them, wincing as they braced for an impact that wouldn't come.

Two arrows marked bulls-eye in a set of glossy brown eyes. *My sister, my girl.* I smirked, taking notice of the intricate carvings Reina added to her arrows when she got bored. We'd waited for Covert Province to approach for an hour. She was bursting with energy at this point.

"My fire is gone," one yelled.

The one next to him shook his hands, searching for a drop of whatever to flow from them. "Wha—my water's gone too! Fucking hell."

I cackled, fire circling the lengths of my body. "Mine's not."

Soldiers pounced down from the trees. Riley stalked through the gas to my side, Shadowstep sword in hand, ax strapped behind him. He pressed his back to mine, helping me kill every motherfucker who dared to take our home.

CHAPTER
FORTY-TWO

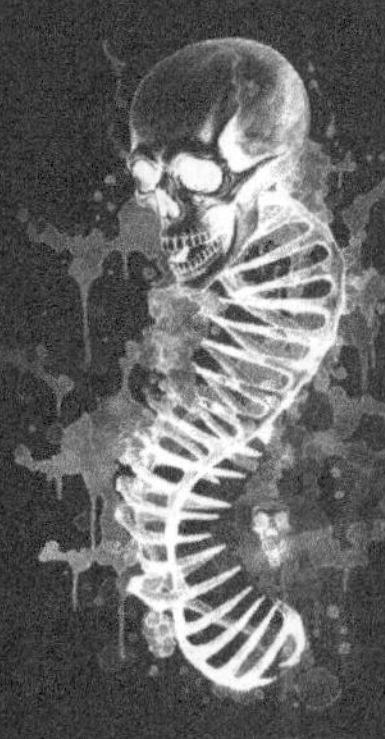

SETH

The roar of this makeshift battlefield was deafening as I fought my way through the chaos, my heart heavy, beating like a stampede in my chest. I knew this moment would come—when I'd have to face my sister-turned-enemy. There was a long period where Amaia had been closer to me than Reina. Despite our inability to agree on most things, we'd had our laughs, leaned on each other when in the face of danger. Now I was the danger and only time would tell who'd prevail in the end.

She raged in the distance, flames covering her body, burning through anyone who crossed her path. Amaia didn't stop there. No one who knew her would expect her to. She was angry.

Vengeance fueled her movements. I sucked in a breath. Those fire-covered kicks and punches had one face imagined on the end of them; mine. It wasn't even a fracture of the power she possessed. Amaia was holding back.

The question was, for what?

My mind raced with the thoughts of the offer my father had made. Either he wanted me dead, or he stupidly believed *I* would be the person to break through to her.

The acrid and sweet smell of gunpowder and death coated the air. Metallic, tangy blood pleased the taste buds of my tongue from the fights I faced to make it this far. Hopefully, the noise had spooked my horse far into Neverland. Don't know what kind of sick operation Amaia was running here now, but I thought animals were off limits.

I slammed in a fresh magazine, clenching my semi-automatic tightly. Sweat and dirt streaked my face as I pushed forward, determined to reach Amaia before it was too late. What I had to offer was as close to an olive-branch as my father would ever extend.

Rehearsing what I had to say made little sense. It would take a few fists and punches to the gut to even get her to let me get a word out. That was if she didn't incinerate me on sight, which was a big fucking if, to be frank.

Getting past Riley was something I'd prepared for. He was a decent enough guy that I'd been able to tolerate his presence in an almost pleasant way for years. Killing him was hardly an option for that reason alone, or the fact that Amaia would burn right through me if she knew I was responsible for his death.

Prescott was already an anchor weighing on the situation as is. They weren't supposed to torture him based on the debrief I'd sat through. Lord knows my father had given additional orders when I was out of earshot as an extra blow to Reina for not coming with me.

I'd jab a sleeping agent into Riley's neck, putting him down for about fifteen minutes, just long enough to say my piece. The blood and gore covering him would be a sure sign of him being dead to any of our soldiers who passed by. What I had not prepared for was him slinging a Shadowstep Blade that Amaia had told *me* she'd ordered destroyed after it was created.

I sneered; even when I was trusted, I wasn't trusted enough to be on the in. Riley, without a doubt, knew. The way he moved through the shadows, appearing behind the unsuspecting, was clear enough—he'd had practice. Extensive amount of it.

The new development meant I'd have to be wary of the other weapons that I'd assumed were destroyed. Amaia had claimed they were unethical, making it an uneven playing field in a world that had already crumbled under the development of advanced weaponry.

On fucking cue, a lean man with red-brown skin fought with veracity behind Riley. His attention was more on covering Riley than on his own ass. Two plasma blades in hand, plasma melting from the blood-covered steel, melting through the bodies of those who got too close. He was quick on his feet, legs reaching behind him, a blade strapped around his heel to slice through the idiots trying to close in behind him, not bothering to glance back as he did it.

This was going to be a problem. I needed a new game plan.

That was incredibly hard to do in the middle of a full-fledged battle while keeping my focus enough to stay alive. I dove behind a tree, slouching down, desperate to think through this, to find a solution, and fast. Minutes passed in what felt like seconds. Men fell at my side, reaching out for help with their final gasp for life. I would not be extending them a hand.

I know what I have to do.

Pressing to my feet, I slid from around the tree, checking to see if my path forward was clear. Dead, battered bodies sprawled around me. Some were pelted with arrows, others were clear victims of magic. Spiders crawled over a body to my right, the poor soldier's face swollen, puss leaking from the array of bites. Bullet holes peppered a few unfortunate, but whoever had unleashed their wrath here, were clearly gone. A second glance at the corpses as I stepped over them let me know Riley and whoever the fuck that was covering him had been here. That little fact meant Amaia had been too, which also meant …

A soft thud hit the earth behind me, making me jump damn near out of my skin. An arrow poised to strike through my forehead. My eyes drifted to the figure behind it. Her face was concealed behind a green bandanna that matched the camo of her hunting gear. The long brown hair I'd known my entire life was gone, now pulled back in two short braids. It didn't matter how different she looked, I'd recognize my sister from a mile away.

"I've been watching you since you ditched the horse, Seth. You may be blood, but if you take one more step toward my sister, you're as good as dead."

As familiar as her physical appearance was, I had no idea who stood before me now. Shame washed over as I realized that I was the cause. Since I'd left, most of my thoughts had been consumed by the fact that Reina was my sister. I was supposed to be her big brother. It was my responsibility to do the protecting. I could do that for her now. That had been the plan thus far.

The woman in front of me was living proof that I'd put on the blinders for far too long. Reina never needed protecting and never would. She had tried to protect me from myself before I'd realized that I needed it. I got it now, the same way I recognized the defiance in our shared blue eyes.

CHAPTER
FORTY-THREE

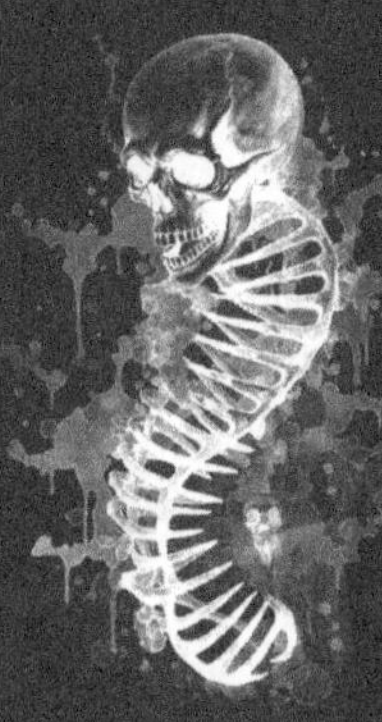

REINA

I'd spent twenty-five years by my brother's side, and right now, he looked like the brother I'd seen time and time again doing something he didn't want to. He stiffened, clenching his gun in his hand. I prayed at that moment that Seth would turn his back to Monterey and walk away. He did not.

"Reina …" my brother said, standing tall before my arrow, daring me to pull it.

I sneered at him, letting him know his dare was accepted. "Yes."

His hands went up above his head, gun dropping on the ground. "Hear me out." He kicked it away from his body.

"Hear you out? Seth, I've been waiting to hear you out for over two months. I thought you'd come back … but you never did."

"I'm here now," he said, stepping forward, hand pushing the arch of my bow toward the ground. "I came back, I'm here."

Seth took my arrow from me, pulling me into a hug. I melted in his arms, not realizing how much I needed this moment, how much I'd dreamed of it happening again. Then anger took over. He'd betrayed me. My brother had set me up to lose my life, our friends' lives too. He'd cost Prescott his. Seth had led our monstrous father on a path to destroy our home. No hug, no love could change that.

I shoved myself back, reaching down for my bow. The tip of my fingers brushed against it as my brother stepped down hard with his boot, grinding against my hand and flattening it.

"Reina, I need you to listen to me carefully. This can end with no blood shed," Seth tried to explain.

While I was born at night, it wasn't last dang night. Ronan Moore wasn't the kind of man to stop short on a path he'd already started down, not unless he was offered something better. If he was willing to halt a war he'd already triggered, then that meant the price of his peace would be high.

My eyes narrowed. Yanking my hand free, I glared at him. "Yeah right. Just go, Seth, you've done enough, taken enough. You're free." I gestured to the world of chaos around us. "Father could think you're dead. We'll claim it if anyone asks, say we burned the body. Go anywhere but here. You don't have to do whatever *it* is that made you hesitate back there."

He winced, my read on him and preposition on his options slowly working their way through his mind. "Reina, you don't know dad anymore. He's not who he used to be. He's not *dad* anymore. It's not that easy to just … get away. It's a fair offer, one life in order to spare everyone here, Amaia included."

"Who's life?" I questioned. Maybe it wouldn't be the worst deal in the world to consider.

I didn't like it, but there were a lot of things I didn't like doing that were necessary now. If it was between one or possibly thousands, maybe it was something to consider.

"You'll get a name once Amaia agrees to the deal," he said, avoiding the question. "I'm sorry, but we can't risk word getting out if she doesn't. They'll know we're coming."

"I doubt she'll agree to do whatever dirty, behind-the-scenes work you and father are up to." I inched back, trying to put more space between us so I was out of his wingspan.

"She has no choice," Seth growled.

That appeared to be a trigger for him. His face reddened, eyes swirling in anger.

"Of course she has a choice," I pressed. "There's always a choice for her whether her opponent knows it or not. What happens when she makes her choice and the answer is no?"

"Then I kill her and Riley and the mission here is complete," he said, the unspoken obvious from the pain radiating off him. *And you and Moe, too*, was what he couldn't bring himself to say.

"I can't let you do that. You want to get to her, you go through me first."

"If it's not me, then it will be someone else, and we're all dead either way. At least the death I bring will be swift," he mumbled, trying to move around me. "Reina, get the fuck out of my way."

I stood firm, making myself an immovable mountain blocking his path. "No."

"I don't want to hurt you." Seth's free hand shifted to his pocket. My eyes followed, the sense of unease from his body making its way toward me.

"No, Seth, I don't wanna hurt you," I said, my magic taking a hold on him. "You will always be my brother, and I will never stop loving you. But I think it's time I live my life without you around."

I worked to pull the water from his body. Tears came streaming down his face as he cried out, falling to his knees, chest shaking with grief. He deserved to know exactly what I had felt for months. My brother, the man who took and took until there was nothing left to take. He'd taken my brother from me, James, then he'd taken Jax, my trust and love. His latest was Prescott, and still, that wasn't good enough for him. Seth had to have more.

Stalking toward him, I stared down my nose, enjoying the sight of my brother kneeling beneath me, on the ground where he belonged. I released that hold, sliding calmly into the mix, letting my brother develop a false sense of hope. That's what I had felt too, for a brief moment.

He looked up at me, words forming, ready to beg for me to stop, but I wasn't done. "Silence," I said, making water flow from his mouth next.

Seth clutched at his throat, water sputtering as he choked. Betrayal stared back at me in his cold, callous eyes. *Good.* Now we were even.

I wasn't my brother. I hated him, but I would never call for his death. If he had learned even a fraction of anything from his time with our father, I hoped it had been to steady his temper. All he needed to do was turn around or stay down. Either option was better than what awaited him or Amaia if he continued on. Only one of them would walk away from that fight.

Amaia winning meant my life, Riley's life, Moe's life. Subsequently Abel's and Alexiares' too, as they would surely try to avenge our deaths. But that also meant the loss of the only brother I had left.

At the end of it all, he would always be my brother, no matter how much pain he'd caused me. It was hard, throwing away twenty-five years of memories over the last few months. The constant battle of it all had left me fractured on the inside.

Seth gasped for air in relief at the pull back on my magic. We locked eyes. As he scrambled to his feet, a reflection of myself stared back at me. I searched them, desperate to find the man I'd spent my entire life with. The one who'd protected me, molded me, had confidence in me, over the years and in our time on the road alone. I thought he'd walk away. He took a step back, turned like he was going to do so.

"I'm sorry, this is for your best interest," he said, lunging toward me.

Years of having to fend him off as a kid gave him away. The small hop he does on his toes when he's about to fake me out. I was ready for him, meeting him halfway with a right jab to clock him in the jaw.

He dodged it, ducking low. Light on my feet, I stepped back, throwing a kick, ready for my foot to meet his ribs. Seth sprang up, reading my next move. He grabbed my leg, lifting me over his shoulder and tossing me down on my back.

My head spun. I pushed myself up, wheezing, as all the air left my lungs. White stars filled my vision, the world in my peripheral a solid black. I panicked, the ability to feel my limbs to protect myself nonexistent. None of them responded to the call I sent out, begging them to listen. Seth's body covered mine. He hovered over me and the last thing I saw was the needle in his hand, now piercing the cusp of my neck.

CHAPTER
FORTY-FOUR

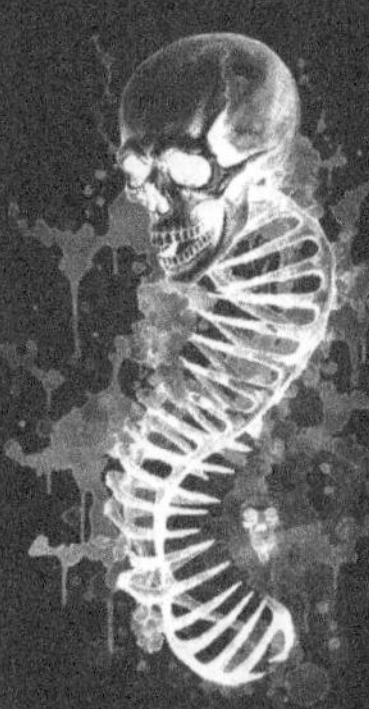

RILEY

This is so fucking bad, man.

I can't see her.

Where is she?

I fucked up big time.

Red stained my hands. It blurred my line of sight, too. I rubbed my face, which only made it worse. There was no pain. In fact, I felt nothing at all. My body moved on autopilot. Slipping through the shadows was taking a toll. I was slowing down, my ax swung slower. I stepped into the shadows at the pace of a sloth.

For me, stepping into the shadows felt like nothing. It was dark for a moment, a blink, then the next I was where I wanted to be within the same vicinity of where I'd slashed through this dimension.

I had to have eyes on where I wanted to go. The space had to be exact or less than a pleasant reaction to the magic would spread across your body. I'd had more than enough practice, but as my magic and this weapon exchanged their power, I became exhausted with the constant ebb and flow of hand-to-hand combat.

They were fighting us five on one. Even without their magic, we were still at a disadvantage given their numbers. Covert Province soldiers were smartly herding us apart. It was obvious they knew who they were fighting by how they chose to assault us. Separating me from Amaia on a battlefield was the number one way to distract me. Keeping Amaia from her family was the best way to piss her off. They weren't aware of who Abel was, but the fact that he fought with intensity beside both of us made him enough of a target to warrant their full attention.

Amaia screamed, a sound fueled by fury. The distraction of the tell-tale distance between her and me cost me. I hesitated a moment too long before stepping into the shadows, no longer moving sporadically in order to not keep a pattern. Instead, my eyes gave me away. I stared at the direction her yell had come from, landing as close as I could.

Pain soared through me, bringing my body off autopilot and rooting it in the present. I looked down, blood trickled from my mouth. A curved blade ripped through my back.

My brows pulled together, I turned, wanting to stare my killer in the eyes. A pale face greeted me, the craters in his skin caked with dirt and blood. He was deceivingly old to be out here in the midst of things. His thin lips pulled into a cruel smile. He shook the blade, bringing me down to my knees. The movement forced me to stare up at him, but the speed of an oncoming figure behind him stole my focus.

I choked on the warm, iron-tasting liquid pouring into my lungs. It was hard to breathe, so hard to speak. He needed to run.

This wasn't his fight, I had to tell him. It was my duty to keep him safe, and I had failed so many already; I didn't want to fail him too.

The soldier turned, sensing the oncoming assault. Abel sprinted toward us, plasma blade in hand. The second blade was missing, lost in a fight. His eyes were hard, focused, raging.

Ready for a kill.

Blood surged into me, the absence of the blade turning my situation into a dire one. Lightheadedness swam over my body and I fell on my back. Leaving me in the perfect angle to watch the little brother I'd sworn to protect be sliced clean through, at my expense.

There was no more air to take in. I watched in horror as Abel reached for an arm that was no longer attached to his body, his plasma blade on the ground with it. The soldier kicked him back, his boot grinding into Abel's chest. He writhed beneath him, howling in agony. His head lolled and our eyes met.

"Tell me where Amaia is," the man demanded, pressing down with his body weight. "Answer me, and keep your pathetic life."

"Fuck. You." Abel growled back.

This was wrong. We weren't together. I promised her together. I won't let them bury another friend. They can't have Abel and they can't have her.

My fingers grasped the shards of grass beneath me, the greenery sticking to the clumping blood on my hands. No magic laid there, the earth did not answer my call.

Death, I dance too close to death. No, I have to get up. If you can still breathe, you can fight.

But I couldn't breathe. No more oxygen found its way into my lungs, only heavy, warm, liquid.

A gun, you still have your gun.

Shakes fought against me. That and the sharp pain radiating down the left side of my body.

You can do this, thirty more seconds, you can do this. Stay alert.

The trigger bent to my will, and the gun fired. And then the world went dark.

CHAPTER

FORTY-FIVE

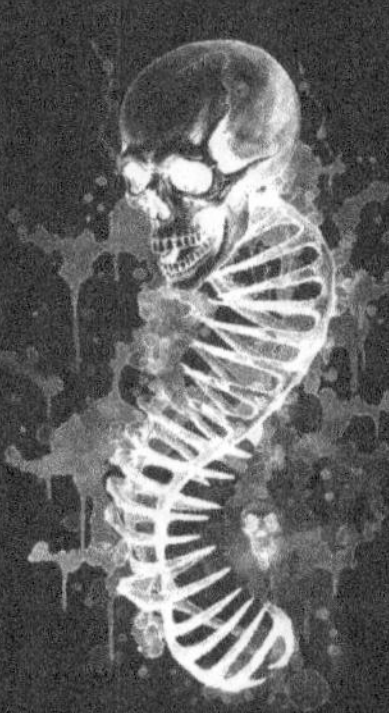

TOMOE

Wrath flew from my hand, the impact from the asshole slapping the shit out of me causing my grip to loosen. His hand closed in on my neck and I took advantage of my opportunity. My arm shot up, slamming down hard on the cusp of his elbow, granting me my release. I grabbed onto his arm, pulling him tight against the back of my body.

His nose crunched under the pressure of the elbow I threw back. I kicked out at his rib cage, but he latched on, tossing me to the ground. He granted me no mercy, grabbing onto my hair, dragging me across the dirt.

Leaning back, I drove my body forward, my legs wrapping around his waist. He landed with a thud and I grabbed onto Wrath. I wasn't in the habit of giving my victims time to realize how the tables had turned before I sliced through his neck, and his head rolled.

Someone grabbed me from behind, their arm closing my airway. Wrath cut through the wind. I flipped her in my palm, jamming her into the side of my attacker. Sneak attacks really pissed me off.

I spun around, sitting on their torso, dropping Wrath at my side in favor of my fist, connecting with their face until the light left their eyes. *Who's next?* I smiled to myself. If Covert Province wanted to take my home, they'd have to do better than that.

Scanning the battlefield for my next victim, I was pleased to find two idiots running right at me. A gun drawn in one hand, knife in the others. It would have been slightly intimidating had I not seen this happen the night before. The one on the left's gun was jammed, he just didn't know it yet.

Light fucking work.

I charged them head on. A silver ball landed at my feet, courtesy of the buffoon with the knife. There was no opportunity to side-step. I kept my calm as Wrath flew from my hands. My vision hadn't shown me using my blade. Bare hands would do just fine, for now.

A few jabs and an elbow later, and the knife was knocked free. He scrambled, trying to come up behind me while his partner initiated the assault from the front. I weaved, ducking in time to land a hard blow to a kidney. Spinning around, I elbowed the one with the gun in the throat.

Whirling around, I kicked at the same spot, collapsing his airway. He'd be dead soon enough. The remaining one barreled toward me but Wrath was already back at my feet. Chuckling, I grabbed onto her, jutting her out at the base of my stomach. He rammed right into it, my action too swift for him to slow down.

Wrath grated through him, I turned my Katana, making his insides ribbons. A vision flickered as I pulled her out. I needed to go to Reina, and I needed to go *now*.

I glanced around, trying to find her location or a giveaway of the general area I'd seen her in. All I saw in my quick glimpse of the future were treetops and Seth, but none of those details helped me scout her out. I was supposed to be headed toward our second location, an area that had no trees, which meant … she hadn't yet made it there.

There was only one place she could be.

Stumbling into a sprint, I didn't let myself stop to think about the choice I would have to make once I found her.

THE MINEFIELD WAS A DEAD ZONE. BITS OF THE EARTH WERE BLOWN out, scattered limbs around them. Chunks of dirt and human meat lay in clumps in tree branches. Piles of flesh littered the ground. It was mostly Covert soldiers. I said a quick prayer, wishing the few of our fallen a peaceful return to the earth.

Some of our field medics had made their way over, mending the people that had a shot of being saved. My vision wavered again, another option of the future washing over me. *Oh, fuck, fuck, fuck, fuck. Reina. I need Reina right fucking now.*

Riley was here, and if I didn't get Reina to him soon …

"Abel!" a voice croaked nearby. "Amaia! Abel! Get off me, I need to get to them."

As clenched as it was, I knew that voice. Relief washed over me. There was still time.

Following the voice, I jogged over to Reina's mentor, Henry. He crouched over Riley, hands pressed to his side, the glow of the healing power nearly faded. Riley clutched onto something but I couldn't get a clear view of it. Henry turned at my presence approaching from behind him.

"I'm … my magic's almost gone, but it's not enough," Henry whimpered, exhaustion all over his face. "He won't sit still, and it's making it worse. It's not enough. It's not enough."

He repeated himself, lost in a trance of despair. I kneeled beside him, my hand pressing against Riley's cheek. His eyes were wide with panic; he stared around me, behind me, through me. Riley wiggled, inching and writhing under Henry's touch. Dirt kicked up beneath him each time he slammed his body to the ground.

"Abel! Amaia! I need to help. I have to get to them," he mumbled.

Riley's skin was clammy, a greenish hue underneath his usual deep brown. His pupils were dilated, gums blue. It didn't look good and his panic wasn't helping shit.

I didn't know how to help. As far as I knew, both he and Abel were supposed to be at Amaia's side. If he didn't know where either of them were, then neither did I.

"Abel was taken back to a med tent," Henry said, breaking through his trance. "He was stable enough to move despite his arm."

My nose scrunched up at that. "His arm?"

"Yeah, what he's holding in his hand. Can't get him to let go." Henry pointed to what Riley was holding.

I focused on keeping my composure. To my horror, Riley held on to Abel's hand, his arm tucked on the other side of Riley's body. His knuckles were white at how tight he held onto it.

"Can it be saved?" I asked on instinct.

"Depends," Henry answered, "if he lets it go and we can get back to a sterile location in the next six hours, then yes. Hopefully," he added, his demeanor lacking the proper confidence to reassure.

I nodded, gripping Riley's free hand. His eyes landed on mine and he fell one step closer to reality, "I'm going to go find Reina, okay? She'll come back here and make sure you live and shit. Stay calm. When she gets here, you have to give her Abel's arm too."

"Reina?" he asked, his pupils dilating.

"Mhmm, Reina. Let's make this the last time we meet on the battlefield under these circumstances, bud. Getting tired of saving your ass." I winked at him, pushing to my feet.

He offered a hoarse laugh, his vision going unfocused again. Pressing my hand against his heart, I faced Henry. "He's pulling in some of my power, but he needs every ounce of magic you have except for the last drop. The ritual I performed … my magic will help support his lifeline for now, enough for me to get Reina, then she can heal the rest. If you can move him, pull yourself to the side, don't go too far—she needs to be able to find you."

Henry nodded, accepting his task without protest. I took off, my decision on what to do now clear.

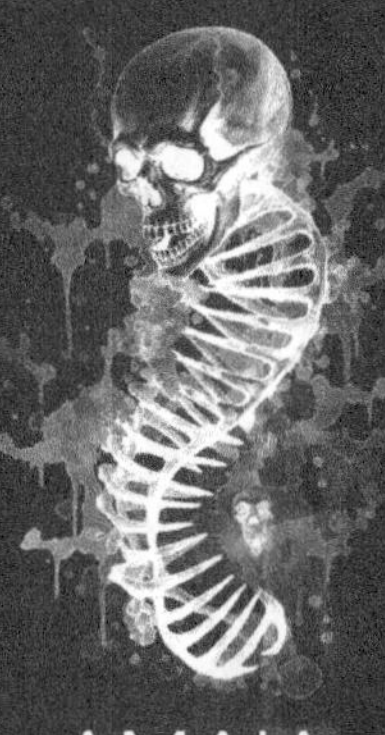

AMAIA

There are five rules to fighting: never move back in a straight line, never take your opponent's energy head on—a fatal mistake the inexperienced tend to make—never and I mean absolutely never set in your stance long enough for someone to guess your next move, always fight your opponent as they fight you, and place the son of a bitch where you want them. Unfortunately for me, everyone who partook in basic combat training understood those principles and now I was facing the consequences of it.

Fortunately for me, most of the soldiers here had been at the sport of kicking ass for a few years, where I'd been at it my whole damn life. Not to mention I wasn't even using my magic. I needed to conserve it. I wasn't sure what for, just had a feeling in my gut. This wasn't my first rodeo; I knew this was far from over despite the die down in soldiers.

If Covert's Province was worth a damn, this would be their first wave. The rest was yet to come. Which meant on top of conserving my magic, I needed to be careful using any ammo too. I was suspicious by the lack of Pansies on the field as well. If not for war, then what was Moore making them for? Most of the first wave of soldiers had used up their bullets and other explosives when they panicked at our ambush. Outside of those who had some sort of metal, hand-to-hand combat it was.

I'd finally worked my way through the football team worth of soldiers working to take down little old me. It was a compliment, truly, to think I needed that many men to contain me. I chuckled. The lone soldier remaining narrowed his eyes, palming me in my fucking face. I kicked his dead friend in the ribs with a cackle, not getting anything out of it other than riling him up a bit.

I'd promised Riley I'd stay close. He was nervous considering what had happened to me last time.

The soldier motioned to facepalm me again, but I grabbed onto his wrist, pulling him over my body and locking my legs around his arm. His bone snapped beneath my weight and I grinned at his blood-curdling scream. I flipped on to his sternum, bringing my arms around his neck. He bit into my side, taking a chunk of my skin off, blood oozing down my body.

"Urgh," I screamed, "fucking bitch." I snapped his neck, pushing his body off me.

I'm sick of this shit. Pounding against my chest, I scanned the battlefield for my family.

I was out near the beach on the other side of our makeshift forest. They'd pushed me out far, which made me nervous as shit at what that meant. There was only one reason to get me alone and with the lack of lethal force that they'd fought back with …

"I don't mind goin' a round, old time's sake," a familiar husky voice said in my ear.

I whipped around, air magic spilling out of me in genuine fear. I hadn't heard him sneak up on me, so much could have gone wrong. Then it would all be over. All of this for nothing.

"Amaia," Seth croaked, "I'm not here to fight you."

"I don't care what *you're* here for, Seth. The point is you're here, on my playground, ready for me to play with," I said, realizing what I was doing.

It hadn't been my intention to steal the air from his lungs, but I found an odd sense of joy at the sight of him clutching his throat. I released some of the pull, letting small bubbles of air escape through, toying with him. He deserved to suffer, deserved for every moment of pain I was about to give him.

Being on the battlefield out in the open was fucking stupid. But I didn't care. All that mattered was him going mad over the exact emotions he'd left me to deal with. In theory, someone capable of doing what he did, destroying our family, risking our lives, was not capable of suffering emotionally. Physical pain would have to do.

"This can … no one else needs to—" he sputtered.

I circled him with a ring of fire, to hell with keeping my magic locked down. There was irony in the fiery pit under his feet.

Reaching down, I pulled my throwing knife from my ankle holster. With a flick of my wrist, it lodged in his hip, the flames bowing out at my command.

"You killed Prescott," I screamed, spitting in his face. "You killed Jax, but that wasn't enough for you, so you killed Prescott too!"

"No I didn't! It wasn't me," Seth yelled, pulling the knife free with a groan.

Taking a step closer, I waved my other knife in his face. "Liar! All you do is lie, Seth."

I tossed the knife through his hand, piercing it to the hip he'd sought to cover up and put pressure on. Something changed in his eyes. They darkened, filling with rage that hadn't been present before. He yanked it out, clutching it tightly in his hand, twitching at the urge to drive it into me.

I welcomed the fight, him refraining from one was unsettling. In the years that I'd known Seth, he'd only turned down a fight once—the day he'd felt guilty for betraying me.

The memory seethed at my soul. I pulled the air back from his lungs, sending him hunching over dropping the knife to the side. That was all it took for him to abandon whatever false pretense of peace he'd come over here offering. I didn't stop there. My fire trailed up his uniform, starting with his stupid fucking boots. I kept the flames over his body at the perfect temperature, not too hot to burn him, but still raging enough to hurt. His hat wasn't as lucky. I burned it to ash with a smirk.

Fury danced in his eyes, his face completely red. "Fight me, Amaia!" He bellowed, "Fight me like the woman you claim to be!"

"Why does everyone say that like I'm afraid to kick their ass?" I seethed, releasing him from my powers.

No magic didn't mean I had to give him a chance to fight on fair footing. I pounced on him, wailing, not letting up as my fist drove home. His face swelled from the impact, and my fist sang with pain.

He caught his bearings, rolling me over, hands squeezing my neck. I choked out air, not pleased to be in the position I'd imposed on him. My feet found his chest, kicking him back and creating space between us once more. Seth reached for the knife, mirroring my movements as I scrambled into a low crouch.

"Amaia," he gasped out, "please just listen."

I swung, ready for him to stop talking. "The sound of your voice hurts my ears," I said between labored breaths. "I don't need to hear about how you hated what we've built here. I couldn't care less about your disapproval of what we've built here. I've seen the company you keep."

Dodging a blow that would have had me pissing blood for a month, I kept light on my toes. I leaned back, throwing him off guard with where my true kick was coming from. "Every day I keep my life, each day that this place thrives despite your father's sorry attempts, becomes the best day of my fucking existence. Starting with the one that ends with you dead."

Sweeping him off his feet, I grinned, dislodging the knife he held in his hand, replacing it in mine. I grabbed the hilt with my other palm, holding it over his chest. *On second thought*, I teased it through the air, settling over the center of his neck.

Seth wasn't even fighting back. He sat beneath me, a defeated look on his face, accepting this fate. That made things slightly less fun. He took my hesitation as a cue, "Just listen okay? If you kill me, if you don't do what he says, then everyone outside the walls will die, which means the people inside will die too when the walls fall. You may not care about what I have to say, but I know you care about them."

"What are you talking about?"

He pushed against my chest, shoving me off him. Seth sat across from me, like we were two friends having a chat in the park. *A park covered in dead bodies.* Memories with Jax and Prescott flashed before my eyes, centering me back in the here and now.

"The last thing I wanted was for anyone to die, Amaia. But shit happened, and then more shit happened, and I couldn't keep up. The lies ran too deep, and then I was in the middle of a mess. I didn't even know where to start cleaning. We may be on opposite sides of things, but it doesn't gotta stay that way forever," he explained.

I sat staring at him, mouth agape. This sure as shit couldn't be what he'd stopped me from killing him over. "What does your half-assed non-apology have to do with saving the lives of *my* people?"

Impulse fought to take over. Years of discipline being the only thing keeping me rooted to the ground when everything in me wanted to tackle him, drive my knife into his body. And claw. And bite. Anything that made him die slowly.

"It doesn't," Seth said, eyes landing on mine, holding my intense stare. "My dad wants to make a deal. I'm explaining why I need you to take it. Monterey was never meant to be my home. That doesn't negate the fact that there are good people here that I didn't do the best job at protecting. You trusted me to have your back, and I was weak. Always have been. I would like to change that now so I needed you to know … I never knew Jax would die, and I wasn't the one who killed Prescott. Let's face it, for a place meant for all, it took me some time to rightfully adjust. I'm not sure if I made a mistake leaving. Regardless, my actions changed the course of everything and there's no going back now."

"The deal?" I pressed, not giving a shit about what poor excuses he chose to offer. It was far too late for that now.

"A life for thousands of lives. My dad has agreed to Monterey's sovereignty under some … conditions in exchange for your support." Seth cleared his throat, staring at me out the side of his eye, nervous his next words would cause me to hit him. "There's someone he wants you to take out. Shut down … for good. They're on the run through Transient right now, hard to track, but dad trusts that between you and the others, you'll get the job done soon enough. He's received word that even if Monterey falls, they'll keep on the path of rebellion. End up causing more trouble. When he looks at the future, it's you on our side, and them dead. It works out in everyone's favor."

"Except for the dead guy and his people," I mumbled. "Who is he?"

Seth smirked through his swollen ass face. "You assume a *he*?"

"She?"

"Does it matter?" he asked. "It's in exchange for Monterey's independence. This place stays untouched. You *guys* stay untouched."

"If *he* wants it done, then it matters. When the bad guy wants someone dead, it always matters. Look around, Seth." I gestured to the gruesome scene beyond where we were standing. "No one's coming out of this untouched. Not a single soul."

"You have to take the deal. This ain't a *this or that* situation," Seth pressed.

"Why me?" I paused, then chuckled. "Because I can get a meeting, lure them into my trap? Because if it's me, that makes everybody under my control bow down too? What's next, putting a fucking crown on his head while taking a knee?"

"Don't you get it? You inspire these people. They speak of you even in Covert. You're a symbol to them. Monterey. Salem. All of y'all are a symbol of what can be. But all of them follow three. Prescott. Jax. You, Amaia." Seth shifted on the ground, no longer wanting to meet my gaze. Something told me at the end of this all, a crown on his head wasn't a far-fetched idea.

"No," I said simply.

Seth winced as he shot to his feet, towering over me. I paid him no mind, dismissing his stature as if he weren't a threat.

His freckled features hardened, fists curling tight. "No?" he asked, his voice a lethal calm.

I crossed my arms, unimpressed with this blackmail over my people and everyone I was now responsible for, disguised as some pleasant offer. The conditions to which I'd even have to meet before taking out this random, not even factoring into my decision. I didn't need to hear the conditions of peace, because whatever they were, they weren't the conditions of my people.

Their right to determine their own futures was one of the main things I'd sworn to protect. There was no negotiating what was a place meant for the ever-changing, ever-evolving Covert

Province's values would never align with that, so neither would I. There were people counting on me, places fighting for their freedom under my command.

I would not let them down. Who was to even say Ronan wouldn't go back on his word? Because that's all they were when it came to Covert Province, meaningless words. A treaty was only as strong as the honor of the more powerful force. That wasn't us, that clearly wasn't us. Not yet. But it could be soon.

Digging my heels into the ground, I found my footing, raising my chin to down my nose at him. "Yeah, tell your father I said he can go fuck himself. My home, my freedom, and my values are not up for negotiation. Never have been, never will be. Then make sure he sends your sorry ass back here so I can finish the job he's likely to start at your failure. Only then will you know how truly unwanted you are."

Seth's face fell, my words striking a nerve. The Earth shook beneath us, and I watched flames light up the sky in the reflection of his eyes. An echoing boom popped my eardrums. I didn't need to turn around to know where it had come from. The last shield. It was too early.

Once that shield went down, the only thing left between them and the inside of The Compound was Alexiares and the soldiers right outside our walls. That couldn't happen. There were not enough soldiers there to hold the line until sundown. We needed to reposition out in the field.

A rough hand firmly grasped my wrist, Seth pulled me back, though I hadn't realized I'd set off running. "We're not done here. You reject this deal, you all die. There won't be another."

"We're already dead; you pulled that trigger when you left. Oh, and Seth?" I asked sweetly, batting my eyelashes. "If you don't come back here after telling your father to back the fuck off, I will hunt you down. There will be no place you can hide, nowhere to run, no scenario where I don't find you. And when I'm done with you, the way you *slaughtered* Prescott will seem like a mercy kill."

CHAPTER
FORTY-SEVEN

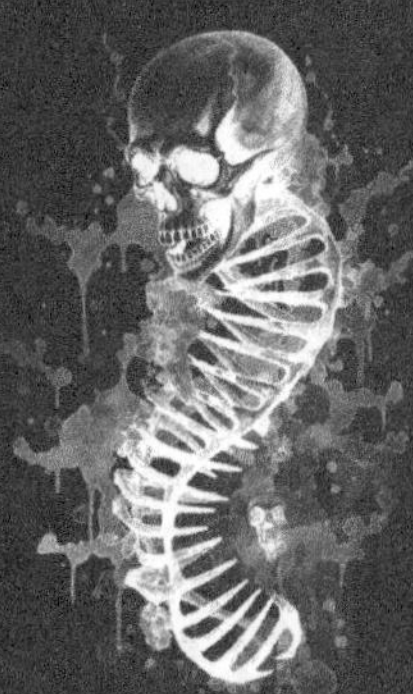

ALEXIARES

I grew impatient, pacing as I watched the battlefield beyond the wall. Thanks to Riley's order of enhancements, we could see them, but the enemy couldn't see us. My girl was out there somewhere, fighting, her life at risk, and I was stuck here, seeing if our stronghold would be dense enough to prevent Seth and his fucktard friends from getting through.

Lying in wait after the fall of our final outer shield made me feel fucking useless. Patience had never been my virtue, no matter how my old man had tried to knock it into me. It appeared we weren't the only one with surprises on deck. Rocks crumbled, earth moving on the side of the cliff, stole prized attention from the battlefield. Pansies trampled over each other, crawling over the cliffside with one target in sight.

Us.

The soldiers placed to guard the wall stumbled, losing their footing at the screeching, rotting creatures surging at them. They spread out, my command not needed when it came to preventing friendly fire. There wasn't anything about this in Amaia's playbook. I wasn't a stranger to being in charge. My father had tried to raise me in his image, hoping one day I'd change my mind and take over the 'family business.'

Calling the shots to *save* lives, however, was never on my radar. I'd been prepared to call the shots when x led to y in order to result in z. Figuring out how to control chaos for some reason had not occurred to me as part of the job. I had zero idea how Amaia would handle this situation.

A new found respect for my girl formed in my heart at her ability to think on the fly. If I didn't know what her next move would be, thinking like her would have to do.

"Watch towers!" I yelled out, my voice coming from the depths of my chest, the hollowed-out portion of the wall amplifying my voice sixty feet up. "Be ready to drop acid on my call. Aim at your twelve and three. Out in the field, hoods up, masks on and retreat, you've got ninety till launch. Archers, hold."

I waited, scoping out the scene, waiting for the perfect moment. Dropping the acid bombs too early could cause loss on our side and minimal to theirs. The key would be getting enough Pansies to get their footing on the cliffside to make them worth it. Reinforced vinyl lined Monterey's uniforms designed to keep the harsh chemicals off their skin. Their masks would take care of their airway and face … from a certain distance. Anything else unfortunate to touch the same air would disintegrate, a highly corrosive acid eating away. Even the dead.

The archers could take out the rest. With the field soldiers on retreat, they could regroup once the assault was over.

Hope and war would never go in the same sentence. The words were like oil and water.

Our soldiers reserved their magic, not wanting to waste it in case a real fight ensued. They fired their guns. Pansies moved in a blur, sprinting toward them at neck-breaking speeds. I had a feeling this batch had been specifically curated for this cause. Their movements no longer had that off-kilter lull. They were precise, unfettered, deadly.

The Pansies ran, arms swinging through the air, yearning for a piece of flesh to pull into their flapping jaws. All of them, with the exception of a few, were *Supras*. We'd barely seen any in Covert ranks on our way back home.

There had been several times when we'd been forced to stop and let their troops pass, or sneak past a few here and there. It allowed us to see what they were working without having to sneak into their camps or their occupied cities.

Supras had nearly been nonexistent because Ronan took it upon himself to create his own super soldiers. Chills went down my spine. Was Seth not creeped the fuck out over this? I mean, not that you should always protect your own, but fuck.

"Acid showers in three … two …" I paused, waiting for that final, slowing leap over. "Drop 'em."

The grenades went off. It wasn't a large bang. One moment over a hundred Pansies lunged, lurking along the cliffside, now maybe twenty remained. The acid grenades disintegrated them on the spot. Those who survived slowed their approach over the cliff to only a few at a time.

My kinda numbers.

"Archers draw … aim … fire." My arm dropped with my command. Being in charge was kinda fun.

Things had quieted out on the battlefield, which was never a good fucking thing this early. I turned my head, straining my eyes, the weight of a lingering threat over taking me. Amaia and the others were still nowhere to be found. They were either dead, injured, or the fight was still ongoing to where my eyes could no longer see. I chose to believe the latter for my own sanity and the sake of everyone, both inside and outside these walls. There was no telling the monster I'd become if something happened to her. If they thought I was a bloodhound now, they'd soon meet the devil.

Movement caught my eye from behind. A soldier dashed toward me, panic on his face. He skidded to a halt, crashing into me like he'd forgotten I was the one he was looking for. I glared down my nose at him, nose pinching at the fact that he was still body to body with me, invading my personal space.

He jumped back at my glare. "Lietenan-officer … er. Sir," the soldier stuttered.

It was obvious why he was on messenger duty. "Alexiares is fine. What is it?"

I actually wasn't sure what the hell I was or what my role was here. To be determined at a future date, I guess. It had to be weird for these guys to go from treating me as a prisoner to listening to my command. No one had protested. I had found that odd, but it appeared no one questioned Amaia's word. When she spoke, they listened, no questions asked, though she'd given them ample opportunity to.

It was more than just the fear from their situation. They respected her decisions, the sacrifices she'd made. They felt a duty to listen to her and it was admirable as fuck.

"They hit South Gate hard, it held. It's holding still, I think."

"You think?" My brow arched. That was a pretty big thing to be unsure of.

He shook his head. "No. I know. It's still good, they're holding fine. West Gate too." The soldier stopped, staring at me with the rest of the words stuck in his mouth.

"You gonna keep me waiting all afternoon? Spit it out." I urged. What did he expect me to do? Hold his hand?

"They're headed here, sir—Alexiares. Covert's making their way around the wall. We're outnumbered three to one, and they'll be here soon."

"Fuck," I cursed. If they surrounded us, there'd be no way for our soldiers out there to get back in. That meant no retreat, no medical runs, nothing.

We had to keep one gate clear to enter through and the North Gate had the power to do so.

"Gonzalez," I said, calling to one of the soldiers in the hideaway between the wall.

Gonzalez came to my side, waiting for the order that could damn us all. It was a finicky piece of junk. They hadn't even had the chance to test it in full capacity, given the chunk out of the earth it would take out unnecessarily. But with the shields that hugged the wall gone, our faith in its capabilities had to be enough.

"Yes, Alexiares."

"Give the order for the aqua-cannons to line the walls. Put the Soulfire in position *C*." I kept my gaze steady. This was some serious shit. No room for any fuckups.

"Copy that," he said, ready to take off.

I grabbed his arm, needing to have verbal confirmation for both my own reassurance and his. "Repeat your orders back to me, slowly, so we're on the same page."

"Aqua-cannons go live, Soulfire position B."

"Position C," the messenger corrected.

I nodded my head at the messenger. "Position C," I confirmed. "Go with him, then spread the word on the rest of the cannons."

They took off, spreading the word to the portion of the wall I could see. I checked behind me to where Elie and Emma had been hiding nearby, the weeping willow and bushes they'd huddled under were now empty. The sky must be on the verge of falling if Elie had listened to a simple request. This was no place for her and Emma to be, not anymore.

SOMETHING WAS WRONG. THE EXPLOSIVES LINING THE WALL ON THE other side of the shield weren't firing off. They were supposed to trigger by tripping the thin wires hidden within the grass. Our soldiers knew where they were, where to step, and what would happen if they fucked up on their way back over the wall.

They'd had to be quick, their training coming in handy as they climbed up the ropes tossed over for them. I whistled, impressed at the endurance Amaia had trained into her troops. They'd been prepared for it all, even when things hadn't gone according to plan. But as Covert's soldiers moved in on us, not a single trip wire blew one of those fuckers to chunks.

I backed up, my eyes trailing along the wires strung throughout the cutaway in the wall. They appeared taut here, leaving the only explanation for where they connected near the gate. The Tinkerers had decided it was the best place to anchor them, given that they would detonate at once if the gate opened and they were still connected.

We were running out of time. Hundreds of Covert's soldiers were now flocking toward the gate, the shield falling at last. There were over two thousand of them. Seth and his father had left no room for failure on their end.

"Light the fuse for Soulfire in forty-five seconds, then take cover," I ordered, my hand slapping against the wall as I took my leave.

Following the line of wires, I spotted the problem, seconds before light brown curls and blonde hair sprinted toward them. Cursing, I strode toward them, pausing at the horror that was about to unfold. Stupid fucking soldiers. I mentally took back my initial compliments. How many soldiers did it take to follow one simple command?

The Soulfire cannon had been lit, placed in position B … right at North Gate. Although it sat at the top of the wall, it had a kickback of flames that would take down that portion of the gate, and anyone who passed beneath it.

"Elie!" I screamed, rage filling me in my desperation to stop her in her tracks.

She waved me off, pointing to her ear and pretending she couldn't hear me. Emma ran to her side, a toolkit strapped to her shoulders. Cute of them to form a suicide pact under my watch, really fucking mature.

"Elie! Emma!" I called after them, "Stop! It's gonna blow. Soulfire is gonna blow!"

Elie's gaze sauntered up, her eyes wide with fear. Defiance crossed her features, "I can make it," she yelled back. "We have to tighten the lines or the rest of the gates will fall too."

She was right. The lines connected to each of the explosives down the entirety of the wall. They were set to trigger one after the other. If the first one didn't go off, none of them would. Soulfire was meant to keep this portion of the gate clear for our people to make their way back home. But the explosives would help lighten the load of enemies we'd be forced to fight off until our troops could do so.

Suddenly, I was left with a decision that could risk three lives and save thousands or screw us all. Racing over, I snatched Emma back by her bag. She yelped, swatting me off and reaching for it from my hands.

"You don't know how to fix it," Elie pointed out over the noise of the commotion around us. "Give it back. We helped build it, we know what we're doing."

And this, Riley, is why kids have no business learning the art of war. Motherfucker.

I sighed in concession. "I'll fix it. You tell me how. Wait back there, and if I say run, you run."

They nodded in agreement, but I didn't buy that shit. If they didn't follow Amaia's wishes the first time, there was no way in hell they'd follow mine. Unease filled my chest. One glance up and I saw our time to fix this was extremely limited. Two minutes at best.

I got to work, following Elie and Emma's instructions as fast as I could, losing my patience at their arguing over which wire crossed where. "*Faster*, you two. Thirty seconds."

"You're almost done," Elie said. "Just tighten up the red one and we're good to go."

"No, it's the black one," Emma protested.

"And who's been making bombs for months? Me. Pretty sure I know more than you," Elie scoffed.

I cut Emma off before she could offer a retort, "The red one is in my hand, so that's what we're going with. Head for cover. I'll be right after you."

To my surprise, I heard their feet scuffling over the cobblestone in retreat. *Got it.* I pulled the red wire back in place, not bothering to gather the tools back up in my mad dash for safety. An ear piercing whir of metal sounded from the other side of the wall, the trembling of the earth beneath me followed shortly after. Whimpers of distress bellowed through the air.

Sparks flew over my head. I was out of time. I emptied my tank, pushing myself to move with the wind. Elie and Emma were now at my side, having caught up to them in a matter of moments. We weren't far enough. When I'd tightened that last wire, I knew our time was up.

I grabbed them by the collar, pulling them into me. Elie peered up, fear and regret washing over her in understanding of what was to come. Her expression hardened to one of pride, proud of what she would have sacrificed for her people. Tears streamed from Emma's eyes. She clutched my shirt.

Pushing them to the ground, I covered my body with theirs. "We did the right thing, Elie."

Heat sliced the clothes on my back before the sound made its way to us. Elie and Emma pushed their air magic out, wrapping it around our bodies on instinct. Against the Soulfire, their magic was nothing.

Fear is a funny motherfucker. It was always right for two very important reasons—it's reactive, something causes that visceral reaction. It has your best interest in heart, usually wanting to keep you alive.

So maybe that's what led me to follow their lead. I covered us in soil, my earth magic coating them, followed by my water, easing the intensity of the fire meant to turn us into ashes.

The final shockwave of the Soulfire cannon firing separated them from under me. My body careened through the air, the ground rushing up to meet me. I landed with a thud, cracks emanating through my body. The impact was fucking brutal. Every fiber of my being screamed in agony, the earth beneath greeting me with a cruel embrace.

Everything around me was blurred, fading in and out of focus as if time itself were slipping through my fingers. The chaos beyond the wall and inside The Pit echoed, Emma and Elie's cries now distorted. But cries were good, cries meant they survived.

Pain seared through my broken body, each slowing thud of my heartbeat a thunderous reminder of how fragile human mortality was. For as long as I remembered, I hadn't cared whether I lived or died, but now I had something that made me want to live. *Someone* who made me want to survive.

Get up.

I laughed, blood leaking from my lips, soaking my hands from touching the gash at the back of my head. There was a bit of irony in finally finding a place in life that made living worth it. It was beautiful to have finally found something worth living for and then dying for it within the same breath.

The distant echoes of war resounded, the aqua-cannons roaring to clean the devastation left in the wake of the Soulfire's wrath. Elie lay beside me, her eyes closed but the rise and fall of her chest told me she was alive. I reached for her, not wanting her to be alone. I couldn't reach Emma, but I could offer Elie some comfort. My palm found hers and I gave it a weak squeeze. The harsh light of day was too much for my eyelids to bear. They were heavy. The darkness that came from shutting them offered me some relief.

CHAPTER
FORTY-EIGHT

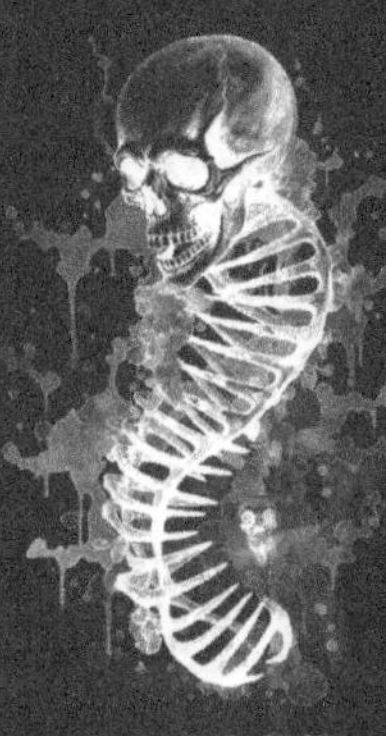

AMAIA

Déjà vu encased me. Almost nine months to the exact date, I was running along the cliffside, racing against time as it threatened to take away the man that I loved. What I thought would be my final time opening my heart to someone had been sealed with my kiss of death.

Fear struck through me. My gut told me I was on the cusp of losing more than just him. Everyone I loved was counting on me, and so many beyond just them, but at that moment all I could think about was how I never wanted to live in a world where Alexiares did not exist.

His name tumbled from my lips, the minefield and forest around me whirling past. It was pointless. Alexiares was back at The Compound, right where the Soulfire had fired, letting any motherfucker who survived it enter my home.

Alexiares would be there, fighting in my home's defense, *my defense*. Anyone who remained outside the shelter would die. We all knew that going into it, every soldier placed at the wall or on our battlefield was aware there was a strong chance we wouldn't see night fall. But if I survived, and they didn't … if *he* didn't …

The field leading up to the North Gate simmered. Brown earth covered in ash. *Good to know it works*. Anyone who was unfortunate to stand on the other side of that cannon was no longer a matter of human anatomy. Limbs scattered the lining of the intact portion of the wall. Feet still stuck within boots, arms within torn, crisp uniform sleeves. The ones who were out of the blast zone of the Soulfire but within our explosives hadn't fared much better.

Covert soldiers flooded in from west of the wall, flocking toward the breach with chants of victory. They clambered through the dusted mess of their fallen, no care in the world. The aqua-cannons fired, sweeping soldiers off their feet, surrounding them in water, then drowning them. It wasn't enough, there were too many, and they were too spread out to put a real dent in them.

Our remaining unit posted at the wall swarmed out, ready to put up a fight. Magic flared out. My soldiers put their training to work effortlessly. Their magic streamed in between their use of combat and weaponry. They were holding their own pretty damn well, but it would only be a matter of time.

I stood at the edge of the tree line, heart thundering in my chest. Alexiares was nowhere in sight. No way in hell that man of mine had turned down a fight. If he wasn't out here in the chaos, there was a reason.

Sprinting toward the gate, I called out for him, "Alexiares!"

Magic seethed from me. Wild, raging blue spouts of fire flew toward anyone in my vicinity. Some screamed, others didn't get the chance to before they turned to fucking powder.

"Alexiares!" I scanned the area. There was so much going on it was hard to focus.

Covert came at me from all sides. Two charged me at the same time, one faster than the other. He reached out, stabbing toward my shoulder with a machete. I ducked down, throwing my body weight into his inner arm with my elbow. His strength gave out with my effort, and I looped a hand around his neck. In one fluent move, I snatched his machete from him, my grip causing his knees to buckle.

Leaning forward, I kicked out to the side, my blazed-up foot jamming into his dick. He flew back, grabbing his crown jewels. His buddy matched the tone of his scream as I slammed him down on the ground.

"Alexi!" My voice broke. "Alexiares, *answer me.*"

The soldier beneath me squirmed, and I saw red. He was a fucking distraction. I needed to find him. *Something is wrong.* There were no orders being given, no commander on the field. My soldiers were relying on the strength of their training and the trust they'd built with one another to guide them through.

Right now, every ounce of my being told me I needed to find Alexiares, but I would be a failure to Jax and Prescott if I walked away. Everything they believed in was on the line.

"It's bigger than you now. You have the responsibility to live for not just you, but them, too." Prescott's words echoed through my head. *Compound first.*

I could do both, though. *Yeah. You can do both.*

Real strength didn't come from being flawless. I understood that now. True strength came from embracing your flaws, owning them, molding them to your advantage. One doesn't get called the best without reason. You get called the best because you're able to turn every imperfection into a weapon of power.

My family, the people whom I loved, were my Achilles' heel. I would do anything for them. It was time I showed Ronan Moore who he was fucking with. The darkness he'd thrust me into nine months ago had only allowed me to find my beast. If he wanted a blood bath, he could have one.

But first I needed to find my *bloodhound*.

The soldier wiggled his arm free, grabbing onto my curls. He yanked my head to the side, attempting to snap my neck.

"Fucking enough," I growled, lifting his head and slamming it into the ground with a sharp crack. His body went still.

I dug into my well of power, stealing the air of every dipshit in my vicinity. They fell to their knees, hands flying to their necks, clawing for air. Their faces turned shades of blue. A path to the gate cleared for me. I followed it, trampling atop their fallen, pretending they were no more than a piece of the earth. Which they would be, when I was done with them.

My magic was draining at a quick pace, so many bodies to control at once. I needed someone to take over. As they realized what had halted their fighting, my army recovered, ending the possibility of Covert having a chance to fight back.

Someone needed to call the shots when I released them from my hold. While my stunt had helped, we were still out-manned.

"Miller," I called, one of the female officers I'd come to trust while out on patrol. If I could trust her with my life out there, then it would have to do when holding the line now.

She slammed her knife into a soldier's throat, that familiar smirk of something bordering excitement and joy, lighting up her face. I found her to be level-headed in her decision-making, with a streak of ruthlessness. Fair enough, that was needed to make rational decisions despite the emotional tax that came from ending a life.

Her long hair was tousled out of her bun, she pulled a strand away from her face, swiping her knife through the gut of another before turning to me. "General Bennett, what can I do for ya?"

"Where's Alexiares?" I asked, my voice a strained mess.

She gave me a pitying stare, whirling ahead of me, hands gripping a soldier's head and snapping his neck. "Last I saw, he was going after two little girls. They were running for the gate before it went off."

No.

There was no surviving the kickback of that thing. *You have to have hope.* The voice in my head was quiet, a barely audible whisper. Yet I felt compelled to listen to it.

I had to have hope, otherwise what was all of this even for?

"You're in command outside this wall. Do you hear me, soldier? This is your field, now own it."

Miller huffed a laugh, a mischievous grin on her face. "Yes, ma'am,"

Air whooshed from their lungs as I released my power, and Miller rambled off a myriad of orders. Howls of agony ricocheted off the wall. I didn't care what was happening behind me, the only way I'd be able to help them all was if my Alexiares was unharmed inside. Getting to the gate was my only concern, even if my worst nightmare may be on the other side.

I didn't know where to look first. At the blonde hair smothered in blood, shrieks of suffering leaving her small, broken body. One of our medics carried her deeper into The Compound. Then there was Elie, who was being held down by a medic and a soldier, a brace secured around her neck. They were pleading with her to be calm, to let them take her somewhere safe to finish healing her. The medic urged her to stop moving, stating he hadn't yet examined her for spinal injuries, that she could still hurt herself.

"No!" she refused, "I won't leave him. He saved my life! I can't leave someone else, please don't make me."

Alexiares' shattered body brought me to a sudden stop. Blood seeped from behind his head, from his ears, streams of red trickled from his mouth. Those beautiful brown eyes welled with tears, staring at Elie, a final request shimmering. Slowly, he released his hand from Elie's, his breaths becoming shallower. *Go.* He seemed to say. *Be safe and go.*

I drifted over, creating a ring of fire around us all for protection. Falling to my knees between them, I brought both of their hands into my lap. "Can you help him?"

The medic peered at me hesitantly. "I would need assistance. Even if I was fully charged up on my magic, I'm not powerful enough on my own."

"Okay, so move him!" Elie spat, glaring at him like it was the obvious answer.

It was a fair point, one I was about to bring up myself. His empty stare settled on me, a small burst of energy flushing his face.

He pointed his finger out along the length of Alexiares' body. "If I move him, he'll die. His body is broken, resonance rupture. He needs to heal a great deal before we move him or he'll have significant damage to his vital organs. Right now, his position on the ground is the only thing holding it all together. We move him now and there is no coming back from that."

"He'll die either way, do something," I growled. The soldier beside him winced, jumping back slightly then pushing back forward at the heat of my flames. "Go find help, go find other healers."

"With all due respect, ma'am, that'll be taking resources away from other soldiers ... ones who have a better diagnosis," the soldier whispered with apprehension.

I inhaled sharply, ready for the pushback. "You will need far fewer *extra resources* if you get help over here as fast as you can. I won't fail you. Now go, that was an order."

They cast a brief glance at each other, inevitably trying to decide whether this would be an order they'd ignore. The medic nodded, accepting his new assignment, nudging the soldier to do the same. I could only hope they would come back, but it wouldn't matter much, I guess. If they didn't, there was a chance I would die right here with him, then they'd never have to answer to their refusal to follow orders.

"Elie, go with them," I ordered, "*now*."

"He saved our lives, Amaia. I won't leave him here to die alone. I won't," she protested.

I scooted closer, my lips kissing her hand still tightly woven around Alexiares'. "Look at me right now, look me in my eyes, and tell me you think I'd let him die." Her light brown eyes narrowed, studying me for a hint of a lie. She shook her head. "Go with them then, let someone check you over, then get to your spot and stay there until I come get you. I'm glad you're safe, Els. I want to keep it that way."

She pushed the medic back with her freehand. He let up, no longer having a reason to hold her back. Her grip on Alexiares' hand loosened. Elie grabbed my hand, dragging it to replace hers.

I gave it a squeeze, holding it up for her to see as I took in the image of the girl I knew would move mountains one day. Broken cobblestone rattled at their departure as I lowered the flames circling us briefly. They disappeared around the corner of the courtyard and I could only hope the medic would keep his word.

Alexiares mumbled something, the blood in his mouth distorting his words. It spattered onto my clothes, the cough pushed from his lungs sounded painful. No sense of pain presented itself in his face, only the slight panic of a death he had no longer asked for.

We were overrun, soldiers everywhere. They began pillaging, throwing open the doors of the rooms around us in The Pit, angry when they found no one. Anything they could get their hands on was tossed. Furniture, paperwork, items of clothing, littered the world around us. I raised the flame up higher around us but it would not protect us from anything shot or thrown our way, only mask our exact location.

His light brown eyes came back into focus, locked in on mine. Cupping the sides of his face, I lifted his head offering him a gentle kiss. "I'm sorry," I cried.

It wasn't fair. He'd given so much, and now I would have to ask him for more. Covert Province was only steps away from finding the locked door of the bunker. The shield was still up, and the door would hold through nuclear war, but in this world, there was no telling what some Scholar or Tinkerer was able to conjure up. For all we knew, Seth had fucked us in every capacity the second he'd run home to daddy.

I presssed my lips to his, over and over again, scared that the next time I kissed them they'd be cold. "You are not allowed to die on me. Do you hear me, Alexiares? If you die on me, I will kill you. Help is on the way, but until they get here, I need you to fight."

He blinked hard, confirmation to my silent request. Guilt swept over me having not been strong enough to say the words but thankful for him taking that weight from me. This wouldn't kill him, I wouldn't let it. He squeezed my hand, a tear dripping down my cheek.

Lowering the flames, I kept my eyes on him. "My heart beats for you and only you," I wept, brushing my thumb over the back of his hand. "Do you hear me, you asshole? Hang on to that, because if you die on me, part of me dies too."

I wouldn't say the words I felt right now. I needed to get them out, but what if, what if those words leaving my lips were truly a death sentence? *No, you can't think that way. Say it.* My lips parted, the words on the tip of my tongue. An ethereal blue hue of flames materialized around us. It wasn't my doing.

Alexiares' power pushed inside my veins, ecstasy briefly passing through me at the orgasmic feel of his power merging with mine. It was weak, yet determination marked his eyes, urging me to do the heavy lifting.

I rolled off my knees, wanting to be able to defend myself in other ways if needed. Keeping our hands connected, I rested his hand on my lap, reserving a small ember of my power to keep his heart going. As long as he had magic, he had a fighting chance.

One breath in. One breath out. Focus. You can do this.

Dropping my walls completely, I let him in without resistance, our gifts making us one. A wave of intense heat and swirling mist emanated from us. The invading army who had been declaring victory were now met with the full force of our Steamfire. Their protective gear turned into a scorching prison, the temperature in the air around them rising rapidly. I closed my eyes, intent on not losing focus. Sheer will and desire to not fucking roast my troops alive the only thing protecting them from undergoing the same fate.

Covert's soldiers' screams echoed around the walls, making my lesson to Moore explicitly clear. We would not go easy. If he wanted war, I'd bring him Hell. Water met fire with incredible precision. Under my command, steam blasts erupted, sending the soldiers flying. Outwardly, they merely appeared burned, but on the inside, they were soup.

There was no kindness in this death. I sent the dark mist further out, latching onto a new body every time our magic was freed up by the loss of life. The world around me no longer resembled my home, I had no idea where my family was, and Alexiares' grip loosened with each second passed.

Sobbing, a final pulse of power surged through the air. It was a gruesome sight, but in this battle for my home, for protecting the ones I loved, there was no room for sympathy. The Compound still standing was a beacon of hope, one I would defend at all costs.

Covert's forces crumbled, their screams fading into the stifling mist. Those who remained untouched surveyed the courtyard in horror, fleeing back out through the gate yelling for retreat. I fell over Alexiares' still body, his eyes flickered one last time before closing. Nothing. There was nothing left, no string of his power left to tug in my soul.

"No! I didn't get to tell you … Come back," I whimpered, crawling over to start compressions, then backing off in remembrance of the healers warning. "Please come back, Alexiares. You have to know that I think … I think—fuck. I can't say I love you, Alexiares. I can't damn you that way. You and I, we were inevitable, and you are my infinity."

I brushed my trembling fingers over the raised letters of my name over his heart. "It took us far too long to find each other, please, live."

Hands gripped my shoulders, and I whirled in response, grabbing the gun from Alexiares' holster, pointing it at the perpetrator. I sighed in relief, putting the safety back on as I took in who it was.

He kept his word.

I fell back, allowing the medics to huddle over him. They got to work. I fell back, gripping my knees to my chest rocking back and forth. "You have to fix him. Make him better. I'll give anything to make him better," I heard myself mumble, pleading with them to do a job they were already doing.

The one in the middle shook his head at the others, pulling back slightly. *No.* I rushed over, throwing my ear to his chest. No heartbeat where there should be. I kissed the side of his lips, tears streaming down the side of my face as I offered pleading eyes to the healers. They placed their hands back on his body, losing their balance as they used some of the final kernels of their magic to heal him.

Alexiares coughed, sitting up with a gasp, clutching at his chest, then his body. He cried out in pain, hell in every part of his eyes. I jumped back, colliding into the medic who'd kept his word.

"He must lie back down. He's not stable," he said.

I pressed my hand through his hair, pulling him into my chest for comfort then brought us both to the ground. I had no intention of letting him go, not ever again.

CHAPTER

FORTY-NINE

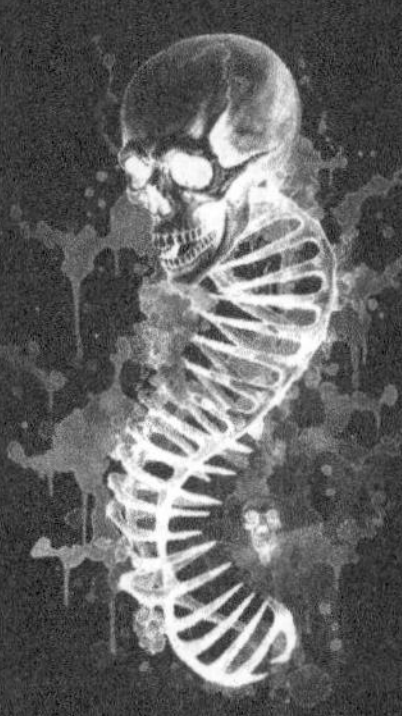

REINA

I'm going to murder him. My head throbbed, pounding incessantly as I tried to will myself to stand up, clutching the blade Alexiares had given me. I froze. Ahead of a plethora of footsteps, different levels of panic knocked me back to the ground. *They were leaving?* Surely this had to be some play. We were vastly outnumbered; I didn't think anyone out here expected to see the inside of The Compound again.

Staying absolutely still was my only option as I listened to their forces pass over me. I kept my eyes closed, avoiding any direct contact that had the possibility of being made. Minutes passed and their steady trail of soldiers slowed. When it appeared only the stragglers and injured were making their way through, I slithered my way back against the tree.

Once I was confident enough to stand on my own, I pushed myself up. My back scraped against the tree. Holes and snags from battle withered my shirt, letting the skin underneath splinter from the bark.

I brushed the dirt from my arms and face, picking leaves out of my hair. *What the heck did I miss?* The woods had gone quiet, and I stilled. A twig snapped, every inch of my body going on high alert.

Rough hands snatched me back, pulling me tight against their hard body, bloody hands over my mouth. Terror overtook me, my arms wailing about dropping the blade. I looked around, desperate for an opportunity of freedom as I forgot all the time that I spent training with Amaia and Jax.

"Shhh," my brother cooed in my ear. "It's me. It's okay, calm down."

It being Seth left no extra ounce of comfort in my heart. Actually, the fact that it was my brother made me want to fight harder. He'd drugged me, or tried to kill me and failed, whatever the frick he'd done had left me susceptible for a far worse death than he'd offer me … I think.

I brought my hands behind his neck, sweeping my foot behind his and pulled down. He fell back but brought me with him. Seth pulled his left hand from my mouth, only needing one to keep me quiet. The cusp of his now free arm slid over my neck, cutting the air out from my throat.

"Reina, stop fucking fighting," Seth urged. "I don't want to put you to sleep to do this, please don't make me."

Desperate from some relief, some God-forsaken air, I nodded my head, making myself go limp in good faith. His grip on my airway loosened, and I gasped for air.

"One, don't put your hands over my mouth again; you know how I am about germs. Your hands aren't clean, I can see the blood." I grimaced, body shuddering at all the guts and bacteria that had violated my oral bio-dome thanks to him. "Two, what the heck are you talking about? Do what?"

Seth sighed, shoving me away from him to create space between us. Like *I* was the one with cooties; I was clean compared to him. He was a mess, his red hair darkened from blood. His boots had a hole in them at the toe and dirt covered him all over. There was a black eye, shattered nose and swollen jaw that hadn't been there before he poisoned me too. Blood seeped through the fabric of his pants near his hip, another forming a handprint on his light colored shirt. Serves him right.

"Bringing you home to your family, doing what's right. Keeping you safe, try to be more grateful." Seth said the word *family* like it meant something to him.

I rolled my eyes, scoffing. "Amaia said no?"

It wasn't a surprise. I knew she would; he did too whether he wanted to admit it or not. Our father probably knew it too, but wanted to at least pretend to give diplomacy a shot. Being a people person had never been his forte.

Seth nodded in confirmation. Those haunting blue eyes that made me hate what I saw in the mirror stared back at me with sadness simmering. *Sad? What the heck does he have to be sad about? This is all his fault.*

"That place isn't my home, Seth, and despite us sharing blood, we aren't family," I ground out, pointing my finger in his face. "Family doesn't hurt each other, *family* doesn't try to get each other killed. Something both you and Father have now attempted several times in my lifetime. That's kinda a lot. All I wanted to do was protect you, but instead of seeing the best in me, the good in me, you set out to destroy me instead. The funny thing is, you didn't destroy me, Seth, all you did was help me grow into who I was meant to be."

His jaw ticked. "Maybe I didn't need your protection, *little sister*." Seth paused, trying to harness his anger. "None of this matters. I'm making up for it now. You can hate me all you want, never talk to me again if that warms your heart. But you need to come with me; that is the *only* option that keeps you safe."

Seth took hold of my arm, yanking me toward him. I pulled free, scoffing at his audacity to tell me what's best after his crappy decision-making skills.

"I don't care if it keeps me safe. I care about doing what's right, and if that kills me, then so be it," I said, planting myself firm in the ground.

"Do what's righ—" He chuckled at me. "Reina, you're a *healer*. There's a hundred of you right inside those walls. What is it that you think you do exactly that makes enough of a difference to lay down your life for a bunch of people who don't even know your name."

I don't know why, but the way my brother said *healer* made me feel less than. Pain flickered through me so quickly, I wasn't even sure it had a chance to root itself in my heart. The thing was, I could never be less than, not anymore.

Between him and my father, they'd put the bar of reasonable expectations in hell. I would always be better than the both of them no matter what I did. Suppose I could even say I was *always* better than. Having a mind of my own had made me the family black sheep for so long.

Even the whitest of flocks can hide the darkest of wool.

"Thanks to you and *your* father, everyone knows my name now." He wasn't my father. I no longer had the desire to claim someone so foul as mine.

"Which is exactly why I matter. I may carry this stupid family name like a burden, but I will use it to do whatever the hell I can to make sure you're both forever remembered as fools. Blood may bind us by birth, Seth, but it's the choices we make, the actions we take, that define family. That is something you will *never* understand, and it makes me feel sorry for you. When you first left, it sucked. You destroyed my heart, and I thought you didn't look back. All I could do was think to myself, *whatever he does, he's still my brother. I just want my brother back, I miss him.* Now that you're here in front of me, all I can do is pity you. The man you had the potential to be, who Momma raised you to be, is right there, waiting for you to *be* him. Instead, I face a sorry, *sad* excuse for a human being, who possesses zero self-awareness for his actions and the consequences they have on the people he claims to love. I'm not going with you, Seth. I would rather die than spend another second on this beautiful green earth, stuck in some screwed up society, known as Reina Moore, Seth Moore's sister."

Hurt washed over his features. Seth sputtered, stammering over what to say in response. When he came up short, anger replaced any remnants of remorse that had lingered. I was starting to see my father's point on how bitter on the taste buds lack of accountability was.

He charged me and I took another step back. "You can hate me all you want, Reina, but I would never hate myself for doing what I could to save the life of the last sibling I've got."

I glanced down, a needle glimmered at his side. Another dose of whatever he'd given me before on deck. Dread chilled my blood. I realized now why Amaia did what she did, why she was always ready to sacrifice herself for the sake of others. It was almost an instinct when put in the position where your options are slim to none. I would never back down.

My decision on not being dragged off to whatever hellhole Seth had crawled his way from was firm. Final. Set. I would not go under any circumstance. One look in those shared blue eyes and I knew Seth's mind was set too. The only way I wouldn't go with him was if one of us was dead.

Despite my current opinions about my bloodline status, he was still my brother. I had spared Millie the pain of having to do what I was now faced with. No one should ever have to take the life of someone they love.

Seth had done it before, and while it tore him up on the inside, he still found a way to sleep at night. My brother had thought me broken, but he was the one who was one more tragedy from breaking. It would drive him mad, but he would survive it. Move on from it one day, just not soon enough.

I knew myself. It wouldn't be the same for me. It would ruin me in a way that there would be no coming back from. I wasn't sure I was ready for that, and unlike my brother, I didn't make decisions when I wasn't sure what the true cost of it would be.

Instead, I would do the world a favor with my death. I would do the only thing I could to break him. Make him kill me. That would be the stick that broke the dam of Seth Moore. He would never be the same again, not enough to be of good use to our father. It would be a mercy on my brother, yes, but also the people of Monterey Compound. Without my brother, my father would be going at us blind. We would have a fighting chance. The soldiers may have been on retreat, but that was only a fraction of the army we'd avoided on the journey here. There were more coming, but this would buy us some time.

Water magic swayed in my palms as I crouched low. It knocked him off his feet. I kneeled on his chest, keeping him from getting up. Seth had seen it coming, holding his breath to prevent himself from drowning in it. I had no intention of drowning my brother, but what was the harm in seeing how long he could fight to keep his life?

The pressure of the water knocked the needle in his hand free. His fingers found his knife, and he slashed my leg, making me jump back with a yelp. I lost my footing, giving him the advantage. Seth scrambled for the needle. It disappeared into the bushes with the nudge of my water magic. The distraction cost me. Seth pounced with my attention now focused on the needle.

I'd have to keep him fighting, anger him. He would never kill me on instinct—I'd have to earn this death. My number one goal in this fight was to simply send him into a blind rage. Messing with his emotions was the easiest way to get there. I didn't want to do this with him, to spend our last few moments together like this.

Fury edged at Seth's emotions, his tan face went red. A sea-storm rage replaced his predator stare. I splashed water up at his face, punching him in the jaw in his momentary blindness. It was my cackle that sent him over. Seth had never taken kindly to being made a fool of, laughed at, like people didn't respect him or fear him. He raised his knife over my chest, ready to drive it home. Face to face, I took one last look at my brother before closing my eyes.

The bushes behind us ruffled. When I opened my eyes, Moe stood over Seth, Wrath grazing the back of his neck, lined up for one swift chop.

"Get the fuck up," Moe growled.

Seth dropped the knife, studying his hands with wide eyes at what he was about to do. Rising up slowly, he turned around cautiously, careful not to spook her. "Tomoe."

Moe's dark brown eyes scanned his body. The grief coming off her was overwhelming. They stared at each other, Wrath wavered slightly in her hand. Then she hardened, her head raising high, giving me a side glance.

"Get up, Reina," Moe said. "Your family needs you."

A demoralized expression crossed Moe's face, replaced by her usual cool exterior within a few blinks. She knew. Our eyes connected for a brief moment and I understood everything she wanted to say. Moe bit her lip, turning back to Seth, determined to hold strong.

"She's coming with me, Moe. You are too." Seth inched closer to her, pressing his throat against Wrath.

"You don't get to speak, Seth," Moe spat, Seth's blood pooling around her blade. "No one's talking to you."

She ushered him back, pressing Wrath deeper to get him to move at her will. When she repositioned herself to my side, Moe extended me a hand, to help me up.

"Riley is six minutes from kicking the fucking bucket," she explained like it was an indisputable fact. "It took me ten minutes to get here and find you. I'm going to need you to use those long legs to get there in five. It's going to take every last drop of your magic, and you're going to have to let it. It's going to kick your ass, you'll almost die, but both of you survive. If you stand here and argue with me the way you're about to, you waste almost a minute of time that he doesn't have. Amaia won't recover, and every territory in this country will fall."

I didn't move. Fear kept me rooted in place. Not the fear one would expect from a ghost or a haunted house. It resembled nothing of immediate panic or adrenaline rush that pushed you into action. This was the lingering tinge of fear that kept you from focusing on one thing and instead a million negative *what ifs*.

Everything that we'd done out here, the stand we had taken would be pointless if I couldn't save Riley's life. It would all be for nothing and I would lose not one, but two more members of my family if I failed. Seth had been wrong—I did make a difference, and everyone's fate lay in my healing hands.

"Do you understand me?" Moe yelled. I winced, her usually small voice becoming large and commanding, bringing me back to attention.

"Yes," I said, cutting a glare to my brother. "Where?"

I nodded, the instructions she mumbled off muted, my mind occupied by making a checklist of injuries to check for and the order of importance that I healed them all in. It would be a band aid until I could get him into a sterile room. He'd need surgery no matter what. If Riley was near death, there was no magical quick-fix.

Why does it have to be me? Tears swelled into my eyes. I couldn't fix Jax. I didn't want to be responsible for the death of someone else I loved. I'd said goodbye to far too many brothers in this life. I refused to leave one more.

"You need to get to Riley NOW!" Moe screamed, spit flying from her mouth.

I gazed over at my brother. He reminded me of everything I once loved in life, of the people I would always love, no matter their sins. Our time on the road together jogged in my memory, a small smile pulling at my lips as a tear dropped warming my cheek.

That time we spent together, how close we'd gotten, I'd hold that close to my life for as long as I lived. I would never stop loving my brother, but I was ready to stop loving the version of the man I thought him to be.

"Goodbye, Seth. I sincerely hope to never see you again. You may think I'm nothing, that I don't make a difference, that the people here couldn't care less if I live or die. But you're about to see how some of us don't have to compromise who we are to protect the people we love."

CHAPTER
FIFTY

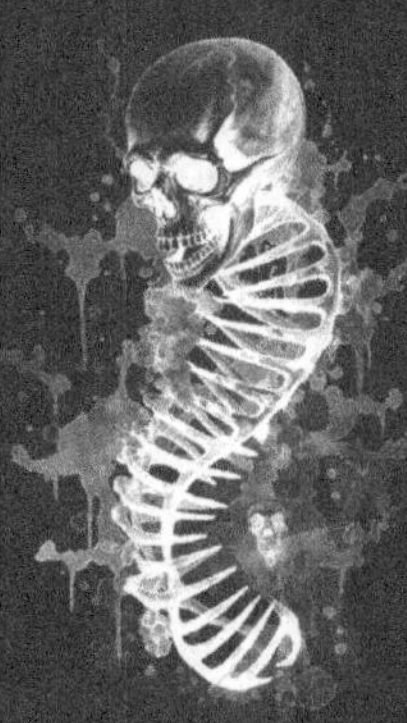

TOMOE

"I know what you are."

He was as handsome as ever. Even with the bruises and busted lip. In fact, it made him look just like *my* Seth. The unpredictability of his mood, along with his hot temper, was what attracted me to him in the first place. *Typical. Guess Amaia wasn't the only one excited by red flags.*

I traced Wrath over his jugular, the weight of her getting heavy in my arms at my reach. "And what's that?"

"You do magic," he said matter-of-factly. "You're a witch. They speak of you—at home. Said you've been casting spells, teaching them to replicate it, changing the structure of their DNA without science."

Well, when you put it that way.

"Sure," I sighed, unimpressed.

His head jerked back. "Sure? That's all you have to say? It's all too hypocritical if I'm honest."

"I've come to understand one thing about you, Seth," I sneered, "and that's that honesty isn't something you're good at. I'm not a witch. I *was* Pagan. I don't practice anymore, not that it's any of your damn business."

Seth's hair fell in front of his eyes, chin resting against my blade. "Make it my business then. Come back with us."

I'm not ashamed to admit that I considered it—what life could be with him outside of this place. Trying to pretend that love was enough and that he hadn't betrayed me would do no one any favors though.

"Did you cast a spell on me, Moe?" He pressed, brows arching.

Taking advantage of my hesitation, Seth closed the space between us. Gripping the end of Wrath, he pushed her down then grabbed my face, tilting it up to hold his stare. He leaned forward, bringing himself closer to my level, his face directly in mine.

Stupidly, I let him. Wanted the safety of his kiss one more time. "If I did, I must've fucked it up," I bit out, closing my eyes to shatter the spell of his charm.

Seth pushed my shoulder back, putting distance between us. "Moe," he growled.

"She's staying here," I ground out, my finger pointing down at the ground. "Reina won't be going anywhere when she has people here who love her unconditionally."

Seth gritted his teeth, sneering as if I'd insulted him. "She doesn't know what's best for her."

"Oh," I said. "And you do?"

Before, I had always assumed Seth had been one of those people who were hard on their little siblings because they wanted what was best for them. Then he'd tried to sell us out, Reina included, so pardon me if I had some trouble believing he suddenly wanted that now.

"She's not thinkin' straight and neither are you," Seth dead-panned. "You're all thinking with your hearts instead of your head. You can't save everyone, Moe, none of y'all can. Amaia may think she can save the world her way, but my dad is more of a *his way or the highway* kind of guy. She's willing to damn you. I'm not. Save yourselves, live to fight another day. At least see what it's like before you hate it."

The audacity. We may not always see eye to eye on methods, but everything Amaia did was for us. If she had decided not to accept the hand Seth was extending, then I trusted her judgment. Not only that, I didn't need Amaia to make decisions for me. I didn't need anyone to when I could make my own. Seth's love had blinded me once. I would not let it happen a second time.

"I don't need to see whatever the fuck is hiding behind your borders to know I'll hate living under a dictatorship with no rights."

"You're powerful," he said, toying with a strand of my hair. "Of course you'll have rights."

I reeled back. "The fact that you can even say that and see nothing wrong with the sentence makes me question everything I ever loved about you. You don't know me at all."

Disgust tugged at my heart. Did I ever know Seth or had it all been a version of him he'd decided to become once he got here? He looked like the man I loved. Physically, there was no doubt that Seth Moore stood before me. That was where the recognition ended.

Everything else about him had changed. The way his icy blue eyes scanned me right now was predatory. It scared me and I was pretty fucking hard to scare.

"That's not true, and you know it." He took another step toward me, taking my breath away.

So badly, I wanted to see the man I loved before me. Instead all I saw staring back at me was a monster.

"There are more fates intertwined than ours. I love you, Seth," I conceded. Needing him to see the truth behind the pain of my words. "But I see a future without you where everything will be okay. I wish I could say I'm sorry, but much like you, I don't think that I am. Not really."

The last bit came out as a humorless, empty laugh.

"I can't accept that answer, Moe." His eyes darkened, lowering as he gazed down at me through half-closed lids.

I should have expected the fight. The defiance in his eyes. The two of us falling in love had been like a fistfight after all.

"Or what?" I said, shrugging off the idea and taking a small step back. "You'll kill me?"

Seth shifted uncomfortably, considering it. He broke our challenging stare, eyes darting at the ground, his usual smirk cleaned off his face.

"I won't lose another family. That's what happens if I go with you. People die." Reasoning with Seth was not possible. I wasn't quite sure why I tried.

This was on him, after all. Him and his kooky, crazy-ass father. Guess that made Seth one of the crazies now that I thought of it.

Reina may have been an idiot for going to search for him, but I'd be a liar if I said I hadn't been holding out hope he was playing both sides. I'd forced myself to shut him out, close any open doors in my mind to keep things Seth-free.

Now that he was here in front of me, it was harder to pretend his betrayal wasn't real, that he hadn't chosen *this* life for us over what we could have had. He robbed me of the choice of the happy ever after or whatever that he'd pretended we could have. I wasn't just sad anymore, I was angry.

Seth recoiled like I'd slapped him. "I thought you said we were family." His mouth hung open.

"Not anymore."

We'd offered that to him once, and he'd spit in our faces. There was no second chance for him and he didn't get to come back as a hero. Scoffing, I turned away from him, opting to walk away from this, from him. The universe had shown me what would happen if this escalated, but maybe, if I walked away, this future would change.

I scraped my tongue across my teeth, nodding at the sight of Seth reaching for his gun in my peripheral. My soul splintered into a million fragile shards. Raising Wrath back in the air, I turned around. Seth's gun pointed in my face. The edge of Wrath taking residence at his carotid artery. I was fast. You had to have a quick draw if you chose to fight with metal against magic or you risked being Pansie chow.

Seth was faster. He'd taught half the cavalry how to quick draw and shoot with accuracy. The men who'd already been gifted with the skill still looked to him for guidance, as he'd shaped them all to be a force to be reckoned with. If he wanted to shoot me, he would have. *Right?*

His thumb trailed over the safety, knocking it off with a click. "You're coming with me, Moe," Seth commanded. "Even if that means I have to beg for your forgiveness again—"

"I don't recall you begging the first time," I said candidly.

"I'll do whatever it takes to make you my woman again. I love you." His eyes glistened at his confession. "You are the best thing that's ever happened to me. I know that now. I don't deserve you, but I sure as hell want you. I'm askin' you nicely. Please come home with us."

"You'd think asking me nicely wouldn't consist of a gun pointed at my head and a blade at your throat."

"You never were one for being wined and dined," Seth chided.

A sarcastic smile teased my lips. "Sorry to disappoint but neither I nor Reina will be joining you today."

"So you're saying there's hope, then?" His usual rough voice was replaced by a lightened, hopeful tone. "That you'll come with me?"

"Why don't you come back? Why do we have to go where we're not welcome? Call your father off, Seth. Let him leave Monterey Compound in peace. He's stolen enough from us."

It wasn't a genuine request. As much as I fucking wished that false dream could come true, it wasn't even a remote possibility. Too much bad had happened between us here for there to ever be a good.

Seth brushed the barrel of his gun through his hair, pushing it back briefly before leveling it at my forehead. "I'm trying to save your lives if y'all would stop being so damn difficult."

"We're not going anywhere with you, Seth." I shook my head. Not understanding what he wasn't understanding about that. "You asked for your freedom from us, said you wanted to go to where you belonged. Well shit, from where I'm standing, you got that. You chose your hill, now die on it."

"I thought I was free," Seth cried out, knees buckling until his skin scraped against Wrath. He glanced down at it with only his eyes. "Thought I was back in control of my life, that I just needed some time to adjust. My dad owns me, Moe. He's always owned me, and he will till the day I die. Ronan Moore is everything I wanted to be, and, Moe, I love you, but I'm too fucked up to walk away. Our minds were intertwined that day. I know you saw what he did to me. It don't matter how much he's hurt me. He's my dad … he's blood. One of the few people left I can call that. We've always related on that, so I know you understand. Now please, either back the fuck down and let me save your lives peacefully, or—"

"Save our lives?" I cackled. "How does stealing our freedom and compromising the place we love save our lives? All you'll be doing is prolonging the long, slow death the rest of us will feel inside, knowing we sacrificed our morals for our mortality. Only one person I know would be okay with that, and I'm looking right at him. I'd argue that he was the one who needed saving."

He was lost, so lost that there was no being saved for him. That was clear to me now.

"It's easy to say that when y'all don't know what you're up against! There're thousands of soldiers headed this way. If I hadn't begged for your life, your heads would be on a fucking stake by noon."

My veins iced, yet I found myself not caring if my death was now impending. I hadn't seen that to be true, but I hadn't known what to search for until now. Death loomed around every corner in our world, especially today. If this was how I met my end, with my family at my side, then so be it.

"You mean like Prescott's?" I sneered.

If he thought I'd forgotten about his role in that death, he was on hard fucking drugs. Just another unforgivable sin of his I'd tried to bury when the pain of his actions cut too deep.

Shame reddened his freckled face and neck. "You should know that I refuse to leave without you or my sister. I will do whatever it takes to make sure you come home with me."

There was no arguing with the determination on his face that matched the certainty in his tone.

"Unfortunately, Seth, I can see the future, so I wholeheartedly believe that you will do whatever it takes. The thing is, I can't let that happen."

My chest tightened as I caught his eye. Moore blue had become my favorite shade of blue. Two of the people I loved the most in this life had it, and both had offered me their own version of peace for so long.

Against my better judgment, I sighed, pushing to the tip of my toes and wrapping my arms around his neck. We shared a few stolen moments, waiting for one to grant the other permission to finish the kiss we both desperately wanted. I gave in, our lips meeting with hesitation.

Seth pushed Wrath away, dropping his gun and locking his hands around my waist. A soft moan escaped me as his mouth drifted to the crevice of my neck. His attention wandered back to my mouth. A tear dropped from above, wetting the side of my face. Cold metal poked into the center of my spine.

If I did nothing now, he'd shoot me, paralyze me, then force me to come with him. There was no version of that future where either of us ended up happy. He'd steal Reina and me away and Monterey would fall. For as many fucking futures I'd seen, few were definite. This was one of them.

"I love you," Seth said with pleading eyes.

With a twirl in my hands, I hacked Wrath at his neck before he had the chance to pull the trigger, severing the connection to his spinal cord. Seth looked up at me from the ground, a haunted stare in his eyes laced with disbelief, but understanding of what was happening. He was still alive. I hadn't had the right angle to finish the job.

Suffering was the last thing I wanted him to do. Seth Moore deserved so little from me at this point, but I would offer him a gracious death. To die by my hand alone was enough to haunt him on the other side, and me for life.

"I love you too."

Raising Wrath, I drove her down. Seth's head rolled down the sloping earth, stopping at my feet. Dropping to my knees with a whimper, I stared in horror at the clean cut from his neck, my hand covering my gaping mouth.

Time escaped me as I lay there in the slowly drying blood of my worst enemy and greatest love and wept.

CHAPTER
FIFTY-ONE

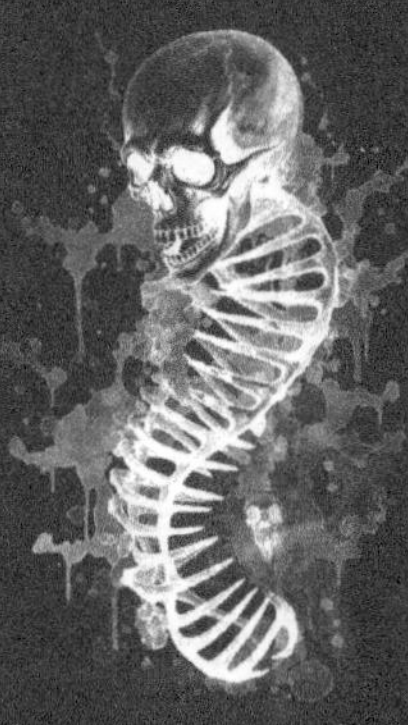

AMAIA

Turns out I did, in fact, have to let him go.

They worked on stabilizing him in the courtyard for what felt like hours. No more than thirty or forty minutes could have passed though, based on the steam coasting from the surrounding ashes. A woman crept through the rubble of North Gate, a black face gaiter covered her mouth and nose. It didn't matter if only her eyes were left visible; I knew Luna when I saw her.

Blood stained her army green pants. The sleeves of her gray shirt were battered, gore splattered across her arms. Concern contorted her prominent features as she searched the courtyard, searching for someone. *Me.*

She sighed in relief, making a beeline in my direction. I stood at her approach, arms wide and taking in the moment of relief at her being okay. My head sank into her chest as she rubbed my back soothingly.

"Sweet girl. Good, you're okay. I was worried I got here too late." She stopped, doing a double take over my body. "I have news and I'm afraid it's not great."

Pain seared my heart at the nickname, but I stomached through it. "What's wrong?"

I glanced down at Alexiares, worried that he'd go somewhere in the brief seconds I'd let go of his hands. He was talking now, nearly coherent, but he still had a long way to go.

"Thousands of Covert soldiers are less than a day away. I was coming back from Denver and ended up keeping pace."

She doesn't know. Denver. She'd been gone awhile.

"I know. It's okay. So we hold them off a little bit longer. Re-inforcements will be here in two days' time," I countered, hold-ing her arms and jolting her a bit. "Maybe sooner. If they caught word of what was happening here, they'd only take rest when nec-essary."

I was rambling, talking more to myself than her, trying to work out the math in my head. We could do this—we had to.

Luna stiffened, making herself immovable. She shook her head, sorrow in her gaze. "No, no one's coming but our own peo-ple, Amaia. San Jose and Fresno surrendered. We're blocked in on two sides. Bakersfield is expected to throw in the hat by evening. They were attacked too, and their leaders weren't as lucky. Their people are scared, Amaia. So are yours. We have nothing left—"

"We have everything left!" I bellowed.

"It's over, Amaia," she said tenderly. "You did well, but if you want this place to see another day, you have to know when to stop fighting. Where is Prescott? We need to gather the council."

The noise of the remnants of what took place here filtered back in. My focus wavered, zoning in and out. Weak groans of agony filled the area around us and beyond. Luna tossed her head toward the gate, centering me back into my responsibilities. "You cannot fight when your people have nothing left to give. Look around us, Amaia. They're out of magic, they're out of ammo, and they are on the verge of death. Look at them!"

She grabbed my head, forcing me to take in the scene. These weren't soldiers scattered about, they were citizens who'd opted out of the bunker deciding to stay and fend for their home. The fact that they were still alive spoke wonders to their training, but in the end, it had not been enough. They had not been able to control their magic use in the face of life or death.

Training had been thorough, as detail oriented as I could get within a few hours twice a week. The fact of the matter was, training would never equate to what my soldiers went through that had allowed them to keep their lives in this encounter. They had learned the mastery of their gifts in the skirmishes along the border or on patrol. Easing into the art of war had not been a gift my citizens had been granted. Instead, they were thrust from simulation into the real fucking deal.

As weak as they were, many of them wouldn't survive the night. Magic had its limitations and you could not refill any empty well with healing. It dawned on me then. Tomoe's protection spell over us was the only thing keeping Alexiares alive. His magic was gone. There was no tendril left for him to pull from. I nodded in agreement. Surrendering today did not mean surrendering tomorrow. It was time I understood that.

Covert Province won the battle. This war, however, would never be theirs. My people were resilient. Inevitable. We would not fall.

That didn't mean we didn't need time to recover.

"Okay," I said, "okay. I know what to do to stop this. Seth offered a deal, one I plan to take. I'll be back. Keep an eye on him for me, please."

Luna studied me warily, nodding reluctantly at the idea of me going alone. "I won't leave his side until you get back," she promised, perking up at something she had yet to say. "Where's Prescott, Amaia? Is he okay?"

MAKING A DEAL AFTER YOUR BEST FRIEND KILLS THE MAN SHE LOVED who also happened to be the son of the man that extended you the deal in the first place was arguably the tensest interaction in my life. The spitting image of Seth stared back at me. A Seth with twenty-something years on him and a shit ton of stress on him, but his mirror image nevertheless.

Ronan Moore towered over me, a projection of patience and calm entrancing his demeanor. "While my method may appear … unethical, I'm only trying to solve a problem that history is inclined to repeat until we get it right. Seth mentioned you're quite the history buff, we have that in common."

"We have nothing in common," I sneered, not backing down from our stare down. "Get to the point."

Screams of injured and dying rang out in the air of the war camp around us. I hadn't a clue where to find Ronan, just followed the straggling soldiers as they made their way back from battle. There was no guarantee he would be there, but if my presence was known, the obvious next step would be to take me to their leader. A man named Malachai slunk from the shadows as I approached, a hand gripping the bloodstained side of his shirt, grumbling for me to follow.

"See, that's where you're wrong. There are two things we have in common, two things that encapsulate who a person is at their core." I watched as he paced over to a bar cart, grabbing some glasses and a flask.

Placing them down on the table, he huffed a breath, pulling at the legs of his pants as he dropped to take a seat. He kicked out the chair across from him, motioning for me to take a seat. A cup of tea in a metal cup was placed before my seat, a small spoon to stir at its side. I remained standing, not interested in whatever power play he intended to drag me into.

"And what is that?"

A cruel smile tugged at his freckled lips. "The desire to create a better tomorrow, a better world, a world where innovation thrives. A world that is great—the next Roman Empire."

"Mesopotamia. Ottoman Empire. British Empire." I yawned, strolling across the room to push in the chair he offered with a smirk. "There has been and will continue to always be a Roman Empire, Ronan. The goal is to always make sure the next one is better than the last."

"See, something you both agree on," Malachai chided, arms crossed, blocking my exit from the tent.

"I have a hard time believing our vision is the same." I arched a brow, my stomach churning at the increased discomfort of being in this room alone. "And the second commonality?"

Ronan poured two cups of bourbon, a knowing glimmer in his eye as he passed it to me. I took it, holding it tight in my hand, refusing to take a sip.

"What all the great empires possessed: A leader who had the will to die to make it all happen. You may not understand my methods, but you do understand my madness." He took a long sip of his drink, smacking his lips after.

"You're running an experiment across an entire territory—"

"Eugenics has been controversial," he interrupted, raising his palm to silence me. "Yes. But it works."

"Until it doesn't. History proves that as fact," I hissed.

"Ah," he stood, striding over and placing a finger over my lips. "But they did not possess the technology or the minds that we have in Covert Province. The minds that you have here, in Monterey.

Minds like Reina. She's good stock. You want proof of the validity of my work: well, there you have it."

I fought off the urge to recoil. "She's your daughter."

"Two things can be true at once."

Malachai chuckled behind me. I turned to glare at him, fear be damned. If I had to put up a fight here, I would.

"So Seth is …" I tried to make it all make sense. It just wasn't clicking for me. He knew Seth was dead, knew Reina hated him. For as much as he talked about family, there were no obvious tells that it had any impact on his day-to-day.

"*Was* an outlier. No experiment is perfect."

I couldn't hide my repulsion. "You're sick."

The sharp stench of blood was consuming my nostrils despite the biting aroma of the bourbon. They had more healers than any territory out there, but Ronan had still ordered them to neglect to heal those whose injuries, by Before standards, were too far gone. Regardless if they were left suffering until they succumbed to their injuries.

"I loved all my children," his voice went soft, eyes distant. "But the mission I have here, this next phase in history, is more important than familiar attachments. Seth had his chance to prove he was worthy of this new world. Reina has her chance now. Just like your chance is now."

I straightened my stance, taking a small sip from my glass, eyes holding his steady, ice-cold stare. "What do you want from me, Ronan?"

A big belly laugh came from behind me, making me jump. Ronan joined in, face reddening at my lack of observation of his end goal. "I want your compound, and I want it turned over peacefully. If that's done, you all may keep your freedom, with conditions. After that is established, I want the promised cooperation of every settlement within your network. Not the Salem Network. I'm speaking of the one formed as you planned an impressive, yet simultaneously disappointing, resistance with each and every one of your allies."

Now I really did need a seat. "Anything else you want to add to Santa's list?" I snarked.

"Don't get smart with me, girl." Ronan shattered the glass in his palm, not bothering to take in the blood now pouring from the cuts in his hand. "There is a level of authority within this deal. You keep your life because you present yourself as being valuable enough to do so. Eventually, everything valuable loses its shine."

He paced back over to a bar cart, snatching another glass as he poured himself a drink. His eyes closed, the contents he just poured already cleared from the cup. Ronan turned back toward me, staring me over, judgment clear in his eyes. "You have knowledge of the *other* part of the deal, no? I presume my son at least got that part out before he lost his head, since you're here."

An odd sense of pity filled me. I felt sorry for Seth. He'd admired this man, clearly respected him to some extent, and this … this was how he spoke of him. "I do. Who are they?" I asked.

"In due time. Until then, there are more pressing requests you have to take on."

"And the conditions you spoke of?" I questioned, not missing a beat.

"See that, Malachai? She *is* a smart girl," Ronan humored. "He didn't think you would be, said not to believe everything that comes down the pipeline. I begged to differ. You made quite the impression on my son. He wasn't the same man who left me behind. Took some real work undoing all that free-thinking mess you spouted off. It takes an intelligent person to change a strong-willed individual at a molecular level. That or a little bit of torture. Or both. You believe in both methods, don't you, General?"

He winked at me. Malachai chuckled at the gesture. *That's not possible. There should be no way Ronan should know about what took place in that room.* A million questions flew through my mind.

"The conditions, Ronan," I urged, willing myself to keep a brave face.

"What goes on in Monterey is none of my business as long as the resources I request are provided within a respectable time frame. You keep your sovereignty. Consider this a sort of tax."

"That's the point of sovereign nations, Ronan, there is no tax. To be sovereign we must be independent. Call it what it is, a territory. An extension without rights on the bigger scheme of things. Why do I get a feeling that by 'resources'"—I motioned air quotes around the word—"You mean actual, literal, human beings?"

"Correct," Malachai grumbled, shifting to Ronan's side. "Problem?"

I wanted nothing more than to grind my finger into the obvious bullet hole on his shoulder that had barely healed. There was no other option. This is what would save my people—that needed to be my focus right now. Nothing else.

"None. As long as those resources don't end up on the wrong side of one of your experiments," I ground out. If there was one point I was willing to fight for, this was it. I would not subject my people to such a fate.

"Of course not." A toothy grin took up his weathered face. "Wouldn't dream of it."

"That all?" I shifted back, the flight in me urging me to ignore the fight.

"Yes, you may go."

"Pleasure doing business with you." I turned on my heels, fingers grasping the olive-green flaps of the tent.

"Oh, Amaia. One more thing before you go. I'll be sending a few emissaries to sit on your council, keep an eye on the place. They may have a few requests, some slight suggestions, nothing exorbitant. I expect they'll be welcomed with open arms?"

I gulped down a slur of insults, head moving from side to side as I bit my tongue. Releasing the flaps of the tent, I plastered a smile on my face, swiveling around to face the man I would mark for death. "With a warm, baked pie."

"You'll be hearing from me soon, take care." He nodded, taking a seat at the table, picking up some sheets of paper, neglecting the wound still seeping with blood. "Send Reina my regards. I am sorry for her loss."

Malachai appeared behind me, a harsh whisper in my ear. "Tell Riley I said you're welcome."

A chill went down my spine on my way out. I would play nice, do what was asked of me. It was the only thing that would allow us a moment of peace to regroup. A lot could change in a year. In fact, my entire life had. The entire structure of what The Compound once was and what we had to offer had been shaken to the core. We were going into a decline at an unsustainable pace and I needed to slow it if there was ever a chance for us in the future.

ELIE JUMPED IN HER SLEEP, HER HAND YANKING FREE FROM MY GRASP, startling me. I sat forward in my chair, relief filling an empty void in my heart that belonged to this girl. Between her, Riley slumped next to me, Abel scowling across the aisle, and Alexiares putting up a fight on Reina's table after refusing to be put to sleep, I was going to have an aneurysm.

It would be of no surprise if they had some secret pact on giving me a heart attack and they'd all done their best work to see it through. Elie had been out cold since the attack yesterday. She'd used a significant amount of her magic, plus her injuries from the explosion. Her body needed a lot of rest.

"What the hell were you thinking?" I hammered, not bothering to keep my voice low for the sleeping patients.

Riley was snoring his ass off anyway. If they could sleep through that, then they could sleep through my lecture. His *beloved*,

Yasmin, glared at me from his bedside, brow arched, daring me to keep up the noise.

Elie groaned, pushing herself up on the bed. I stood up, pulling her forward to fluff up her pillows before tossing her back. She whimpered, grabbing at her neck. "Ow! Aren't you supposed to be nice to the injured or something?"

"Not how this works," I said, crossing my arms. "You had me worried sick! Eleanor, I trusted you to listen to me, trusted that you would be safe."

"Elie," she corrected.

I rolled my eyes. "You could have died!"

"Yeah, shoulda, coulda, woulda. Surprise, I'm safe. I'm alive. And I'm also a fucking hero." She smirked, reaching out to grab my hand in excitement. "I'm like you, Amaia, a soldier. Prescott said you have no one left but Riley, but that's not true. You have me too. Which means I have a responsibility to him the same as you guys. I took care of this place, just like he asked."

Sorrow inundated my heart. I motioned for her to scoot over, cuddled next to her, bringing her under my wing.

"You're just a kid, Elie. You aren't supposed to be a hero."

CHAPTER
FIFTY-TWO

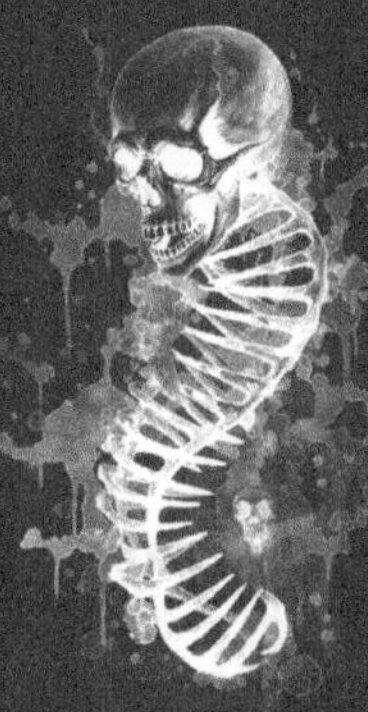

AMAIA

"You know better than to be out here alone."

I turned to swim on my back, grinning at him, already having sensed his presence fifty feet ago. The waves crashed into my body, submerging me in the icy water long enough for the only thought to consume my mind being how freezing it was. That was the only moment of reprieve I'd had in the last seventy-three hours, five minutes, and twenty-one seconds.

There was much to do to prepare, but little time to do it. It didn't help that much of my plan consisted of waiting, pretending to return to normal before we made our final move. With still time came anxiousness and I couldn't afford to be scatterbrained when it came to this.

Those damned eyes that I loved so much trailed my clothes on the shoreline. Alexiares wiggled his thick brows at me, unzipping his pants and tossing them to the side.

"And you're supposed to be taking it easy," I teased, reaching out my hand, signaling for him to join me.

It'd been an impulse decision to get in. A swim wasn't necessarily scheduled into my day. I needed to breathe. Despite my desire to save the place I called home, being out here just felt so … fresh. Or maybe it was freeing that was the right word? No, I suppose it was a mix of those two. In being free came fresh starts, new beginnings. Two things I would never get to have but would secretly wish for.

Sinking into the water, leaving only the top of my head peeking out, I watched him shed his clothes. For someone who'd been on the brink of death three days ago, he looked like a fucking Greek statue, to be honest. He turned his back to me, feigning to be shy while taking off his shirt, but it only made me stare more. I smirked, imagining his broad shoulders and toned back flexing in that manner for a very different reason in a more private setting.

There were no new physical scars lining his skin from his wounds, thanks to the healers. The real scars were in his haunted stare. Alexiares' gaze rarely left mine when we were within the same vicinity. When they did, mine fell into place in its absence. I knew exactly what he was thinking. If I took my eyes off him again, that could be the last time I'd ever see him. So I watched him, kept my eye on him, because if I didn't look away, I wouldn't have to worry about never seeing him again.

He waded over to me, picking me up, offering me a break from treading water. Alexiares gave my ass a squeeze, smirking unashamed.

"This is taking it easy, I can finally relax," he jested back. "You're here to take care of me now."

I unhooked my arm from around his neck, splashing him with water. "Guess chivalry really is dead. You're supposed to be the scary boyfriend who protects *me*."

"Nah," he said, kissing me firmly on the lips. "My girl doesn't need any protection. *Bloodreina and the Bloodhound.*"

"They won't stop calling me that." I rolled my eyes. Truly though, I didn't mind. It was a little badass.

"Well, when your body count rises over a hundred within a few minutes, you get nicknames you can't kick. It's part of the notorious, scary girlfriend package."

I leaned myself back, pulling us down into the water. Alexiares' grip broke at the impact of the wave. His hair was plastered in front of his eyes, a dead stare on his face as he fought off a laugh. Splashing obnoxiously, I swam back over to him, clinging to his waist until he forgave me, pelting me with kisses across my cheeks and supported my weight.

"What are you cheesin' for?" he asked, pausing in his assault of affection.

We hadn't had much time alone over the last few days; he was only cleared from the infirmary today. I'd visited when I could but everyone needed me in so many ways and there was only one me. Figuring out how to be General and leader of this place was going to take a lot of effort. The pace of which would be unsustainable if I weren't only doing it for the short-term.

"Because," I said, guiding his lips toward mine and biting down on his bottom lip. I kissed the spot after, holding it for a few seconds, not wanting to put more distance between us than this. "You're alive. Riley is alive. Reina is alive. Moe is alive. Abel is alive and back home."

Alexiares' head tilted, wondering where I was going with things. Yes, we were alive but to any sane individual, being alive just meant another day of suspended death.

I rested my chin on his shoulder, connecting our heartbeats. He waited, letting me gather myself before finishing my thoughts.

"Prescott is dead," my voice shook. "Jax is dead. Both are Seth's fault. Seth is dead. And now, all that's left is to kill the person who made him this way. That makes my mission clear, simple, one-tracked. With a clear mission, makes a clearer path for everyone's happiness. I'd say, that's reason enough to smile."

He chuckled, the sound vibrating through my chest. "Sure, princess. If you say so."

The words caught in my throat, unsure if I were brave enough to force them out. "So the question becomes, Alexiares, you say you're falling in love with me because I make you feel alive, that I make you want to be better. But how about feeling alive from bringing death? Would you do that not *for* me, but with me?"

"I'd do anything for you if it meant doing it with you," he said, body going stiff. "But I don't like where this is going."

Burying my face into his neck, I finished my thought before it remained stuck in my throat forever. "I'm not done. I have a plan, one none of you are going to like. Which is fine by me, as long as you respect it. We need to find out who Seth was talking about before Moore has the chance to tell us himself. If they're threatening enough for Covert to work out a deal with me, then that's someone I want on our side."

"I'm not seeing the part of the plan that is supposed to make me angry."

"Give me a second, I'm getting there," I said, huffing out a sigh. "The rest of you guys will stay here. I have to go alone. After Prescott, how can I leave these people vulnerable, Alexiares? They need support, to think there's something left to fight for, especially with Covert here watching our every move."

"If you think Reina and Moe would ever let you go somewhere without them, you've lost your fucking mind. The only way Riley will ever let you out of his sight again is if I'm at it, which leads to my final point: I'll knock you over the fucking head if you ever mention leaving me behind again."

Alexiares grabbed my waist, prying me from around him to look me in the eye. His stare was heavy, searching, but for the first time in a while, I couldn't read the emotion behind it. The lines of worry that usually etched his face were replaced by relaxed features. Slowly, those honey brown eyes lingered over my mouth then found their way back up, his pupils dilated.

"You once told me that you think I deserve the world, happiness or whatever. That I'm not a bad person, that I've changed for the better. Here's the thing, princess, I'm not a good guy. I have no desire to be better outside of being worthy of you. A *good guy* would let you risk your life to keep everyone you love safe. To keep this place safe, Compound first and all that bullshit. I'm not that guy. I care about them. Would die for them, clearly. But you? I'd kill for you. I have killed for you." His brows pinched, face reddening as his grip tightened against my skin. "And I'd do it again. I'd burn this world for you. This world, and the next. My only desire is to keep you safe, to keep you alive."

One, singular tear fell down my smile ridden cheeks. "I don't need a hero, *Alexiares*," I said teasingly.

"How many times do I have to tell you, I'm the villain of this story?" He smirked, pulling me into a tender kiss.

CHAPTER
FIFTY-THREE

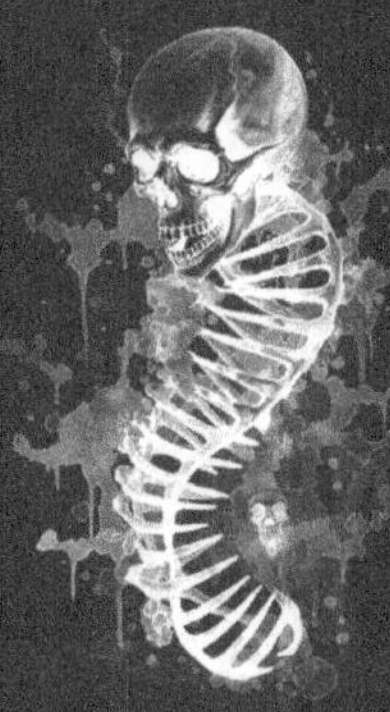

TOMOE

Hiraeth.

Noun. It's Welsh. In my studies I'd come across the word and never been able to drop it. There was no direct English translation for the word. The Welsh define it as a homesickness for a home to which you cannot return, a home that possibly never was—the nostalgia, the yearning, the grief for the lost places of your past. That deep longing for something that is infinitely out of reach.

When I'd first read about it, I had thought it odd how it was a noun and not an adjective. The look in Amaia's eyes made me see the tangible, complex emotion that it was. Made me think if I reached out and got close, I could hold in my hand, mold it, make it mine.

She sat near the fireplace in Prescott's old quarters, a cup of coffee, a slice of pie, and mancala board sprawled across the coffee table. I hadn't exactly been quiet upon entry, yet Amaia didn't bother to meet my stare until I was right on her. It wasn't that she didn't know who approached her; I knew my sister. She'd probably known who I was before I even opened the door.

Instead, she reverted her eyes back to the coffee table, playing both turns of the beaded game. Amaia paused thoughtfully between each play, thinking through what Prescott would do.

"It doesn't have to be that way, you know." I asked, stopping a few feet away, wanting to give her some space.

Sometimes Amaia was all predator, and other times she was a scared fawn. If you got too close, cracked the wrong stick, she'd flee. A scattered Amaia, a startled Amaia, served to no one's benefit. It wasn't often I'd seen her go the irrational route, but when she did …

Her body stilled as I spoke. "Doesn't have to—what are you talking about, Tomoe?"

I risked an inch closer. "Amaia. You know *exactly* what I'm talking about. It does not have to end that way. There are options, other avenues to make this end." I kept my tone even, voice soft, nurturing.

"And how many of those options guarantee the least amount of people die? Which ones ensure the freedom of these people for longer than even you can see? Tell me, Tomoe, how many lives make sure evil stays down, stays dead?" She was so detached.

Anger was an emotion Amaia thrived on. Anger for the sake of peace. Anger for justice. Anger for revenge. Anger for the sense of normalcy that had been stripped from us all. Anger to bring a sliver of normalcy and hope back to our lives. Anger for a better world.

There was no longer any anger in her eyes. The only thing that remained was the same self-sacrificial grief that made me want to shake some common sense, some self-preservation, into her.

"How does any of that fall on your shoulders?" I snapped, "No one likes a martyr."

The side of the board that housed Prescott's pieces went empty. A sly smile teased the corners of Amaia's mouth as she completed his turn, winning him the game. She closed the board, packing it back into its wooden case, the silence between us thick in the air.

I'd broken the number one rule—speaking on the path of death. It could change the entire future; there was also the possibility of my words being the binding motivator of them taking said path. This was worth the risk though; fate had already offered the worst hands.

I wouldn't let it win this too.

I studied her demeanor, trying to figure out what she would say. No vision came to me of her decision, which meant deep down, she was still undecided. There was still time to take her off this path. My chances weren't great, but there was still a chance, so I would take it.

Amaia pushed past me, placing the game back to where I assumed it belonged on Prescott's bookcase shelf full of trinkets and history books. Her hand brushed along them, touching the broken compasses and other knickknacks he'd sworn to everyone he'd fix one day. She chuckled, eyes wondering back over me, taking me in.

"That's the thing, Moe, everyone loves a martyr. Martyrs move armies, rally people. Martyrs win wars."

EPILOGUE

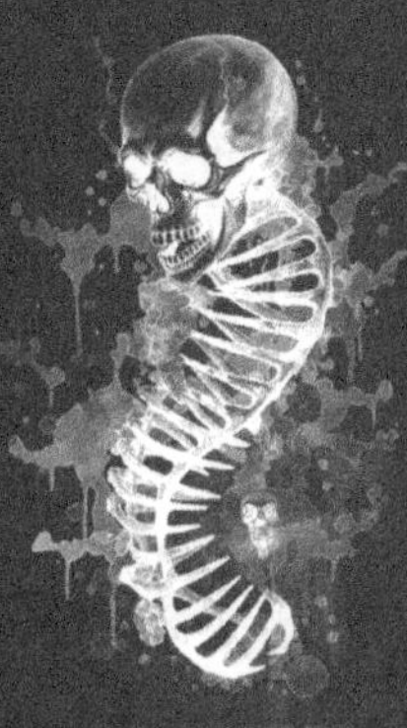

AMAIA

Vincere aut mori. Conquer or die.

That had been the way of the world since the dawn of civilization. I'm not sure why I thought this go-round could be different. Perhaps it was a stupid way to live. Maybe Transient Nation had it right.

It wouldn't be long now before I would never see any of this again. I would be immortal. The girl who destroys armies and ends wars. Prescott's dream.

When I first became General, I knew there was a chance of that, especially if we did things right. History that isn't recorded was lost. If we failed, then maybe someone else would be able to learn from us and prevail. That had been the extent of my expectations, however. I mean, how many people remembered who George Washington was *before* his Presidency?

Poor example, but my point stands.

Now here I was, Commander-in-Chief of a third of what was once the continental United States. This much power in a twenty-eight-year-old woman's hands was about one of the stupidest fucking plans I'd ever heard of. But I suppose most of the greats never wanted power—they just wanted to help. That's what made them so great.

My revenge would be sweet, but the reward of getting it would be sweeter.

The windmill Riley had carved weighed heavy in my hand. I wanted to bring Jax something that would last. His family home in Ireland had one. As a kid he'd spent a lot of time hanging out there, playing in the grass with his dogs and friends. That was before his father went to jail and his mom lost the house. Then he lost his mom.

He'd told me one night that he still dreamed of getting our own house, with our own windmill … for the kids we both knew we would not have. That was Jax though, always the dreamer. For a while, most of his dreams had come true. And then they'd been cut short.

Alexiares grabbed my hand, intertwining our fingers. Rubbing the back of my hand with his thumb, he kept his focus forward, recognizing I needed a moment to collect myself but offering support anyway.

I'd been on my way to Riley's handy little earth slide, Harley and Suckerpunch in tow when he'd stopped me, suspicious of where I was going. Riley had without a doubt snitched when I forbade him from coming with me. I swore he'd get a mouthful for it later, but I knew he had my best interest in mind.

Alexiares had asked if he could come with me, to pay his respects. To my surprise, a smaller windmill rested in his palm. Not as detailed, but still clearly Riley's work on a rushed job. His cheeks flushed as he caught me staring at his gift to the man I'd loved before him.

Impulsively, the word *no* formed on my lips, but when I thought about it—nothing in the world at that moment could have made me happier. Outside of Ronan Moore's head on a fucking stick and my territory left alone. And some cornbread. Maybe a shot of tequila, but hey, maybe those were gluttonous given the times.

The sound of the waves soothed my nerves as I knelt down at Jax's grave. Grinding it into the dirt, I gave it a spin with my finger, watching until it came to a halt. Harley let out a soft whimper, circling behind his tombstone three times before finding rest. I couldn't even fight her on it, I wanted to stay too.

Huffing down next to her, I leaned against the back of the snake-shaped tombstone, the details of Riley's work scraping against the skin on my lower back. Alexiares took a seat next to me, laying down to rest his head on my lap, gazing up at the clouds above us. Suckerpunch stayed on guard, too wary of our relaxed mindset to get comfortable. Harley had apparently taught him a few things while we were away, the two falling into a sort of pack.

I bit my lip, fighting the urge to glance to the other side. Come Wednesday, Prescott would be right there next to him. Then I'd have two graves to visit instead of just this one. Seth had been burned with the rest of Covert's soldiers. We did not bury traitors. It wasn't worth this effort. The windmill next to me went wild, spinning uncontrollably to the point of shaking.

The thing was, there was no wind.

"Is that you?" Alexiares asked, head lifting off my lap to scan the area.

It was just the two of us here. For as long as the eye could see by the looks of things.

Tears welled in my eyes as I realized what was happening. What it meant. "No. It's Jax … he had air," I said between choked breaths. "He's happy to see me … I think."

Alexiares didn't question me. He offered me no frown of doubt, not a single side-eye. Instead, he grinned, relaxing again, hands combing through his hair.

"Well, if that's the case, Jax," he teased. "Let me tell you what you missed. By the way, I've been wanting to ask, how the *hell* did you find a way to deal with her before she's had her coffee? Talk about a menace to society."

Without missing a beat, he started at the beginning. We sat there for hours. Talking and laughing, Alexiares caught Jax up on the last few months of our lives. The windmill spun out of control each time Alexiares cracked a joke or talked about the crazy things I'd done that he disagreed with.

"I think he likes you," I said, not hiding my astonishment.

Alexiares was … Alexiares. First impressions weren't really his thing.

"No. I think he misses you just as much as you miss him and he wants you to know that. But also yes, who wouldn't like me?"

ACKNOWLEDGMENTS

So this is it? The end of book two. What a journey, what a ride. There's a lot of thanks to go around, it isn't often a girl can claim to have the best support system in the world.

Ben, thank you for your endless support. The plan to retire by thirty has never been so clear, you're welcome. In all seriousness, thank you for being my soundboard, my calm, and my peace through all the chaos of marrying an author. From staying up late into the night with me just so I wouldn't feel like I was in this alone, to picking up in the places I had to let slip during the process. Thank you, and I love you.

To my brown author baddies, Mikayla D. Hornedo, Allie Shante, and Amber Nicole. I couldn't ask for a better group of badass women to lean on for support and laughs whenever they were needed. A special, special, shoutout to Mikayla for getting me through the finish line, this quite literally, would not be possible without your help.

Kenzie, Nyree, Jessica, and Lara; never did I ever imagine I'd be blessed with a crew of absolutely hilarious and insanely intelligent Alpha readers. Without your feedback, Echoes of War wouldn't be what it is now. Thank you from the bottom of my heart, and I hope to have you around forever!

Thank you, Emma Jane, for always keeping me honest (and realistic). I really f*cking scored in the editor department. You're stuck with me for life, I'm not open to negotiations.

Jolee at Satisfiction; the world needs more people like you. Your support in the indie author and BIPOC communities does not go unnoticed, let me be the voice to say thank you from many.

To my ARC readers; I've stared at the screen for awhile, yet I can't seem to find the words to express the level of gratitude I have for you all. My team has nearly *tripled* since book one. It is moments of reflection such as this, that makes it all, so, so worth it. Thank you for supporting my work, having me on your e-readers, and saving a space for me on your bookshelves.

If you've read this far, my loyal reader. Thank you for reading. Thank you for being here. Thank you for opening your heart to my world and to the band of misfits.

Mom and dad, your endless support means the world to me. I know you don't understand what I'm doing, or how this all works, but supporting me without question has been a great blessing.

To my sister, thank you for being my biggest hater and biggest fan. To be the sister of a Gen Z romance reader, is an extremely humbling experience, and I love you for it.

To myself, you wrote this during a time when you had every reason to doubt yourself. Cheers to never letting passing moments and the tribulations of life determine your self-worth.

Forever dedicated to my Papa and Drew.

ABOUT THE AUTHOR

Nelle Nikole was born in Corona, California, spent time in the battlefields of Virginia, and now lives in Atlanta with her soon to be husband, Ben, and their furkid, Sophie. A lifelong reader, she began writing thrilling stories to share with her classmates as early as elementary school.

Having lived a little bit of everywhere, Nelle took her studies internationally and completed her anthropology degree by researching abroad in Rio de Janeiro and throughout Cuba. Driven by an insatiable appetite for knowledge, Nelle pursued a Master of Arts in Public Policy, specializing in Global Affairs. Often stuck within the realms of daydreams and her imagination, Nelle is inspired by all things fantasy, apocalyptic and anything in between.

9 7 9 8 9 8 7 8 5 0 8 1 7